POYER   Poyer,David

DAVID   Louisiana Blue

DATE DUE			
MY 24 '94			
JE 01 '94			
JY 28 '94			
AG 11 '94			
AG 23 '94			
DE 1 '94			
SE 0 6 '95			
SE 18 '99			
AUG 1 8 2007			
SEP 2 2007			
JUL 1 7 2010			
FEB 2 1 2012			

LOUISIANA BLUE

DAVID POYER

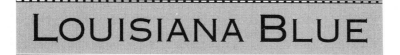

LOUISIANA BLUE

A Tiller Galloway Thriller

St. Martin's Press New York

4/94

Design by Judith A. Stagnitto

Permission granted for quoting from "Against the Wind", written by Bob Seger, copyright © 1980, Gear Publishing Company.

Library of Congress Cataloging-in-Publication Data

Poyer, David.
    Louisiana blue / David Poyer.
       p.   cm.
    ISBN 0-312-10494-4
    1. Galloway, Tiller (Fictitious character)—Fiction. 2. Offshore oil industry—Louisiana—Fiction. 3. Petroleum workers—Louisiana—Fiction. 4. Divers—Louisiana—Fiction. I. Title.
PS3566.0978L68   1994
813'.54—dc20   93-44055
                                                CIP

First Edition: April 1994
10 9 8 7 6 5 4 3 2 1

Books are available in quantity for promotional or premium use. Write to Director of Special Sales, St. Martin's Press, 175 Fifth Avenue, New York, NY 10010, for information on discounts and terms, or call toll-free (800) 221-7945. In New York, call (212) 674-5151 (ext. 645).

*To the men and women
who go down to the sea
to work*

ACKNOWLEDGMENTS

E*x nihilo nihil fit.* For this book, I owe much to Joe Adams, James Allen, Mike Brown, Junius Crochet, Danny Dossett, Carol Edwards, Dale Fakler, Marilyn Goldman, Frank Green, Richard A. Haines, Steven Hall, Glenn Hundley, Mary Hunter, William Hunter, Robert Kelly, the *real* Robert Kelly, Lillian Kiffe, F. Gary Martin, Gene Miller, Will Miller, Larry Pipes, Lenore Hart Poyer, Lin Poyer, Drew Ruddy, Keith Van Meter, Jack Vilas, George Witte, and many others who gave generously of their time to contribute or criticize.

Thanks especially to John Buscemi, without whom this novel might not have been written.

As always, I claim all errors and deficiencies for my own.

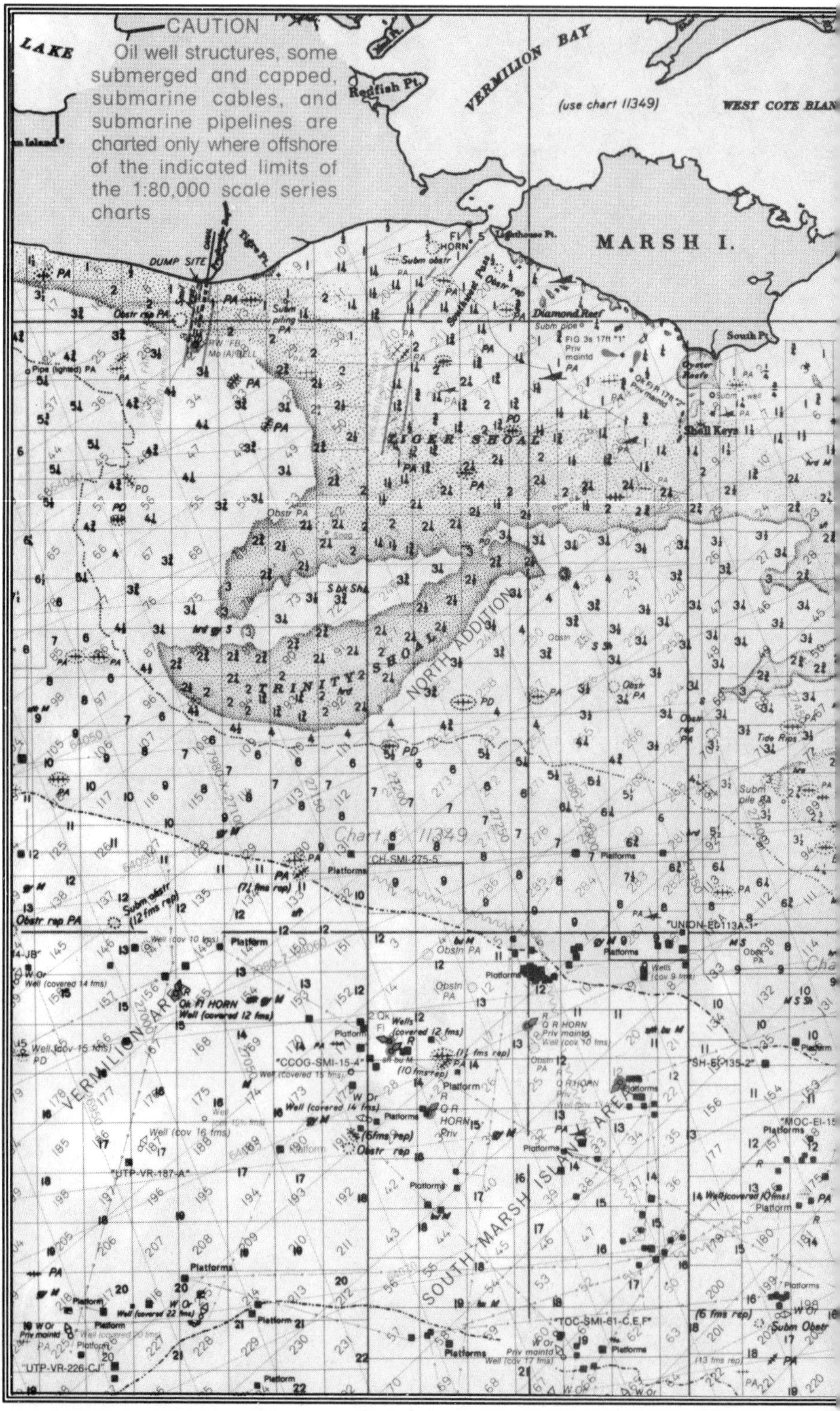
CAUTION
Oil well structures, some submerged and capped, submarine cables, and submarine pipelines are charted only where offshore of the indicated limits of the 1:80,000 scale series charts
LAKE
VERMILION BAY
(use chart 11349)
WEST COTE BLAN
Redfish Pt.
MARSH I.
DUMP SITE
Diamond Reef
South Pt.
Shell Keys
TIGER SHOAL
TRINITY SHOAL
NORTH ADDITION
VERMILION AREA
SOUTH MARSH ISLAND AREA
"UNION-EI-113A-1"
"CCOG-SMI-15-4"
"UTP-VR-187-A"
"UTP-VR-226-CJ"
"TOC-SMI-61-C,E,F"
"SH-EI-135-2"
"MOC-EI-15

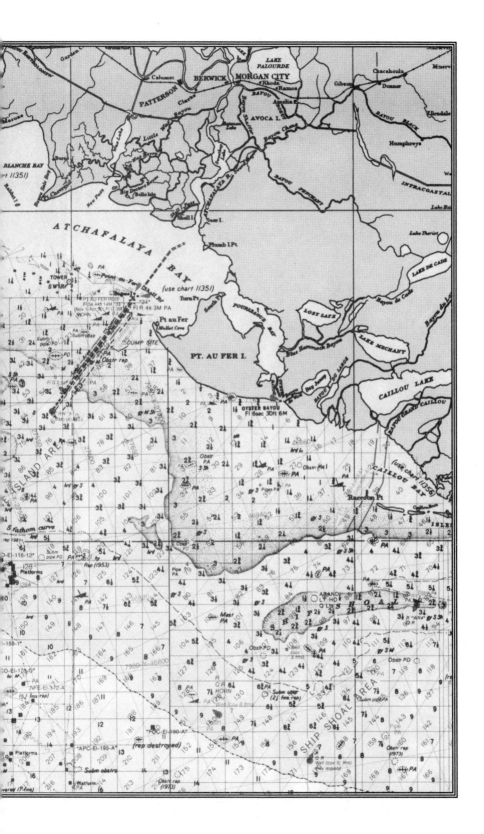

ONE

They'd covered eighty miles from New Orleans since dawn, rolling at a no-risk fifty-five past Gretna, Boutte, Paradis, Allemands, Thibodaux, Chacahoula. Miles of sugar cane slid by, surging like a stormy sea in the morning breeze, then miles of swamp. Shrimp boats reclined drunkenly in the bayous; egrets stalked among the cypresses; willows draped rusting barges. Beyond them was more swamp and jungle, more Spanish moss dripping from the live oaks. . . .

Then, as they neared their destination, refineries and chemical plants; the chemical stinks and the bayou smells merged till they were the same, crammed hotter and hotter into the windows of the Silverado.

Now the highest bridge of all lifted them in the lazy parabola of a rifle bullet, and the stocky white man in the passenger seat jerked awake. Tiller Galloway squinted into the blue glare of a Louisiana July. He rubbed his eyes as the truck kept climbing, higher and higher, till he could make out the far-off glitter of open sea.

"That's it," he said. "The Patch."

"That so?" grunted the black man, who was driving. "What river's this?"

"They call 'em bayous, Shad. This here's Bayou Boeuf."

"I know what a bayou is, goddamn it. Same's a sound, back home. What I want to know, is we there yet? Three days from Hatteras, long enough on the road for me."

1

"Another couple miles. This's Amelia, here when we come off the bridge."

Galloway stared down. He remembered "Bayou Buff" with workboats, crew boats, tugs moored six abreast off the jetties. Now the flat water was deserted, save for a late-morning sand barge.

"Till, you really think Nuñez's got his second string out gunning for us?"

He grunted, recalled to the present as the pickup nosed over. A cluttered jagged river edge of scrap yards and steel-works scrolled into view over the hood. It wasn't ten years ago. It was now, and he and Shad were broke and on the run. "I don't know," he said. "But it isn't something I want to gamble my life on."

"It wasn't him wanted you dead. It was that Troy Christian."

"He worked for Nuñez, Shad."

"Yeah, but basically, there at the end, all he wanted was to have that Cuban wasted."

"I killed Gonzalo for him. But I sank his boat, too."

"He sank yours first."

"His cost twenty-five million more than mine." He rubbed his mouth. "No, I think I better stay out of sight for a while. But I don't think he wants you, Shad. Just drop me on Front Street, you don't want to stay."

"How'm I gonna get home on thirty bucks?"

"We'll see this guy owes me money. Then you can—"

"Forget it." The other man ran a big scarred hand over a stubble of black hair. "We're partners, right? Whither thou goest, there goes Shadrach Aydlett, too. I just as soon see what this big-time oil-field diving's all about, anyway."

Tiller leaned back, remembering how little was left for him back in Hatteras. The mess in the Bahamas had left them thirty thousand dollars in debt and looking over their shoulders for hired geeks. He and Shad had raised *Miss Anna* from her muddy grave in Pamlico Sound but couldn't afford repairs. They'd left her in the Seafood Industrial Park at Wanchese, sad and abandoned on blocks.

He'd left Bernice behind, too. He'd thought things would be better when he came back. Instead, she told him they were through, that she'd had enough of his drinking and fighting

2

and not even thinking about settling down. The last time he'd seen her was when she signed his parole release.

The only way he'd been able to figure to catch up was to get back on Route 90 again.

He straightened, fighting the depression that grapneled his soul. If he could hook up with the right outfit . . . five or six months and he could go back with enough to settle his debts and medical bills and get *Miss Anna* overhauled. Enough so he and Shad could go chartering again.

"What's those steel things?" said his partner. Galloway glanced to where four huge columns towered above a bargelike hull loaded with platforms, cranes, and a huge red-and-white derrick.

"That's a jack-up rig."

"How's it work?"

"You tow it out to the site, then jack those legs down to the bottom. That hoists the platform out of the wave action so you can drill. You can only work in about three hundred feet of water with those, though."

"That's deep."

"Out in the Patch, that's a bounce dive, or a no-sweat saturation job."

"You lost me."

"I mean, they go a lot deeper than three hundred feet out here. A hell of a lot deeper."

After the bridge came pipe yards, acres of drill string and pipeline, casing and thick-walled conductor pipe. Then another fabrication yard and scrap yards and piers. Shad asked why it was all here, and Tiller told him how offshore drilling had started in the thirties. They'd begun in the marshes and bayous, then followed the oil, slowly leapfrogging out into the ever-deeper bays of the Atchafalaya and Terrebonne and Vermilion and finally out into the Gulf of Mexico.

"You up for breakfast?" asked Aydlett. "I'm about starved out, myself. Someplace with the air conditioning."

"Just a little farther. Turn left here. This's the old part of town."

"Look at the little houses. Reminds me of Ocracoke."

Galloway remembered that except for the Bahamas, his boyhood friend had never been farther from the Outer Banks than Norfolk. "Used to be a fishing village. Till the boom hit."

3

Paralleling water again, this time the Atchafalaya River. The shadow of a huge old steel bridge fell like cool water across their sweating faces. "This's the Huey Long," Galloway said. "I remember hundreds of guys used to sleep under it. You'd see 'em in cars, vans, cots in packing containers they rented by the hour."

"I ain't sleeping in no packing container. Tell you that right now," grunted Aydlett.

"Comin' up on it. Slow down, now."

Tiller, looking out, thought Bayou City's Front Street wasn't much different from a dozen other Louisiana and Texas towns he'd crewed out of. A mile-long seawall of splintered oak. Past push boats, barges, and shrimp boats eddied the brown eternity of river. In the spring floods, the street was just a shallower part of the Atchafalaya, and coffins would pop out of the low, swampy soil of the Catholic cemeteries and float past the storefronts, accompanied by plastic flowers and hollow Virgins, like some grisly Mardi Gras parade. A line of beaten-looking men slumped in front of a crew service agency, smoking, waiting for the doors to open.

"Who're those guys?"

"Crew. Deckhands, cooks, mates."

"That where we check in?"

"Hell, no. We're divers."

"La Petite Lounge . . . Tony's . . . the Blowout. These bars is all closed."

"Keep going. Oh. There's one to stay away from."

"Which?"

"With the green door. The Moon Pool."

"Where we headed, anyways?"

"Right there." Tiller pointed to a shabby, windowless corner building. "The Brass Hat."

Suddenly, he felt afraid.

TWO

The Hat served a Cajun breakfast, shrimp omelets and rice and grits. One sip and Galloway remembered Community coffee. Everybody drank it out on the rigs.

"What we doin' here, anyway?" Shad muttered.

"This's where the divers hang out. Anybody hiring, this is where we'll hear about it first."

Aydlett looked around. Behind the bar was an ancient brass-and-copper diving helmet, metal and fittings tarnished till it blended into the shadows. Blended with yellowing photographs of men with fish, with girls, with diving gear, while behind them derricks punctured a cyan sky. A scuffed dance floor echoed in the empty glow of a cigarette machine. An old man crept out from the back with a broom, rested against the wall, then began following it across the floor. He moved as if his joints were full of sand, shuffling on bowed legs.

"They hang out here, huh?" he muttered. "Well, where the shit are they?"

"It's early yet." Galloway looked at his wrist, then remembered: He'd lost his watch outside Mobile playing poker for gas money. "I wonder where Miss Jill is. You want to meet her. Every diver's mama in Bayou City."

"Uh-huh."

"See that bar? I seen a hundred thousand dollars on it more'n once. Guys flashing it for the girls, playing poker and bourré. A diver can make that in five, six months."

"Bo-ray?"

5

"Cajun poker—the loser gets to stuff the pot for the next hand. It gets heavy fast if you stay in longer than you got cards for." He glanced toward the bar again. "Yeah . . . used to be you could hitchhike in here, or drop off the freights when they slowed down for the bridge, and in a couple days you'd be a hundred miles out at sea. You heard of Jack Abbott, the murderer—he worked on a rig here."

"Yeah, looks like a great place to get lost," said Aydlett. "Except if it had the air conditioning—"

"Forget air conditioning, okay? Hey, want a beer?"

Some others drifted in, no one he recognized. One went to the jukebox. Coins rattled, and the music started. Bob Seger. "Against the Wind."

He took another sip of half roast and all of a sudden a door opened to some back room in his head and a thousand faces tumbled out, people and memories he hadn't thought of for ten long years.

The people. Like Jerry Cutrona, who'd given him a 90/10 helium-oxygen mix one time when he was supposed to get 50/50 . . . Hacky Stover, an ex-Marine who loved to drink and smoke dope. They'd been at one-atmosphere school on the West Coast when Stover got stinking drunk one night and slit his esophagus open eating glass . . . "Top Cat" Webber, one of the smartest, most aggressive guys he'd ever met. Webber had gone to the Honda dealership one payday and bought a Gold Wing. Took it off the lot; the throttle jammed; he went across four lanes and the divider, under an eighteen-wheeler, and through the window of a Mexican restaurant. And never walked again.

The jobs. The time out on the Flower Garden, a reef east of Texas, when he'd gone down to burn off the upper half of a platform that'd collapsed in a blowout. At 460 feet, he'd cracked the hatch, flipped on the bell's outside lights, and looked down into what looked like slowly oozing black mud. Puzzled, he'd sealed his helmet and dropped through. Only when he was standing among them had he realized that the boiling darkness was thousands of six-foot conger eels.

Doing inspections on platforms, when the engineers had no idea what was down there. The divers would get caught in Halliburton wire, or lost in the spaghetti mess of trash and cable that accumulated under a platform.

The LOOP job, when nobody'd been in charge and Uncle

Otis had no idea what was coming down. That was the job where Rick Osteryound had gone blind and nobody had ever figured out why.

The accidents. Water blasters blasting out thighs. Compressor handles shattering arms and kneecaps. Guys getting lost under a barge doing an inspection and never coming up, or coming up dead.

And the fun. Getting drunk in the chamber on the *Seaway Eagle*, singing Christmas carols over the intercom. Hazing the tenders: putting towels over the chamber portholes, and saving the catsup from dinner and putting it in the outlet valves. Then screaming when the tender vented, and how they'd panic, seeing catsup flying out onto the deck, thinking they'd blown up a diver. Bringing barmaids and dancers from the titty bars back to the boat. Waking up with two girls from Fouchon, Louisiana. Not knowing where he was at first, then the two of them going around the world on him. He'd been married, but that hadn't mattered, not then, not to him.

And the years rolled slowly past,
And I found myself alone,
Surrounded by strangers I thought were my friends,
I found myself further and further from my home. . . .

The old man, who'd worked his way gradually across the floor to them, hit a patch of spilled water, slipped, and went down. Shad helped him up and steadied him on his legs. "You okay, old-timer?" he asked. The old guy nodded and started to shuffle off.

But Galloway had half-risen, studying the weary, veined cheeks, the twisted mouth.

"Bill?" he whispered. "Jesus *Christ*."

The last time he'd seen Bill Claunch, the man was young, blond, and built like an Olympic swimmer. He was smart, too, going places. Now, staring at the man who propped himself on the broom, eyes on the dust, Tiller shivered.

"Who're you?" The voice was slurred.

"Galloway. Remember me? We were on MOXY-Sixty-two, East Cameron—and we were, I forget, fixing risers—"

"Pipeline," Claunch said, and the left side of his lips was

7

rigid. "Laying twenty-inch off a barge. We did that on air, didn't we?"

"That's right. I remember now. But, Jesus—"

"You don't look so good." Something flickered behind the sanded-over eyes. "Shit, I prob'ly don't, either. Where the hell you been?"

"Here and there. Away. Want a beer?" He looked for a spare chair, yelled to the guy behind the bar, "Hey, a cold barley pop for my friend, too."

"I don't want one," said Claunch hastily.

"Sure you do. Hey, you! Another long-neck over here."

Claunch folded himself shakily into a chair, muttering, "Tiller Galloway, Tiller Galloway, Tiller Galloway. Say it, say it, say it, maybe it'll stick. . . . What you doing back?"

"Keeping our heads down for a while."

"Who you hiding from?"

"A former business associate."

Claunch pointed a palsied finger at Aydlett. "Who's the nigger?"

"Look, buddy—"

"Shad, take it easy—the guy's not all here. He's my friend, Bill. My partner." Galloway exhaled and turned back to Claunch, who was sucking beer rapidly through the right side of his face. "What happened, man? You were one of the best in the business."

"Took a hit. Screwed me up. Can't jump no more."

"When was this?"

"Don't ask me—can't remember no whens. Short-term memory, doc said. Remember perfect ten years ago, but can't remember shit happened yesterday. In-farts in my brain, he said. Necrosis in the joints. That's why I move all stove-up like I do."

"What happened?"

With a fierce, focused intensity, Claunch chanted from one side of his mouth, "I was out in the South Addition, doing an inside burnout on a platform leg."

"*Inside* the leg?"

"That's right. Cheaper that way, I guess. The leg's thirty-six inches wide. They drop you down inside it to two hundred and eighty feet, then snake down the burn gear.

"So I start burning. And when you burn like that, electrolysis of the water, you know, makes hydrogen. It must have built up in a pocket. And finally it flashed—kaboom. Blew my faceplate right off. Knocked me out, too.

"So here I am stuck in the leg two hundred and eighty feet down, committed to a decompression, and they can't get the standby diver to me. No comms, they don't know what the hell happened.

"Well, I had my free-flow on, and I must have kept my face down, because I was still breathing when they got me up. They didn't do no stops on the way. Just yanked me, then rush me into the deck chamber.

"Well, might of been okay if they'd pressed me all the way back down and brought me up easy. But they rushed it.

"Oh, and I remember looking down at myself. Weird as it sounds, that's what happened. Thought it was all over. And you know, funny thing, didn't feel too bad about it.

"I wake up in the chamber. The tender's kneeling on my shoulders, holding an oxygen mask on me. I guess convulsions. Me just shaking, shaking. They call the beach, talk to the safety officer. 'Bring him up on a table five; he's okay.'

"Get to the dock. The company's got a carryall and a driver, local hotshot with a sixth-grade education, drive me to Jo Ellen Smith Hospital. An hour-and-a-half ride, he gets lost, turns into well over three hours. I'm vomiting the whole way. The hyperbaric unit, in New Orleans. But I guess it was too late by then.

"The docs say the right vestibular system's gone. Spinal-cord damage. The bone's dyin' in my knees and arms.

"Well, all that I didn't know then. So they let me out, an' the safety officer gets after me, and the company docs. 'Nothing wrong with you. Just sign the paper and we'll take care of you.' I settled for ten thousand. Signed it all away. They let me go two weeks later. Said I was late one day too many."

"Late?"

"Shit, nobody ever come in at seven-thirty, less they had a shop assignment. But that was it, pink slip. I asked for tender; they said they didn't need a tender couldn't remember what the mix was without writing it on his hand." He hesitated, head cocked toward the bar. "Now it's sweepin' floors. And glad to get it."

"Hey, Lurch! You spent enough time cooling your ass!"

9

"Back off, Jack. I'm talking to Mr. Claunch," said Galloway.

"My name ain't Jack, Jack. Who the hell are you?"

"Who am I? I'm one son of a bitch you're gonna remember if you don't shut your goddamn mouth, I promise you that."

The barkeep stared back for a second, then dropped his eyes. He started taking apart a stack of glasses.

"Hey, uh, Tiller," said Aydlett.

Claunch said, without missing a beat, "I remember him; Killer, they called him, ole Tiller Killer Galloway. Real name was Lyle. From North Carolina, one of them ex-SEALs thought they was hot shit. Big guy, mustache, I remember him sellin' dope and that girlfriend of his exposing herself. Mean when he was drunk or stoned. Last I heard, they fired him, caught him with a bunch of shit. Some say he went into the smuggling full-time."

He felt sick. "Bill, that's me. I'm Tiller Galloway."

"Give up, Till," muttered Aydlett, drumming his fingers on the table. Four more men had come in, and Galloway realized that now there were twenty people in the Hat, and Aydlett the only black—and that the men at the bar were looking their way.

"Okay, that's it," said a voice. He looked up, to find the barman standing over them, a bottle in one hand. His other hovered near his belt. "Back to work, Pappy."

"I thought I told you to get out of my face," Galloway told him.

"I don't know you. You a customer, ain't make you God."

"I'm a personal friend of Miss Jill's."

"Every goddamn kitten around the dumpster's a personal friend of Miz Watson's. Somebody's got to watch out she don't get taken every goddamn minute."

"And that's you, huh?"

Claunch plucked at his sleeve. "Take it easy. He lets me drink what's left in the bottles. Boss, I'll sweep an extry half hour, make up for talking time. Okay?"

"Make it snappy," said the barkeep.

"You better leave, Tiller. Maybe I'll see you later. Where you going?"

"Thought I'd try the old outfit first."

"They're all the same," muttered Claunch. "Use guys up, throw 'em away like blown gaskets. It's a shitty business."

Galloway finished his beer and got up. "Look, I wish I could—"

"Ain't nobody can do nothing for me, mister. You a diver?"

"Yeah, I'm Tiller—"

"Galloway. That's right. I remember you now. You just watch out for yourself down there, now. You hear? Too many good men wasted, down there in that blue."

"The blue?" said Aydlett.

"That Louisiana blue. It'll get you sooner or later. Eat you up from inside, first little by little, then all at once like a charge of plastic goin' off inside your head. Just don't sign no papers from no company doctors. You hear?"

"Look, you hang loose, all right? Say, is Miss Jill gonna be in today?"

"Mister Boss?" Claunch hoisted himself with rapid lurches. He glanced furtively at the man behind the bar. "Mister Boss, you know that, what he wants to know?"

"Told you, asshole, she's not doing so good. Might be in later, might not."

"It was good seeing you, Bill."

"Good luck in whatever," said Claunch, looking after them. "Hey! You didn't say—how's Ellie doing? How's your boy, what's his name, Thad?"

"Tad. They're . . . okay."

"That's the only thing worth riskin' your life for. I used to look at her and that baby and envy you, Till. Envy you like a son of a bitch."

"Yeah, well, we . . . I don't see much of them anymore."

The eyes faded again, emptied, went blank. Claunch coughed, coughed harder, spat. He turned away. "Well, you watch y'self, mister."

"Yeah," said Tiller, looking after him. The broom made a dry rasping, pushing up a little heap of cigarette butts, dust, pop tops. "You, too."

11

THREE

Tiller drummed his fingers on the wheel as he surveyed the brick sprawl of Sea Systems Incorporated's Bayou City facility. The old-fashioned diving bell still sat on the lawn. Beyond the admin building was a crayon yellow crane and the white tank the welders practiced in. Nothing had changed but the grilles on the carryalls.

"Jeez, Till. Way you was talking, I was expecting some huge yard full of gear."

"Diving gear doesn't take up much room. This is the biggest damn diving outfit in the world."

"Well, let's check it out." Aydlett reached for the door.

"Uh, Shad—maybe I ought to go in alone. Then when I see how things are going, I can bring your name up."

Aydlett shrugged. He slid into the driver's seat as Tiller slid out, and the truck took on its usual port list. "You got it. How long?"

"An hour?"

"Okay." Shad hesitated. "Hey. That stuff your buddy Claunch was talking—"

"Bill screwed up, Shad. He started burning without making sure the hydrogen could vent. It's his own fault he got hit."

"Oh. Well—okay. See you."

Tiller looked after the pickup, rubbing his mouth. Then he faced about and strolled with a quick swagger down the neatly trimmed walk.

The receptionist asked him to wait, saying the employment manager was in conference. He sat awkwardly, staring around the room. Same cheap laminated paneling. Same fish tank. Probably not the same fish, though. Not after ten years.

People drifted through in the divers' uniform of Red Wing boots, heavy-cased watches with rubber wristbands. He didn't recognize them. He picked up a copy of *World Oil* and pretended to read.

"Galloway?"

He looked up. "Al?"

It was Al Jaxon, a little heavier, a little grayer, in a suit instead of jeans and a plaid shirt. "Well, I'll be damned. Where the hell'd you drop out of, boy?"

"North Carolina."

"What brings you back?" Jaxon looked at the receptionist before he could answer. "I got him."

"Yes sir, Mr. Jaxon."

" 'Mr. Jaxon,' huh?" said Tiller, following him along the worn green carpet. "And a tie, suit—you're doing okay."

"It's been up and down, but that's diving, idn't it?"

The door read OPERATIONS MANAGER. Jaxon got them coffee, then settled behind his desk. "This's unexpected."

"I should've called ahead."

"Ain't that I'm not glad to see you." Jaxon's eyes went to the wall, then beyond it. "I still get a ... shudder sometimes. That job on Sackett Bank."

Tiller remembered it. He and Jaxon had been partnered on a rush job. The helo dropped them at midnight on a Grace jackup twenty miles south of where the Mississippi ran out of land. They'd dressed each other out while the company man briefed them and the tenders fueled the compressor. The rig jockeys had been trying to set an anchor when they lost control of the bitter end. They'd been grappling for it for twelve hours.

The divers' job was to go down, find it, and shackle it to a block attached to tugging wires so the barge guys could get it up on deck again. One would dive; the other would be standby.

Jaxon had won the flip. He'd taken the shackle and the wrench and the sheave with the wires running through it, grabbed his mask, and jumped. The black water had closed over him instantly, leaving Galloway watching umbilical and tugger wires leading down into water that glittered and heaved under the work lights like liquid obsidian. Even then—watching the bubbles swirl away, out of the light—he hadn't really thought about it, about how fast the current was.

Jaxon told him later he'd gone to the bottom like a concrete-coated mobster, barely clearing his ears as the shackle and wrench and sheave dropped him 210 feet. He'd groped around in the black mud and found the chain. Got the wire in place, lined the pin and shackle up, and torqued it closed. Then keeper-wired it, all in the dark, working by feel.

Then he'd asked for slack.

Tiller had stared at the tender, who was throwing slack out, coils of it. "You stupid son of a bitch! He's trying to climb his umbilical! Get that slack in, fast!"

It came in loose, and he felt scared. Then it went taut. No give to it. Jaxon wasn't answering the phones.

He sealed his mask and jumped, too fast, hitting the water so hard, he almost bit his tongue off. Fifty feet down he hit a massive snarl of wire and hose. Total darkness—he couldn't see a thing. If I get caught in this, he thought, they'll be looking for us both in the morning.

Just then Jaxon slammed into him. Limp, swaying on the end of the line. He grabbed him with one hand and with the other started climbing his own umbilical.

Halfway to the surface, the current had grabbed him, too, caroming him off the drill string so hard red galaxies wheeled in the blackness. But somehow he'd kept going, hauling them both up foot by foot. He'd come to the knot of wire and hose and shoved it ahead of him.

The next thing he remembered, they were on the edge of the moon pool, the enclosed access to the sea through which the drill string ran, and the tenders were taking Jaxon's mask off. His face was blue-green, like a newborn child's, and for a while they weren't sure he was going to start breathing again.

"Yeah," said Jaxon softly. "I didn't think the first thing that current would do, soon as there was an ounce of slack, was snarl my lines around the tugger wires. I still owe you that one."

Tiller said, embarrassed, "Shit."

"How long you been back?"

"Just got in."

"Seen anybody else?"

He decided not to mention Claunch, trying to remember who else he and Al had worked with. "Just you. I was gonna ask, what became of some of the guys—"

"Who? Give me names."

"Bacon Bits?"

"Him and his wife, they saved every penny he earned. He bought into a bank, but it went broke. Last I heard, they were in Santa Barbara, living on a sailboat."

"Jack Frost?"

"Jack went to Brazil on a job for Petrobras. Got involved with the daughter of the guy that owns the biggest diving company in Latin America. Haven't heard from him in six, eight years."

"Paul Galt? How's he doing?"

"Not a happy story. Paul was on deck in the chamber, eight hundred feet of pressure, waiting out his decompression time. He went to take a crap, okay? Just sitting on the can. The tender turned the wrong valve and vented the bowl to atmospheric. Sucked his guts out and sprayed them into the Gulf. Nothing anybody could do for him. It took him five hours to die."

"Jesus Christ."

Tiller couldn't think of anybody else to ask about. "You here looking for a job, right?" Jaxon said at last. "Or is this just a sentimental journey?"

"I heard oil was up. Drilling's up."

"It's up a little, but it's nothing to buy futures on. Everybody out here's still hanging on by their teeth." Jaxon hesitated. "You know, you were a good diver, had good skills, but . . . you rubbed people the wrong way. Especially getting busted with a satchel of pot. That was dumb. I mean, Johnny just had no choice."

"I understood that, Al."

"What about your drug problem, Tiller? You still doing that stuff?"

15

"No. I quit." He took a deep breath. "In prison."

"Prison." Jaxon's face stayed neutral.

He decided to let him have it all at once. "When Johnny let me go, I went in with a guy smuggling grass. Maybe you heard of it. The Silverberg organization. Then another guy, running hard stuff. I got caught. Pulled five years. Now I'm trying to get my frigging life in order, okay?"

"Take it easy. I had to ask. How'd Ellie take all this? She still with you?"

"No. She left when I was in Central."

"I'm sorry to hear that." Jaxon gave him a beat, but when he didn't respond, he went on: "What's your legal status? On parole?"

"Just off."

"Things have changed, Tiller. There was a wage cut, for one. No more thousand-dollar days. And the industry's evolved. Specialized. It never took a lot of talent to blow bubbles and turn a wrench. When things got tight, Johnny decided to deemphasize saturation diving." Jaxon put his fingers together, as if he was the secretary of state live on CNN, Tiller thought. "We do most of our work with ROVs now. Remotely operated vehicles."

"How do you untie a knot with an ROV?"

"We design the job without knots."

"You still have divers, don't you?"

"Yeah, we still got divers. But now they learn to cut and burn and rig in Wilmington or Houston. We work them in the shop, then they tend offshore, then they start diving. It's a profession. We don't hire transient anymore. Another thing, you know the old attitude—'Get the job done, and if you don't get hurt, great.' We got a safety program now."

"I know that, Al. And I'm not looking to start at diver one. I'm steadier now than I was ten years ago."

"We've all changed. Some ways good, some not."

"Goddamn it. What do I have to do? Who do I have to see? Johnny?"

"Johnny's in Corpus Christi."

"Then what?"

Jaxon said reluctantly, "You'd have to pass a physical."

"I keep in shape."

"You sure you want to go through with this?"

"Yeah. I do."

Jaxon sucked a tooth, then leaned to the intercom. "Medical, front office. Got time for a physical? ... Thanks." He leaned back. "Okay. You got your chance."

"I appreciate this. Say, I got a friend with me—"

"Pass the physical first, Till. Then thank me. If you still want to."

The doctor took a history, asked if he smoked, if he drank. Tiller fudged the latter question. No, he wasn't taking any drugs.

The doctor did a vital capacity, an audiogram, and an EKG. Then he ran him for fifteen minutes on a treadmill and took another one. Then he sat him down naked and stared at him.

"Ever been bent, Mr. Galloway?"

"I've had pain."

"How about weakness? Loss of sight? Tremor, nausea, hearing difficulties? Paralysis of limbs, shortness of breath, fatigue, collapse, coma?"

"Just pain."

"Ever had any back problems?"

"No," he lied.

"What about that scar at the fourth vertebra? That looks surgical to me."

He didn't answer, and the doctor made a note. "What's that on your right hand?"

Tiller said reluctantly, "I handled some radioactive metal once."

"Your cheek? What did that? Bottle?"

"Knife," he muttered.

"Who stitched it up? A sail maker? Mr. Galloway, I'd say we're about done here."

"That's all?" He stood, surprised.

"Not exactly. We haven't gone through the standard ADC long exam. But I don't think we need to waste your time, or ours."

"What do you mean?" he said, though he had a feeling he knew. He started pulling on his pants.

"Let's put it this way. I have no doubt you're an experienced diver. Unfortunately, experience has left its marks."

He put on his shirt, feeling the guy's eyes on him as he fastened the cuffs. He was wise to that one. That was an early sign of nervous-system degeneration, when you fumbled getting your cuffs buttoned. "All I want to know is, can I dive?"

"You can dive. But not for Sea Systems." The kid leaned back. "We have fifty recent dive-school graduates on our waiting list. Young guys, full of napalm and testosterone. Trained on the latest gear. No bad habits. No back problems—like you're going to have."

"My back's fine."

"It's an injury, and when you decompress again, that's where the bubbles will lodge." He studied Galloway's EKG. "We have a saying: Visible damage is extreme damage. It makes me wonder what else is there I'm not seeing. Or getting told about."

"I've put in a hundred times the saturation time they have."

"We don't do much sat work anymore. Maybe they told you that at the front office." He paused. "But . . . if you insist, we'll do the rest of the exam."

"Forget it," he said. He pushed his feet into his boots, flipped off the doctor and walked out.

He stood outside, fighting an urge to kick in a window in one of the cars in the executive parking.

"How'd it go?"

He spun around. Jaxon stood waiting, jacket over his arm, tie loosened.

"Crappy. Why'd you—"

"Let you do it? Because you weren't listening. Come on. Let's take a walk."

"Where?"

"Out back."

They went back into the shop. Under a high ceiling, technicians in coveralls were working on rigid suits on upright stands, the clear bubbles removed, their heads and shoulders thrust inside. It looked to Galloway like they were being devoured by giant white grubs. Across from them, other techs were servicing the ROVs. They ranged from twenty-foot frames covered with motors and manipulators to tiny self-propelled underwater cameras. He and Jaxon came out the far end and the sun bounced off the concrete of the open yard and hit him in the face like a fast pitch.

"That's where the industry's going, Tiller. It's not glamorous, it's not the big payday, but it's steady work. You want to take a couple minutes, think about it?"

"That's not diving. I'm a diver."

"You really determined to get back into it, huh?"

"Yeah."

Jaxon just shook his head. "I can't get you in here, Till. Our insurance guys would crawl up our ass with spikes on. I doubt if any other reputable company will, either. I'm sorry, that's just how it is."

He didn't say anything. Through the window, he saw the gleaming camera bubble of an ROV. It seemed to be watching him.

Later that afternoon, he slammed the door to the Global office so hard, the glass shivered. As he swung himself up into the pickup, Aydlett said, "Any luck?"

"Shit. I was to third base with Mike Brown. Getting ready to steal home when Cleveland came in."

"Who's he?"

"A guy I don't get along with." Tiller rammed his fist into the dash. "He's their superintendent now."

"Maybe this'll help."

He cracked the tallboy and foam flew onto the windshield. When it came down again, it was empty. He crushed it in one hand and whanged it off the GLOBAL DIVERS & CONTRACTORS sign. "Okay, let's drive."

"Where to? Oh, and another thing I thought of while I was waitin' out here." Aydlett pointed to the sun. "Where we gonna sleep tonight?"

"Shit."

"You said some guy owed you—"

"Christ, yes. I forgot all about him. Let's go."

Creaky wooden floors, an office area, a step down to the shop. He rubbed his mouth, then turned around. Aydlett stood outside, examining his wallet. When he looked up, Galloway motioned him in.

"Good presentation," said Aydlett, casting a professional eye around the interior. He tapped the display counters, looked at the racks of spear guns and dive flags, the laminated posters of tropical fish, the block and rig charts shading from land white to the purple of the Mississippi Canyon. He looked wistful.

"What's the matter?" Tiller asked him.

"I miss retailing."

"We'll get our shop back, Shad. Remember the plan? Get offshore jobs, take the hitches the married guys don't want. Six months, we go back with a nest egg."

"Uh-huh. Hey. This diving helmet. Plastic?"

"Fiberglass."

"You don't use masks?"

"You get in black water, cables and shit whipping around, you want protection. Plus you get better comms."

"What's this one?"

"That's called a Superlite. Or a Kirby-Morgan."

"It's heavy. Bolts on to the suit, like?"

"There's a clamp, seals to a rubber neck dam. Actually, in the water it's neutral. . . . That's a Rat Hat. A Ratcliffe. That over there's a Miller."

"These look complicated. Which one's the best?"

"Any of those'll take you to fourteen, sixteen hundred feet. If you got everything else right, you might even come up again."

"Scuba diving's one thing. I don't know if I'm up to this stuff."

"Don't worry, goddamn it. I'll take care of you." Galloway tapped a bell.

A heavy, tall man with a black beard answered it. "Help you?"

"I came for the money you owe me, Larry."

It was as if a plate-glass shutter snapped down across his eyes. "I owe you? That what you said, pal?"

"Uh-oh," murmured Aydlett.

"The cash for the gear I left. Dry suit, hat, set of spares, Miller weight belt, a welding shield. Easy a thousand bucks. I won't even ask for ten years' interest."

"I don't remember that." The bearded man folded his arms with amused tolerance. "An' I barely remember you."

"This is how Larry operates," Tiller explained to Shad. "A guy's a good customer, deals with him for years. Then one day he runs into some hard luck. Larry sells his gear on consignment. Keeps promising to send the money. He'll promise you anything on the phone. He figures you'll give up, forget about it." He leaned back on the counter. "You going to tell me you don't remember me calling you?"

"That gear you left here was shit. I had it on the shelf for a while, then I had to throw it away."

"Who're you kidding? You never threw anything away in your life, Larry. I bet you even hate to flush."

"You working, got a card? We maybe can arrange some credit."

Aydlett picked up a Nikonos and squinted through the viewfinder.

"That was a new Superlite I left with you. Kind of like ... this one here."

Tiller picked up a new helmet. The smooth fiberglass gleamed like a huge yellow pearl in the fluorescent light. The stainless-and-brass regulator and valve assemblies glowed.

"Put it down, man. Unless you going to make me an offer."

"I'll make you an offer." He raised it, getting a grip, balancing it just above the glass counter.

"Uh, Till," said Shad. He put his hands on the helmet. Galloway looked startled. Pulling it out of his hands, Aydlett turned to the owner. "Noticed that rack of wet suits you got back there. Nice markup on those."

"That's cost. I sell those at cost."

"I know what wholesale is. But that ain't what was interesting about it."

"What do you mean?"

"I mean, that ain't Dacor. Got Dacor tags on it, but it looks to me like one of those Korean trademark rip-offs."

21

"That's Dacor gear," the big man said sullenly, but his hand came up to his beard. "You with him?"

"Partners. Now, what I was about to suggest is, there's some used gear over on that shelf. Maybe we could arrive at some kinda compromise. Like, say, Tiller picks out the same kind of helmet he left with you. That way, you ain't out as much as if you paid him cash."

Tiller recovered. "Shad, he owes me the goddamn—"

"Bottle it, my man. You getting too hot under the collar." He turned to the owner. "How's that sound?"

"Lousy. That gear's a lot better than what he—"

"Be a shame to have guys find out you was selling them cheap hinky rip-offs, wouldn't it? 'Specially with that big 'Buy American Because You're an American' sticker you got on the front door. Till, he got anything you like?"

Galloway drifted to the counter and looked down at used helmets, used band masks. "This seventeen. Kind of shape's it in?"

"That goes for eight fifty."

"You got to be kidding."

"I don't run no junkyard. Just overhauled. New O-rings, new diaphragm in the regulator, even got a new faceplate."

He made up his mind. "One used Superlite. Set of spares. Weight belt." He pushed Larry back, crossed to the rack. "And a suit. This Parkway looks to be about my size."

"You gonna be explaining this one to the cops, Galloway."

"Figured you'd remember my name sooner or later. Just remember, I learned a couple things since I left the Gulf. Like how to make an alcohol bomb." The owner's face paled.

Outside, in the dying evening, Aydlett said, "Jesus, Till." He almost flooded the engine getting it started. "What were you gonna do with that helmet? Were you gonna do what I thought you were gonna do?"

"I just got fed up. He owed me money. He doesn't come across, I take it out in damages."

"All you had to do was show him the receipt—"

"I lost that years ago."

"Jesus. What if he calls the cops? They check your record, and back you go."

"Don't sweat it," he said, but he was thinking Shad might be right. In his mind, he'd seen it a fraction of a second ahead, the counter shattering under the blow, glass flying across the room in a glittering cloud. Then he'd two-arm it into the guy's chest—

"You got to control yourself, Till."

"It was an *act*, Shad. Didn't you get that? 'Killer' Galloway, about to lose it. You played your part good, though."

"That's all it was? An act?"

"Didn't you learn that in the line at Hatteras High, Shad? Best defense is a good offense?"

"Yeah. I learned that." Aydlett glanced at his partner. "Okay, what now?"

"Let's backtrack, hit the Hat again. Maybe Miss Jill's in. You'll like her. From Mississippi. Funny to hear her tell it— raised a Baptist, didn't drink, didn't dance, never been in a bar—married a guy loved it all. She ran Randy's, the Elbow Room, then started the Brass Hat when he died. Heart-of-gold type, you know?"

"I don't mean tonight. I mean, what are we gonna *do*, man? We don't have jobs; we still don't have any money—"

He said patiently, "There's other companies, Shad. We'll score."

Aydlett looked at him. For a moment, he seemed about to say more. Then his face closed, and he drove on, through the falling, peeper-creaking Louisiana night.

Four

But Jill wasn't in, and they spent the night in the bed of the truck, parked in a blind alley behind a boat yard. In the morning, they ran three miles in the mist curling up from the Atchafalaya. As usual, Aydlett kept up the pace for the first mile, lagged for the second, then came back in a lumbering sprint that had Galloway panting to keep up.

At eight, he slid back behind the wheel, feeling desperate. After breakfast and a paper-towel bath in the rest room at McDonald's, they had twenty-six dollars. Shad leaned out of the passenger side, sucking the last coolness from the damp air.

"You feeling more like yourself today?"

Tiller blinked. "You mean that with the helmet? I told you, that was an act."

"Uh-huh. Well, I got no business tellin' you what to do."

"Never stopped you before." He was careful to grin. His boyhood friend was sensitive about that, had been for as long as he and Shad went back.

The Aydletts had a history on Hatteras almost as long as the Galloways. In 1862, when the Outer Banks had been seized by the Union Navy, thousands of slaves had fled across the narrow sounds to what they hoped was freedom. Instead, they'd found concentration camps, condemned rations, and the demeaning designation of 'contraband.' After the war, most left again, scattering or headed west. But a few stayed on, finding the fishing and farming life of the Banks to their liking.

Aydlett's great-grandfather had pulled an oar at the Pea

24

Island Station, the only all-black crew in Lifesaving Service history. Shad's grandfather had inherited three miles of shorefront land near the bight of the island, between Buxton and Frisco—land that went now at a quarter million an acre, for oceanview homes built in the shadow of Hatteras Light.

Captain Cliff, Shadrach's father, had started with nothing, after his father died in a storm and the land sold for taxes in the Depression. Before he was done, he owned a fleet and was famous from New York to Key West as the finest charter fisherman on Hatteras Island.

When Galloway was a boy, he'd run away from his dad's strap to bait and gaff for Captain Cliff. He remembered the aching hours of boredom as they trolled for swordfish and white marlin, dolphin, tuna, wahoo. Then the sudden, disciplined panic of the hit. The daylong battle they'd fought with a huge black marlin late one July through thunderstorms and line squalls, the lightning all around them like white-hot lizards running down a vine; they'd ended it at dusk with the fading fish on deck, a massive beast that weighed out a heartbreaking ten pounds short of the IGFA all-tackle record. How Meshach Aydlett, Shad's older brother, had saved his life once when he'd slipped in a patch of chum and fallen overboard into a boil of makos.

Years later, Galloway had killed him.

That was the last trip on the *Victory* from the Golfo Triste, when they'd been towing the dicked-up drogue "Dr." G. Q. Lee had built to haul shit without customs or the Coast Guard being able to detect it. It had turned out to be the voyage from hell, and not only because of the drogue, which had almost killed him all on its own. Each man suspected every other aboard. Even those who were satisfied—as captain and owner, Galloway would have netted over half a million dollars—had to guard their backs.

But he'd won, and at the same time lost; brought *Victory* in to port, only to find the Coast Guard waiting. He'd never found out who'd turned them in, though he'd sworn someday he would.

His father had shot himself the day the verdict came down.

He'd walked out of prison five years later, to find himself as welcome as a ghost. His brother and stepmother wanted no part of him. He'd been drinking the hours away, till one day a man named Keyes had come to Hatteras, and his and Shad's lives had become entwined again.

Now Shad Aydlett was the closest friend he had. But sometimes he still felt Mezey's shadow between them. If only he could never recall the past. Never see again Meshach Aydlett's face when Galloway's bullet hit him. . . .

"What you thinking on so deep over there?"

"Oh." He shook his head. "Just remembering when we used to fish together, on the *Princess.* You know, I'm starting to wonder if this is doing us any good. Seems like they don't really want divers. Or want me."

"How many companies it show in that Yellow Pages you got there?"

"Eleven."

"And you hit four of 'em yesterday. Seems like you only about a third to where you can make a decision."

"A lot of these are shallow-water outfits. Nickel-and-dime, family operations. Mostly specialize in wheel jobs."

"What's a wheel job? Prop?"

"Yeah, checking the propeller on a tug, clearing lines, that kind of stuff." He sucked his lip, watching Route 90 speed by; they were west of Bayou City, on their way to Lafayette. "Easiest wheel job I ever did was for a woman captain. She was towing a barge on six-inch braided nylon. The second she knew it was in the wheel, she shut the engines down and picked up the radio. I unwrapped it and she was back in business. But some of these coon-ass captains keep backing and filling, thinking they can bust loose, and all they do is get it so tight, you've got to—"

"What was that word you just used? Did you say 'coon-ass'?"

"Relax. Means Cajun. Coon-ass and Cajun, same-same."

"Call 'em that to their face?"

"They use it."

"Well, I might call a man 'nigger,' but that don't mean I smile when some white asshole says it." He cranked the window down and Galloway kept quiet, looking out to the south as they topped another bridge and the vast blue shimmer of the Cote Blanche planed the horizon smooth. "These Cajuns, they're like French, right?"

"That's right."

"What they doing in the U.S. of A.?"

"The English threw a bunch of 'em out of Canada 1700 and some. They came down here and settled along the bayous. This where we're going—Lafayette—hell of a lot of 'em up there."

"Tell me again why we going there."

"Two more diving companies." He looked in the rearview, at the road that up till then had been empty, shimmering asphalt under the blistering sun. "Holy smoke."

Aydlett twisted around just as the black convertible hauled into the left lane and whipped past, engine howling, so fast that they caught only a freeze frame of black hair and sunglasses. Then it was a dwindling speck.

"She's got to be doing at least a hundred."

"I hope she's got a detector on that thing."

"Least we got a nice day." Aydlett leaned back and tilted his Oregon Inlet Fishing Center cap over his eyes. "Well, maybe we'll get lucky."

"Let's hope so," said Tiller, but he didn't feel lucky. In fact, he was starting to feel pretty bad.

When he came out of Acadiana Divers and Salvage, he stood blinking in the sunlight, feeling like the lowest of the low. He hadn't known anybody there, and the first thing the manager had asked him was for his logbook. When he'd said he didn't have one anymore, he'd gotten a look that said plainly they didn't believe him, didn't believe he was a diver at all.

"Shit," he muttered. That left just two more major companies, in New Iberia and Houma. The rest were small outfits working scuba or surface-supplied air. If he'd wanted to scrub hulls and retrieve outboard motors, he could have done that out of Virginia Beach.

Maybe it was time to think of heading west, to Port Arthur and Houston. He chewed his lip, looking around for Aydlett. Where had he gotten to now?

The pickup swung in and slid to a stop, tires squalling. When he got in, Shad pulled out again, laying more rubber.

"Do any good?"

"No." He rubbed his mouth, wishing he had a beer.

"Well, how about crew? They got boats. Boats need crew, right?"

"I'm a diver. I want a job diving."

"Yeah, but at least we'd be eating while we're waiting for something to open up."

He didn't answer. He knew he was being illogical, but he didn't want to clean out suction strainers all day. He remembered the men standing in line on Front Street. Then he noticed the street signs.

"Where the hell you going?"

"There's a party west of town. Read about it on a poster."

"Shad, we don't have time to—"

"Lighten up, man. You need a break, you know? You starting to get on my nerves. Goin' to be Zydeco there, Beau Soleil, Bois-Sec, Evangeline. We are going to this 'Cadian Village, and we going to have fun, you hear?"

He heard the music before they could see where it was coming from. They parked on grass and locked up, then made their way on foot toward the low gray buildings. The sun-soaked crowd was in the oil-patch uniform: gold Cross pen, gold Rolex, Red Wing boots, baseball caps that read TEXACO or MARATHON or SHELL. Everybody carried plastic cups and paper plates. It looked to Galloway as if they were all five drinks ahead of him. Banners read BIENVENUE AUX DANSEUSES BRETAGNES DE LEURS COUSINS ACADIENS.

Aydlett shouted above the babble, "Listen to this! This is great. Hey, beer stands. You want a cold one?"

"Yeah."

He unbuttoned his shirt and followed his partner down the grassy, furrowed street of the old village. The cypress-sided, shake-shingled houses had long front porches and shelves outside the windows. They reminded him of Nags Head cottages. Above a stand of pines twinkled a hurtling aluminum sliver—a Learjet on approach to Lafayette Regional, on its way in from Houston or Corpus Christi or Nigeria.

Out in front, on makeshift stands and awnings, were the

bands. He stood and watched, and after a while his foot started tapping.

Accordions, guitars, and violins, the occasional triangle and banjo. With just the fiddles out front, it sounded like bluegrass with a beat, but then the accordion began wailing with a hell-with-it joy. It felt strange hearing it again after so many years. Before, it had seemed happy. Now it sounded desperate, a protest against the foredoomed ferment called life.

When he looked around, Shad was gone. He left the bandstand and wandered through the craft booths. Looking at a handwoven brown cotton shawl, he wondered whether Bernie would like it, then remembered: That was over.

He got his beer topped up, then stood out of the stream of people, drinking and scowling.

After a while, his partner came by carrying two plates. "Where you go, man? This crawfish gumbo, I got to learn me how to make this."

"Shad, this is fun, but we got to get on the road."

"Told you, man, unpucker yourself. Have another beer. Have some of this jambalaya. Hey, we'll get jobs. Do like that sign there says. Let the good times roll."

He gave up and had a plate of rice and green gumbo and another beer and stood in front of the pavilion tent, watching the dancers. In antique Breton dress, aprons, and headdresses, they slammed down their blocky heels like the clog dancers out of the Carolina hills. Shad was right, he thought. Enjoy it. Trouble was, it wasn't working. He wished they sold whiskey here.

Brooding, he wandered among the revelers.

When he finally got Shad pried free and out to the lot, there were even more cars. More people, drinking and fondling one another. The black man searched his pockets for keys. "Wanna drive? Who had more, you or me?"

"You drive; it's your truck. An' where the hell is it?"

They were standing there puzzled, looking out over the sea of cars and caps and campers, when he heard a throaty purr behind him.

When he turned, the black car was almost on him, bumping and growling over the grass. He blinked. The top was up now. He caught only a glimpse through the windshield, but it was her. A lavender print scarf covered the dark hair, and the sunglasses dangled on keepers. She didn't slow and he flattened himself against a van at the last second. Looking down as she slid by, he saw a hand resting on her leg. Long fingers. A heavy gold military-style ring with a gold initial inset on a dark stone. He couldn't see its owner.

"That the doll passed us on the way up?" said Shad, looking after her.

"I think so, yeah."

"You like those little Miatas?"

"Too small. Not for me."

"She looked good in it. Check out those plates." Tiller looked back, blinking to focus through sun and sweat and beer; the Louisiana license said JDVIVRE.

Then, as he watched, the little car hauled hard right and parked, and he saw their truck and nudged Aydlett. "Hey. There we are, over there. Beside that limo."

They were almost to it before a heavily mustached man in a dark suit stepped in front of them and said, "Where are you headed, guys?"

"Say what? That's our truck over there, man," said Aydlett.

"Go have another beer," said the guy. "On me. Here's a twenty. Come back in ten minutes, okay?"

Galloway said, "What? To hell with that. That's our goddamn truck—"

But at the same time, he was looking over to where the Miata sat beside a huge Mercedes with diplomatic plates. The doors were open, and he could see in. The men inside were all in dark suits, too, though they were older than their muscle, and sunglasses, and they all had either mustaches or small beards. He switched his attention back to the gorilla. "That's our goddamn truck and we're getting in it, whether we have to go over you or not. Shad?"

Aydlett said, "I don't know where you're from, buddy, but in the U.S. of A., you don't get between a man and his pickup."

"Okay, which one's yours?"

"The white Silverado. See it?"

"Okay, go ahead." But they could feel him watching them as they went on.

Tiller glanced again at the Mercedes as Shad unlocked the truck, but now the doors were closed. The windows were darkened so that you couldn't see inside. There was no one in the Miata parked beside it. "There we go," said Shad. He hauled himself in, reached across, unlocked the passenger door. "That was weird. Where you figure he was from?"

Galloway checked behind the seat for his duffel and gear bag, then shook the map open with a snap. "A long way from here, I'd say. . . . Okay. You got that out of your system? Get on One sixty-seven. We got two more places to hit today."

There were no openings in Houma or New Iberia, either. They were back at the Brass Hat late that afternoon when the door jingled and a small woman with white hair came in.

A few seconds later, Galloway was making introductions. "And this here's my partner from Carolina, Shad Aydlett. Shad, Jill Watson."

"Pleased, Mr. Aydlett. Tiller, I'm sorry I didn't recognize you right off." Jillian Watson was fine-boned as a bird, with wispy white hair and skin that looked as soft as a gardenia petal. Her hands had a fine resting tremor as they lay on the polished counter, and her old voice was deep Mississippi, like mountain honey. "How's Ellie and the baby? Though I guess he ain't no baby now."

"They're fine." He looked away. "How are you? We figured you weren't feeling good, not coming in."

"I don't come in every day now. Sometimes my hip hurts me. I fall down sometimes with the Parkinson's. But I'm all right. Thank the Lord." She smiled.

"How's Janet? Still painting?"

"Doing real well, got her a little baby now. She named her after me. Little Jill . . . and you're back lookin' for work?"

He nodded. She drifted behind the bar, her expression placid, as if whatever happened, she'd seen it all before—or, if not, then heard about it a hundred times. Heard it and understood it and, more compassionate even than her God, forgiven

31

it all in advance without any necessity for contrition or sacrifice. She said gently, "Well, don't think I know of anybody who's hiring now, but I'll keep one ear open."

Tiller cleared his throat. "Uh ... I know you've always been good for a couple bucks, if a diver needed it."

"And I always knew, if I needed a couple dollars, where I could go to get hold of it."

"Well, Miss Jill, that's what I wanted to see you about. If you can spare it, that is."

She rang the old mechanical register open and fanned five twenty-dollar bills down beside his hand. Behind her, the bartender crossed his arms and looked away, heaving a sigh.

"Thanks, Miss Jill. I'll pay you back as soon as—"

"There's no hurry on it, Tiller. It ain't a hundredth of what you left in tips. Where are you boys staying?" She must have seen the answer in their faces, because she went on: "We still got the back room. You know the rules: no bathing in the can, no girls, and if you make a mess, you clean it up."

"Thanks," he said again. He folded the money and put it in his jeans.

She reached across the bar and patted their hands—both their hands—and Aydlett looked faintly surprised. "Now, what else?"

"What else?"

"Don't make me drag it out of you, son. Is that enough? Are you two going to be all right? I want you to tell me when that runs out. I don't want you doing anything stupid just because you need money. Hear me? I don't want you to think there isn't anybody who cares about you."

Galloway had to look down at the floor. "We'll make out," he said. He cleared his throat. "Thanks, Miss Jill."

"Okay." She gave him a final pat, a penetrating, bird-bright stare, and closed the register with a bang. "Mr. Aydlett, it has been nice meeting you. Now, you boys will have to excuse me. I got some business in the back."

When she was gone, Aydlett murmured, "What a woman."

"She's a goddamned treasure."

"How old is she, anyway?"

"Damned if I know. Nobody ever had the guts to ask."

"How's she cope when things gets wild?"

"She just expects you to behave. If you don't, the other guys'll throw you out." Tiller grinned. "She's a good listener. Been through a lot, too. Good times and bad, lost her husband, her kids dying—"

"She lost her kids?"

"Two, in a fire. The oldest one, she's an artist in New Mexico. Keep your good-heartedness through all that, kind of makes you wonder."

"Well, what now?"

"I wish you wouldn't keep asking me that. Because right now, the only thing I can think of is to get drunk."

FIVE

When the phone started ringing, he couldn't remember where he was. Nobody else answered, and as it rang on, he struggled up from a hard, flat surface. It was a long way from the billiard table to the floor, and he stumbled over a recumbent form that grunted and struck out at him.

Memory crept back as he groped toward the insistent ringing. "Shut the hell up," he muttered. Fragments whirled like bubbles on a black current. Borrowing money from Miss Jill. Cheap tacos at a stand. Stopping at a drive-in daiquiri place with Shad, drinking by a bayou till the stars came out and the mosquitoes with them. Then back to Front Street. A bottle of bourbon, full, then empty . . .

His head felt like a nuclear reactor past critical. The air smelled of flat beer, stale smoke, curdled vomit, and Pine Sol. Daylight leaked around the boarded-up windows. He jerked the old-fashioned black handset off its cradle, its final close-up ring flashing pain through his brain as if the magneto was connected to his ears. "Brass Hat," he snarled.

"This Lyle Galloway?"

"Who wants to know?"

"Understand he's looking for a job. He there?"

"Just a second. I'll get him."

He put the receiver down as gently as he could and slid behind the bar. He valved himself a paper cup of Coke and gulped it down. Then went back out and picked the phone up again. "Galloway."

"Lyle Galloway?"

"I go by Tiller. Yeah."

"Understand you're a sat diver, looking for a job."

"Yeah, sort of," he said, wondering whether he knew the voice. He was pretty sure he didn't. Jesus God, his head . . . "I've got a salvage business up in Carolina, but things are slow."

"Who'd you work for here?"

Galloway told him.

"You clean now? Or still using?"

He swallowed. "I've been clean for years."

"Got gear?"

"Most of it. What kind of work you do?"

"It's a small outfit. But we go deep. Fact, that's our name. DeepTech. Got a major contract and we need some bodies fast, guys we don't have to teach the alphabet to."

"I'm your man."

"Good. Thinking longer term, we want to get into one-atmosphere work down the road. Understand you've done some of that."

One-atmosphere meant rigid suits. "Some. I dove JIMs and WASPs. Trained on the West Coast."

"You willing to do some here?"

He'd never much liked it—they made him feel clumsy and claustrophobic—but this didn't seem like the time to be too choosy. "Uh . . . yeah, probably."

"You know Summerland?"

He slammed his head with his free hand, but nothing came. Well, he'd ask Claunch. "Summerland, yeah, I know it. Sure."

"Half mile up that road, on the left. They'll expect you around nine."

The receiver clicked just as he was about to ask who this was. He still didn't recognize the voice. But the guy seemed to know all about him. Especially that question about whether he was clean. Well, anybody who'd spent time in any bar in Bayou City in the old days would have asked that.

He suddenly realized he had a lead. More than that, a guy interested enough to track him down. He felt so good, he went behind the bar and had a beer. Just one, to get the headache under control, he cautioned himself.

35

The door jarred open. Dust floated in beams of sunlight as a bent figure shuffled in. "Hey, Bill," said Galloway. Then, remembering, added, "It's Tiller."

"Killer Tiller! When you get back in town, man?"

"Yesterday."

"Oh, we already done this, huh? How about fillin' me in, then."

When he was done explaining, Claunch said, "Oh yeah. Remember all that now. Where the hell you been? I—"

"Listen, I got an offer."

"Yeah? Who from?"

"Outfit called DeepTech. Ever hear of 'em?"

Claunch looked at him for the first time, really, that morning. "That's Roland Boudreaux's outfit."

"Yeah?"

"He's the guy put me down there in that platform leg. That's the son of a bitch got me hit. Roland—'Bender'—Boudreaux."

"Is that right? They're in Summerland. Remind me where that is."

"Forget it. You don't want any part of that, man."

Galloway looked at him for a second. "Maybe not. But it won't hurt to take a look. I already been everyplace else."

Claunch angled his twisted mouth grimly toward the stamped-tin ceiling. "Okay, you want to know . . . Summerland, that's down on the Bayou St. Marie. Remember where there used to be the dance hall, and that barbecue place? You take the fork before you get there and go left instead. Half a mile down that road, where the St. Marie hits the 'Chafalaya."

"I got you."

"But I'm telling you, you don't want to—"

Galloway slapped his back. "Relax. I'm just gonna see what they want. Hey, want some eggs? I'll help you on the grill."

After breakfast and a change of clothes, he borrowed the truck and drove out alone, leaving Shad two twenties in case he needed anything. Halfway there, he had to flick on the wipers. Then he put them on full speed as the heavens let go and the road erupted in a cloudburst. The windshield fogged and he opened the vents to the smell of rain. Semis blasted past, trailing scarlet-lighted mist.

When he made his left, the traffic dropped off, and for the last half mile the pickup rocked and bucked, bottoming out in mud holes. He pulled into a muddy lot where carryalls and sedans nosed a lime green prefab.

He cut the engine and sat for a moment listening to the rain. Don't sweat it, he thought. If it don't happen here, Shad's right—something'll turn up.

But another part of him said, Ex-cons don't get jobs after interviews.

And still another remembered Claunch's warning.

It didn't look like a big outfit. He wanted to look around, see what kind of gear they had so he could tailor his pitch, but the rain was coming down harder, cutting off sight. Finally he ducked out, hunching his shoulders, and jogged past a nodding border of dripping azaleas as the sky opened again.

"Appointment at nine," he told the receptionist, hoping she wouldn't ask him with whom. She didn't, just told him Mr. Hohmann would be right out.

Chet Hohmann introduced himself as the operations manager. Short and stocky, in work greens and a scuffed hard hat, older than Tiller by ten, fifteen years. His hand felt oddly rigid, but it was a second before Galloway realized why.

"That's right, it ain't real. Was flooding a jacket, setting a rig. Learned once an' for all not to get my hand near a valve when it comes open." The voice was cement-mixer rough, as if he'd had some kind of larynx damage; it definitely wasn't the voice on the phone. Hohmann looked him up and down with faded, sun-crimped eyes. "Galloway, huh?"

"That's right."

"Understand you done time," the manager said around a Tampa Nugget, lighting it with a paper match from a folder that read "HYBOR GEL: The Most from Every Well."

"Yeah."

"An' dove for Sea Systems. That before or after?"

"Before."

"Got sat experience, one-atmosphere experience?"

"Yeah."

"Sounds like you'll do. Get in trouble, call the number on this card. I'll come bail you out."

"Uh—thanks."

"Can't rate you any higher than a diver three to start. Base pay's five hundred eighty a day sat, dollar a foot over four hundred feet. You furnish hat and gear up to the umbilical."

"Look, I got a friend—"

"He a diver?"

"Sport work and light salvage. But he's a hard worker, and he learns fast." He swallowed. "We go together."

Hohmann raised his eyebrows. "That so? Okay, we'll look at him for a tender. Go see the doc. Get your paperwork done, then come back and find me."

The doc's name was Van Dine, and he hovered expectantly as Galloway got undressed. "Very good," Van Dine said, patting him after taking his blood pressure and pulse. "Excellent physique, young man. You a runner? Swim a lot?"

"I stay in shape."

"Various marks and scars, such as we all accumulate, in body as well as soul. . . . Read the letters, please, from the top of the chart down. . . . Now the colors . . . that's perfect. Very well, you've done the spread-and-yank before, haven't you? Stand, please." He did, steeling himself as behind him he heard the snap of latex gloves. "The fellows say, 'Dr. VD, I wonder how you do these with both hands on my shoulders.' . . . Bend over, please."

He grunted as Van Dine grabbed his penis with the left hand and drilled his right index finger where it hurt most. It was a standard test for spinal-cord damage; the anus was supposed to contract when the penis was stimulated. But instead of a quick pinch, Van Dine stroked it. He let go as Galloway opened his mouth to protest.

"Everything seems normal. Sign here. Go ahead and get dressed."

"That's it?" he said, surprised. "D'I pass?"

"I said so, didn't I? Here's a little kit I made up for the boys. Decongestants, analgesics, Band-Aids, that sort of thing."

He patted Galloway again. "See Virginia in the front office for your paperwork."

Virginia wasn't in; the girls said to come back later. Still shaking his head, he went out back.

He found Hohmann under a prefab metal roof behind the main building. The manager was looking thoughtfully up at a twenty-foot-tall assemblage of metal cylinders covered with piping and valves, the whole freshly painted a pale lime green and mounted on skids. Not looking at him, Hohmann said, "Guess you seen these before."

"Mostly from the inside." The rain drummed on the roof as he circled it, hands thrust into his jeans. Hohmann waited, working the cigar around in his mouth as if he was cleaning his teeth with it.

It was a fairly standard saturation-diving system, made up of two large units, the deck chamber and the bell. The deck chamber, which rang faintly when he rapped it with his knuckles, was an eight-foot-diameter welded steel cylinder lying on its side. It would stay on the barge or drilling rig, wherever the divers were operating from. At one end was a transfer lock and mating assembly; at the other, a smaller air lock for food and medical supplies. Without looking inside, he knew it contained a small head, spartan berths, and enough lighting, heating, and communications to keep four or five very tough men alive and working for up to forty days.

The second part of the system was a vertical cylinder six feet in diameter and fifteen feet high. This was the SDC—submersible decompression chamber—which divers usually just called the "bell" or the "pot." It mated to the deck chamber through a side lock. Atop it were a sheave and lifting pads; below were detachable weights to counter its buoyancy, as well as a wide lockout hatch, through which the divers could emerge in full gear.

The way a saturation system worked was that the divers compressed on deck, in the larger cylinder, breathing a carefully monitored mix of helium and oxygen, till they reached ambient pressure for the depth at which they'd work. They then transferred to the bell, which was lowered to the work site by a crane or winch. After putting in a shift there, they returned to the bell, were hoisted to the surface, and locked back into the deck chamber still pressurized.

Essentially, the team lived in the deck chamber and commuted to work in the bell for however long the project took. Just looking at it made him feel itchy. He came back around it, to find Hohmann still waiting. It felt like some kind of test. "Not new, is it?"

"Not exactly."

"How long you been operating it?"

"This'll be first time. Bought it from SubSea in April."

"You check out all the valves? Pressure-test the locks? Comm gear and ECUs work?"

Hohmann nodded. He worked the cigar around some more and let go some smoke. Galloway tried again. "Where's the handling gear?"

"On the boat. Loaded that out this morning."

"Chamber control?"

"In that control van."

"And the life-support stuff—"

"Finishing checkout this morning; it'll go out with the chambers."

"Well, it looks like it ought to work."

Hohmann nodded at last. "That's what I think. Everything go okay up front?"

"Not quite. That doctor of yours . . . "

"The answer's yes."

"What was the question?"

"You know what the question was. Knuckles gets too friendly, just belt him. He won't, though."

He was about to ask Hohmann about the paperwork when a carryall splashed into the yard. Four doors popped open. The manager pulled the cigar from his lips and spat to the side. "Introduce you to the team. Hey! Get over here a minute."

They pulled gear bags from the back, then drifted over to the shed. They wore slickers or nylon jackets over work clothes, greens and denims or cutoffs, and heavy boots. They had knives on their belts.

Galloway stood waiting, surveying their faces. A dive crew was about as close as you could come to a squad in combat.

He'd be living cheek by jowl with these men. Depending on them for his life, as they'd depend on him. They were studying him with the same casual intensity.

"This here's your new diver three. Name's Lyle Galloway. Don't know if he's got a nickname—"

"I go by Tiller."

"He used to dive for a couple of outfits here. Been up north running his own show for a few years, come back to see what's changed. He'll be going with y'all Monday out to Pandora."

He shook hands, trying to place names with faces. Derick Winslow, a gaunt, gloomy-looking fellow with sparse brown hair retreating from a vast domed forehead. "Porch" Porchellacchia, a huge, ugly customer with tattoos covering his forearms below rolled-up blue denim sleeves. Ernesto "Ace" Rodriquez, a well-built Latino who wore his hair pulled back in a John Paul Jones ponytail. Jay McCray, shorter and slighter than the rest, whose eyes darted past Galloway's as they clasped hands. "Porch and Ace are divers, Wildman and the Captain are diver tenders," Hohmann explained, smiling as he watched them circle one another.

"Glad to meet y'all," said Galloway.

"I hearda you," said Porchellacchia. His accent was pure New Jersey. "Di'n't you use to crew with Lee Cleveland?"

"Yeah. Once."

"What, you don't like him?"

"Where's the boss?" Hohmann interrupted. Porchellacchia shrugged his massive shoulders like Atlas relieved of the world. "There's one guy left, the head hammer. Roland Boudreaux."

"He's still on the boat," said Rodriquez. "Probably goin' to stay there, too, ride it back out, I know him."

Galloway: "Boudreaux. Coon-ass?"

"You got it, from Chauvin. How'd it go out there this morning, Ace?"

"Okay. Most everything's on the boat. Roland's makin' sure the crew's getting it stowed right and griped down hard."

"Everything look good for Monday?"

"Far as I can see, just get the chamber aboard."

"Truck'll be here at noon. Want you all here, lend a hand if we need you. Knock off after that. Rest up tomorrow; it'll be hot and heavy come Monday."

41

"Loadin' gear, that's tender work," said Rodriquez, but when Hohmann looked at him, he smiled.

Hohmann waved them away and the knot broke, the men picking up their bags again and heading inside. The slight guy, McCray, lingered behind. He said, still avoiding eye contact, "Guess I'll be tending for you, then. What kind of hat you use, Tiller?"

"Got an old Superlite."

"Got it with you? Want me to check it out?"

"Thanks. I'll get it from the truck."

When he came back, McCray looked at it closely, turned it upside down, fingered the valves. "I'll crack it apart, check it out. Got your telephone, umbilical, all that?"

"I thought the company—"

"Yeah, just checking. I'll get it all together for you, get it out to the boat Monday."

McCray left. Galloway looked after him. He wasn't sure he liked the small man's ingratiating, anxious manner. What was McCray's nickname? "Captain." Had Hohmann intended that mockingly?

"Galloway, got a second?"

"Yeah."

Hohmann asked him if he minded checking out the air compressor on the life-support pallet while they waited for the truck. Tiller reminded himself he wasn't a diver first anymore. He was back to a third, only one jump ahead of a tender. He said okay quietly and went to look for the toolroom.

The toolroom smells—spray paint, Darathene, WD-40—took him back years. He checked out wrenches and compression gauges from a blue-smocked woman named Earlene. He took them back out to the shed, located the compressor among the gas-storage banks and the mixing units and recovery units, and went to work.

It was a Quincy, the standard workhorse used to compress air for diving or to pressurize the chamber. No electric starters on these. You spun it up manually with a long crank, a bitch of a job on cold mornings. He checked the air system first, the volume tanks, piping, the compressor. Everything was tight. He moved to the engine. He checked the oil and filters, then the compression. It was low on one cylinder and he pulled the head to check it out.

One of the rings had picked up a nick somewhere. He went to the toolroom and got a replacement and a striker hammer in case he had to apply a little force.

As he was fitting it, Porchellacchia came over and stood watching him. Tiller glanced his way, but neither spoke. They were about the same height, but the other was built so massively, Galloway wondered how he got into a wet suit. His upper arms were huge. He had his shirt off now, showing more tattoos. On one shoulder, an eagle screamed from the handlebars of a Harley-Davidson. On the other, the Pagan colors and a "1%" patch. Blazoned across his chest was a Nordic warrior defying the heavens from the bow of a storm-tossed long ship, a screaming woman slung over his shoulder. From the deck howled the skull-faced crew. It was in five colors, skillfully done.

Porchellacchia put his boot up on the compressor Galloway was working on.

"Mind taking your foot off there?"

Porchellacchia didn't answer. Instead, he put his boot right on the ring.

Galloway picked up the hammer. He hefted it, then, when the other still didn't move, bounced it off his instep, aiming above the steel toe. Porchellacchia snarled and jerked his boot down.

"So you don't like Lee Cleveland."

"Nobody likes Lee Cleveland."

"He's a good diver."

"I think so, too. But nobody likes him. You like him?"

"No."

"There you go. Something else we agree on."

Porchellacchia looked baffled. He scratched sweat above the warrior. Gradually a scowl grew. "That kind of mouth don't go from diver threes, asshole."

"Anytime, buttwipe." He kept the hammer swinging casually. "Anytime you're ready."

Porchellacchia moved slowly away, like a gradually departing thunderhead. Galloway started putting the compressor back together. He topped off the oil, lubed the compressor section, and put a gallon of diesel in the tank. He fitted the crank, backed off, and gave it a whirl. It started rough, but the pressure gauge climbed steadily. "That's old fuel in that can," Hohmann shouted over the roar. "It'll run better with fresh."

43

"Truck's here," someone else shouted, and the drone of an air horn came from the gates. Galloway cut the compressor off as a crane blasted black smoke.

Before too long, the whole tons-heavy mass of the deck chamber and after it the bell lifted off their concrete pads and dangled, swaying on steel threads in the drizzle, then descended to a temporary lodgment on the flatbed. Hohmann and Rodriquez directed the griping down. When the manager had climbed up and tested each steadying line, the eighteen-wheeler blared again. It backed carefully out the gate, made a three-point, and headed off down the road.

"Okay, that's it. See you guys Monday. The Gaudet dock in Bayou City, five A.M. That's zero five hundred for you ex-pogeys too dumb to read a watch right."

"Up yours, Chester."

"*Chinga tu madre.*"

Rodriquez came over, his ponytail curled limp and damp against his neck in the heat. His smooth, swelling arms glistened dark. Tiller noticed a gold stud in his ear. "Look, after work, rest of us going to end up at the Rack Box, probably. You know where that is?"

"You don't like the Brass Hat?"

"We like someplace you can cut loose, have some fun. *Laiss' les bon temps rouler,* like they say around here."

"I'll be there. Oh, I got a buddy, too. Okay if he comes along?"

"Sure, why not? We'll get something t'eat at Elmo's, then go there."

Galloway hesitated. Something about Rodriquez, the way he talked . . . "You from California, Ace?"

"I'm a Chino hand, if that's what you're askin'."

Chino was the California Institution for Men, a prison east of Los Angeles. It had a training program for commercial divers.

"Thought so."

"You done time, too."

"How'd you know?"

"Way you hammered the Porch right off, didn't take an ounce of shit. Way you figure quick to act in the joint. Where you was at, man?"

"Central. Raleigh."

"Where's that?"

"North Carolina."

"Never met anybody did time there. Hard?"

"It's never easy, is it?"

"You got that right. Well, see you tonight, *chico*. You an' your buddy."

"Yeah," said Tiller. "We'll be there."

Six

So why'd you didn't give me a call?" Shad said, stalking around the barroom. "I was waiting all day. Went out, some redneck son of a bitch in a tractor-trailer throws a bottle at me. Maybe I ought to get in the damn truck and go home."

"Take it easy. Look, I told you, the manager said he'd take you on as a tender. Okay? Soon as you learn the gear, they'll break you out to a diver third, same pay I'm getting. Just report to Hohmann Monday."

"I could have gone in today, you'd of called."

"Well, I didn't think of it, okay?" Tiller tried to smooth him down. "I'm sorry. You're right, I should have called. But it's all fixed now. Let's grab a burger, then go meet these guys."

The Rack Box was on 90, near the Honda dealership. A Miller's sign blinked from the window like a beacon. The air conditioning was on so high, opening the door was like walking into a beer cooler. It was newer than the Hat, chrome and Formica, overhead fans, a tank of tropical fish near the back. Galloway craned around the Saturday-evening crowd, caught a raised fist, and headed over.

McCray lifted a glass in welcome. Rodriquez and Winslow nodded. Porchellacchia sucked a tooth and said nothing, his visage indifferent and hostile. McCray said, "This guy here you

46

don't know's 'Pinhole' Guidry, a welder from Crew One. He's some kind of second cousin to Ron Guidry, the pitcher. Plays a good game a softball himself. Well, guess we're all here, except—"

" 'Ceptin' Roland," said Rodriquez.

"He coming? I need to meet him," Tiller said.

"I think he flew back already, out to the rig. He don't ever stay ashore very long." McCray half-lifted his beer. Then all their eyes lifted, moved past Galloway, and he saw them go still.

"Guys, this is Shad Aydlett, friend of mine from Hatteras Island. He's hiring on as a tender."

"With *us*?" said Porchellacchia.

"With DeepTech, yeah." He grabbed two vacant chairs from a nearby table; the drinkers at it looked up, frowning, then saw the ring of divers and looked away.

Rodriquez resumed talking, gesturing with an empty shot glass. "So I say to him, 'Look, you talk whether I got the balls, hey, *chinga tu madre*, hey? It is not a matter of balls. It is a matter of do you like to screw a goddamn piece of ice or not.' And he say, 'You take the job, you dive the job—that is what divers do, no?' So finally I say yes.

"Well, this is in the goddamn East River. Dead rats, dead cats, white eels—rubbers floating in the water. In January. We have to chop holes in the ice to dive. Two months we work in that goddamn river. That was my leas' favorite job, you know it. I just don' like to be cold."

A girl came by for their orders. Galloway noticed she stayed clear of the divers' hands. "It don't matter," said Porch. "Ain't a bad bottle up there. Bring me whatever gets in ya way. Ace, whassa matter, you not drinking tonight?"

"Jose Cuervo is not drinking? Hombre, you do not know what drinking is. You try some of this, no?"

"Refill this coon-ass china," said McCray, holding up his plastic beer cup. "Tiller, Aydlett, what you want? This's Porch's round."

"Shit it is. I didn't sign on to buy for tube-suckers."

"I'll pay for ours," Galloway told the harried-looking waitress. He thought for a moment of just getting a soft drink. He'd fried his brain the night before. Then he saw them watching and shrugged inwardly and said, "Double bourbon. Shad?"

"Sounds good."

47

"Two double bourbons . . . wait a minute . . . make it four. I never dive without a backup."

The Crew One guy, Pinhole, started a story about Saudi, about a friend of his who'd gone there. "Deke Swenson. Another Chino hand, Ace."

"Yeah, I hear of him. He graduate three, four years ahead of me."

"Good guy but a slow learner, you know? He started with Oilfield International, and they had this group going to Saudi Arabia. The company sits them down and give 'em this briefing. One thing they tell them, don't bring any booze. Under no conditions. There's no drinking in this country we're going to, understand? So what does Swenson do? He packs some pot to tide him over and gets caught at the airport soon as they arrive. He served two years and then he had three days to get out of the country."

"Saudi, it is hot there, no?"

"You'll sweat your brain right out your ears. But there's work there. A lot of work, I hear. That's why things are so slow in the Patch, crude prices so low, they're pumping like mad. You thinkin' of going to Saudi, Ace?"

"I might, somebody makes me the right offer."

McCray said, "I know a guy was out there. On a dive barge working over by Kharg Island. This was back, you know, we're not supposed to be helping the Iranians, right? But they kept upping the offer and finally somebody figured out how. Set up a dummy company in Switzerland, hire a few Aussies and Brits, but the rest were just the regular guys from Houston. Only the divers talked in a bar and somebody overheard them. The Iraqis hit the barge with an Exocet. One guy killed, forty-five hurt."

"Where you pick up diving, man?" Rodriquez asked Galloway.

"Coast Guard. I was a diver there, then did a tour with the SEALs in Vietnam."

"How can Coast Guard be a SEAL? Thought they was Navy."

"They had this volunteer wartime cross-service program, since they needed divers."

"Volunteer get your ass shot off, sounds shit-stupid to me," said Porchellacchia.

48

"How about your friend? Shad, where you learn to dive?"

"I got a PADI certificate."

"A what?"

"That's scuba talk. That's tube-sucker talk there," said Porchellacchia contemptuously. "What makes you think you can come down here with that kind of rooty-poot, fish-spearing, bottle-baby bullshit?"

"Who is this mother?" said Aydlett to the table at large. "He always like this, or is it PMS?"

There was a scrape as McCray scooted his chair back. "Where you two stayin', Tiller?" he said quickly.

Galloway kept his eyes on the big man. "Right now, sleeping at Miss Jill's."

"At the Hat? What, she got bunks there?"

"She got floors," said Aydlett. He tossed off his double and reached for the reload. Porchellacchia grunted and pulled out a pack of ultralights, tilting his head back and squinting as he torched one. Tiller relaxed; the moment had passed, though he couldn't tell how. But he stayed alert.

"The Clauncher still over there?"

McCray: "He's a sad tale."

Porchellacchia: "He's a shithead."

Guidry: "That's right. He dicked up. It was his own fault."

McCray said angrily, "How was it *his* fault? The company put him down there without a backup, in a situation he couldn't get out of if something went wrong."

"It wouldn't have gone wrong if he'd used his head before he started burning."

"Smart guys don't get hit, that's all," said Guidry, nodding like a judge.

"Nobody'd get hit if there were rules and everybody followed them."

"What kind of diver are you, Cap'n? We followed the goddamn rules, we wouldn't never get any work done."

There was no mistaking it, Galloway thought; the way Porch and the others used "Captain" for McCray was an insult. "Were you in the service, Jay?" he asked him.

"Army."

"What branch?"

"Diver."

"Mud-sucker," Porchellacchia said.

49

"Why do they call you Captain? Were you an officer?"

"Because they're assholes." The little man glowered, then drained the last of his beer.

"You callin' me a asshole, Captain?"

McCray hesitated. "No, Porch."

"How about Ace? He a asshole?"

"Knock it off, Gary," said Winslow. Galloway flinched; he'd almost forgotten that the gaunt man who sat with a foil pack of Mail Pouch and an untouched glass of clear liquid in front of him could speak. Even more surprising, the big Pagan dropped the subject. He got up, chains jingling, and stamped off. "Be back," he called back to them, shoving men into table edges. "Gonna get me some of that pussy-ass Ho-zay Queervo Ace keeps darin' everybody to try."

Tiller started on the second double. He stretched out, listening lazily as the others traded bullshit stories and diving tips. He felt at home with these people.

Maybe it was because they were like him. They weren't comfortable in a nine-to-five tie-and-jacket job, or in the stamped-out ranks of the military. There was just something about them. . . . He thought about that for a while, adding bourbon from time to time to maintain the glow.

There was just something about divers. Not what most people thought, that they enjoyed danger. Divers didn't take risks for fun. They took them, sure, but because it paid.

It was more a matter of the personality matching the career. You sort of had to be a boisterous, arrogant, egotistical son of a bitch, unable to imagine doubt or apprehension . . . or you were worthless in the water. Like that movie about the astronauts. You had to have the right stuff. You didn't need a Ph.D. or even a high school education. But when the shit hit the fan, you had to be able to make the right decision fast. If you couldn't, you wound up dead, or dicked up in some even more unpleasant way. Whatever McCray said, nothing was ever going to change that. Down there, face-to-face with—what had Claunch called it?—the blue, no regulation was going to save you. You had to depend on yourself, and on your buddies.

" 'Scuse me."

When he looked to see who was poking him, he saw that the bar was full. The table behind them was full, too. Two men stood by it, short, squat guys who looked like brothers. "Yeah?" he asked them.

"Give us those chairs back."

"What chairs?"

"Those chairs you took. We didn't need 'em then. Now we want 'em back."

"Hell with that. We got 'em; you get some others."

"Or sit on this," said Rodriquez, giving them a hand sign that was not strictly limited to underwater communication. "We're divers, Pierre. You want to make trouble, get set for a shitload."

Porchellacchia came back with a half-gallon bottle of tequila. The twins scowled as he towered over them, six feet by three of leather and silver and black T-shirt and a hopeful, vicious, drunken grin. "Hi," he said.

"Let's go," said one of the men at the table. They all got up, scowling. One spat at Galloway's feet.

"Hey, you want some of this tequila?" Ace asked Shad. Aydlett pushed his glass over. Rodriquez filled it till the top held a convex lens of clear liquor, then, with a flourish of his butane lighter, lighted it.

"Son of a bitch," said Shad, staring down at the dancing blue flame.

"Drink it down, my man. Do not hesitate. You all right, long as you have no fear."

McCray was talking about the first job he'd done for DeepTech. "This fella was just an accident waiting to happen. On the beach, he'd drop motors on his foot. So this job, we were gonna stab a conductor in the northwest corner of the template. Space Man stabs the conductor in the southeast corner, comes up, and tells everybody topside he has it in the right one. So we broke down the gear and left. The drilling company went down, proceeded to drill in this hole. I mean, exactly one hundred and eighty degrees opposite where it should be.

"Six months later, they call us in to set another conductor, in the southeast corner. Porch goes down and looks. 'Can't do it,' he tells the supervisor. 'There's a conductor here already.' 'Can't be.' 'Tellin' you, there's one here.' They figure he must be narced, doesn't know what he's doing. Send me down. 'Hey. It's in the southeast corner.' "

"What's a template?" said Aydlett.

"When they drill, they do directional drilling out from the well head. Go down, then turn the string and strike out horizontally. If you're in the wrong corner, you've just cost the company mucho mucho dollars."

"How come? As long as there's oil?"

"Because there're other holes in the template, but you've wasted every one your well runs across. Instead of producing twenty wells, now you can only produce fourteen. Space Man got fired, and his supervisor, too."

"Supervisor? It wasn't his fault."

"Now you're getting it," said McCray. "But the oil company laid it on the line: If you don't fire the supervisor, DeepTech will never work for us again. He had no protection. See what I mean?"

"No," said Galloway.

"Cut the chatter, Captain." Porchellacchia leaned across the table. His eyes were red now. "Let's get back to Galloway and his shade friend here."

"You looking for trouble?" Aydlett rumbled. "You just found it."

"Ain't talking to you. Talking to your asshole-buddy."

"Yeah, you talk to me, fat man," said Galloway. He got his feet under him. It was coming down. He was ready, and now it was coming down.

"I say you ain't a diver. You ain't shit. You one of them hotshot SEALs can't rig a comealong or do an underwater burn. Hell, you ain't even a real SEAL."

Porchellacchia laid a five-dollar bill solemnly on the table. Galloway squinted at it. "What's that say?"

"Abe says you can't even drink."

"Ain't I been knocking back double Turkeys all night?"

"I'm sayin' we can make up something you can't drink."

"If you can put it in a bottle, I can drink it," said Galloway. He'd done this before. They'd mix up some horrible concoction of gin, vodka, whatever was behind the bar. It would taste like kerosene, but—

Guidry got up, grinning. An empty Heineken stood where the others had left. He grabbed it and brought it back. Worked his throat, hawked, and spat.

He passed it to Winslow. The gaunt man sighed, worked his chaw into his cheek, and expectorated several tablespoons of brown drool. McCray hesitated, then added beer; under the scowls of the others, he added Tabasco and two envelopes of Sweet 'n Low.

The bottle got to Porchellacchia. An evil grin distorting his stubbled cheeks, he eased it under the table. He stared at Galloway for several seconds, then slammed it back into sight. He stood and zipped himself ostentatiously.

"Okay, drink that," he said.

Galloway caught the waitress by the arm. "Two more doubles."

"Till, you ain't seriously gonna do this."

"Nothing serious about it, Shad. Just a little game." He searched the faces around him as the woman put the heavy glasses down and retreated. He positioned one in front of the bottle and one behind it. He took a deep breath, a four-minute breath.

Before he could think about it, he tossed down the first glass, the raw straight liquor burning its way down his throat. Then, without a pause, he grabbed the slightly warm green glass of the Heineken bottle and aimed it at the ceiling fans.

Swallow, swallow, swallow, done. He slammed it down empty and grabbed the chaser, poured it down, too, and closed his eyes and sneezed.

When he opened his eyes, they were reaching out to clap his back. Porchellacchia looked dumbfounded. Galloway grinned back at them, a big drunken shit-eater, and scooped in the five.

The grin was a mask. A volcanic eruption was building up in his stomach. He staggered upright, but knew in that second he wasn't going to make it more than a couple of steps.

He turned back, leaned over, and let go onto the big Pagan's lap. Porchellacchia jerked away, roaring and flailing. "You son of a bitch. You pig-loving son of a bitch!"

"Sorry. Took me all of a sudden."

"I'm gonna hammer you for that, you prick."

"I got a better idea," Tiller said. He felt like shit, but anger came from somewhere he'd forgotten about. "Stand up. Back-to-back, here."

"What the shit is this?"

"Eskimo duel. Back-to-back. Thass right. Now hook your finger in my mouth here."

He felt the Pagan's broken fingernail dig into his gums. He got his own securely hooked in the corner of the big man's mouth. "Aw right," he mumbled, "last son of a bitch to yell or let go wins. Go!" And he gave a terrific pull.

The other took a second to understand, but when he did, Galloway felt as if his head was coming off. He locked his neck muscles and yanked on Porch's mouth, scraping his nails along the gums. He was rewarded with a pained grunt. "That's a yell," shouted Aydlett.

Guidry: "That ain't a yell."

Porchellacchia grunted. He shifted his feet and Galloway locked his throat on a howl as connective tissue started ripping. He could hear it in his head, like a piece of cloth being torn apart. His lips were slowly being torn off. The thought crossed his mind that maybe this wasn't a good idea. He couldn't resist the big man's strength.

He relaxed his neck suddenly. The slack took the Pagan by surprise, and in that fraction of a second, Galloway got his molars locked on the big man's thumbnail—right at the base—and chomped down with everything he had.

Porchellacchia's bellow of agony silenced the bar. Instantly, Tiller let go and spun around.

"Sounds like the new guy wins," said Winslow. He had a deadpan delivery, like Buster Keaton.

"Nobody ever beat me at nothing before."

"It builds character. Anyway, now you know the trick, they'll never beat you at that, either."

"Ah, son of a bitch," said Porchellacchia. He sat down, holding his thumb and looking sad.

McCray popped to his feet. He staggered over to the fish tank and groped around in it. He pulled out one of the gobies. "Hey guys," he said. "Watch me snort this fish."

"Go for it, Captain Skidmark."

"Only counts if it comes out the other side."

McCray shoved the fish up his nose, then tried to pull it out. He struggled with it for a second, and they heard a muffled "Ah, shit."

"What's the matter, Jay?"

"Help him out there."

"You know how the fin spreads? On a fish? It's caught. He can't get it out."

Galloway started to laugh. For some reason, it was funny as hell. Porch and Ace trying to tease the dorsal fin down with toothpicks while they worked the minnow out tail-first. McCray with his head back, whimpering, blood running down his chin.

At his elbow, Aydlett muttered, "Till, these guys is crazy drunk. Let's get out of here."

"Don't be a goddamn bottle baby, Shad. You don't mind putting away a few and tearing up a bar, as I recall."

"This ain't fun. This is stupid, man."

"Wait till we start sucking heads."

"Sucking heads?"

"Old Louisiana tradition. Sucking crawfish brains till one of you pukes."

"Don't that sound like fun. Look, I think we ought to get out of here, head back to the Hat, get some sleep—"

Somebody was yelling at them. "Divers! Hey! Any you assholes divers?"

"No, none of us divers are assholes."

"Call for you."

Rodriquez loped over to the pay phone. Galloway watched him frown as he listened, then gesticulate as he spoke. "What's goin' down?" asked Pinhole as he came back.

"Some bastard wants to see us at the Moon Pool."

"Kind of bastard?"

"Don't know. Just said come over there and we'll see what kicking ass is all about."

"You hear that?" screamed Porchellacchia, and Galloway slid his chair back in sheer awe. All at once, the huge Pagan's face streamed with sweat. His eyes glowed like a video game booting up. His hair stood on end. He jumped to his feet and threw two hundred-dollar bills on the table. "Who they think they're talkin' to! Let's travel."

The carryall wove and jolted through the dark streets, wheels slamming over lane dividers, crashing through bushes when McCray hauled the wheel over too soon. In the back, Aydlett muttered as he and Galloway slid around on the slick, oily bed with toolboxes and lengths of rusty chain. Tiller watched the facades going by. The sky flickered from the flare-off towers, out of sight over the horizon. He felt lightning in his fists, the familiar excitement before a mix-up. Christ, it felt good.

"These guys is frigging crazy, Till. And you're just as crazy as they are."

"Man don't take a challenge lyin' down. Least a diver don't."

"You don't know who these people are."

"Don't care, either."

"Moon Pool," McCray announced. The tires squalled and the Suburban made a graceful sliding pirouette across gravel and stopped three feet from the black lightless windows, the green door.

"It open? Don't look open."

"Saturday night, gotta be open."

"Open or not, we going in," said Porch.

"Weapons," said Winslow.

"No, Derick."

"Stop him, somebody."

"No knives, nothing like that, Wildman. 'Less they pull them first. Hear me?"

Rodriquez grabbed the door. Past him, Galloway saw nothing but darkness. Then Porchellacchia charged and they followed.

The door closed behind them, and in the sudden dark, Galloway heard the lock click shut.

"Uh-oh," someone muttered.

The lights came on, blinding him. But not enough that he couldn't see twenty guys in a ring around them, holding pool cues. They didn't look like oil-field guys. They didn't look like anything, really. Just mean-ass rounders in jeans and dirty clothes, white, black, even an Indian. Square in the center were the twins, smiling and tapping the heavy butts against their palms.

"Welcome to the Moon Pool, cher."

Porchellacchia charged with a roar. The next second, he was covered by a crawling, shouting, hammering horde, like a bumblebee attacked by ants. Galloway started forward, too,

56

then realized that was exactly what they'd been expected to do. The two wings of the opposition folded inward, cutting them off from the exit. Shit, he thought, these guys have done this before.

A face loomed up and he swung, missed, and spun as the other's eyes went past him; got his left up just in time to block the descending cue from the guy who'd closed from behind. The blow hit solid bone, sending an agonizing shock up his shoulder. He grunted, ducked under the second swing, and punched the guy as hard as he could in the throat. He went down and Galloway kicked him in the side as he bounced.

Another face. They traded blows, both missed, and they staggered apart. His left arm was limp as pasta. He stared around, rubbing it, at tables and chairs rapidly being reduced to kindling and rubble.

A stick caroming off his skull reclaimed his attention. He ducked and came around, bringing this one up from the floor, and almost punched Shad. Aydlett had the cue around the guy's neck from behind. The guy's tongue came out, then he sagged. Tiller grabbed the cue as it fell, took two steps, and broke it over one of the heads in the bellowing, jerking, struggling heap that covered the still-standing Porchellacchia.

A gleam wicked past his head, and he jerked back. Then another—so fast, it hummed. He followed the flat deadly trajectories back to Guidry, by the bar. The Cajun hefted another tumbler, then reared back into an overhand pitch and fired it across the room at a man who was trading punches with Rodriquez. It bounced off his skull with a sound like a thumped cantaloupe. He looked startled, then his eyes rolled up. Rodriquez stared down, fists still raised, as if some bolt from heaven had struck in front of him.

A little guy moved in on Galloway, grinning like a death's-head. He moved his half-open hands rapidly, feinting. Tiller circled wide, suddenly wary. The guy was too small to come in on the attack like that. He moved his hands too much. He reminded Galloway of a Vietnamese kickboxer he'd fought in Saigon City. He shifted his attention just in time and caught the kick in midair. He twisted it, then got his other hand under the guy and lifted him off the floor and slammed him over the bar into the bottles, the mirror, the stacked pyramids of glass. It sounded like a truckful of plate glass hitting a brick wall at sixty miles an hour.

He leaned on the sticky wood for a second, breathing hard, and his hand found a heavy ashtray. When he turned, another cue, the tip this time, came out of nowhere and raked his forehead. Suddenly, he couldn't see. He swung the weight blindly and was rewarded with a cry of pain.

Can't see, Christ, my *eyes*... He staggered toward where he hoped the door was, clawing at his face. Then it cleared and he saw blood smearing his hands, dripping away. As he watched it fall, he noticed a face down there. It was McCray, hugging the dirty carpet under the pool table. He didn't look proud, but he didn't look particularly ashamed, either.

From the corner of his eye, he saw the central struggle moving parallel to him. Porch was down to four passengers, but they were sticking like ticks. Fists and the butts of shattered sticks rose and fell like the frenzied jerking of insect antennae. The face of the second twin rose up, screaming curses, and came at him with the jagged end of a busted cue. Galloway crouched, flinging blood from his eyes like a horse shaking away flies.

"Banzai!" screamed Aydlett, and charged. He caught the man in the gut and carried him backward. The window exploded around them as they went through it into the parking lot.

Behind them came more crashing, a lot of glass breaking. He glimpsed Winslow with a smashed bottle in his hand, he and a man circling, the man reaching smooth as silk for his belt and coming up with a honed glitter. Shit, Galloway thought. We better wind this up before somebody gets cut. "Outside!" he yelled. "Outside!" He grabbed the tall diver from behind and dragged him toward the door.

They gathered outside, panting and wiping off blood. He blinked in the lights of cars pulling in. Between him and the lights, a woman's silhouette, a woman kicking somebody on the gravel.

"That was close."

"They were laying for us. Those bastards."

"Porch, you just about—"

"Ace," Porch panted then. "Ace! He's still in there."

Howling, they charged in again, crowding each other in

the narrow door. Tiller saw the shattered window gape and lurched toward it instead. Two steps, then a leap. The leaping part went okay, but as he hurled in, he felt his boot catch on the sill, felt his body wheeling forward and down into a graceless nosedive, saw the dirty, blood-spattered floor come up. He had only a moment to reflect with resigned, drunken awe on how incredibly hard he was going to hit.

When he came to, horns were blowing. For a second or two, he thought they were in his head. Then he was thrown onto something that boomed metallic, hollow, that smelled of oil. Another body landed on top of him. He fought to push it off, but it was heavy, immovable, limp. Then he heard the carryall start and let go, and he slid downward then, into the black.

SEVEN

He jerked, coming back from a hazy, red-flickering midnight.

With consciousness came pain. Even breathing hurt. His head felt fragile as the translucent cocoon some reef fish weave at night. "Shad," he muttered between dry lips. "Shad."

No answer. He lay with his eyes shut for a while, enduring it, then had to move. Had to open his eyes first, though. He groaned in advance and forced the lids apart.

They blinked at an unfamiliar ceiling: pressed acoustic tile, with brown water stains in vaguely threatening forms. Morning glared from a small metal-gridded window. A motor of some type whined and roared on the far side of the wall. The air was so hot, it burned his lips when he breathed. His hand explored the surface he lay on. It was a bunk, narrow and hard.

He felt perspiration needle his forehead. Was he under way? Was this a boat, a craft of some sort? But he couldn't feel any motion.

He rolled off the bunk and sank to the floor. On hands and knees, he dragged himself across a scratchy polyester carpet smelling of dry mold toward an impossibly distant metal door. He hesitated, then elevated his head cautiously. His pulse hammered his temples with a ball-peen and he groaned again, then suddenly went silent.

Someone was breathing hoarsely on the far side of the door.

He looked around the cubicle for a weapon. Nothing of-

60

fered itself but a strip of aluminum edging peeling off the jamb. He tore it free—it was very flimsy—and bent it around his knuckles, sharp edge out. He pulled himself to his feet and balanced there, dripping sweat in the airless heat. He cocked his fist and jerked open the door.

The gray tomcat, bristly as a bottlebrush and ugly as a Jerusalem artichoke, jumped back and hissed. Spread out in front of the door were the disassembled, bleeding remains of a large mole.

Galloway felt his gorge rise. He groped rapidly along the short, narrow passageway toward the whisper and drip of water. He found a startled Porchellacchia, naked except for a greasy leather vest, sitting on a toilet. He pushed by him, muttering, " 'Scuse me," and threw up into the shower stall.

"Guess that's better than last time," said the Pagan. He wiped himself and flushed. "You feelin' okay?"

Tiller clenched his teeth. "Want to die."

"What you need's a nice long crew-boat ride in ten-foot seas. Then you won't be afraid of dyin'. You'll be afraid you won't."

He hung to the shower edge, breathing hard. When Porchellacchia left, he unwound the metal from his fist and dropped it into the wastebasket. He confronted himself in the spotted mirror. Nothing that looked like it needed stitches, but his mouth hurt like hell, and when he spat, black clots spotted the rusty porcelain. He splashed cold water on his face and drank ten mouthfuls of it. It tasted of iron and oil.

When he found the little kitchen, Porchellacchia and Winslow were sitting there with the Sunday *Times-Picayune* spread over the table and floor. Coffee was chuckling into a not-very-clean carafe. He pushed the cat off the remaining chair, noticing as he did so that it was missing a front paw. It bit his hand and he kicked at it, but it evaded his foot easily.

"Don't dick with Windex," mumbled Porch. "He got some very nasty ways of gettin' even, people he don't like."

"Where the hell are we? What am I doing here? Where's Shad?"

"Who?" said Winslow.

"His jungle buddy," said Porch. "You hung over, man? Hey, that's too bad."

"People who drink have only themselves to blame."

"Derick don't touch that nasty alcohol," Porch told Galloway. "Hey, you want some coffee? You mean you don't remember you and him arguing?"

"I don't remember anything after getting thrown in the carryall after the fight."

"Hell, that was only about ten o'clock. Evening hadn't even started then." Porch sipped from a Care Bears mug, considered, then reached for a pint carton of half-and-half. "Try some a this between roast; this'll bring it all back."

Tiller rubbed sweat off his forehead, trying to remember. No matter how he tried, he got only flashes. Yes, there was something there about Aydlett—an argument, Shad walking out. Out of which bar? Hell, he couldn't remember. "So where's this?" he asked them.

"Where's what, man?"

"Where are we right now?"

"Oh. This here's our trailer, man."

"*My* trailer."

"Yeah, I mean, it's Derick's, a'least it's rented in his name. Him and me, we live here, when we're not out on a job or shacked up."

"Isn't that an air conditioner?"

"The fan works. The air-conditioning part, we ain't got that fixed yet. Derick, you was going to fix that before summer got here."

Winslow didn't answer. He was reading *Parade* magazine.

"So what am I doing here?" said Tiller patiently. He felt like crawling away into some dark crevice and dying like a poisoned roach.

"We invited you to live here. An' you said okay. Di'n't you see your duffel and shit there under your bed?"

"What about Shad?"

"We only got room for three."

He felt, if possible, worse. Had he accepted an invitation when Aydlett hadn't been included? He hoped he hadn't really done that. "Where's he staying? Did he say?"

Porchellacchia shrugged. "Probably still at the Hat. What you sweating it for, where he lives?"

"Just go back a ways is all. Our families—"

"You tellin' me you're related?"

"Forget it. Just forget it." He reached a shaky hand toward the coffee. "Gimme some of that half-and-half."

He got two cups down and then part of a cherry Pop-Tart. He tried to read the sports section, but the print vibrated too fast. He refilled the mug with water and wandered around the trailer, then found a sliding door and stepped outside.

He was on a weathered salt-treated deck, the same toad gray as the cat. Beyond heat-withered hydrangeas and a silent set of wind chimes, a parched lawn stretched down to a pier jutting into a narrow bayou. The water was brown and still, reflecting a scrubby jungle beyond.

On impulse, he went down the steps, past beetle-gnawed rosebushes. Dry grass crackled under his bare feet, then squished as the ground sank. There was a little dike at the edge of the bayou. A levee, he remembered. Boards balanced on concrete blocks led up to and over it. Frogs hopped and rustled as he negotiated it, arms outstretched, scanning the tall grass for gators.

A squadron of pelicans stretched their wings, eyeing him, then launched heavily into flight one by one as he stepped onto the dock. At the edge of the bayou, a shoal of rubbery-looking water hyacinth lay tangled in marsh grass and alligator weed. The pier ran out over the grass and the brown still water, and he stepped carefully on the sun-warmed wood, not wanting a splinter. He squatted there and looked out for a long time in the insect-clicking, drowsy heat.

Gradually, he became aware that something was behind him. He turned his head slowly to avoid startling it.

Nothing there. Nothing but the pier, the levee, and the overgrown lawn rising heat-faded green to the trailer and the deck, and off to the right of it a rusting radar antenna on a steel pedestal. Past that were more trailers, a parkful of them. Back and forth by the closest, a pit bull loped like a tireless machine, dragging a wire loop along a line.

He lowered his eyes to the levee verge. The water was still, but here and there the glossy dark green leaves of floating hyacinth bobbed, as if beneath the murky surface something was moving among the roots, betraying its presence only by their occasional twitch and stir. Nothing . . . yet still he could feel it waiting, smell its presence in every breath of the steamy, rotting air he snorted through his flared nostrils.

Suddenly, something moved to his left, at the very corner of vision. He jumped back, turning to face it, his fists coming up. But again, there was nothing there, just faded boards, a sun-bleached shatter of jagged shell.

Till the buoy twitched again. He hesitated, then moved to it.

The polyethylene line was smooth against his palm. The cage came into sight, galvanized chicken wire knitted into a cube. Inside it dark horny shapes scrabbled frantically in the sudden glare. The smallest lay motionless on the bottom of the trap, shell split and legs pulled off.

The larger crabs, trapped, had turned on the weakest for food.

When he got back to the trailer the TV was on and the beer was out. He turned his head away when Porch held up a can. Porchellacchia and Winslow were sitting in two ripped BarcaLoungers that drooled stuffing onto the carpet of the living area. The Westerner had the remote control. They watched half a second each of the Nashville channel, CNN, Turner, Headline News, and MTV, then paused at the weather channel to watch a dying hurricane off the Georgia coast. When the dizzying flicker of images started again, Porchellacchia stirred. "Christ. Let's just watch something. What you want to see? Want to watch some golf, Tiller?"

"Shit, no. There a ball game on?"

"Rangers and Brewers."

"Who?"

"Hey, can I use your phone?" he asked both of them. Winslow aimed the remote back toward the kitchen and clicked it twice.

The phone rang and rang out at the Hat. Nobody answered. "Shit," he muttered. Where the hell was Aydlett? He went back into the living room. They were watching golf. "What happened last night?" he asked the Pagan again.

"Las' night we kicked some righteous ass, boy. What you mean, what happened last night?"

"I remember the Rack Box. Then I remember the Moon Pool. But after—"

"You remember throwing that guy over the bar? And then, when what's-his-face went through the window? Well, his wife was out there—the guy's. And she musta been drunk out of her head, because she started kicking him in the balls, the guy, not your buddy, and screamin' her head off about how they were killin' her husband. She had those pointy heels on and I bet that son of a bitch don't get it up for a year."

Tiller sat down and watched Curtis Strange tee off. "Hey, lighten up," said the Pagan, belching. "Want a beer?"

"No."

"Smoke?"

"I don't smoke."

"Yeah, me neither," he said, looking around for the pack. He torched an ultralight. "So what were you askin' me?"

"What happened last night."

"Like I told you, nothin'. We just went to a couple nother bars and you and your buddy had a argument and he split. Then we partied some more, then come back here." Porch shrugged. "An' here we are, end of story. Don't worry about it. He's a big boy—I mean, a *big* boy. He c'n take care of hisself in a fight was my impression." He grinned. "That's mostly what counts for a Pagan."

"I noticed your tattoos."

"Like these?" He turned around to show off more on his back.

"You still ride?"

"Sure. Got a piece a iron out front. But I ain't really what you'd call full-fledged scooter trash no more. There's a club up in N'Orleans I do a little trick ridin' with once in a while, but I ain't a member. Once you a Pagan, you never wear another patch."

Trying to include the other man, Tiller said, "How about you, Derick?"

Winslow raised his eyes slowly from the comics. "Me?"

"Yeah, where you from, that kind of stuff."

The gray eyes in the gaunt face studied him for a few more seconds. Then they went back to the brightly colored pages.

"Ol' Wildman, he don't talk about hisself much. He's from Utah or some such of a place. But what he says he'll do, he'll do. . . . Well, you ready to head out and start tomorrow?"

He thought with relief of diving. Sometimes it was just too complicated, trying to live on land. "Yeah. I guess so."

"Roland should be out there waitin' for us. . . . You ain't met him yet."

"Boudreaux?"

"That's right. The boss, he ain't the kind of guy you meet every day. Ol' Roland, lemme warn you on this, don't make no jokes about his wife. Or cracks about Jody."

"Jody?"

"Jody's what you call the guy comes in the back door when you go out the front. Moves in when you move out, drinks your liquor, drives your car. Roland's wife, she's a major-league fox, and she don't exactly believe in locking it in the freezer while he's out in the Patch. You know what I mean. An' he don't like it one little bit. He don't have much of a sense of humor at the best of times, ole Bender Boudreaux."

"Nice nickname."

"You'll see why. He don't like to be called that, either."

Galloway said, "Talkin' about divers . . . how about Mc-Cray? Why do you call him Captain?"

"Short for Captain Skidmark."

He remembered the Moon Pool, a face looking up from underneath a pool table. "He's a squirrel."

"The nuttiest."

"When I was out in the Patch and a guy squirreled, that was his last dive with that crew."

"Well, he's a strange breed of squirrel. Before a dive, he'll quake in his pants. One time, he took his skivvies off in the bunk room after. And he had skid marks in them. So we started calling him Captain Skidmark.

"Then one day we were out doing a job for Shell, cuttin' up a buckled pipeline so they could lay new. There'd been rough seas for a while, and suddenly just all hell broke loose. We had the chamber chained down, on the barge, you know, and it broke loose. Chain was going across the deck like to cut a man's head off. Then all of a sudden there was McCray, running in there with an armload a chocks to stick under the skids. So we grabbed the comealongs and hoists and went in after him. The barge was rollin', wires were poppin'. But we finally secured it."

"That don't sound like a squirrel."

"No, but he an' me were out on a platform inspection for Chevron. He was down. I was in the control van, running the dive. And he starts to see sharks. Like, 'Pick me up. I see a shark.' 'Jay, I don't see any sharks.' 'Pick me up. I'm not going any deeper; there are sharks down here.' Hell, if we got out of the water every time there was a shark around, they'd laugh us out of Louisiana. Nobody else saw any fins or anything. I said, 'Jay, listen. If there's a shark there, it's not going to bother you.' 'No, no, I don't care. Get me up.' The tenders made a drawing of a shark and a diver, taped them on sticks. So Jay's in decompressing, and they do the puppet theater in front of his port. The shark comes up, and there's these little captions—'Help, pick me up! This is Captain Skidmark. Pick me up!' "

"Well, how do you figure—"

"I *don't* figure it. I'm just tellin' you how it is. Yeah, we got some off-the-wall puppies in Summerland. But you ain't met the number-one main man yet." He grinned. "You ain't met the Bender."

"What exactly is he, anyway? Supervisor?"

"Shit, no. I mean, he supervises on the big jobs, but he's the frigging owner. He come out of the shrimp fleet, started with Cal Dive."

"How is he as a diver?"

"He's good, sharper than he looks. Went from tender three to superintendent in three years. Then quit and set up his own outfit. It was touch and go for a while. We thought we was gonna go broke, 'specially after oil went down to about two cents a barrel. But then this Coastal contract comes through and we've been busy steady since then. . . . You guys want somethin' for lunch? I got clam strips we can nuke."

Tiller said, "Whatever." Winslow shrugged, watching an eighteenth-hole face-off between Fred Couples and Nick Faldo.

The big man shuffled into the kitchen. Miscellaneous clatters and curses, the scrape of a freezer lid and the beep of a microwave being programmed. Then "Hey. Wildman. Thought you was gonna get the garbage."

"Your turn."

"Screw it. This is a real mess under here."

"I'll get it," said Tiller, putting his hands on the armrests.

"Naw, I got it. . . . Where'd you put the garbage bags?"

"Sink," said Winslow.

"What you say?"

"Under the sink."

The thunk of a cabinet opening, and then, suddenly, Porchellacchia was shouting, "Snake! Snake!"

Tiller came out of his chair fast. At the door, he halted, watching the big man ease slowly back from the open doors beneath the sink. From a tumbled mass of black polyethylene and empty cans, a fat-bodied, rough-scaled dull brown stream was flowing smoothly out onto the vinyl tile. It took his brain a second before his eyes convinced it he was looking at a cottonmouth, a big one. It was between Porchellacchia and the door, head weaving and tongue flickering. He looked around for something long—a stick, a broom—

Winslow pushed him aside and lifted his arm. Galloway had just time to jump back before he pulled the trigger.

And kept pulling it as vinyl leapt up and cabinetry disintegrated and plastic drainpipe exploded. Empty brass glittered in the air. The snake tried to coil and strike, jerking as it was hit, but even after it stopped moving, Winslow kept firing. The rounds plowed up the flooring, tracked to and fro into the sink, punctured the stove, blasted out the window, and punched neat holes through the wall sheathing. Tiller started to reach out but stopped. It seemed safer not to interrupt.

The slide locked back, empty, and the racket stopped. For a second Winslow held the pose, combat-style, blue smoke hazing his motionless figure. Through the ringing in his ears, Galloway heard a dog barking. Then Winslow lowered the gun. "Did I get 'em?"

"You sure did," said Porchellacchia. He came slowly out from the partial shelter of the refrigerator and stared down at the remains.

Tiller slowly became aware that shouting had joined the barking. "Is that somebody outside?" he said.

When they went out on the deck, people were standing warily by the other trailers. Two held rifles, and more were gathering behind them. The pit bull loped crazily back and forth, barking and snarling frenziedly in their direction. As

68

Porch and Tiller came out, the women ducked inside. "What the hell's goin' on over there?" one of the men called.

"Just shootin' a snake. Cottonmouth got in the kitchen."

"Well, goddamn it, some of those bullets hit our trailer. We got kids over here. You coulda killed one of them easy."

"Hey, we're sorry. We'll pay for the repairs," shouted Porchellacchia. He started walking toward them, spreading his hands. "I'll take care of them," he said over his shoulder. "Make sure the Wildman's under control, all right?"

Winslow was sitting at the kitchen table, reloading the automatic from a green-and-yellow box. Galloway saw it was a nine-millimeter, the fifteen-round Smith & Wesson.

"Couple shots went wild. But I got 'em, all right."

"That's one dead snake."

"There were two of 'em. They had Porch cornered. They were gettin' ready to strike."

"That so?" said Tiller. He wasn't sure that's what he'd seen, but he could have missed one of the snakes. And it hadn't looked to him like the snake was after Porch. It had probably been trying to get away.

Windex came in. The cat checked out the bloody mess on the floor, sniffing delicately here and there at the tenderized remains; then began eating it. Tiller swallowed again, looking at the holes in the stove.

"What you want?" asked Winslow, not looking up as he slapped the reloaded magazine back into place, worked the slide, and sighted the gun.

He cleared his throat. "Mind if I have that beer now?"

EIGHT

At three thousand feet, he floated like a seed on the summer wind. Above him, almost within reach, the sky was a canopy of azure silk, stretched taut above the dark blue bowl of the Gulf.

Galloway shaded his eyes against the sun, as if flickered through a circle of scratched plastic. The aluminum fuselage of the Sikorsky S-76 buzzed like a beer can full of wasps. The muted drone of the turbines made his ears itch. Made him think of Vietnam, hurtling through the night before an op drop over Ben tre. Something back in his mind buzzed, too, some trapped hornet of memory from Nam.

He didn't try to retrieve it. There were too many things back there he never wanted to remember. Most of the time, he succeeded. He leaned forward, watching the Gulf of Mexico expand like a huge blue soap bubble.

The copilot, craning back, a dark face shouting: "Y'all okay back there?"

The only other man in the passenger compartment lifted a thumb to the Ray-Bans. After a moment, Galloway did, too.

They'd exchanged nods as Tiller had climbed in a few minutes before. The other passenger was middle-aged. Steel-framed bifocals. His work jacket and trousers looked like they'd absorbed a lot of stains in their career. A pale gray briefcase was wedged under the seat. He was sitting back now, adjusting one of the inflatable Mae Wests the pilot had handed back before takeoff.

70

The helicopter canted, seeking a new heading, and Tiller looked down, down at the Patch.

From this high, it looked like a forest, not of trees but of steel—hundreds of oil and sulfur platforms, their derricks prickling the curving blue as if the sea grew thistles. Single platforms, clumps, then gigantic clustered mangroves in circle shapes and spider shapes, whole cities perched on spindly steel legs. Here and there glimmered pinpoints of flame: flare-off towers for excess gas and cracking by-products. The sky grew murky, shading deeper as it approached the horizon.

He stared down, remembering when he'd been curious about what lay beneath it. Curious enough to quiz the engineers and geologists.

They'd explained how hundreds of millions of years ago this had been a vast swamp. The plants and animals that died in it were gradually covered with mud and sand and compressed till they became a porous rock filled with petroleum. The oil percolated slowly upward till it pooled in traps, natural gas at the top, then oil, then water.

So that now, throughout southern Louisiana, off the pendulous jut of the Mississippi Delta, and hundreds of miles out into the Gulf, the fleeing shadow of the helicopter traced one huge province of petroleum, a submerged reef of liquid energy, the richest offshore oil field in the world. Drill down to it—however deep—and up it came. Like magic, flowing on and on as if inexhaustible, as if the planet itself down to its core were turgid with oil.

It was the drilling that cost money, and lives. . . .

"Headed out?"

The other passenger was leaning forward. He nodded.

"Roustabout? Pusher?"

"Diver."

"Cameron?"

"No, Pandora."

"That's South Addition, East Cameron area. You know West? Gaston? Shattuck?"

"Haven't met anybody yet. First time out. How much farther?"

The other lifted his head slightly in understanding, held up five fingers. Five miles? Five minutes? Anyway, probably not long. Galloway leaned back into his seat, adjusting the belt

71

of the bench seat that was all the luxury a charter oil-rig chopper offered.

He tried to relax, but it wasn't easy. His arm hurt, and it was spreading. Hell, he thought. Of all the times to get inoculated.

He'd reported in with Winslow and Porch at 5:00 A.M. at the dock in Bayou City, like Rodriquez—senior guy till the rig, where this Boudreaux would take over—had told him. He remembered it from the last time he worked offshore, and when Winslow's van turned off Front toward the pier head, it was just as if he'd never left.

In the early dark, the tenders and mechanics were getting everything loaded. Everything—compressors, burning gear, cylinders of gas, ROVs, bailout bottles, suits, pallets of taped-up umbilicals. The truckers had gotten it there over the weekend and it was all supposed to be loaded now, ready to go, but somehow it never was. Now the quarter-mile dock was like a cross between a carnival midway and an invasion beach at D+2. Trucks grunted past, the splintering planks of the quarter-mile wooden pier giving off a hollow rumble. He followed Porch and Winslow toward the boat, shivering in the cold fog off the Atchafalaya.

It was a 175-foot workboat out of Amelia, with North Sea stacks and a high white deckhouse. He stopped as they went aboard and stood there, hands thrust into the pockets of his leather jacket, just looking.

It was all so familiar it gave him the creeps. Boats were growling into the slips like nursing bulldog pups. Cranes were jerking gear off tractor-trailers, crews rattling chains and shouting in hoarse voices padded by the fog, securing the pallets and tie-downs. Greenish floods lighted the pier with Kryptonite radiance. Between the pilings, the water was dark brown, black, green-gleaming where the light hit. Diesel fumes, yes, goddamn it, that was all you could smell after a while in this business. If somebody marketed a perfume that smelled like it, every whore in Bayou City would buy it. Not only divers were going out but all the different rigs' supply boats, with food, drilling pipe, concrete, mud and milk and light bulbs, everything an entire industry offshore had to have to keep producing. The *beep-beep-beep* of cherry pickers needled the back of his neck. He sucked air nervously. About the only difference he saw was that there were a few women now, operating the machinery, mostly.

"What you doin' here, Galloway?" somebody said behind him. He turned. Rodriquez had on a foul-weather jacket and a lime green hard hat with the DeepTech logo—a diving helmet and dragonfish. His earring twinkled in the emerald light. "You not get the word?"

"What word, Ace? Aren't we going?"

"Shit yeah, we're goin' all right, but not wit' chew. Hohmann tell you to check in at the front office Friday?"

He recalled with a grimace that he'd been supposed to check back with Virginia before he left. "Uh."

"Yeah, 'uh.' You better get over there soon's they open. They got some paper they want to wipe on your ass. Gear truck up the pier, going back to the yard."

"You gonna hold for me?"

"No can do, man. We got to get under way or Bender'll have my ass."

"How am I gonna get out?"

"Hey, this is not my freakin' problem, that's all," said the other diver. "Come a think of it, ain't yours, either. Just see Slack Ack. That's his job, get you out to the job."

"Who?"

"*Slack* Ack. Hohmann. You know, the manager."

"Shit," said Galloway. "Time is it?"

"Five-twenty."

"When do they—"

"Eight, office open at eight. That your gear? Throw it aboard; you can pick it up when you get there. Hey! Skid Man! Over here. This piece a shit is our boat, I think. Let's get this shit inventoried."

Galloway went up the pier and found the driver on the gear truck. He told him to wait for him, then went aboard and helped load, put his back to it with the rest of the crew for half an hour. Then cast off their lines and watched them churn off into the darkness.

The driver dropped him at the admin building, but at six-fifty the windows were dark. He sat out on the steps, watching dawn ignite like an oil fire over the bayou.

He spent two hours carrying a smeared check-in sheet around. Insurance. Bonding. IRS withholding form W-9. Next of kin. He thought about that for a second, then put down Shad. Damned if he wanted his brother to get his death money. Then he remembered a quavering voice, a shaking hand. *You got kids. You got something real.*

He crossed Aydlett's name out and initialed it and wrote in above it, small but legible, "Theodore Galloway, in trust of Eleanor Schuster, Elizabeth City, North Carolina."

Van Dine wasn't in when he went to medical. Instead, an unsmiling woman gave him a tetanus booster and a flu shot.

He was sitting there rubbing his arm when Shad came in.

His eyes fell first. He kept rubbing his shoulder, and after a pause, Aydlett said, "Tiller."

"Hey, Shad. You here for shots?"

" 'S what they tell me." He looked around, then took a seat. The silence returned.

"Look," said Galloway at last. "I understand—I mean, the guys told me I said some things. I guess I must have been so drunk, I don't even remember what I said. 'Cause I don't, but they tell me you got mad, and"—he was groping—"shit, what am I tryin' to say? I guess just that whatever I said, I was shit-faced drunk, and, man, I'm sorry."

"Yeah, you was drunk, all right."

"Hey, give me a break. I wake up Sunday morning at Winslow's; I don't even know where the hell I am. Nobody answered at the Hat. Where were you?"

"I got a place." Aydlett looked away, toward a frosted window where light came in, polished cold and pale. "Don't bother about Shad Aydlett. I got a place, got a job. I can take care of myself, man."

Galloway got up. He bent over Aydlett and put his hands on his shoulders. "Like shit. When I get back from this job, we're getting a place together. Hear me? We're still partners."

"You sure?"

He searched his mind for something to say. The times Shad had saved his life, stood by him in bar fights, pulled him out of wrecks. And the times he'd saved Shad. But those weren't things you brought up. If you mentioned them, it proved they hadn't meant anything. It had to be deeper. Had to go way back. . . .

"Remember the time you took me out to show me where your granddaddy died?"

"Out in the inlet."

"Uh-huh. And what we said then?"

Aydlett said unwillingly, "Somethin' about bein' friends for good, or something."

"And what your daddy said, about you and me?"

"Yeah, I remember."

"What was it?"

"That . . . when you goes in halfs with a white man, make sure your X is on all the papers."

"And that you stick with him. Right?"

"Guess so."

"Goddamn it, are we still partners or not?"

"I guess we is."

"Well, shake, then."

The big warm hand wrapped itself around his reluctantly, but it was there. He felt a stone roll off his chest. "Okay, god-damn it."

"But, Till, you got to stick, too. You keep sayin' you gonna help me out, but when I look around, you ain't there."

"From now on, I'll be right behind you. So, you checked in? They took you on?"

"Uh-huh. Tender three, that Chester say."

"That's what I figured. Gonna be kind of dull for a while. You got to learn the gear. They'll give you the shit jobs. But a company this small, they'll have you diving pretty soon."

"Another thing: The girl in the office, she say it's only six-fifty an hour, tender. That ain't shit, Till. I could make more than that crewing down at Oregon Inlet. Where's all this money you said we was gonna make?"

"Divers make money. Tending, you don't make that much."

"What're you getting?"

He told him. Aydlett whistled. "Five hundred eighty a *day*?"

"There's a depth bonus, too. Hang in there. Six months, you'll be raking it in, too." He slapped him again, feeling the iron-hard muscle of his partner's arm. "Gotta get going. We'll get together when I get back."

"Okay," said Aydlett. But Galloway could feel Shad's eyes following him as he walked out.

When he'd finally found Hohmann, his arms already throbbing from the inoculations, the operations manager stared at him like a long-lost bill collector. "What the hell are you doing here? You're supposed to be out on Pandora."

Two sentences into his explanation, Hohmann glanced at the wall clock and shoved his bulk up. "Follow me," he said, and ran outside.

Past the pole barn, past the muddy gear yard, a whistling roar was growing. Tenders and mechanics straightened to watch Hohmann as he waved and shouted across the grass field. A man in Mickey Mouse ears lifted his arms, signaling to the pilot. The roar steadied, then throttled back a notch as Galloway had run out, ducked under the blades, and settled himself across from the mild-looking man who now sat across from him, eyelids drooping closed.

When he glanced out again, the Gulf filled three-quarters of the window. A paler dot moved slowly through it, headed east. It rolled out of sight, then rolled back, closer now as they sank toward it. He recognized it then and smiled. A sea turtle, stroking its way doggedly across the vast blue plain.

The fuselage tilted slowly, settling, and a shudder wormed through the airframe. A sideslip pressed him against the seat belt. They were dropping now. Leaving the clear brilliant blue, sinking like a drowned body into the smoky air that lay close above the sea.

He reflattened his forehead against hot acrylic as below him Pandora 12 scrolled across the curved screen of the sea.

At first it looked like a toy, a Lego-and-Tinkertoy assemblage of colored blocks and sticks set on aluminum foil smoothed over the living room rug. Then, the eye realized it was gigantic: a steel square bigger than a football field, growing

76

from the serrated silver blue on four huge cross-braced legs. The dominant color was a pale cream, but here and there glowed the red-orange of primer. Yellow-and-black cross-hatching picked out elevators. Along with the derrick, this platform was packed with squat towers, miles of varicolored piping, boilers, smoking uptakes. Cottony manes of steam faded into invisibility as they rose. At the end of an outstretched boom, a huge bloom of dandelion-colored flame writhed in the wind. A landing platform jutted from the opposite corner. Not far away from the platform rode two dark low rectangles he recognized after a second look as a pipe-laying barge and a jet barge.

The helicopter banked again then, and the platform and barges slid out of view. The pitch of the rotors changed, and the sunlight through the window slowed its flicker.

He was wiping sweat from his hair when he heard the muffled thud above him. The jolt wasn't hard. Like being bumped by another cart at the Food Lion. The tail pitched up gently and the sea started to rotate outside the window.

He grabbed for nonexistent armrests, seeing red lights blast into life ahead of him, in front of the flight crew. Arms stabbed out, jolting switches down, palming red buttons. The pilot shouted suddenly into his throat mike: "Losing the tail rotor—losing power. Help me out, left rudder—aw, shit, no flight controls. Unable to autorotate. Looking at a hard water entry here—"

All at once, they pitched up and dove headfirst for the blue. He hung like a spun-in spider as the seat hammered his rump. Parts were shearing away, clattering along the aluminum. Suddenly he heard wind through the skin, saw daylight where metal should have been.

Through the fogged circle of plastic, the sea stared him in the face. They were falling into it, tumbling and wheeling, like a huge, crippled metal dragonfly. His gut told him desperately to do something, do something *now*. But he wasn't underwater or on land. They were in the air, and he had no idea *what* to do.

His hands clamped helpless on the seat, but it was falling, too. Everything was falling in a crazy vibration-blurred whirl of screaming sound, hammering noise, wheeling sunlight, shouts, and the hail clatter of metal. Across from him, the older man was yanking frenziedly at his life preserver. Galloway screamed a warning, but it was too late; the burrowing hands found the release toggle. Yellow nylon tautened as gas bulged into it.

In the seconds before they hit, his brain felt frozen, holding no thought at all, no more than a stone. Then he did, forcing the words through the endless ancient terror of the fall.

Sorry, Bernie, he thought, clutching the frame as hard as he could to keep his hands from doing what the other man's were doing. His eyes squeezed closed as the waves hurtled upward, like a door slamming closed, a blue rippled lid closing on his face. Tad. I'm sorry. Sorry for everything. Thought I'd have time. Thought someday I could make it right.

Looks like I was wrong.

The sea wheeled, suddenly no longer blue and distant but white and green and violet and streaked brown, multichrome, close and intimate as a lover's irises before they are too close to see. Then it crashed upward into his still-unaverted face.

It didn't knock him out, but the shock shorted something in his skull for a second or two. Yellow-and-white sparks, like an exploding firework, only he was inside it. Then it faded. He shook his head, and his eyes started working again.

He almost wished they hadn't. Everything loose or breakable had smashed free and lay in a tumbled mass against the pilot and copilot's seats. The fuselage was tilted forward and he could feel them dropping, nose-down. Through the access door, he saw blue past the slumped figures of the pilots, blue-green sea gushing in through the shattered windscreen. One of them stirred and groped out. A side door popped and thudded back. Bad move, Galloway thought, sucking the air in the compartment in and out, fast as he could, building up blood oxygen. The incoming water reached his boots.

His ears began to hurt, all at once, a lot.

He swallowed automatically and when they popped, it was like some kind of signal, like when the hypnotist snaps his fingers; he came suddenly back from paralysis to an instant, instinctive determination to escape. The fuselage was leaning to starboard. In a second, they'd be upside down. Someone was moaning.

"Get out!" he shouted, and tripped the belt and fought free of the seat straps. The light was going, the interior getting dimmer . . . the blue darker. . . . He slammed at the door beside him, then remembered what they always told you before a helo ride: Push outward at the top of the window and it'll pop right out. He did, but it didn't. He stood up, braced his back against the overhead, and hit it again, this time harder than he'd known he could. It gave, the sea flooded in, and his legs shoved him out with a great gulp of air.

Then he was outside, kicking upward, looking down as a few feet away the silver bird shape rotated slowly. There was nothing else around them—no fish, no sign of the platform. Just him, hanging in azure space, and the sinking machine. The sun lanced down in searching, sparkling beams, probing downward through great gouts of silver bubbles. When they hit the fuselage, it flashed like a fishing lure, falling slowly away into the blue. They had to be twenty, thirty feet down already.

His hands stopped sculling upward. He hung there, watching it.

Then he jackknifed and began swimming down.

As he reached it, the spin stopped. Blades sheared off, with engine and transmission mounted high, now the S-76 was sinking nose-first, upside down, tail boom pointing surfaceward. The copilot's side door was open. He grabbed the sill and hauled himself in, his body screaming, *Need air now. Got to have it NOW*, staring around in the maskless blur for what he knew had to be there.

The bottle was green and had a white band with directions on it. He couldn't read it, but he knew what it said. He tore it off its mount and thrust the mouthpiece between his lips. He twisted the valve savagely and blew out and sucked in and got a mouthful of seawater and then a lungful of stale but wonderful air.

The copilot was hanging upside down, still strapped in. Galloway searched his lap desperately with one hand, gripping the sill with the other. He swallowed and his ears clicked again. Forty feet? Fifty? The sea around them grew abruptly colder, and he knew they'd left the sea-mixed zone of warmth near the surface. Begun the long fall to the deep cold that never, even in summer, varied by a fraction of a degree. *Got to get this loose....* At that instant his fingers found the buckle and he tripped it, pulling the man outward and pushing them both away with the same motion. The fuselage rocked slowly away as he shoved the limp body about, found the toggle, yanked it. The vest popped and he let go, letting the sagging body in its loose flight suit rise toward the flickering brightness.

Then he dived again and frog-kicked downward once more, knowing even as he did so that he might not be as lucky this time. But there were two more men still in there. The other passenger, the older man—he'd inflated his vest too soon; he'd be pinned against the floor. The pilot—he hadn't moved since the crash. They needed help. He bit the mouthpiece hard as he saw a sea-blurred arm emerge through shattered Perspex, flail around, then disappear from sight as the fuselage began to spiral.

But something had changed. It was falling faster now, as if the last of its buoyancy was gone, arrowing downward into the indigo. How deep was it here? Too deep to follow it far, he knew that. The champagne bottle–sized emergency unit he sucked breath from held only enough for four or five minutes. He might have been down that long already, fighting to drag the copilot out. Yet still he tried, kicking harder, digging himself through the sea with his arms.

Below him, gouts of bubbles leapt suddenly from inside the tail boom, and the fuselage rolled gently into an inverted dive. It accelerated away from him and faded gradually into the darkness.

Shit, he thought. At just that moment, his air stopped, without the warning constriction he'd expected; faster than it would have from a standard scuba tank; just air one minute and a useless mouthpiece he bit with sudden savage dismay the next. When he looked up, he couldn't see the surface.

Okay, time to take care of himself. He let go of the bottle and was immediately sorry; it might have given him one more breath closer to the surface, when ambient pressure was less. But now it was gone, sailing upward in a shrinking wobble above him. He struggled after it like a man climbing a rope, kicking and hoisting his way against the cold dragging hands of the sea. If only he didn't have his boots on. If only he had *air—*

He realized suddenly that he wasn't going to make it. If only he hadn't—wait a minute—

He cursed himself and fumbled for the toggle. He'd forgotten his own Mae West. His stiffening fingers found the little ball and yanked with despairing force.

A soft *bam*, succeeded by a hiss. Christ, it worked. Jesus, he could feel it inflating. Its buoyancy lifted him like a mother's arms, but far too slowly. He was too heavy, his clothes soaked. Through dimming vision, he still saw no surface, no aid, nothing but the hazy gold-shot glow that meant the sun existed somewhere, but far, far away.

He clawed at the cold sea, but it slipped through his fingers. Then they went limp, drifting flaccid as seaweed. Bubbles came from his mouth. He screamed and closed his throat as salt water rammed down it. Then something red and hot as blood closed tightly over his still-upward-staring eyes.

NINE

Fumes in his lungs, fire in his eyes. He clawed at them, struggling to keep his face out of the water. Then something soft struck him. He blinked through the burning and saw the copilot being lifted and dropped by a two-foot chop. He sucked for air and got more fumes, noticing only then the iridescent slick that surrounded them, gentling the waves but choking him with the heavy kerosene stink.

He tried his arms and found that though they were feeble, he could move them. But it was the vest that was holding him up. He was glad of that. He could scull a bit, but he wasn't sure he could hold his head out of the waves. He was just about done.

Gradually, he became aware of shouting.

When he looked up, his head went back. Up and up, blinking at the sheer size of what towered skyward for hundreds of feet above him, the sun blazing down through derricks and piping and pierced metal. Then the shouting was cut off by sirens. A boat emerged from behind the massive legs, water leaping into cream at its bow as it turned toward him.

He had enough breath back, by the time it loomed over him, to breast-stroke clumsily toward it. Men kicked over jacob's ladders; one crewman climbed over the rail and stretched out an arm, clinging to the gunwale with the other. Galloway shook his head and got his foot on a rung, then stalled out. Finally he accepted the hand. Hauled like a gaffed shark onto the afterdeck, he staggered two steps to a locker and collapsed.

They had to use a boat hook on the copilot. His face was purplish gray. When they stretched him out on deck in his sodden Nomex, water ran from his mouth. A medic knelt with oxygen, but the way men stared down and then turned away abruptly told Tiller all he cared to know. He dropped his head and coughed, fighting nausea, fighting the sick taste of defeat.

"You okay? You MMS?"

"Say what?"

"Who are you, buddy? You Todds?"

"No. Galloway."

"Who else made it out?"

"Just me and him. The other two are still in it." He coughed again, got something that tasted like lighter fluid. He spat over the side. "Tried to get to 'em, but it went down too fast."

The medic straightened, tucking his stethoscope back into his shirt, then went over to Galloway. He said, "Get this man some dry clothes."

"They'll dry. And I don't need a corpsman—I'm not in shock or anything."

The guy pulled out his stethoscope again and tried to put it to Galloway's chest. He shoved him away, snarling. The medic backed off, looking surprised. "Take it easy, fella. Just trying to help."

He thought of apologizing, then just looked at the deck. He felt angry. He should have gotten them all out. He should have done it before he exited the aircraft. He'd screwed up again, and maybe cost some people their lives.

The boat slid under the shadow of the rig and made up very cautiously to a dangling bird cage. Four men got on the elevator with him, carrying a litter. They rode up in silence, swaying gently in the wind.

When they reached the platform, the litter disappeared, and the crewmen with it, and he found himself alone. He braced himself against a stack of drums—his knees were still trembling—and looked around. He'd forgotten how noisy, and at the same time how empty, a production platform was.

There were scores of people aboard, but the thing was so huge, it seemed deserted.

Okay, let's find somebody. He shambled into motion. His boots squished, and he shivered. Maybe dry clothes were a good idea. He took two wrong turns, was confronted by blind alleys of gear or blank masses of hissing piping, and backtracked. On the third try, his arm was grabbed by a bushy-bearded guy whose gut bulged through a plaid shirt. "You the diver?" he yelled. "Guy just outta the crash?"

"Yeah."

"Tool pusher wants you."

The tool pusher was the top man on a rig, except for the company man, when he was around, and usually then, too, as far as anything practical went. The pusher ran the platform. Galloway said, "Sure. Which way?"

"Follow me."

They climbed three levels, and he had to rest twice. The drone of diesels running at full speed got louder as they climbed, and so did a whining rumble. The air smelled of steam and oil. Finally, they got to the base of the draw works. He stopped, watching four men in muddy T-shirts and jeans and slickers and yellow hard hats and work gloves—*dancing*, that was the only word that fit.

The drill string was coming up. Lifted from above, ninety feet of hollow steel emerged with a grimy glisten into the light. When the joint came into view, the men moved in, fast and easy and sure. One maneuvered a huge wrench slung on chains. The others pushed the string off center as the stand twisted off and unlocked. A tiny silhouette, eight stories up on the monkey board, lowered the upper end. Liquid mud cascaded onto the gridwork as a thousand pounds of iron swung out and then down to clang and settle beside the derrick. Then the block whined downward and the dancers caught and steered it the last few feet till steel jaws clamped shut. The motors whined and reversed and cables slid and hummed and came taut and hauled the next stand glistening slickly up into the sunlight.

Plaid Shirt looked around, then shouted to another muddy figure, "Where's West?" It jerked a thumb. Their boots rattled on grating. When Tiller looked down, he was gazing through it, down at the sea. The slick was still there, and white-and-orange fragments bobbed on the surface. The boat nosed through them, the crew reaching out now and then with boat hooks.

"Talkin' to you, mister!"

"Sorry." He looked up from muddy boots to greasy jeans, a Tulsa sweatshirt, clipboard, big shoulders, dented yellow Holden-McOwen hard hat, red beer drinker's cheeks, pulled-back reddish hair with strands of gray. A big knot of keys and a knife sheath hanging from a leather tool belt.

"West," she said around a chew, and clamped his hand hard enough to hurt. "Saw you go in. Saw you come up. Too bad about your buddies. You the diver?"

"That's right."

"Got a name?"

"Galloway."

"Gassy says you the only guy made it out."

Gassy had to be Plaid Shirt. "That's right."

"What happened?"

"I don't know. We were coming in for a landing, then all of a sudden everything went to shit. I tried to get the others out." He hawked and spat through the grid. It sailed downward, curving in the wind, and disappeared under the platform. "But I couldn't."

"I thought those seventy-sixes were good birds. Well, you got luck, anyway." She eyed him, and he waited.

But she didn't say anything else, and after a beat, he asked, "Are our other guys here? The other DeepTech guys?"

"You mean your boat, it's still about an hour out. You mean Boudreaux, he's down in the dive office. The squid locker, we call it."

He looked up at the draw works. It smelled familiar: the dense aromatic stink of oil, barium mud, grout, rubber, sweat, and diesel exhaust, all mixed with the salt sharpness of a hundred miles at sea. Gulls wheeled above the derrick, rising to stay clear of the wavering plume of flame on its boom extension. Ninety feet up, the traveling block clanged against its cables and another length of drill string slid sideways to be stacked. "Think you'll hit oil?" he asked her.

"What kind of jackshit question's that?"

"Well, I thought—"

"Oh, forgot you're new." Her tone softened. "Thought you were jerkin' my chain. No, these are more production holes going down. We're in full-scale production on Twelve." West shifted the tobacco and reached for a red paper cup. He noticed missing fingernails. "Anyway, look around now, 'cause you ain't gonna be here long. You boys are headin' out tomorrow."

"What's the job?"

"Roland ain't told you? Okay, scope of work: We got thirty miles of DOT line to lay out to One Thousand. That'll be the production platform for Pandora South. Should be interestin', nice deep job. Lump sum. I know you people like that, cut down on the spread, get y'self some a that bonus money."

"As long as it's safe."

"That's his business. I run the rig; he runs the divers. We all work for the company man. Anyway, you guys was low bidder, but we got a six-million performance bond."

"How deep?"

"The new line starts here at three hundred–some feet. Runs out to the southeast, kind of half-assed parallel to the Galveston ship channel. Gradual decline at first, couple of ups and downs, then you hit the Canyon. I think the deepest's about eleven hundred feet."

"That's—not shallow."

"Thought divers did it deeper." She chuckled. "You know, you not a bad-lookin' piece a shit, for a squid."

"ROVs, what they usually use now that far down."

"Yeah, but they're no fun in bed."

He didn't want to follow wherever she was leading with that. "This transmission line. You say it's to a new field?"

"Not exactly new. Some of the holes out there are five, eight years old. Drilled by Met Sulphur, when they were tryin' to get into oil. But they didn't pan out. Then the bottom fell out of the market, so they stacked up and sold out. Couple swaps later, Coastal ends up with the lease. They hold it for two years, then decide to start drilling again. So far, it's pannin' out; they found two nice half-million-barrel fields. Now we need to develop. Okay, platform rules. You hearin' me, Galley?"

"Galloway."

"Whatever. One: no spear guns. You're here to work, not shoot fish. Two: no drinkin'. Three: same for druggin'. No grass, no white dust. Four: anything else I happen to say. You hear me?"

"I don't like threats, Ms. West."

"That's no threat, squatty. That's a promise. You don't think I'm serious, try me. You'll think you're a windshield wiper on a duck's ass." She squinted at him. "You union?"

"Not anymore."

"What's that mean?"

"Means no."

"That's another thing I don't want on my rig. I don't want to hear the word. Understand me? No spear guns, no juice, no drugs, no union. Any questions?" She glanced past him, and he turned, saw the bearded man waiting.

"Just one. How'd you get to be head hammer?"

"Because I don't go anyplace 'less I'm in charge. It's a new world out here, Gallows. I like this company. My daddy put in forty years in the field and never made pusher. I was workin' for Unocal. Brad Shattuck comes to me; he says, 'Hannah, let's see if you can hack bein' on top for a change.' "

"I never saw a woman pusher before."

"It's not so hard, long as you're twice as tough as a man and twice as smart." She grinned and lifted the spit cup again. "See, I figure like, shoreside maybe four hundred women gettin' sexually harassed right this very minute by their asshole bosses. Right? An' they got just me to even things up."

She grabbed his upper arm suddenly and dug in. He winced—she had a grip like Aydlett's—and slapped her hand off. She chuckled and turned away, cocking the hard hat back. Halfway down the passageway, she turned again and hollered, "You remember what I said. It's a long way to Juarez. You find a drill bit in your pants, decide you're tired of playin' pocket pool, come see Hannah. I don't make no secrets about who I like."

Gassy directed him to the divers' compartment, on one of the lower decks. Tiller thought of making a joke about West but decided he'd better not. Instead, he asked, "How's the chow out here?"

"Hot."

"Spicy, huh? What, got you a Cajun cook?"

"No. It's just—warm."

He gave up and followed him down oily metal ladders and

past a battery of holding tanks. The steady drone of engines grew, then faded. Finally he pointed at a metal door. DIVING SUPERINTENDENT was stenciled on it. R. B. BOUDREAUX. "Thanks," said Galloway, looking after him. His rap echoed on steel. He waited a second, then undogged the door.

The guy inside was standing over a plank table, looking down at a set of prints. When the door opened, his hand went to his face, then to his pocket.

When he straightened, Galloway saw a big man in his thirties, with black glossy hair combed back long, well-built except for a swelling belly. His nose had been broken a couple of times. He had a good tan. Dark hair covered his bare chest, slabbed with muscle, gleaming with sweat. "What you want?" he said angrily.

"Galloway, new hire on Crew Two."

"Oh yeah. Jesus, I hear you almost didn't make it." Boudreaux came out from behind the table, and Tiller saw bowed divers' legs, khaki shorts with lots of pockets, a black web belt with a knife on it, broken-in deck shoes without socks.

"Almost. Lost the other guys on the chopper. I got one out with me, but they couldn't CPR him."

"You see the medic? You hurt?"

"Just some scrapes. And a dose of JP-four."

"What you do, swallow it?"

"Breathed it."

"That shouldn't bother you." Boudreaux glanced at a digital watch. "Boat should be here soon, crew and gear. Meet anybody on the rig yet?"

"West and uh . . . Gassy."

"Oh, you met the pusher?"

"Uh-huh."

He expected Boudreaux to say something else, at least introduce himself, but he didn't. Instead, he bent over the prints again. Past him, Galloway saw a steel desk. On it were a computer, a marked-up calendar, and a framed photograph of a dark-haired woman leaning on the hood of a black sports car. He blinked, but before he could speak, Boudreaux said, "You know what we got to do?"

"West said, jet in a new pipeline." He moved to where he could see the diagrams. It was a chart of the Gulf, NOAA 1116A, overprinted with the locations of platforms. He stared at it, realizing how extensive was the steel net that stretched from Galveston to the Mississippi Delta. "Christ. Where are we on this thing?"

"Here." Boudreaux pressed a big thumb down firmly at the outer edge of the web. "Hundred and twenty miles out. Edge of the South Addition. Just short of the hundred-fathom curve."

"How big's this complex? West said it was new—"

"Yeah, and the company's still buildin'. It's based on an older network, meters into the Unocal line back to Marsh Island. Coastal's extending it out into their lease in the Garden Banks area. They call it Pandora South."

Tiller leaned closer. To seaward of a grimy oval, Boudreaux's thumbprint, were a scatter of black squares. The print beside one read "WELL (cov 388 fms)."

"These producing?"

"Don't go by that. Company chart over here." Paper sighed as Boudreaux unrolled it. "Grab that end. This's Coastal's two-year plan. Current producers in black. Dry wells in brown. Capped holes they got to lay line to in green. Locations the rock guessers say are worth a gamble, down here, in red. They got three rigs out there punchin' them out. Operating stations and production platforms, here and here and here."

Tiller looked it over, knowing he didn't have to memorize it but that he should remember the basic layout. Pandora 12, the steel they stood on, was one of five production platforms, from each of which colored lines spidered outward to the submerged wellheads. Some were "on stream," already drilled, connected by subsea pipe; the pumps whose throb shivered the metal walls were thrusting their product shoreward toward the refineries of Louisiana and Texas. Others had been drilled, hit oil, and needed only to be tied in with undersea pipe. And still others, dotted out past the snaky curves of the hundred- and even the two-hundred-fathom line, were red, meaning, Maybe there's a payday here, maybe not.

Just looking at it, he had a sense of the gigantic concentration of capital and brains and muscle that had to go into a subsea oil field. Steel and power and money and lives, and at the end of it maybe fortunes, but just as probably nothing but dry rock. He knew oil had never been what you'd call a low-risk business, but this far at sea, this deep, it was a gamble of such proportions he felt uneasy just trying to imagine how much it all cost.

Boudreaux moved his hand south from 12. "This is the DOT line, the big transmission line, starts going down Wednesday. Thirty-six-inch-diameter pipe, concrete-coated steel. We'll follow a ridge here for the first few miles."

Tiller raised his eyebrows. "Big."

"Sized for three hundred producing wells. Going to jet it in till we get deep enough, then just inspect as it goes down after that. Gonna be a tight schedule, cher. Hope you're up for some bottom time."

"That's what I'm here for."

Boudreaux looked him over from half-lowered lashes as he asked him where he'd worked, what he'd done since then. Tiller gave it to him straight. The other man said nothing when he mentioned prison, just drummed his fingers on the chart. When he was done, Boudreaux said, "You a fag?"

"What?"

"I heard something about you and some colored guy."

"We're friends. That's all."

"You take orders?"

"If they make sense."

"Okay, lemme make a couple things clear. You work for me. West, anybody from Holden-McOwen, anybody from Coastal, inspectors, customer's reps, whatever—they ask you something, you smile and refer 'em to me. *Comprends?*"

He nodded. That was standard. Boudreaux continued: "I don't like squirrels, but if you got real problems, let me know before you go bellyachin' to somebody else."

"Okay."

"I'll be workin' two crews on this job. Got two weeks to get it done. Under fourteen days, we pull a bonus. It's not gonna be easy, but we can do it. Me, I'll honcho the topside team myself. Where's your gear?"

"On the boat."

"Yeah, the boat." Boudreaux checked his watch again, then grabbed a jacket and hard hat from pegs. He found another one behind the desk and flung it at Galloway. Hard; if he hadn't caught it, it would have hit his face. "Okay, cher. Let's go see if they're in sight."

They looked down as the boat made up outboard of the jet barge, nosing in, then swinging to lay its starboard rail against the huge black rubber fenders. Smoke jetted from the twin stacks and drifted downwind. A bell began ringing, and high on the platform a crane pivoted deliberately. Boudreaux whipped a walkie-talkie from his jacket and began directing the off-load. Tiller leaned on the rail, watching.

It felt familiar, as if he'd never left. Leaning on the gritty, cool steel, one boot propped on the lowest horizontal, he remembered all the hours he'd spent just like this, a joint in his hand, or just watching the waves.

For the first time since he'd come down off the bridge into Bayou City, he felt relaxed. Despite having come so close to drowning. Or maybe it was that, almost dying, that made it feel so good every time he sucked in a breath.

You could watch the sea from a boat. You could watch the sea from shore. But watching the sea from a platform was different from either. From a boat, you scanned the sea suspiciously, aware at any second that gray cloud on the horizon could flicker with lightning; that your speeding, dipping prow could suddenly rip into a floating log; that the bilge pump could fail, a seam open, a tanker come left instead of right and press you down into eternity. You watched the sea like the French watch the Germans. From the shore, the ocean was awesome but unthreatening; you turned away from it for a beer or hot dog, to eye passing girls on the boardwalk.

From Pandora 12, you looked down on the sea. Around you soared massive steel legs, thick as sequoias, and below you a web of I beams fell away till it met the tiny-looking waves. The jacket—the supporting framework—went all the way to the seabed. It wasn't going anywhere. It had been designed to take 150-mile-an-hour winds and hurricane-height seas.

Yeah, he'd spent a lot of time on platforms like this, watching the evening come, or the dawn. Between shifts, there wasn't a hell of a lot to do. Watch fuzzy TV, too far from land to get a decent picture. Read the creased Louis L'Amour and Mack Bolan paperbacks that passed from hand to hand. Wait for the mail chopper. Eat. And then, because you'd eaten too much, work out, savagely, till the sweat dripped and your muscles vibrated in a strange numb zone beyond pain.

Actually, it wasn't too different from prison. . . .

He stopped that line of thought. He shifted one boot for another and leaned again and thought instead, for some reason, about Bernice Hirsch.

Shit, was it true, that the first thing a man wanted after almost dying was to get laid? He had a—what had West called it—anyway, a hard one available right now.

He remembered how Bernie used to look aboard *Miss Anna*, wearing a thin T with no bra or, even worse, that tiger-striped bandeau thing. How she lay in the sun, glistening with sunscreen and tanning oil, legs spread as if daring him to attack her.

Sometimes he'd wondered whether she was too young for him. But she'd taken care of him after his back operation. Defended him at his cousin's inquest. Admitted at last that she loved him, and then gone in partners with him and Shad in the dive shop. Then one day she'd asked him casually why he didn't just move in, he was around her place so much.

For a little while there, he'd had it all, everything he wanted, right in his arms. But somehow it had slipped away . . . and he'd felt it going, but hadn't been able to get a bight around it in time. . . .

You blind, arrogant asshole, he thought, gripping the salt-gritty steel till his fingers hurt. He couldn't think about that. He couldn't keep reproaching himself for that.

He looked up as the crane swung across the bright sky like a mobile gallows, a battery of helium cylinders rotating slowly beneath it. It swayed the length of the jet barge, then descended smoothly toward where a tiny figure he recognized even from this height as Ace Rodriquez pointed it.

What was it he'd been thinking, about what West had said? . . .

Not that about spear guns or unions, or even the invitation, but about the field. Something about it had bothered him at the time, but now, thinking about it, it made even less sense. Something about it not "panning out" for Met Sulphur. How could a field not produce for one company, then come through for another? The throbbing pumps behind him, roaring so loudly that it was hard to hear, proved they were pumping oil. Well, maybe Coastal had better geologists—or better luck.

And something else: this pipeline. He'd laid lines before. It was a dirty, tough, dangerous job. The jet sled had to be watched, and sometimes the pipe was damaged as it went down; the coating cracked, the welds broke, and sometimes it even kinked and whole sections had to be cut out and replaced. The part that didn't make sense was having divers do it. Deep as West and Boudreaux were talking, it was safer to use ROVs, at least to keep tabs on things; if repairs were called for, the crew could go down then.

A whiff of hot gas washed his face, exhaust from the flare stack, blown down by a stray gust. That was a hell of a flare-off out there. Its hollow roar underlay every sound on the platform—another proof that the wells fanning out from Pandora 12 were producing.

Okay, he had the answer to the ROV question: DeepTech didn't have any. It specialized in warm, human, blood-and-balls saturation divers. Buying, renting, or leasing the complex and expensive remotely operated vehicles, along with the control gear and trained operators, would wipe out any profit from the contract with the oil company. So naturally they'd use divers on the line job, even if it meant more risk.

And naturally, he thought with a grimace, they'd crew at the lowest possible level, and work that crew to the bone. It was how you made a buck in the Patch.

"Killer!"

"What the hey? I thought we shook that squared-off son of a bitch, and he turns up here ahead of us!"

"What you doing up here, *baboso*? Hiding from work already, anh?"

He grinned, turning from the rail to Rodriquez, Porchellacchia, McCray, Winslow, and Guidry, carrying tote bags and gear. The others called insults and kept going, but McCray set down his burden. "How'd you get out here, Till? They fly you out?"

He didn't feel like explaining it all again, so he just nodded. "Uh, what's the drill, Jay? Should I help off-load—"

"It'll get done, man. We worked off this barge before. Just swing it on and bolt down, that's all we got to do. The chamber and stuff, they'll have an area cleared for us."

"I better get my gear—"

"Taken care of." He jerked his head at a teenaged seaman trotting up the ladder, Galloway's tote over his shoulder. "Come on, show you the bunk room, then let's get some chow. Say, you look tired, Till. I'd turn in early if I was you. Last decent night's sleep we're gonna get for a while."

With a last look back, Galloway followed him inside.

TEN

He went to bed at eight and slept fitfully, awakened once by the pain in his arms and again by a nightmare. Both times, he eased himself back down into the bunk, sweating, and listened to the snores in the compartment and the distant roar of the flare and the whine and rumble and clatter till he sank again.

In the galley at breakfast, he piled his tray with eggs and grits and steak and fried red potatoes from the steam tables. He'd been drinking too much and not eating enough. From now on, it would be hard work. He carried the tray out into the noisy, packed, smoky room. The divers were sitting together at a table apart from the roughnecks, and the drillers, older men, apart from both. He saw Hannah West studying a flimsy piece of what looked like fax paper as she shoved bacon into her mouth.

Porch, McCray, and Winslow were all eating as if they'd never seen food before. They glanced up and grunted as Galloway joined them.

Boudreaux came over from West's table with coffee as Galloway was finishing. He looked angry. "Where's Rodriquez?" he asked Porchellacchia.

"Las' time I saw him was in the shower. Prob'ly still there. You know Ace, he—"

"We got a change of plan. The lay's pushed back twenty-four hours."

"Shit!"

"Crap!"

"Is it gonna count on the bonus?"

"I got a radio call in now. Asking that." Boudreaux looked at Galloway as if all this was his fault. "There's gonna be some people coming in this morning, investigate that crash. They want to talk to you."

"Me? Okay."

"Only you're not gonna be there. You're gonna be down with me doin' a snatch. They're coming in around nine. That's when we'll jump."

He felt confused. "You're talking a body snatch?"

"You got it. Jay. Jay! You listening?"

"Yes."

"Rig us for a heliox bounce to three hundred sixty. Wildman, double-check his figures an' the mix. Porch, you're safety. Look, I gotta get back to West. Tell Ace he's got the rack box, when he comes in."

"Wait a minute. Roland. What's their hurry?"

Boudreaux hesitated, half-turned away. "The other passenger," he said.

"Who, the old guy?" Galloway said.

"That was Mr. Derleth Todds. GS-fourteen. Head of Gulf Coast leasing for Minerals Management Service, U.S. Department of the Interior."

"Major honcho, eh?" said Porchellacchia around a finger. He pulled out a string of gristle and flicked it at Rodriquez, who had just come in.

"MMS assigns the offshore leases. Ace, where you been? I want you on deck by eight from now on. You guys fill him in."

When he left, the divers looked at each other. "Shit," said Porchellacchia, rubbing the tattoos on his arms as if he was cold. "That don't sound good. It wasn't enough, fourteen days, to get thirty miles laid. Now it's thirteen?"

"*Chingada madre*. What we get paid for bounce dives?" asked Rodriquez, looking around eagerly as he set his tray down.

He sat naked except for socks, watching another copter circle the platform before landing. The breeze felt cool as it dried his skin, but somehow more sweat was always there. Beside him in the dive area, Boudreaux said, "Let's go over it again."

"Okay." He sucked a tooth. "This is gonna be a three-hundred-sixty-foot surface-supplied mixed-gas dive. Bottom time'll be about thirty minutes. Air to fifty feet; eighty-four percent helium and sixteen percent oxygen to two hundred feet; then switch to a bottom mix of ninety-three/seven."

He thought about that for a second, then went on. "We got to get pictures, check out the helo, get the crew out, get anything else looks interesting, and attach a lifting line. Decompress in the water."

"Safety?"

He vaguely remembered something about bells. Coast Guard regs specified a Class II bell over 220 feet and a Class I over 300. "Well, you said something about a bell—"

"Stand up," said McCray, behind him, and he stood up and McCray held the suit as he stepped into one leg and then the other and then zipped it up. It felt tight, but he knew it would feel loose once he got down there, got moving around.

Boudreaux said, lifting his head as Winslow, his tender, helped him with his suit, "Yeah, they're droppin' an open-bottom bell between us and where the chopper went in."

An open bell was a Class II. Strictly speaking, they should have had a Class I, but Tiller decided it wasn't worth mentioning. None of the other divers seemed to think anything of it. He said, "And we got bailout bottles."

"How long's your bailout good for at that depth?"

A seventy-two-cubic-foot tank lasted about an hour at sea level. At 360 feet of salt water, that was twelve atmospheres, divide by twelve—"Uh, around five minutes."

"Close enough. Follow me at first—it's a mess near the platform and I know the layout. Once we find the chopper, you get the pictures and jerk the bodies. I'll take care of the lift line."

"Sure." It sounded like a quick job.

Rodriquez strolled up. "What you got?" Boudreaux asked him.

"Twenty tanks of bottom mix, twelve decomp mix, and a cylinder of oxygen."

"You gauge 'em?"

"Yeah. An' checked out the console, and made sure I got treatment tables. How you wanta decompress?"

"In the water."

McCray handed him his helmet, telling him he'd checked it out and put in a new neck dam. Tiller put the nonreturn valve in his mouth and sucked, then sealed it with his tongue. It held vacuum.

Above them a bell began ringing and the pedestal crane swung out. The open bell went down slowly from it. It wasn't much, just a clear Perspex bubble maybe three feet in diameter and a framework and iron weights to hold it upright on the bottom. It hit the water, rocked, flooding, then submerged. He could see it for a long time as it went down, a pale, wavering blur, but at last there was nothing there, just the lift lines and water hoses running straight down into the blue.

McCray was checking the umbilical, running yard after yard of taped-up hose through his hands. Breathing-gas supply, phone cable, pneumofathometer hose, and a good, sturdy safety rope in case they had to haul a diver up. Galloway breathed in and out, balanced, waiting, as beside him Winslow dressed Boudreaux.

"Lemme have that back." McCray cradled the helmet in his lap, connecting the hose. Tiller watched; he did it right, hand-tightening first, then torquing down with two crescent wrenches, and checking the fitting with his thumbnail for cracks. He'd had tenders who forgot that, and it hadn't been fun. It tended to interfere with getting enough to breathe.

McCray held up his bailout bottle, a standard scuba tank, with the gauge attached. He read it and nodded, watching as McCray checked the first stage and the whip.

Hands under his armpits. He stood and shrugged the harness on. He patted himself down: knife, spare knife, work light, spare, all clipped to D-rings. A face he didn't know held up a Nikonos; he nodded; the camera went on his diving harness, too.

Getting hot now. The sun was deadly. He tried to relax as McCray settled his weight belt over the harness and guided his hand to the release buckle. If he needed to drop weight, there wouldn't be time to grope around. The bailout bottle went on next, upside down from the way sport divers wore it.

"Want a shot?"

98

McCray had Afrin. "Okay."

"Tilt your head back. Sniff."

"That's enough." It tasted bitter at the back of his throat. "Okay, gimme the hat."

The helmet came down and suddenly he was inside looking out. The sun had heated the metal and fiberglass and it smelled close and rubbery. He snuggled his face into the oral/nasal and cracked the free-flow valve, sniffling as the decongestant ran back out his nose. The helmet joggled as the neck clamp closed. Then it joggled again as McCray connected and tugged on the hose-to-harness snap shackle.

A click, a hiss, a voice—Rodriquez's. "Comm check, guys. Gonna try this crossover switch, see if we can get everybody on the line at once."

"Loud 'n' clear."

"Hear you. Till?"

He turned his head, to see Boudreaux looking at him through flat safety glass. The other diver was using a Rat Hat, slightly larger than his own and with a square face port. "Hear you."

"The unscrambler work on that spare set?"

"It did last time."

He felt McCray connecting the whip from the bailout. He reached behind him to grab it, in case it wasn't connected right; a loose whip could take a man's eye out. He cracked the bailout valve. It held.

A hand on his shoulder. He sat down again, carefully, because of all the weight on him, and stretched out his feet as McCray duct-taped his work boots. Working divers hardly ever used fins, because there was no way to brace yourself with them. He was sweating hard now. The suit sealed in body heat at the same time it absorbed sunlight.

Something occurred to him then and he asked Boudreaux, "Roland, we got hot water?"

"Got a hose running to the bell. We can pick it up there."

"That's good." No matter how hot he was now, they'd be freezing at depth.

"All set?"

He held up his thumb. Faintly, through the helmet, he could hear the hiss and rattle of the tugger and then a clang as Winslow and McCray swung the gates of the stage open.

A pause. He waited patiently, hands on his knees. His back was starting to hurt from the weight of the bottle. Finally, he turned his head awkwardly and saw Winslow at the diver's station telephone. If he held his breath so the rush of gas stopped, he could just make out what the Wildman was saying through the fiberglass shell clamped over his skull.

"Galloway? Yeah, he's here. What? You want him where?"

Over the intercom, Ace said, "Roland, we got a call from West. They want Galloway in the galley."

"Shit they do. Who wants him?"

"Hold on a second . . . investigating board, they say."

"He's dressed out. He can't come. We're all set to jump."

"They say hold the dive till they're done talking to him."

"Who says?"

"Hold on . . . somebody named . . . Shattuck, I think it was."

Boudreaux cursed in Cajun French. Galloway waited. Finally, he snapped, "Tell McCray, get him up there. *Merde!* Get this helmet off, Winslow."

Helmet off, tank off, weight belts, harness, suit. He stood naked, bathed with sweat in the sudden cool.

"Here's your shorts," said McCray. "Want your shirt?"

"Nah. I'll be right back." He clump-squished after his tender up toward the galley.

The room was empty except for four men and West, sitting at the drillers' table, papers and a cassette recorder in front of them. As Galloway came in, West pointed to the chair across from them. He sat, feeling underdressed in khaki shorts and sweat-filled boots and bare hairy chest. McCray lingered; West said quietly he could go.

Then he was alone with them and the hum of the soft–ice cream machine.

"Mr.—Galloway? I understand you're the only survivor of the crash."

"I am. The only survivor, I mean."

The guy who was asking questions, in the center, was kind of tall, kind of bald, and entirely in charge. He said quietly, "I'm Stan Duckworth, FAA. This gentleman is Bob Kelly, Sikorsky Aircraft; James Richardson, National Transportation Safety Board; and this is Brad Shattuck, Coastal Oil."

Tiller nodded and Duckworth turned the recorder on. "This is the preliminary investigation of the crash of Offshore Air Service Twelve sixteen, an overwater-modified Sikorsky S-Seventy-six A, which took place yesterday, July 12. Third witness is Lyle Galloway, a passenger, employed by DeepTech Diving, Incorporated, of Summerland, Louisiana. He is the sole survivor of the crash.

"Mr. Galloway, the purpose of this investigation is to find out what happened to Twelve sixteen, so that we can make sure it doesn't happen again. Do you have any problems helping us with that?"

He said he didn't. Duckworth went on to ask him what had happened. He rubbed his hand across his mouth, collecting his thoughts, then told him. It didn't take long.

When he was done, Kelly said, "Think back to when you said you 'heard a thud.' Was it behind you or ahead of you?"

"Above us."

"Directly above? Forward and above?"

"Directly above."

"Rotor brake system?" asked Richardson.

"Let's finish with Mr. Galloway first. Now, after that: Did you see the pilot reach up and to his right and snap a switch?"

"He might have. I don't remember."

Richardson interrupted. "Are you at all familiar with helicopters?"

"I've flown in them a few times. Jumped from them. Took ground fire. Aside from that, no."

"Let's go on to after you hit the water." Kelly again. "Are you aware these aircraft are equipped with inflation bags?"

"You mean like air bags?"

"No, I mean for buoyancy. There are four, total—two in the wheel wells, two under the chin window, forward of the cockpit. When you're looking at an emergency water landing, the pilot hits a switch and the bags deploy."

"I didn't see any bags. Besides, we hit hard."

"I understand you tried to rescue the others."

"I got the copilot out. But he didn't make it."

Shattuck spoke for the first time. He was the only one who

was wearing a tie. "Hannah told me about that. It was damned brave."

"Maybe somebody else would have done a better job."

"You're pretty hard on yourself, Mr. Galloway."

Tiller shrugged. He looked at Shattuck again. His voice sounded familiar, as if he'd heard it before somewhere.

"Let's go back to the bags," said Kelly. He unfolded a diagram and pointed to where they would have deployed from. Tiller thought back carefully, closing his eyes. He could see the sinking fuselage, twisting and glittering like a fishing lure on its way down. He could see it pretty clearly. Divers cultivated visual memory. He opened his eyes. "Nope. I didn't see anything like that. Maybe they deployed, but the collision broke them. Or the pilot just didn't have time."

Duckworth reached out and turned the recorder off.

"Two things I don't get," said Kelly, the man from Sikorsky. "Why they went in so fast, no control, and why the buoyancy bags didn't deploy. It wasn't the pilots. I knew Gracie; he had two thousand hours."

"Well, maybe we'll get something from the wreckage, Bob. Mr. Galloway, thank you."

Duckworth stood stiffly, and so did the others. Tiller did, too. He was starting for the door when Shattuck came around the table and held out his hand.

"Brad Shattuck, Coastal Oil Corporation. Vice president of offshore operations."

"Good to meet you, sir."

"I meant that, about going back down. That took balls."

"Thanks."

"You work for Roland, don't you?"

"That's right. New hire, Crew Two."

"They've done good work for us. Going to help us with the line to One Thousand?"

"Starting tomorrow."

"We've got to get that done on time. Or ahead of time, if possible. Roland's assured me you're the men to do it."

Shattuck paused, as if waiting for objections. Galloway remembered Boudreaux's warning, about talking to anyone outside the company. "Well, we'll try like hell. Look, I better get suited up again. The guys are standing by—"

"I understand. Good luck."

He held out his hand again, and this time when Galloway took it, Shattuck put his other hand on top of it, like a politician, and he felt something hard and large. He looked down and saw it on Shattuck's left hand.

The dark blue stone and gold initial *S* of a massive military ring.

Back at the diving station, Winslow was spraying water on Boudreaux from a hose. The supervisor was still dressed out, sitting stiffly with his hands on his knees. The Cajun's eyes followed Galloway down the ladder. When he got close enough to be heard over the diesels, he shouted, "Hanh?"

"Let's jump," said Tiller, bending to peel off his shorts as McCray moved in again.

The diver's stage was just big enough for two if they crammed their gear-laden bodies close together on the little bench. Open metal, rusty, it swayed as Rodriquez stepped back from the edge of the platform and signaled to the tugger operator on the deck above.

Then they were dropping, and the stage was swinging, a little open elevator rocking down on two cables from the overhanging cliff of the platform. The jacket framework moved by steadily, huge steel tubes interlocked with I beams. Rust bled down the lower ones. Looking up, he could see men watching them. The clatter and roar of the draw works sounded distant through his sealed helmet. McCray, already tiny, was leaning over the life rail, waving. Tiller lifted his glove, careful to keep a grip on the handrail with the other.

Below them, coming up fast now, the morning-glittering sea. About a two-foot chop, not bad. The drop accelerated. They'd hit fast, but that was normal; the idea was to get divers through the turbulent interface of air and water before they got shaken up too much. Dry air hissed through dry lips, and he sucked his teeth for moisture.

A splash and roar, a cloud of golden bubbles, a shock of welcome liquid cool. The stage swayed, then steadied. When the cloud streamed upward and away, the blue flooded in to surround them. He swallowed and his ears popped, and the sounds he heard changed; the texture of hearing itself changed, became intimate as a whisper in the dark. He heard a faint grinding: the cable, running through the sheave above him. A hiss and roar of bubbles as he exhaled. A click and jingle as Boudreaux shifted, a creak as the cage flexed, yielding their weight to the all-encompassing sea.

"Everything copacetic down there?"

"Roger." Another creak, a soft jolt and sway. Looking up, swallowing again, he could see the cables leading up to the silver-shot surface, then disappearing. Nothing under the sea could look out of it from below. That ever-changing mirror gave you back nothing but the distorted image of yourself.

The stage stopped. "Fifty feet," said Rodriquez in his ear. "Gas coming to you. Ventilate, ventilate. Gimme a count, voice check . . . Taking you down at sixty a minute, loading the rack a hundred and fifty pounds over ambient. Tiller, hear me?"

"Yeah." He cracked his free-flow and let it blast till he got heliox. The first breaths always tasted strange, flat and thin.

"Then talk, *baboso*. Ears doing okay? You feeling all right?"

"I'm fine." There it was, the squeaky pitch heliox gave your voice.

"You feel unusual in any way? Talk to me, man. That's the only way I—"

"I know what I'm supposed to feel like. I'll tell you when anything goes wrong."

Ace subsided. Tiller worked his jaw, keeping his ears clear. The assistant supervisor had a point; you had to keep checking yourself, thinking not just about the job but about how you felt. A little shortness of breath, a dizziness—if you noticed stuff early, it could save you grief later. But he just didn't like guys yammering in his ears.

The surface vanished gradually into a light blue haze the color of a spring sky. A school of snappers glittered like silver coins as they maneuvered through the framework. School-masters or yellowtails. Mussels and seaweed haired the painted steel. Pandora 12 was overdue for a cleaning, he thought.

The sway had stopped now, damped by the sea. They traveled straight down, canted by the current. The suit shrank around his body, molding itself to him. He relaxed his grip on the frame, worked the fingers of one hand, then the other as the blue deepened. His breath went *hush, hush* in his ears.

Rodriquez: "Hundred feet on the pneumo."

Boudreaux grunted acknowledgment. His voice was distorted by the thin helium, electronically corrected to intelligibility by the interphone, but still weird, echoing.

Tiller turned his head, to find his partner looking at him. Behind the big flat faceplate, Boudreaux's face was unsmiling, harsh, all but hostile.

"So, you grow up in Bayou City?"

"Huh?" The dark eyes narrowed. "No. Chauvin, me."

"That's on the Bayou Lafourche—"

"P'tit Caillou."

"We were up to Lafayette couple days ago. Had a good time. You ever get up that way?"

"No."

"What your folks do?"

Boudreaux said grudgingly, "My father, he was a shrimp fisherman."

"I've done some commercial fishing. That's a tough life."

"No shit, cher. Brothers an' cousins still are. Then one summer, he rented his boat to Texaco."

"That how you started?"

"Helpin' the divers on deck, yeah." Boudreaux let it ride as the sea around them deepened toward twilight.

"Say, about this crash, Roland. They asked me, at the board, did some kind of bag inflate. You know—"

"Goddamn it, Galloway. Let's talk some other time."

He returned his attention to the passing sea, understanding; Boudreaux wanted to keep it curt. Okay, he could do that. He checked his gear again, making sure his weight belts were fastened, that he could reach his bottle valve and EGS and freeflow. Looking up, he saw the long snake of the umbilical bellied out, well clear of the tugger cables. That was good.

"Two hundred."

"Two hundred aye," grunted Boudreaux.

Ace: "How far off bottom you want to stop, Roland?"

"Stop her at three fifty. Jus' shy of the mud."

"Stop at three fifty, you got it."

Through the flat glass two inches in front of his eyes, the world had aged through the blue dusk into a twilight dim. The cold came more slowly, but he knew it was out there. An icy chill that penetrated gradually, till at last you were shuddering.

He remembered going deep on air and how silly it made you; a weird lighthearted high that made you think foolish things, take dangerous chances. But you didn't care, because you knew nothing could ever happen to you, and even if it did, who cared?

But on helium and oxygen, your brain was lucid and cold as the sea around you.

There was room for fear.

The dry, cool gas hissed in and out of his lungs. He thought of the hundreds of feet of hose between him and the rack box. Say six hundred feet, to allow for the horizontal excursion. How often did a hose rupture? If it blew out and the nonreturn valve worked, he'd have five minutes to get to the bell. His hand moved back, checked the bailout again. There were a million things that could go wrong down here. Too little oxygen in your mix, you blacked out; too much and you went into convulsions. Carbon monoxide, oil vapor, even paint fumes in the mix could do you in. He tried to reassure himself. He had good gear, a good tender, an experienced partner. He was back in the water and pulling down over six hundred bucks a day.

But it was getting *dark.* . . .

After what seemed like a long time, the cage jostled to a stop. They hung motionless, centered in a gray-black gloom. He turned his helmet slowly. Which way was the rig?

"Ready?"

"Yeah."

He clung to the cage and let Boudreaux detach himself first. The lead diver tilted his helmet back, held his umbilical away from the cage, and stepped off. Disappeared.

Tiller hesitated. He didn't like the idea of a drop. That was how divers got squeezed. But Boudreaux had just stepped off.

He took a deep breath, made sure his hose was clear, and followed him.

He sank for perhaps three feet before his feet hit silt. He didn't see Boudreaux till a beam of light cut through the dark, sweeping back toward him. He pulled his own Super Q and gave him a flash back, then began struggling forward, leaning into the muck that sucked at his boots.

Pulling his umbilical along, he kept following the light, shining his own ahead of him. Fifty feet on, he came to a stop, playing it up and down till his eyes made sense out of the huge looming shadows their lights threw on rusty, bent wreckage, snapped girders, kinked drill string. The glassless windows of a crushed bunkhouse module stared emptily out at him.

"Careful now. You get into that mess, you'll wish you hadn't."

"What happened?"

"The first platform here collapsed in a storm. They blew it up, what was left."

"Ten minutes," said Rodriquez.

"Let's get moving. You getting cold?"

"Shit, yeah."

"We'll stop by the bell, get the hose."

Tiller milled after Boudreaux as the boss clambered on along the sea bottom. He paused, orienting himself somehow relative to the looming saw-edged junk, all of which looked alike to Galloway, then struck out into the dark again. He slogged after. It was slow going through the muck, and now and then loops of scrap cable and old wire snagged his boots.

The junkyard faded into blackness behind them. It was succeeded by flat bottom, littered with the detritus of industry: half-buried drums, cans, more cable, torn sandbags. The corner of a plastic bag writhed slowly in the current. Looking back, Tiller glimpsed his trail as a zigzag in murky haze, a staggering furrow of already-half-obliterated footmarks, like a man groping in a midnight blizzard.

The bell came into view, canted on the bottom, lighted with a white two-second strobe that plucked shape from darkness for fifty feet around it. Two hoses were duct-taped to the down line. Boudreaux sliced them free and handed Tiller one. He shoved the hot-water hose down into his suit. The wave of warmth flooded along his body, driving out the chill that had already numbed his feet and fingers.

When he looked up again, Boudreaux was back at the lift line. He was sawing again. Another line, a heavy shackle at the end of it, and two flat packs with dangling pull toggles.

"Time, Ace?"

"Thirteen minutes."

"Let's see if we can keep the hoses with us," Boudreaux said. "Getting cold, all right. Maybe we should have done dry suits for this."

Tiller thought it was his longest speech of the dive.

There was no pinger or anything on the chopper. They'd just have to find it. Galloway climbed through the bell frame, dragging his umbilical after him. That way, he'd be sure of getting back. He tried to remember the orientation of the platform when he'd popped up, and then reverse it, going out from where the bell was. But Boudreaux was ahead of him again, moving away at a slow lope. His light probed here and there in a blurry emerald fan ahead of him.

Bingo, Tiller thought.

The crashed chopper lay upside down, like a dead silver roach. Its smooth belly gave back their lights. Part of the windscreen lay twenty feet from the rest of the wreck, but he saw right away they weren't getting in that way. The impact had driven the cockpit area deep into the fine brown silt.

Boudreaux was looking back, making a funny hand gesture Galloway took a second to interpret as taking pictures. He found the camera on his harness and squinted through the viewfinder. A pop, and for just an instant, he saw everything.

The light glinted off a square face port; Boudreaux was still looking at him. He made a circle with his glove, pointing right. Galloway started that way, then was yanked backward. "Slack," he told them topside, tugging at his umbilical. "Have Jay gimme about fifty more feet, Ace."

"Paying out fifty feet."

"Where you headed?"

"Passenger door, this side."

"Big enough?"

"For one of us."

The door was slid back and buckled. He had a bad feeling as he grabbed the jamb, the same place he'd grabbed before as they'd tumbled down from the regions of light. Now the interior was a black well. He made himself not think about it.

"You goin' in?"

"Yeah. Gimme some illumination, uh, Roland."

The first thing he saw when he stuck his head in was fish.

A shadowy stir of them, packed inside the canted narrow interior. They froze as his light hit them. He let go of the jamb and clapped his glove. The little shock wave blew them apart in a flurry of fins and tails.

"You inside yet, Till?"

"I'm inside, Ace."

He found the civilian right where he'd expected: pinned against the floor of the inverted chopper. An arm floated and wobbled, white and swollen in the stare of his light. He moved in cautiously, watching for sharp edges or dangling straps, and got a leg. The sock came off in his hand. He got the bare foot and hauled. At the same time, his hot-water hose pulled out of his suit. He let it go. No progress yet . . . he saw what was wrong.

A gush of bubbles erupted when his knife ripped into the vest.

Derleth Todds slid out into the beam of the flash, bumping against aluminum with the sound a canoe makes when it brushes a floating log. Tiller swallowed as the open blank eyes rolled past, then flinched at a sudden slam and grate above him. He backed, dragging the body, and shoved it through the door. It settled gently into the mud beside the helicopter, facedown, beside his heating hose, which was wriggling like a live thing, burrowing into the muck as the hot water jetted out.

"Got it?"

"I got it."

"We got body one, down here. Mister passenger."

"You see any briefcase?"

"Any what?"

"Any briefcase."

"No. The door was open. Could be anyplace."

"Take another look," said Boudreaux.

Ace Rodriquez, chipper and bright, and the bluster of wind across an open mike: "Hey, Roland, what's going on, *baboso?*"

"Don't call me that, Rodriquez. Getting this lift line on the chopper."

"Why not? You talking Cajun alla time. Where you putting it?"

"Where you told me. Around the rotor head."

Searching with the light again, Tiller caught a pale gray

glint. He pulled it out. Yep, the very briefcase. Samsonite. He shoved it out the door, too. It hit the body, tumbled slowly, and came to rest on the mud beside it.

"Tiller?"

"Inside the fuselage. Going for the pilot now."

"Watch your umbilical."

"Roger."

He didn't like being inside. It was disorienting. Everything was upside down. Things kept bumping into him. He knew it was only luggage, but it was just too close in there. Like cave diving, except cave divers had four of everything, and gear designed not to hang up. He was breathing too fast. No hurry, he told himself. Slow down. He wished he had something to wet his lips. He pulled ten feet of slack in after him and faced forward. His light was getting dim. Cold did that, faster than you'd think—killed the batteries. He snapped it to his harness and got out his spare.

That was better. It showed him the way to the cockpit, the back of the pilot's and copilot's seats, and a black, light-absorbing mass. Green glints from instrument faces. He was hauling himself forward, upside down, when he thought he saw something move. He started to say, "There's something up there," then remembered Porch's story about McCray seeing sharks no one else saw.

"What, Till?"

"Nothing." Another rattle and scrape, forward and above him, then a clank.

"Where are you now?"

"Inside. Going forward."

"Bottom time: twenty-four."

Neither diver answered.

Okay, let's get this over with, he told himself. It's getting cold; you're building up decomp time. Let's get it done. He passed a glove over his helmet to make sure he wasn't hung up, grabbed the back of the seat, and somersaulted awkwardly under it into the cockpit.

More fish, scattering. Little crabs, raising their claws like boxers, then retreating into circuit-breaker panels and upholstery and behind a CO_2 extinguisher.

The pilot was waiting for him, belted in upside down, staring forward with his visor down. He still had one hand on the collective. The crabs had eaten his eyes and started on his lips, and his tongue, which protruded about four inches, was a mass of gnawed pinkish white gristle.

Galloway looked away, swallowing, and found himself looking up at the center console: the banks of switches and indicators, their positions, gauge readings. Was that the kind of data the investigating board wanted? He groped around, looking up past the motionless, dangling head, and found the camera again. He framed part of the console and squeezed the lever.

The back flash seemed to balloon the compartment, blinding his wide-open eyes with about a megaton of white light. At the same moment, the cockpit shuddered. He tensed, blinking, waiting for the purple afterimages to dissolve. No, the metal beneath him was perfectly solid, motionless, as stable as the basement of the deep it lay on.

"Tiller?"

"In the cockpit."

"Thirty minutes. Better hurry it up, hombre."

He let the camera go and started on the lap and shoulder belt. First, he tried to release it, but something was screwed up, or maybe his fingers weren't working too well. Christ, it was cold. . . . Finally he sawed the webbing apart, glad for the edge on the little stainless knife. They were cheap, too, so he didn't mind when it slipped out of his hand, clacked as it struck his helmet, and disappeared. By then, the pilot was free, drifting down on him like the video clips you saw of guys dicking around inside the space shuttle. Tiller kicked him back up, but something black was gradually moving between them. He waved it away, but his glove went right into it—and disappeared. He frowned.

"Galloway?"

"Here. You got the other guy? The passenger?"

"He's on the wire, going up. You need help?"

"Coming out now. Hey. What is this shit?"

He couldn't see anything now. The black was everywhere. He could feel it now, too, when he tried to touch his helmet—soft, mucky goo. Mud, he recognized suddenly. It was coming in through the busted windshield.

The airframe groaned, settled. Something brushed him, a

flying boot, he guessed, though he couldn't see it. Where was his light? The blackness gave no hint of it.

"Galloway! She's startin' to roll. Get out of there!"

He could feel it then. The wreck was rotating slowly, pressing the open door, the only way out, down into the mud. For a moment, he didn't understand. Then he remembered his hot-water hose—burrowing into the bottom, percolating, jetting, softening the mud under one side of the fuselage. Till it rolled, trapping him inside, 360 feet down in the dark and cold.

Damn it, he thought. Well, no real problem. They could get a boat over here and winch the wreck up to the surface, now that Boudreaux had attached the shackle and mating line. Take a couple of hours, but that just meant it'd take him longer to decompress. Unless it . . . aw, shit, he thought, rolling his eyes inside his helmet and feeling his throat suddenly constrict. Unless it rolled over onto his *umbilical* . . .

Just like that, his gas stopped. No hiss, no click and rush of mix. His desperately sucking lips found nothing to breathe.

"Tiller!"

"No air," he wheezed. "Roland! Ace! Get me out of here."

Voices, all talking at once in the dark. Then a scrabbling, a scratching, closer than any of them. For a moment, he thought it was in his head. Then he knew it wasn't.

It was a hungry crab, searching across the outside of his helmet.

As if he was already dead.

ELEVEN

I'm not dead yet," he whispered into the oral/nasal.

The claws and legs scrabbled frantically as he gripped the thing. The shell cracked, then squished. Take that, you scavenging son of a bitch, he thought.

His other hand found the bailout valve. Gas clacked pressure back into his regulator. He took a half-strangled, infinitely grateful gasp of the dry helium/oxygen, knowing even as he inhaled that he had only seventy-two cubic feet of it. About five minutes, at 360 feet.

Lying on his back, unable to see, he took another long, slow breath. The 80/20 in the bailout was richer than the bottom mix he'd been breathing. It seemed to fizz as it hit the adrenaline in his blood. He was charged, *charged*; his body wanted to claw its way through the aluminum skin. But he couldn't panic. Had to figure this right, and do it right the first time.

Or Mister Crab's mourners would have a feast.

No question he was in trouble. Even underwater, the wrecked chopper had to weigh four or five tons. He didn't see how they were going to move it in the time he had left. He was trapped like a bee in a jar.

"Tiller, you there, amigo? You okay?"

"I'm on the seventy-two now, Ace. Still getting nothin' from topside."

"Porch is on his way down. What else can we do?"

He grunted and forced himself to think. First: the umbilical. He had comms, so it was probably intact. Just crimped, enough to cut off his mix. "Topside, Galloway: Try this. Come in on my umbilical, then slack off. Do that a couple, three times. I'll haul on my end. Maybe we can saw past whatever's constricting it."

"Standby . . . hauling in. Now . . . slacking."

He pulled with the one hand he could get on the hose, so hard that his elbow and shoulder cracked. Then let go. "Forget it. It's fouled hard."

"Roland?"

"I'm looking at it. Outside the hatch. Mud's real silty here. Like quicksand."

"Can you get his hose free?"

"I'm tryin' to."

He had a sudden urge to get out of his helmet. Forget that, he told himself. It was a saying in the Patch that dumping your lid was the last thing you did—and probably would be. Shouldn't there be another emergency bottle in the cockpit? Like the one he'd used during the crash? But this deep, it would give him about three breaths. A bubble? No, helo fuselages weren't airtight. And even if it did hold a little air, it wouldn't last much longer than what he had on his back.

He had to get out, and fast. But that meant he had to follow his line out, find the door, and dig under the side and up again. That didn't sound like something he could do in five minutes. But it was all he could think of. He grabbed at his helmet but reached it only after groping through a foot of mud. Slowly, inexorably, it was flooding in around him, burying him alive in the freezing dark.

"Galloway."

"Yeah, Roland."

"You on your bailout?"

"Yeah."

"That ain't gonna hold you long. What you want to do?"

He reached to his left, blindly groping, stretching his fingers. No good. Held back by the pinned hoses, wires, and line of the umbilical. Well, it wasn't doing him any good now.

Okay, he had it. Not what you'd call a sure thing. But the best he could come up with.

114

"Roland, start digging at the nose. I'm gonna try coming out the front. Cutting loose now."

"Tiller—"

"Galloway, wait—"

"See you topside," he said, and pulled the phone jack. Sudden silence: he was alone.

He got the spare knife—man, he'd done one thing right, packing spares—and opened it and placed it against the hose by feel. Sure hope that non-return valve works, he thought. Okay, here goes.

He sawed through the hose fast and hard, hoping he wasn't amputating anything. It separated with a squirt of bubbles and a hard welcome *clack* as the valve seated. Last, the lift line. This was harder to get to, a snap shackle on his right side. Finally he had to pull his glove off and probe with dead numbed fingers. Still no good. Shit, if he couldn't get this off he was screwed. Finally he cut it, too.

A lunge to port again. This time, his blundering hands hit something hard and rounded. He found a handle and yanked. It came free. He grabbed the pin and pulled it, got the handle, and squeezed.

The CO_2 fire extinguisher burst into a bubbling rumble. Galloway's lips twitched. He hadn't been too sure about that, whether the internal pressure was higher than ambient pressure at 360 feet. Apparently it was, at least a little. Hoping it was enough, he twisted, got his other hand on the top of the windscreen, and shoved the nozzle ahead of him into the mud.

Kicking himself forward against the pilot's body, scooping the wet, heavy blackness backward like some tunneling worm, he thrust himself out the shattered windshield. The nozzle rumbled and then faltered, dying. Still he could feel the soil more liquid ahead of him, a narrow, slightly softened tunnel next to the aluminum. The CO_2 stopped and he let go, digging now with both hands, scooping silt and mud backward like a mole. His breathing was getting ragged, but he couldn't stop. He rammed his helmet into the mud and got his knees up against the dash, still on his back, and shoved as hard as he could. Like some ugly, misshapen infant desperate to be born.

He couldn't see, but suddenly he could turn his head. Then his shoulders emerged. He thrust his arm up and hit something that boomed hollowly.

115

He pulled free, kicking and scrabbling as the seafloor opened above him, and slammed his helmet so hard on the fuselage, his ears rang. Then he was clear, but he still couldn't see. Waterborne silt, bubbled into a turbid soup, surrounded him, absorbed all light.

A hand closed on his leg. Couldn't tell who and couldn't ask. It let go, came back, clutched his arm. He tried to get free, but the bailout was going dry now. Had to have air. Had to get to the surface. Drop weights, that was what he had to do. He clawed at his waist.

The hand tightened, became an iron grip. He fought with diminishing strength as it drew him closer. His throat closed. A moan filled his ears as the black slowly dissolved into blood-red shot with silver lightning. The hand found the bail that unclamped his neck dam.

Suddenly too late, he understood. The other man was trying to kill him.

But he was too weak to fight, too weak to move. He gave up, sinking away into the silver darkness. . . .

A roaring blast of icy water needled his face, succeeded instantaneously by lancing agony in his ears and sinus. He inhaled down to his toes, shuddering in a seconds-long, indescribably beautiful orgasm. The gas howled in his ears, bubbling around the loosened neck into his suit. His head was splitting, but he didn't care. There was nothing better in the world than air.

The hand returned, fumbled at his helmet, and suddenly there were voices in his head. He broke in, shouting over the roar. "Hey, guys. I'm . . . alive."

Rodriquez, sounding excited: "That you, Till? *Oye!* Talk to us, *cabron!*"

For a second, still pumping his lungs full, he was confused. He was breathing, but where was it coming from? "I think somebody jammed a hose under my neck dam. Porch?"

"I'm still on my way down, man. This cage is the slowest thing I ever rode."

"It's Roland. He told me to give him mix to his pneumo hose. You're on his phone line, Till."

"Ah," he said. Now it made sense. The pneumo line was smaller than the mix hose; it was really just so the guys topside could get depth readings on the diver. But free-flowing, blowing gas down to him at a few pounds over ambient, it was giving him just enough to breathe.

Suddenly he saw a blue balloon of fuzzy light. Then all was black again. Two seconds later, the blurry flash recurred— a strobe, lighting the moving silt like a police cruiser in fog. "Okay, we're coming up on the bell. Porch, hear that? Meet us at the bell."

The hand returned. The jack came out and he was alone again. Gas blasted in and roared out, making his helmet dance around, battering his shoulders. He craned around. The next blue-white flash showed him Boudreaux's Rat Hat, face port aimed grimly forward, toward the bell.

The rest of the dive was pretty dull. Actually, Tiller thought, sitting in the cage on the way up, the most exciting part was arguing over the partial pressure of oxygen. That determined where they went into the decompression calculations, which determined where and how long they had to stop on their way up. Finally, Rodriquez and Boudreaux agreed on which tables to use, a partial pressure of oxygen equivalent of 360 feet and a bottom time of sixty minutes.

After getting to the bell, he'd ducked under the plastic dome, yanked off his helmet, and thrust his nose up into a tiny pocket of air at the top. He sucked in as gas bubbled up from the pneumo hose, still free-flowing, gradually displacing the water till he stood in a nipples-high bubble at the bottom of the sea.

After a while, Porch had emerged from the twilight, slogging across the silt bottom. He waved slowly, then passed the spare umbilical he carried under the lip of the dome. Galloway uncapped it, connected it to his helmet, plugged in the jack, and put the helmet back on. He twisted the valve and got a spray of water mixed with gas. A lot of water. He went to free-flow and lifted his neck dam. The water receded and he breathed more easily.

"Thanks, Porch."

"No problem. Look, gotta go."

"Gotcha."

When he and Boudreaux got back to the cage, it had been lowered again and now revolved slowly a few feet above the bottom, waiting. They hoisted themselves in and got as comfortable as they could. The cable vibrated, the sheave began to grind, and the ascent began.

They crept up at 25 feet a minute to 170 feet, topside switching them back to the descent mix as they passed 200. Boudreaux passed him his hot-water hose. He needed it. They stopped for seven minutes at 170 feet, then went slowly on up to 150 and waited for five minutes.

Tiller broke the silence at last. "Thanks for getting me."

"You got out on your own."

"I mean with the pneumo hose."

"*N'est rien*, cher. How was the pilot?"

"Not so good."

"Eels?"

"Crabs."

"Crabs make a mess. Eels burrow in, you can't see the damage."

"Tough on the family."

"Well, they'll get what's left when they lift the chopper."

Tiller remembered the old guy. "You got Todds, though, didn't you?"

"Yeah. Sent him up on a lift bag."

The flat plastic packs. "And the—you got his briefcase, too, right?"

"Didn't see no briefcase."

"Wait a minute. It was right beside him. If you got the body, you had to see it."

"I didn't see nothing, me. Ground was soft there. Might have got buried when the chopper turned over."

That was possible. It must have sunk into the silt, there where his water hose had burrowed in. He didn't feel like telling Boudreaux about the hose, though.

They spent another five minutes at 140, six at 130, eight at 120, eleven minutes at 110. At a hundred feet Ace switched them to compressed air. With the first shot of it, he felt warm and slightly drunk. He didn't sound like Donald Duck anymore, either.

Sixteen minutes at ninety feet.

Nineteen minutes at eighty feet. Sitting in the cage, he stared up into the gradually brightening glow of the sun. Dancing beams came flickering down, chasing over his hands when he stretched them out.

Twenty-three endless minutes at seventy feet. A school of tarpon sped by, fat, swift bodies glittering like platinum studded with diamonds. They watched the fish till they faded in the blue.

Another twenty-three minutes at sixty feet, the sun so bright now, it was like being on the surface. They told topside to cut the hot water, they didn't need it anymore.

Sixteen minutes at fifty feet.

At forty feet, Rodriquez cut in oxygen. At the first hit Tiller felt the elation strip away, blown free like a tatter of silk in a gale. Odorless, tasteless, the pure gas that fed the body's flame made his brain work all too well. He saw how stupid he'd been, and how close he'd come to dying. If Boudreaux hadn't been there, he'd have suffocated. Or, if he'd managed to drop his weights before he blacked out, died on the way up.

They hung there for a full hour and a half, watching the barracuda on their endless patrol. When they finally broke the surface and swung upward, the sea reeling and swaying below, he pulled his helmet off, though you weren't supposed to till you were safe on deck. Lifting his face to the sun, he sucked in every atom of clear, clean wind his bared teeth would let past.

TWELVE

Porch patted his back as he stripped off his suit. Rodriquez actually hugged him. Tiller stood stiffly till he let go. Then suddenly it was back to normal. They turned away and started talking, and McCray led him over to the overturned lubricant can they used as a stool. "Gear work okay?" he asked.

"If it hadn't, I wouldn't be here. You're a good tender, Jay."

"Thanks! Stand up. Arms up. Okay, sit down."

When the suit zipped off, he looked down at his own puckered white skin. It seemed suddenly very dear. "What about chamber time?" he asked Boudreaux.

"You don't need no chamber time."

"Tilt your head." A trickle and sting in his ear. "Other side." He bent obediently and smelled alcohol.

"Got a shot of that?"

"You don't want a shot of this. It's isopropyl."

"A beer'd be nice. I'm all dried up."

Ice rattled and he found a sweating ginger ale in his hand. McCray's personal supply, apparently. He slammed it down in about three gulps.

Beside him, Winslow and Boudreaux were talking in low voices. He glanced over. Boudreaux tilted his head back as the tender lighted his cigarette. The exhaled smoke drifted downwind, toward the everlasting roar of the flare.

The phone buzzed on the bulkhead. Porchellacchia, naked

except for white socks, waddled over. "Divers . . . yeah. Yeah. No, I think your boat guys were supposed to pick him up, check with them. Yeah. Yeah." He hung up. "They want you guys back in the galley."

"Who?"

"The divers, they said. Guess they mean you two."

"Wear a shirt, Roland," Tiller told the supervisor.

"A shirt?"

"Believe me. You'll be glad you did."

The board was reconvening when they got there, gathering around a table a teenaged boy was still wiping down. Trays and flatware clattered in the scullery. The smell of steam and food reminded Galloway they'd missed lunch. "What time's it, Roland?" he muttered as they pulled out chairs.

"Don't worry, cher. I asked Gassy, told him we were gonna be down over lunchtime. He had the cooks hold us out trays."

The steward brought an insulated server and cups, sugar in packets, creamer. He got coffee as the last members arrived. Duckworth, the FAA honcho. Richardson, the safety-board guy. Shattuck, Coastal Oil. Kelly, from the helicopter company. West came in, setting her spit cup by her place.

Duckworth cleared his throat and punched the cassette recorder, and they were, Tiller thought tiredly, on the air again.

"July 13: continuing data collection on the crash of OAS Twelve sixteen. Interviewing the divers who have just completed a postcrash dive for photography and body recovery. Mr. Galloway, you've testified before. You, sir, are—"

"Roland Boudreaux."

"Your employer?"

"DeepTech Diving Corporation of Summerland, Louisiana. I'm the owner."

"Current contract?"

"Coastal Oil Corporation."

Duckworth thanked him and explained what the investigation was, the same spiel he'd given Galloway. Tiller sipped his coffee and waited.

121

"Mr. Boudreaux, please describe the condition of the wreck as you found it."

"It was upside down, tilted to the right. No blades visible. Lot of debris around."

"Did you get photographs?"

Tiller put the camera on the table. It was still wet and a little pool formed underneath it as they looked at it.

"Did either of you note any external or internal damage inconsistent with damage caused by impact?"

"No."

"Mr. Galloway?"

He said slowly, "I'm not sure what you mean."

"I mean holes in the exterior, burnt patches, evidence of internal overpressure."

"No."

"You recovered the body of the passenger, Mr. Todds?"

"Yeah. Couldn't get the pilot out, though."

"The reason?"

"It took me a while to get to him. Then while I was taking a picture, the wreck shifted and I had to punch out on my bailout bottle."

"What was the condition of the body?"

He described it. Duckworth said, "You say he had his hand on the collective?"

"That's right. A good grip, too."

"Interesting. All right, anything to add?"

Boudreaux muttered, lighting another cigarette, "Can't think of anything."

Duckworth reached out then and the recorder went off. "Then let me bring something up. I'm not pointing any fingers. But the fact is, when Mr. Todds's . . . remains were brought up here and we asked about personal effects, there were none."

"None?"

"No watch. No wallet. No briefcase. Did you see anything like that?"

Boudreaux said he hadn't seen them. "Anything missing, it must have disappeared in the silt, after Galloway shoved him out. It was soft there, like sugar sand. Maybe it *was* sugar sand, under the mud, and that was why it gave way so sudden."

"Any chance of finding it? The briefcase, I mean." Shattuck asked him.

Boudreaux shrugged. "We'll look if you want, sir. Don't think there's much chance, though."

Shattuck looked down at the tabletop, shaking his head. Galloway looked at him with new interest. He checked out the gray slacks and light blue short-sleeved shirt, the combed-back blondish hair above a long, alert face with rimless glasses.

Because he recognized him now. Had just remembered where he'd heard that voice before.

It was Shattuck who'd called him that morning at the Brass Hat.

But why was Coastal Oil, the company DeepTech was under contract to, interesting itself in who it hired?

The FAA man said, "Okay, that explains why there's no briefcase. But what about the wallet, the watch?"

"Just a minute," said Tiller, forgetting Shattuck in sudden, disbelieving anger. "Are you accusin' us of stealing the guy's goddamn *watch*?"

"I didn't say—"

"I heard what you *said*, and I understand what you mean, and I don't like it. We hit *hard*. He was thrashing around, fighting for his life. He lost his watch, his wallet—that doesn't surprise me at all."

Richardson said, "I've investigated a lot of crashes, Mr. Galloway. Probably three or four hundred. You'd be surprised how tenaciously a corpse can cling, so to speak, to its personal items. A lot of time, that's the only way we can make an identification."

"Always?"

"No. Not always."

Duckworth dropped his eyes. "Okay, maybe it was out of line. Sorry. Gentlemen, any further questions for the divers?"

Shattuck and Kelly shook their heads, so Duckworth went on. "I don't know if we need to proceed to a formal investigation. We'll have to wait on recovery for that. Right now, there's a lot to be said for a catastrophic failure somewhere in the vicinity of the tail rotor drive or the rotor brake system."

"That's a highly unlikely failure mechanism," said Kelly. "You know the stats on the S-Seventy-six. It's the safest turbopowered commuter flying."

"We'll go into it thoroughly, Mr. Kelly. Like most crashes,

it's probably due to a complex of causes, not a single point of failure."

"How about the nondeployment of the emergency flotation?"

"Pilot error." Duckworth stood. "All right, let's view the body. I don't think we need you men anymore. Thank you."

"That's okay," said Galloway. He was still angry. "You better check your wallets before you let us go, though."

They gave him a sharp look, but no one said anything. "Good lick," said Boudreaux, letting out a stream of smoke as he watched them exit. Then he stubbed the cigarette out. "Let's get somethin' t'eat."

"Just a minute. Roland—"

"What?"

He was going to ask about the watch. He was almost certain Todds had had it on when he shoved him out the door. But now that he thought about it, he wasn't sure. He'd been worrying about more pressing things.

"Nothing," he said. "Yeah, let's eat."

The cooks had saved them rice and grilled liver. Porch and Wildman, Ace, Boudreaux, McCray, and Galloway ate without much talk. When Tiller finished, he was still hungry. He eyed the soft–ice cream machine. Finally, he went over and built himself a sundae with gooey pineapple topping and pecans.

When he got back, Boudreaux was telling the tenders what had to be done that afternoon. "We ain't gonna be back here for a while. So I want it broke down, all of it, and make sure everything's under cover and lubed up good. Drain the fuel tanks on the compressor. Check the valves on the gas bank. Regauge all the tanks. Make sure there's at least two hundred psi in the empties and tag 'em 'Used.'"

"Check, check, *baboso*."

"Tole you about that, Ace."

"Sorry."

"Everything else goes aboard the barge. Everybody aboard by nine tonight. We're gonna start early-early. They're setting the risers today; that's where Pinhole is."

He remembered what that meant. A tricky job, first jockeying the lay barge to align the first section of pipe relative to the platform, then cutting and welding until the tube turn—the huge steel weldment that bent the flow through nearly a right angle upward—fit just right into where it would attach to the platform legs. "They're doing that now?" he asked.

"Told you, this's a hurry-up job."

"No shit," said Porch. He scratched his belly where his T-shirt rode up. "Han' me that Tabasco, Ace."

"I better check on that," said Boudreaux, wiping his face and throwing down the paper napkin. "Make sure Guidry don't weld it in upside down an' ass-backward. But before I do, one more thing."

"Allus is."

"Ace, you gonna be eating tamales with false teeth. Company man wants to see us. Five o'clock, dive shack. Before that, I want you all to go down and take a look at the pipeline cross section I got up on the wall there. Read the statement of work. Then maybe you can ask some intelligent questions." He got up. "See you then. An' get some sleep—you're goin' into sat tomorrow."

"Sho, boss," said Porchellacchia, venting a belch like an oil tanker's horn.

McCray said, "Want to go down, look at that thing?"

"What, now? We got time, Cap'n."

"You want to lift some iron, Till? They got a nice weight room here on Twelve."

"I better not, thanks." Hard exercise after a deep dive increased the chances of the bends.

Rodriquez got up and so did McCray. "You going to the shack?" he asked them.

"Uh-huh."

He got up, too, and followed them down two decks to the dive shack. He was starting to learn his way around the platform, but it was confusing—like a ship, but there was no compartment numbering. You just had to follow your nose.

Rodriquez unlocked the office and they filed in. McCray and the assistant superintendent glued themselves to the blueprints. Galloway glanced at them—the words PANDORA 1000 caught his eye—but wandered over to Boudreaux's desk instead. He picked up the framed photo, studying the dark hair, pale oval face, brightly painted lips. Yeah. He couldn't see the plates on the Miata, but he was pretty sure this was the same woman he'd seen in Lafayette with this guy Shattuck.

"Good looker, huh?"

"Who is this?"

"That's Roland's wife."

"Oh yeah. Porch was tellin' me about her."

"Whatever he said, it's true."

"Don't say anything about her in front of Bender, Till."

"Touchy, huh?"

"Ole Roland don't have much sense of humor about Arden."

He put it back carefully. Next, he eyed the telephone. "This work?"

"Sure it works. Coastal's got a cellular link back to Bayou City."

"Can we use it?"

"Official call?"

"No."

"We didn't see you touch it," said Rodriquez.

"This is sure a long piece of pipe," muttered McCray.

"The better to pay us with, man."

"You guys know the number there at Summerland? The company?"

McCray gave it to him. He got a woman's voice. "Shadrach Aydlett, please," he told her.

"Who?"

"He's a new hire, a tender. Probably be back in the shed."

Finally, he heard Shad's voice, slow, a little suspicious. "Aydlett."

"Hey, Shad, it's me."

A pause. "Where you at, man? You back in?"

"No, I'm jumping a company phone out here on the platform. Can't talk long, just thought I'd call and see how you were doing. Probably be out of touch for a while, out on the barge." He paused, but Aydlett didn't say anything. "Anyway, how you doing? They put you to work?"

"Yeah, I'm at work. Say, know what I'm makin'? After they take out for taxes and Social Security? About three-fifty an hour."

126

"I told you it didn't pay much at first, Shad. It's diving gets you the full envelope."

"Well, this here is shit. You know what I found in my hard hat this morning? A big handful of grease. Lucky I didn't put it on; that's what they were all hanging around waiting for. . . . How you doing?"

He wanted to tell Shad about the crash, about a lot of stuff, but he didn't know when Boudreaux might walk through the door. So he just said, "I'm okay. Looks like a tough job. Tell you about it when I get back. Look, you got a place? Where you staying?"

"I'm roomin' with your buddy Claunch."

"You're rooming with Bill?" He couldn't keep the surprise out of his voice.

"Ain't much of a room. Up above the bar. It's actually pretty shitty here, Till. I don't think they want me around the shop."

"Shad, every new guy goes through that. Stick it out till I get back. We'll get a trailer or rent a place. Hey, why don't you do that? Get a copy of the *Daily Review*. Look in the classified. Find us something. Look out toward Ricohoc, or maybe Calumet."

"Think it's a good idea, me trying to rent it?"

Tiller knew what he meant. "Just find us a couple of possibilities. All right? Look, I gotta hang up. See you in a week and a half, two weeks. Okay?"

Aydlett said so long, sounding more cheerful than he had when he'd picked up. Tiller blew out, rubbing the back of his neck.

"That your colored compadre?"

"Yeah."

"How's he makin' out?"

"Fine." He dismissed Aydlett from his mind and went over and looked at the prints with them. Then he read the statement of work.

"Hannah move on you?" Rodriquez asked him.

"Huh?"

"I said, the pusher grab your dick? Ain't she a piece a work?"

"I don't like aggressive women, Ace."

127

"Hell, man, Hannah ain't aggressive; she just got more *co-jones* than the whole rest of her crew. I don't know where they come from, but they're about the most ragtag bunch of loose bolts and spare change I ever seen. Her drillers are about seventy years old. Some of 'em can hardly get up the ladders."

"So it ain't the J. R. Ewing Oil Company. They produce, don't they?"

"Seem to. Lot of oil going out of here."

Tiller put the folder back beside the photo on Boudreaux's desk. He couldn't help looking at it one more time. "See y'all later, guys."

"Where you going, Till?"

"Later, Jay." He was in no mood to have McCray tagging after him. He could get along with him, but not on a cheek-by-jowl basis.

Unfortunately, that was exactly how they were all going to live for the next two weeks.

He strolled around the platform, thinking about the job, then about Aydlett, then about nothing in particular. He came to the dive stage and leaned on the rail, stuck his hands in his pockets and stared out.

To his right, the pipe barge lay to anchor a few hundred yards off, men boiling purposefully about the pipeway. The first few lengths were on deck, being assembled from forty-foot sections. The stinger jutted toward him from the barge's stern. It was a long set of twin steel pontoons, compartmented and valved so they could be inclined at different angles by flooding. Fitted with rollers and guides, it supported the pipe as it came off the stern and began its curve downward toward the bottom. Beyond it was anchored the jet barge, the one they'd be diving from.

The Fourth of July sparkler sputter of welding started up below him. He looked through the open gridwork and saw Guidry. Cascades of hot metal burst from under his torch. They fell in heavy drops, cooling from white to orange to red as they made the long descent, then exploding in a cloud of steam when they hit the blue below.

Leaning out, he could see the tube turn being lowered slowly into place, the crane poised above it, the cables tending straight down under the terrific weight. Steel screeched as it descended. He made out Boudreaux, then Hannah West on the tender boat. She was holding a walkie-talkie and pointing to the crane operator far above. Shattuck stood beside her. Vice president of offshore operations, he'd said. That made him the one they all worked for. Him, Boudreaux, West, everybody on the barges, chopper crews, tug crews—everybody out here.

Far out, a bobbing orange mote caught his eye. He shaded his brow and made out the buoy Boudreaux had placed over the helo. He shivered as he remembered the crabs. It'd almost had him then, the—what had Claunch called it?—the blue.

No, that was superstitious shit. He had a close call because he screwed up. He hadn't forseen the hot-water hose would soften up the bottom. That was all. Fate, providence, bad luck— all bullshit losers used to justify losing.

He grinned into the wind. Now it was his turn to win. Two weeks at $580, round that off to $600—hell, that came out to $9,000. There'd be a depth bonus and an end-of-job bonus on top of that, if they made schedule. No fortune, but a decent paycheck. They could rent a house. Once Shad had a place to bunk, he'd feel better about Louisiana. Maybe he, Tiller, could call Latricia in Hatteras and fly her down here for him as a surprise.

A clank and hiss behind him. When he turned his head, Winslow was bent over the gas bank. The Westerner caught his eye and nodded. Galloway smiled but didn't speak. It was no use trying to make the Wildman talk. It was as if he had to pay for each word he used.

He was still standing there when McCray stuck his head around the corner. "Tiller? It's almost time for the meeting."

"Oh yeah. Sorry. I don't have a watch yet."

The second he said it, he knew it sounded wrong. What better reason to steal a watch? But McCray apparently hadn't heard about the missing stuff. He just said, "Well, I got an old Timex if you want it."

The guys were already going in, the first two getting the chairs. Boudreaux took his seat behind his desk. Galloway went in last. He leaned against a wall and crossed his arms.

Close up, Shattuck looked fit. Tall and tanned, he didn't look like he spent much time in the office. His thinning blond hair was slicked back, cut short around the ears. He fished in the pocket protector of his shirt and extended a chromed pointer.

"Everybody studied the job?"

They nodded. Porchellacchia lighted an ultralight; Shattuck glanced at him. "Close quarters in here, son. Mind putting that out?"

The big diver looked around, then slowly crushed the butt out against the sole of his boot. Shattuck waited, watching him.

Meanwhile, Galloway studied *him*. The way he stood reminded him of something. Back straight, head up. Fiddling with the pointer. The slicked-back hair and rimless glasses looked familiar, too. Then he had it. The intel officers in Vietnam. That was exactly how they stood when they briefed you before a mission.

Shattuck cleared his throat. "Okay, I thought before y'all got started, I'd go over a couple of things with Mr. Boudreaux, make sure we're all working the same job, and he suggested you men sit in, too. So here's the plan. You'll board the *J. C. Rice* tonight. You'll blow down then and stay down as long as it takes to finish the job. Roland, I understand you put a helmet on today. You boss your company the way you want, but on this job, I hope you'll mainly manage from topside. Unless, of course, there's some operational need for you to suit up. Okay, over to you."

Looking at a piece of paper on his desk, Boudreaux said, "The dive teams will consist of two shifts: Rodriquez, McCray, Guidry; Galloway, Porch, Winslow. Eight-hour shifts, but that don't mean eight hours off in between. You know that, you all worked sat before. We start off setting the riser. Got to check it, align it, then clamp it off to the first section of pipeline."

Rodriquez said, "How about the shackles, Roland? That they use to lower it with. We gonna have to get them off?"

"Bang 'em soon as it's in position. It takes too long to do that by hand. That's another thing: I want to use explosives whenever it saves time."

Shattuck said, "The first phase starts as soon as connection's completed. The bottom goes up and down, but we'll just trench it all till Mile Six. After that, there's four miles we don't have to trench, then the bottom rises again. That's the Galveston safety fairway, a lot of tanker traffic, so Coast Guard regs require the pipeline be buried. That's between Mile Ten and Fourteen—the fairway's two and a half miles wide and we have to give it three-quarters of a mile on either side. Past that, we're deep enough to lay right on the bottom. All you have to do then is fix any problems, clear debris, sandbag the crossings, et cetera and so on."

The men sat with their hands on their knees. Tiller rubbed his teeth with his knuckles. He wondered again why they were using divers for visual inspection rather than ROVs. Then he thought, Who cares? Better us than some can of electronics and an armchair jockey with a degree from Nintendo University. Then he decided, No, I've wondered long enough. He raised his hand.

"Galloway, right? Got a question?"

"About the pipeline. I understand why you need us on the jet sled. But why are we doing visual inspections on the deep sections of the lay?"

"In case there's a problem, cher," said Boudreaux.

"I mean, why not use an ROV?"

The other divers twisted to examine him, with varying degrees of interest and disgust. But Shattuck nodded. "Good question. The kind I have to answer in advance, when I bid out a job. The answer is, I think human divers are still better than machines. You can just about turn a bolt with an ROV, if the bolt's specially designed to mate with its manipulators. If it isn't, or if that robot craps out and you have to bring in another model, you're back to square one.

"Second, this may sound funny, but the robots aren't as tough as you guys. One gets caught in a bight of cable, you got to have a guy standing by to go down and rescue it. And you got to pay him anyway, whether you need him or not.

"Third and last, they don't have any sense of touch. We're talking mud bottom between here and One Thousand. There's going to be a lot of silt kicked up. You guys can work in black water, but if a robot can't see, it's helpless. You have to wait till the water clears, and meanwhile you got a lot of expensive capital equipment sitting around waiting."

The ring flashed as Shattuck snapped the pointer shut. Tiller expected him to say something about light at the end of the tunnel, but instead he just smiled. "Yeah, we could have ordered in ROVs. But I think you guys can do just as well at about half the cost. And that's why Roland got the job. Make sense, Lyle?"

"Uh, I go by Tiller. Yeah, thanks for the explanation."

Shattuck grinned and, sure enough, gave him an offhand salute. Galloway felt as if he should be wearing fatigues and combat boots.

Boudreaux stood. "Any other questions? Okay, time for chow. Remember, bonus for every man if we make it to connection in twelve days."

Nobody said anything else, and the meeting broke up.

Thirteen

Galloway."

He came awake instantly in the darkened compartment. "Yeah."

"Time to jump."

He sucked a deep breath and heaved himself out. McCray handed him his boots. He stuck his feet into them automatically as the tender asked, "You got a kit?"

"A what?"

"A sat kit. What you taking into sat with you?"

For the first time, he remembered: He was going into saturation. He sat up straight and cracked his head on the frame of the upper bunk. "Shit. What time's it?"

"Eleven."

"Thought we were gonna get some sleep."

"Bender says get you up, you and Porch and Wildman; you're going down first shift."

"Hell. No, that's it, that bag. Oh, my gear—"

"I took it over to the barge. Rinsed it and dried it; it's ready to go. You got any spray cans in here? Deodorant, anything in an aerosol can?" Galloway shook his head, buttoning his pants as McCray rummaged through his shaving kit. "This all?"

Irritated, he didn't answer. It wasn't that he wanted to travel light, he was carrying everything he owned. McCray grabbed his tote and they went out onto the deck.

Outside the rig lights were bright and hard and the night beyond them was so dark, it felt for a moment as if he was

133

falling. A rainbow halo of humidity glowed around each bulb. The filaments burned fiercely, trembling to the hammer of the diesels, fire skinned with glass; brilliant close up, but negligible and lost in the windy immensity of besieging night. The wind rushed and moaned through the works and braces, smelling of smoke and oil and the sea. He sucked it in and out, in and out as they clattered down steel stairs to the cellar deck.

The bird cage rattled as it hit the deck of the crew boat. Engines rumbled, cables hummed again, and they were under way, the boat rolling hard as it motored out of the lee. He sat on a capstan and looked back at Pandora 12, adorned with lights like some huge black Christmas tree. The thirty-foot plume of fire wavered and danced, grinding yellow sparks off the tossing waves.

"Where's the rest of the guys, Jay?"

"Bender an' Kimball and the bell techs, they're on the barge already. The others are getting some sleep."

"Nice for them. How about us?"

"Somebody's gotta take first shift."

"Wait a minute. Who's Kimball?"

"You met him . . . when we came aboard. The professional tender."

He didn't remember any pro tenders, but he let it go. They were all going to get to know one another real well. The boat swung right and the green sidelight and rows of white work lights of the barge came into view, close aboard. They coasted in and lurched to a stop against big black rubber Yokohama fenders. He followed McCray over them to the platform, waited for the roll, then jumped across two feet of open water to a ladder. A handpainted sign read GET LAID FAST. WELCOME TO THE JOHN C. RICE, FINEST JET BARGE AFLOAT.

Boudreaux was waiting at the top of the ladder. He nodded to Galloway and said to McCray, "He sober?"

"Wait a minute—"

"You ready to dive?"

"I'm ready. And goddamn it, you want to find out if I'm sober, you ask me, not my friggin' tender."

"You and Rodriquez, all you want to do is mouth off, hanh? Better remember who's boss of this outfit. We're gonna blow you and Porch and Winslow down in the bell. You know what to do?"

134

"If I don't, you can tell me over the interphone."

"Get him suited up," Boudreaux snapped, looking at his watch. "I want you down there blowing bubbles in fifteen minutes."

"Let's go, Tiller," said McCray, tugging at his arm. Galloway looked after the boss, then turned to follow him.

A few minutes later, he and Winslow and Porchellacchia were standing next to the chamber and the bell and the gas shack, out on deck on the starboard side. They were waiting for Boudreaux to get done talking to the barge captain. Even near midnight, the *Rice* was noisy as a foundry. Clanging steel and the crackle of welding echoed around the superstructure. The compressor was running and the bleed air was hissing and he was sweating already in his sweat gear, the heavy hotwater suit, harness, and boots. McCray and Kimball, a short, fat guy with a mustache, stood holding weight belts and hats and the rest of the gear.

Winslow stretched. Long and rangy, when he stretched he seemed about eight feet tall. Porchellacchia was sucking hard on his last ultralight for a long time. Tiller stretched, too, feeling the tension in his back and neck. He took a last look at the sky. A few stars showed here and there, but the work lights on the barges and the huge torch of 12's flare all but eclipsed them.

A trembling explored the back of his legs. It was always like this going into sat, he thought. You couldn't get a needle up your asshole with a hammer.

"I wouldn't do it," said Kimball.

"What?"

"I wouldn't dive sat. It's no good."

"You little shit, nobody'd ever ask you," said Boudreaux, coming around the bell. "An' if they did, you couldn't get through the hatch, I guarantee. We lined up for a pop? Let's get moving, goddamn it. We got thirty miles of sewer pipe to put down. Galloway, get in the pot. Quit wasting time."

He sucked a last lungful of sweet air. Down in his gut, a thousand black eels were tying themselves in square knots. It felt like his first time all over again.

135

"We're gonna blow the first shift down in the bell. To save time."

"Okay." He understood. The bell held a smaller volume; it would be faster than blowing down the whole chamber.

But Boudreaux was still talking, pacing back and forth. "You pressurize in the bell, on deck here, then we lower you in it. You go out and do the job, then back in the bell, up to the deck, lock into the chamber."

"I know all that, Bender—I mean, Roland."

Boudreaux gave him a vicious stare. "Wildman, you lead, till we see how Turbomouth here handles himself on the bottom. Porch, how about you take bell tender for now."

Tiller sighed. No, you didn't joke with Bender Boudreaux.

The bell was disconnected from the chamber, sitting alone in the middle of the deck. The work lights glared down like opening night on a stage. They lighted up the lift cables, gas lines, and power lines, dangling below the crooked shadow of the crane. Pierced-metal steps led up to the entry hatch. Sweat squished in his boots as he went up them. Without looking back, he bent and crawled through the hatch.

The interior of a six-foot-diameter sphere, curved blank walls without view ports. He looked carefully around, noting the locations of the gas panel, first-aid kit, hot-water panel, weight-release lever. The looped coils of umbilicals. The interphone box. CO_2 scrubber. Then he crawled in the rest of the way, got his boots on the flat ring around the slightly bigger hatch that was the floor itself, and fitted his spine to the concave steel wall.

Winslow and the Pagan crawled in and settled themselves. A light came on below them, behind a thick shield of steel-reinforced glass. Shadows etched Winslow's eye sockets, the queer bulbous outthrust of his forehead. Porch sagged back, gut drooping. Galloway could smell him already.

"Gear," said McCray at the hatch, and they leaned forward and pulled in weight belts, a coil of half-inch rope, snatch blocks, a box of shackles and pins and wire and J-bolts, a hydraulic impact wrench, more hose, charged bailout bottles, their helmets. Winslow's leather gear bag, McCray grunting as he handed it in. Three paper sacks.

"Snack. Case you get hungry."

"Thanks, Jay."

"Nose drops?"

"I'm okay, thanks."

"Porch? Wildman?"

Porch took some, but Winslow shook his head, shoving the gear bag under the seat. McCray asked him, "What in hell you got in that thing, anyway? It's heavy as hell."

"Tools."

"What kind of tools weigh fifty pounds?"

Winslow said slowly, "A sixteen-inch steel crescent. Sockets. Spare fittings." He unsnapped the padlock and groped around. Held up a hand-powered drill. "Stuff you might need in sat, or out on the job."

Boudreaux's scowl replaced McCray's smile at the hatch. "Okay, listen up, you. We're gonna blow you down to four hundred and fifty feet. Storage depth in the main chamber's gonna be around four eighty, five hundred to start. That'll give you enough shallow-end excursion for the riser job, and the other guys'll be set for the first leg of the lay."

"Whatever you say, chief."

The hatch swung closed with a thump. There were no handwheels, just dogging levers. Gas pressure kept the sea out, not lock work. When it sealed, they were closed in watertight, airtight, gastight. He took a deep breath, reached out, and rapped his knuckles softly on the interior of the bell.

It was like rapping a granite wall.

"Standby in the pot." The interphone, hollow, above them. "Comms okay?"

"Five by."

"Bell umbilical master valve open?"

"The green one, Tiller," said Porch. "No, to the right. Yeah."

"Master valve all the way open, check."

"Starting pressurization."

The hiss started low, then increased to an ear-blasting roar. Tiller started chewing air. His ears popped, but not all the way. The roar increased, and so did the pain. He grabbed his nose and blew. If you fell behind the rise in pressure, you'd lose eardrums easy.

His ears equalized with a squeak and pop. He pulled his hand across his face. About a quart of sweat came off on it and he rubbed it on the plastic he sat on. He twisted, looking around the bell. The repainting hadn't gotten to here. The white paint was yellowed, the cushions crinkled like the skin around an old man's eyes. He found the internal-pressure gauge. The needle was already swinging past one hundred.

"He's taking us down fast." Already his voice was going squeaky with helium.

The other divers didn't respond. Maybe they hadn't heard over the blast of incoming gas. Winslow was unwrapping a chew. Galloway refused with a shake of his head. The Westerner tucked it into his cheek, put his hands behind his head, and leaned back. Porch looked asleep.

A fine whirling mist formed as the cold expanding gas hit the humid air of the compartment. It dissipated almost instantly. Sweat squeezed out of his pores. The hot-water suit felt like a lead sausage casing.

The roar grew louder and louder. Finally, he put his hands over his ears and closed his eyes and sat rigid.

He remembered the first time he'd heard about saturation diving, back in diving school in the Coast Guard.

The theory was simple. Everybody knew about nitrogen narcosis and the bends. Air was a mixture of nitrogen and oxygen. When pressure increased—as it did when you dove—the nitrogen dissolved in the bloodstream. Dissolved nitrogen was an anesthetic and an intoxicant. Beyond about two hundred feet, most divers got too drunk to work. And the longer you stayed down, the more nitrogen built up. When you came back up, the dissolved gas had to come out of solution again. If you rose too fast, it formed bubbles. This was what caused the bends: bubbles blocking the capillaries and pressing on the nerves.

If you replaced air with a helium-oxygen mix, you eliminated narcosis. Helium wasn't an intoxicant. It still dissolved in the tissues, though, and you still had to spend a long time decompressing after a heliox dive.

The Navy had pioneered saturation diving in the sixties. Beyond a certain point in time, your body had absorbed all the helium it could. After that, you could stay down as long as you liked—days, if you had enough to breathe and a place to sleep.

But there were problems with helium, too. It conducted heat better than air, so you got cold faster. It was hard to talk. You still had to decompress. You had to compress slowly, too. Or else—

Clearing his ears once more, he reopened his eyes to the gauge.

Suddenly, he tensed. They were going down too goddamn quick. What the hell was going on? A 450-foot pop, that wasn't shallow. But it looked like topside was taking them all the way, straight down, one long blow-down. It couldn't have been more than ten minutes since the hatch had sealed, and the needle was swinging past 150 feet and the air was getting hot, hot, hot.

When he looked at Winslow again, he saw that the other man's hands were shaking.

Oh, shit, he thought. He held up his own hands, saw them trembling and dancing. The palsy spread, grew to shaking, then to uncontrollable jerking.

Porchellacchia's eyes popped open.

Suddenly the interior of the bell went out of focus. His inner ear told him they were upside down, or spinning, though he knew they weren't. Across from him, Winslow's head was juddering like he was driving over cobblestones.

Topside told them to stand by for lift. A scrape, a jostle, a drone, a grind; the bell tilted. He felt heavy and then his stomach dropped away and he felt light.

A splash and gurgle, faint through an inch of solid steel.

Not fully pressurized yet, and they were on their way down. He ground his teeth, fighting for control against the panic that came not from himself but from some weird reaction of a body squeezed too hard, too fast—

Winslow screamed, the sound tearing into his eardrums in a weird helium keen. "They're gonna kill me!"

Porch's eyes popped open again. "Wildman!"

Winslow wailed and clapped his shaking hands to his face. For a second, Tiller thought he was going to claw his eyes out. "Shit! Get them *out* of here!"

"What's the matter with him?"

"It's HPNS." Porchellacchia grabbed Winslow's arm. "Man, listen, there's nobody here but you and me an' Tiller here. You know what's going on."

"They got me. They're gonna kill me!"

"It's high-pressure syndrome. Cool it, Derick, nobody's gonna—"

"They're gonna lock me in and kill me. Just like before! It's gonna be gas!"

Winslow suddenly lunged for the side hatch. His hands were inches from it when Tiller got his arms around him. He smelled like urine and Skoal. Porch had his legs. When they had him locked down, he went rigid, choking and gurgling. "Goddamn it," muttered Tiller into his ear. "Look, calm *down*. We got to get used to it. It goes away after you're pressurized. You know that, goddamn it!"

Winslow was panting and shaking as if he'd just run a hundred-meter sprint. He seemed to be staring into hell. Then he blinked and wilted. His eyes flicked this way, then that. Tiller held the bear hug for a second longer, then both he and Porch eased off.

"Everything okay down there?"

He looked around for the intercom. "Shit, no! What the hell are you people doing up there?"

"Tiller? That you? You're too close to the mike. You're talkin' too fast. Slow down, man. Take it easy."

"Jay, that you? What in the hell's name is going on? Why're you pressing us down so fast?"

"Wasn't me. Archie's on the box. And Roland's standing right over him."

"You got to slow down. Shit! We almost had to—" He was about to say, "coldcock Wildman with a wrench," but he stopped himself. You didn't say things like that about your partner, not if you expected to work with him again. And Winslow looked better now, rubbing his face and blinking. "Hey, we've got the shakes. We got the high-pressure heebies here."

McCray's voice went low. "Jeez, I'm sorry, man—look. We get five eighty a day, in sat, right? Plus your depth bonus."

"Yeah, so what? What's that got to do with—"

"You're at depth five minutes before midnight—that's a day. Not just divers, but the superintendent gets depth pay for that day, too."

"So it was—"

"So we had to hurry up to get you fellas blown down and in the water. Roland wanted you over the side before midnight."

"You're shitting me," Galloway said.

"Is it bad? You want me to tell him you want to come back up?"

He glanced at Winslow, who was staring at his hands. The

140

trembling was easing off. Porch had his hand on his partner's shoulder, muttering to him. "No, forget it. I think he'll—I think we'll cool down."

"You sure?"

"Think so. Hey. Derick. Derick! You okay?"

Winslow looked around the inside of the bell. He nodded, managing a sheepish half smile.

He didn't know whether McCray said something to Boudreaux or whether this was the original plan, but the last hundred feet to the bottom went slower. There was no bump, no jostle, nothing dramatic to signal their arrival. Topside just told them they were there.

Time to go to work. Top hatch, first. He took a second to go over it in his mind before he did anything, just to make sure.

The bell had a two-hatch work lock beneath where the divers sat. The "top hatch" was actually the one his boots were resting on. The upper hatch opened upward; the lower exit hatch swung down. They were just wide enough for a suited diver. When you were at depth, the pressure should equalize, the gas inside the bell matching the water pressure outside.

He tried to pull the top hatch up, but it wouldn't unseal. Winslow fanned his fingers from side to side, palm down— "hold off"—and cracked a valve.

They watched the interior-pressure needle twitch upward. At 365 feet, the upper hatch unsealed with a hiss. Porch hauled it up—it was spring-loaded, but still heavy as sin, a two-and-a-half-foot disk of cast steel—and locked it. The sea appeared around the edge as he did so, then flooded up, a dark, noiseless welling-in of cold water.

"Topside, gonna blow out this water." Tiller reached up for the bell blow-down valve. The sea retreated sullenly, the restless black surface dropping till it no longer licked their boots.

"Okay, I'm going out. Helmet going on."

He lined up the supply valves on the umbilical and flemished it out so that it would run out without snarling. He checked his helmet and put it on. The inside of the used helmet was almost homey by now. He swallowed with a dry mouth.

Boudreaux's voice inside his head: "Got your bailout bottle on?"

"Uh-huh," he lied. The divers always put their bailouts on outside the bell. It was a pain to get them on inside. The super knew that, too. It was just a game. The bailouts were kind of a game, too. At the depths they'd be working, a seventy-two was just a puff or two before the big bedtime. Barely enough time to wish you'd picked a safer career.

"Locking out." He slid off the seat and dangled his boots in the water. Made a last check. Tools. Super Q. Knife. Getting heliox. Getting hot water. Geronimo. He grabbed the lip and went in feetfirst.

It was like sliding into an inkwell. There were lights on the bell and he could see for fifteen or twenty feet. Then the glare came back at him. Beyond that, just black, like deep woods beyond a camp fire. He clicked his light on. The beam cut a narrow wedge out of the cold chocolate pie that was the sea at midnight at 360 feet.

"You outside?"

"Uh-huh." He swung himself around big tanks of onboard gas that the bell carried for emergencies. He sat on the drop weight, leaned against the tool basket, and got his bailout strapped on.

When he stepped off his boots sank into the bottom. Muck. It was going to be a long job. "Leaving the bell," he grunted.

He waited patiently while Winslow slid out, born into the deep wriggling, like a shark. Porch would stay inside the bell this shift, handling their umbilicals and running the hot-water panels, ready to switch to onboard gas in an emergency or come out after them if they needed help.

There was supposed to be a work line rigged to the site. He tramped around the bell, moving with the nightmare slowness of depth and mud, and found it. Yellow propylene, floating in coils, already snarled. He hated poly line, but it was cheap. He fought till it came taut, then half-walked, half-pulled himself into the darkness.

The pipeline took shape under the touch of his light. More immense than the eye could grasp, running from blackness to blackness, it lay half on, half under the mud. It seemed incredible that something so big had been put here by men. Even more incredible, they might have to move it—unless the riggers had placed it perfectly the first time, which was unlikely. A flash of light; Winslow on the far side of the line, moving along parallel to him. The other diver seemed to have recovered from the episode in the bell. Pressure syndrome hit different people different ways. Shakes, dizziness and nausea, those were the most common symptoms. Winslow just moved along, and once in a while Tiller could hear him breathing. Topside had the crossover switch on so they could all talk to each other.

"Porch, you there? Give us some more slack."

"Roger."

They came to the end of the yellow plastic and there it was: the riser. A light lowered from the platform illuminated the work area like a searchlight in fog. Tiny living things, little filmy jellyfish-type guys, drifted through its beam like a horizontal snowfall. He noted the direction of the current: northwest.

He snapped his attention back to the job. The shape of a huge letter L, the riser came down from the top of the rig, made a curve here at the bottom, and headed outward for about twenty feet before ending in a flange. The outboard end had to butt up against where the pipeline, which had been laid the night before from the barge, began. He slogged his way slowly up to the meeting point and stopped, putting the beam of his light on first one and then the other.

"Shoot," Winslow muttered. Galloway shook his head slowly. The horizontal alignment looked close. But the end of the pipeline, leading back to the lay barge, was five feet from the open end of the riser and offset from it by a couple of feet.

"It's dicked up," he told topside. He heard somebody moan, couldn't tell who.

Boudreaux: "What you need down there?"

"Gimme a minute. I want to think about it." Then he remembered that Winslow, not he, was lead diver, and said, "Derick, what you want to do?"

"Kind of clamps they got on this riser, Roland?"

"Just two, they set it up quick. Top and bottom. Gonna set the rest later."

"How tight they torqued?"

"You can probably snatch it around, if that's what you're gettin' at."

143

"Well, we got to get this end of the line moved first, anyway. It's too friggin' far away."

A little later, they discovered that the rigging was dicked up, too. The lifting sling, the main one that went up to the bow crane on the barge, had slipped off the end of the pipeline. It took them a while to dig down with their hands to the bottom lip and get the sling around it again. Then they had to get the hook on it and moused with a piece of welding rod.

When they had that done, they took a short break, leaning on the pipe and breathing hard, blowing out all the CO_2 so it didn't build up. Then they moved back toward the barge, inspecting the lift points for the davits on the way. When Winslow was sure they were clear, where no debris would fall on them if anything parted, he told topside to take a strain.

It took an hour and a half of talking to the barge captain and the chief rigger and Hannah West on the platform, through Boudreaux, to get the end of the pipeline lifted, shifted five feet, and dropped again. When it was close to position, Galloway and Winslow moved in and attached two sets of snatch blocks. As the crane operator relowered, they braced themselves and ratcheted in the hand levers of the chain hoists with all their strength, first one side, then the other. After about an hour, they'd jimmied it in close enough that they could think about the angle problem. They measured it and thought for a while, then asked topside for more line and two air tuggers.

While they were waiting, Tiller rested. The cold was getting to him despite the hot water Porch kept flowing out to them. It didn't get all the way to his gloves, so his hands were always cold. He wished he'd gotten more sleep the night before. He cracked his free-flow just a bit, wasting gas, but what the hell. He dozed for a little while there in the water.

When the stuff came down, they rerigged, this time snatching the outboard end of the riser to one of the jacket legs. They rigged the line from the air tugger, an air-driven winch. But when topside took a strain, nothing happened. He and Winslow studied it for a while, then ascended twenty feet to the lower riser clamp. He loosened the bolts one turn and descended again. This time when they ran the tugger, the riser creaked and slowly pivoted into position.

"Not bad."

"Yeah, that worked."

"Why don't you two *babosos* congratulate yourselfs or something?"

"Hi, Ace. What you doing up?"

"Getting pressed down. Me an' Pinhole and the Captain gonna be takin' over from you clowns."

The realization his shift was almost over made him feel stronger. "Well, we just about got it into position for you."

"How about breaking this down," said Winslow over the interphone. His voice sounded tired even through the electronic filtering. Tiller said sure. He started pulling pins out of snatch blocks, then changed his mind; topside could take it apart faster on deck. He unhooked the gear from the jacket leg and left it lying in the mud, then trudged through the muck over to Winslow. His partner was bent over the gap that remained between the end of the pipe and the end of the riser.

When he saw it, he grinned. Only a three-inch gap between the flanges. Cocked, but close enough for the next shift to square up, shim up, bolt together, and torque down. They spent the last minutes cleaning off the O-ring grooves on the flange faces.

They left their tools, the tuggers and line and blocks, in case the next shift needed them, and struggled back toward the bell. By the time they got there, Tiller was exhausted. He let Winslow enter first, then pulled himself into the lock with the last of his strength. He collapsed on the bench, streaming muddy water, and worked his helmet off.

"You guys aboard? Ready to lift?"

"Let us close these—okay, get us outta here."

The bell went up fast. They clung to handholds as it swayed, then clanged down onto the deck. Looking at Winslow, Tiller saw himself: exhausted, cold, a growth of stubble accentuating his pallor. A reddened patch around his mouth, where the oral/nasal rubbed. Another at his neck, where the dam chafed. Porch looked better, but then he'd spent the shift sitting in the bell. A pause, a thud, then: "She's mated. Standby to open."

When the pressure equalized, the side hatch unseated with a pop. They stirred, groaned, and got up. Cradling their helmets like injured football players limping off the field, they crawled across into the chamber.

The second shift, looking fresh, slid out past them as they staggered upright. The lock slammed and sealed behind them and Winslow closed and dogged it. A clang, a rush of gas, and that was it, their shift was over. They sagged on a bench and just blew heliox in and out. Their suits were covered with mud and yellow-black grease from the cables. Tiller shoved his into the transfer trunk for the outside crew to clean.

As he toweled off, he looked around at where he'd be spending the next two weeks. The chamber was roomier than the bell, but not by much. Enough steel-wrapped cylindrically shaped space for bunks, a sink, and a fold-down table. Valves and gauges like the inside of a submarine. It smelled already of damp and sweat and chewing tobacco. Pale green walls. The distant clatter of the compressor starting up outside. Aluminum deck battens above a trickle of bilge water. Personal gear stuffed under the racks. The flush toilet was in the transfer lock, giving them a little privacy at least. He tilted his head, dripping alcohol and acetic acid first into one ear and then the other.

He was dragging himself toward his bunk when a pale gleam stopped him. He shoved his face close to the little saucer of Lucite set into steel and peered out.

The sun was rising. The sea seemed to lie flatter in the imminence of morning. The sky glowed pale, nearly white, except for wisps of golden cirrus near the horizon. Then all was eclipsed as some rigger's tattooed back slid in front of the porthole.

It occurred to him that he was wasting time. Eight hours and he'd be back out there. Back face-to-face with that Louisiana blue.

But balanced against that was over a thousand bucks he'd made. Thanks, in part, to Boudreaux. Greedy shit, he thought, but wasn't sure who he meant.

Out of no place, he remembered something the Baptist had said to him once. Before he'd left the Golfo Triste on that last trip. Risk versus reward, he'd said, standing there in his spotless white suit. That was what everything human beings did came to in the end. Business. Economics. Sport. Love . . . no, he was getting tired, getting confused. . . .

For a moment, he wanted to think about that. It seemed important. But the next minute, whatever thought had teased him was gone, vanished like the mist when you pressurized.

To hell with it, he thought. A hook had been welded onto the steel over the port. He hung the towel over it, blotting out the dawn. Before the bunk stopped swaying, he was asleep.

FOURTEEN

The flange-up? We got that done."

Tiller mumbled around a mouthful of congealed eggs, "How'd the rest of it go for you guys?"

McCray said, "We cleared a lot of trash out of the way and started jetting out under the riser. Used hand jets. Had a hose burst on us, took a half hour to get a new one. But we got most of the mud out from under the first fifty, sixty feet of pipe. It's just about ready for you guys to set the sled."

Winslow and Porch were getting dressed out as Galloway swallowed the tepid coffee Kimball had locked in before he hit the wake-up buzzer. McCray and Rodriquez and Guidry had just come in, dirty and tired. He thought, Glad I missed that part. Jetting by hand was about the hardest work in diving. The nozzle was heavy, the water hose stiff and too buoyant; it was always trying to pick you up off the bottom. The recoil was counterbalanced by back-thrusters, but the back-thrust was touchy, too. You could lose tools and gloves or even the boots off your feet.

"Who's gonna ride the sled?" Ace said. "You? Galloway?"

"Who you want?"

"You'll do. There's just a little jetting left to do while you get that set up. I left the jet tied off to the riser."

"Is the sled on the bottom?"

"Should be. They were lowering it when we wrapped up. So we knocked off, figured we'd let you *culos* set it."

"*Culo.* That mean what I think?" asked Galloway.

147

Rodriquez smiled. "Not in your case, man."

"Then don't use it to me." He stood up and zipped his suit. It was clean, but he winced at the clammy feel. Nothing ever dried in the chamber, and if it was dry when it came in, it picked up moisture fast from the humid atmosphere.

Winslow said, "How's visibility?"

"Shitty. About five feet till you start jetting. Then it's zip."

"How's topside doing?"

Strictly speaking, they were topside now—the chamber was on deck, on the barge—but in terms of pressure, hundreds of feet separated them from the men outside. So when a diver said *topside*, he meant the supervisor. "Ole Bender, he was on our ass the whole time out there. Man, it gets tiring having him in your ear all the time."

"But we gotta keep at it. What we got, twelve days to get this line down."

"We'll get it done." Porchellacchia stood up and grabbed his helmet off the rack. "Ready?"

"Let's go," said Tiller.

On the way down in the bell, Boudreaux came on the interphone. Tiller wondered when he slept. Maybe he didn't. "Wildman, Tiller, Porch. You guys there?"

"Team two, on deck."

"Ace tell you about setting the sled?"

"Yeah."

"Who's gonna do it?"

"Me," said Tiller. "Any special way you want it rigged?"

"Got a soft bottom here. Make sure there's nothing under the sled it's gonna hang up on. Check the hoses for slack."

"How about the riser? You want those clamps loosened some more?"

"Don't worry about that. We'll get that later. Get this sled sledding, cher."

"I hear you. How's the lay barge doing?"

That was the first stage of the lay: assembling the sections on the lay barge, welding them, sealing the joints, and running the pipe off the stern. Crew One was up there, checking pipe as it spun out for cracks, bends, and kinks. Crew Two was the second stage, cutting a trench and making sure the line was buried properly.

"They're about two miles ahead of us. We got to keep up."

"A-okay." Winslow drawled it out, and Galloway looked at him, nodding three feet away in the dim incandescent light of the bell. Hard to believe he'd flipped last night. Even after diving with him, he had no idea what the real Derick Winslow was like.

As he thought this, Porch asked him, "You set sleds before, Till?"

"Yeah."

"I ain't. How about Wildman takes the bell this time, and I'll finish up the hand-jetting. You lead on this one, and we'll just not tell Bender."

"Okay."

The bell reached the bottom. Like subway riders reaching their stop, they got up and shuffled about, getting gear, going over the valve settings for their umbilicals.

"Locking out." The pressure equalized and he hauled up the upper hatch. He checked his helmet and gear, then slid through. He got his boots on the frame and raised his gloves for his bailout. It bonged on the hatch edge as Winslow passed it down. They all winced; a charged tank could go off like a bomb.

The sea was indigo today, a deep dark violet. He was surprised daylight penetrated this far. It was just possible to see the mud he waded through. It seemed softer. He guessed he was walking in the stuff Ace and Jay had jetted out of the trench.

The sled took shape ahead of him and he stopped, looking up at the dim bulk suspended on slings.

Two big floodable steel pontoons about fifty feet long formed the base. Couldn't see it from where he was, but they curved up at the front to form skids. Above that was the claw. It fitted down around the pipe and had vertical rows of jet nozzles at the front and rollers inside to align it as it was dragged along. The hoses for the jets dangled down from above, connecting at the top of the claw.

His job was to get the sled set on the pipe and aligned properly fore and aft. He trudged over to his right and found the end of the riser and the flanged joint. It looked solid, and

149

when he bent and felt under it, there were a couple of feet clear there and then more mud.

He slogged back to the sled and hauled himself up onto the pipe just behind where the skids would come down. He straddled it like a cowpoke. He rubbed the rough concrete coating with his gloves and checked himself out. The suit gave him a good hot-water flow around his trunk. Plenty to breathe. No chafing. His umbilical ran back to the bell and there wasn't any way he could see that it'd get sucked into the jets, tangle in the sheaves, or otherwise embarrass him.

"Topside, Galloway."

"Yo."

"I'm on the line, got the sled in sight. You talkin' to the A-frame jockey?"

"Got him on the phone."

"Can you patch him to me?"

"No can do, not from here. Anyway, it's hard to make out what you're saying. I better interpret."

"Tell him the bottom of the claw's twelve feet off the top of the line. The sled's about five feet to the left and pointing three o'clock."

Tiller stuck his hands under his armpits, keeping them warm, and waited. After a while, the sling wires came in on one side and the pontoons swung slowly around. He watched it, ready to move out fast if it swung over him. But it just rocked, swung right, and settled down about three feet too far to starboard.

He passed that word topside. It moved back and halted pretty close to where he wanted it. He looked it over thoroughly, sticking his head in to peer up at it from below, making sure there were no fouled hoses. Then he put his gloves on the pipe and scooted himself backward. "Okay, that's pretty good. Tell him to come on down," he told Kimball.

The sled descended slowly, stopped halfway. "He wants to know, how's it look," the voice inside his helmet prompted.

"Keep coming . . . keep coming . . . hold it."

The sled had twisted as it dropped and hung up on the pipe. He decided to try to push it around till it slid off and set properly. He told the winch operator what he was going to do. Then he scooted up close again, got his feet under him, and stood up on the pipe. Brace; both hands on the rear horizontal roller; shove hard.

The sled pivoted, catching him off balance, and he toppled off. He hit the mud on all fours. He tucked his head as grinding and grating came from all around him. Then he scrabbled backward, kicking up muck. Through it, the pontoon came down slowly with more shrieking and grinding. It rotated slightly, then the claw found the pipe and slid down around it with a boom and clatter.

He breathed out, letting go of the breath and a half a diver took whenever he thought anything might go wrong. The murk drifted away, showing the sled sitting in pretty much the right position, at least from the back.

"Galloway, you okay?" said Winslow, back in the bell.

Tiller said, "Yeah. Need some slack . . . I'm going to do a walk-around."

He had 150 feet of umbilical. It ought to be enough to inspect the sled. He headed forward, then stopped. The current would take his slack right into the mass of hoses and sheaves. He bent, got a spare lanyard from his harness, and tacked his hose to a crossbar. Not tight, loose enough so if Winslow had to pull him in, it'd rip free.

He slogged forward, peering down. The forward left corner was cocked up a bit. He poked around under it till he discovered a rusty, crusty piece of grating somebody had heaved overboard years before. He got the winch operator to lift the sled a foot or two and dragged it out. He was puffing when it was clear; ten by three feet of steel was heavy, and the barnacles didn't help.

"You ready to go, down there?"

"Hey, Roland, where you been? We missed you."

"Sure you did."

"Sled looks good, chief. What now?"

"Is it clear under the riser?"

Porchellacchia: "Yeah. Got about two feet of play till you bottom out in the trench."

"We're gonna cut about two, three hundred feet, then back-blast by hand. Then we'll drop the riser and check everything out before we go any further."

"Where you want me?" Tiller asked.

"On the sled, cher. Stay out of the claw."

Okay, he thought, let's get some ditch cut. He stepped up on the pontoon, remembered his tie-off, and went back and yanked it free. He crossed to the downcurrent side. Aft and downcurrent was the safest place to be. Forward, you could get sucked into the claw. Aft, if you lost your grip, at least you'd be blown clear. He found a spot for his boots and double-wrapped his arms around a sling.

"Let 'er rip, Roland."

The jets cut in with a rumble that took a few seconds to build up to a scream. The whole sled shook, and he clutched the sling, wondering belatedly whether he hadn't ought to have sat this out in the bell. The whole sea was roaring now and the bottom was boiling under him.

The sled jerked and began to move forward. It slammed from side to side, scraping on the concrete jacket of the pipe, riding over hard spots in the bottom. All he could see was a black boil of mud and bubbles. It was like riding a carrot down a garbage disposal. The operator must have turned up the hose pressure, sensing resistance, because the sound grew to a shaking bellow that vibrated in his lungs. The sling played crack-the-whip as the sled dipped and bucked, almost flinging him off.

Somebody was trying to talk to him, but he couldn't make out a word. Noise hammered his ears as if the helmet wasn't even there. Then the scream dropped a note and things seemed to smooth out, though everything was still shaking and howling. He got a leg around the sling as well and felt more secure.

The pumps were still running when Kimball's voice said, "Okay, that's the first cut. How about checking it out."

"You wanta shut the sled down?"

"You can check it while it's running. The jets are off."

"Well, okay. Make sure the foreman knows I'm off the sled."

"Roger."

He kicked free and dropped into the bottom again, sinking through a bean-soup muck. It seemed lower here. Sure, he was in the furrow the right pontoon made, dragging across the bottom. He trekked across the back, jerking his umbilical after him, and fell into the trench before he saw it. Nice going, he thought.

He felt clumsy, shaky. "Hey, Porch, I'm gonna need some help on this."

"Want me up there?"

"Yeah." He hated jetting by hand, but it looked like his turn. "We got some backfill here, need to blast it out. Bring the nozzle."

Waiting for his partner, he lifted his face port for just a moment, aiming it toward the surface.

He knew the sun was up there. But the only light now was the faintest wash of dusk, gloomy, vague, and sourceless. He lifted his gloved hand and looked at it. Only a shadow. He was a shadow himself, moving in a gray world of murky night.

Like they used to say about hell, he thought. Back when no matter who you were, prophet or poet, warrior or king or beggar, you went to the same place when you died, deep beneath the foundations of the world.

But this wasn't Hades. This was just a job. He and a lot of other people on barges and platforms, flying helicopters and shipping pipe and planning and welding and laying and inspecting: They all had a job, a boss, and a deadline to meet.

And a paycheck to go with it.

Smiling a little inside his helmet, he bent and went back to work.

By the end of their shift, they had the back trench jetted out and had detorqued the riser clamps. They climbed back into the bell and rode it to the surface in the numbed, staring silence of utter fatigue, then stumbled into the chamber. It was a long time before they could pick up the trays Kimball had just locked in.

FIFTEEN

For the next five days, they rode the jet sled, trenching in the pipeline. The bottom deepened, then shallowed, rising to two hundred feet, then resumed the long slide downward.

They worked around the clock, crawling past each other on their way to the bell or their bunks or the bell again. At first, they taunted one another, but gradually the grab-assing stopped and they just worked. Eight on, eight off, and the eight off locked in the chamber. They could see the sun, but only through two inches of reinforced view port.

Gradually, the days blurred into a gray haze, distinguishable only because they were grease-penciled in on a calendar of a massively endowed redhead Porch had brought. They duct-taped it on the curved ceiling of the chamber so they could all see her from their bunks.

Trenching mainly meant hour after hour of riding the sled. Ace figured out a way they could clip their harnesses onto the pipe bracing. After that they felt safer, though when you finished a shift you still felt, as Porch said, "like you'd been ridin' a hog with concrete tires from Miami to Maine."

Every half hour or so, depending on the bottom and the rate of progress, the jets would wind down, though the pumps kept throbbing. It reminded them to be careful as they unclipped themselves and swung to the bottom and slogged back to check the cut. As they walked, they checked each field joint. They made sure the claw hadn't knocked off any of the zinc anodes. They shot pneumo readings, depth readings, and did a last visual for kinks, cracks, and dents.

From time to time, progress was interrupted. They'd find a crack and have to fix it, wire-brushing it and slapping on epoxy. Or they'd have to replace an anode, or sandbag sections so they wouldn't sag and crack.

The statement of work called for valves for future tie-ins to be placed every mile. The lay barge spliced them into the ongoing line, with a sonic pinger attached. When the divers heard one coming down, they stopped the sled and plodded ahead till they found it.

Each valve was laid with a cover to protect it as it went down the stinger. The covers had to be removed before the valve body was buried. Galloway had seen this done before with burning gear. DeepTech did it with Broco explosive cutters, which were more expensive but took about a quarter of the time.

Boudreaux did the rigging, preparing the cutters topside and sending them down on lines. Rodriquez attached them the first time as they all watched. After that, Galloway did it, too. The cutter was an explosive-filled split ring a little bigger than a man's fist. You unsnapped it like the clasp of a woman's necklace, slipped it around whatever you wanted cut, and fastened it. You wired together all the cutters on all the bolts that you wanted cut with Primacord, then went back to the bell, unreeling the detonating line from a hand reel. You attached the detonator a few feet from the entry lock. Then, after making sure the area was clear, you pulled it, let it sink toward the bottom, bubbling and fizzing, and made for the lock. When the thud-SNAP came through the thick steel walls, you locked out again and dragged the neatly detached cover out of the way.

At Mile Two and again at Four, they hit crossing pipelines, old, buried lines that the new line had to go over. Crossings were even worse than valves. At least they knew where the valve was. But this far offshore, the positions on the MMS charts were off by as much as a quarter of a mile. Slamming the sled into someone else's line could be costly. So, long before the sled reached its charted position, one of the divers was out in front of it with a piece of reinforcing iron, like some pilgrim of the Middle Ages making his way with a staff through deep snow. This got old fast. Not only was it slow going through the mud but the sled was cutting right behind them. Tiller had images of it crawling right up his ass and sucking him in. He *might* make it through without being hammered to death by the jets, but he didn't want to bet on it.

Once they found the other pipe, they had to pull up the sled and put it on the other line and jet it in another five or six feet deeper. Then they hand-jetted away the mud under the new pipe.

Finally, the riggers swayed cargo slings of sacked cement mix down to them and they spent a full shift or maybe two building a viaduct over the old line. The first time they tried this, one of the nets tore and unloaded on top of McCray; they had to dig him out fast, because he kept whispering he couldn't breathe, that the cement was crushing his chest.

When the crossing was finished, they went back and shot pneumo readings everywhere. They got pictures, too, just in case the company that owned the other line decided Coastal had damaged it and unleashed its lawyers.

After Mile Six, they were deep enough so that they didn't have to trench. The rate of lay sped up after that. The jet barge moved up directly behind the *Catherine Rice,* which was the name of the lay barge. Both crews alternated checking the line as it rumbled off the stinger. And, of course, they were still on call for crossings or repairing cracks in the weight coating.

Porchellacchia complained he was so tired that he couldn't sleep. McCray had pains in his chest. Galloway had saltwater sores. Guidry had a persistent ear infection, and every fifteen minutes they heard the whisk-snort of Rodriquez's Afrin inhaler.

"You getting addicted to that shit, man," Porch told him one day when they were lying in the chamber on deck, waiting in irritated boredom for the lay to resume; the X-ray machine had blown on the lay barge and everybody was counting the minutes, waiting for the helo to arrive from Bayou City with a new tube.

"I *need* it, man. My nose just swells up and then I can't breathe at all."

"You don't need that stuff."

"Look who's talking. Mister Big League Chew."

Winslow paused, his head already dipped to the red paper

156

cup. They all looked at him. Then he smiled slowly, and the other divers did, too.

Tiller leaned back on his bunk and locked his fingers behind his head. It was hard making out what the others said. You could understand helium speech, with practice. But a conversation still sounded like a fight between Donald and Mickey. He looked around the interior of the chamber.

Ten feet by twenty—over a week of habitation, it had changed. Become a little world to itself, a world of cold food and no smokes and everything wet.

That was the worst thing in sat, the damp. Everything got wet and cold, except like now, when they were all sweating from the sun beating down on the outside. The environmental control units were supposed to cool and heat the chamber, but they weren't working right. They could lock in all the towels they liked and in fifteen minutes they were dripping wet. The water soaked the mattresses and lay in a stagnant pool under the deckplates. The men pissed and crapped in a little toilet, but inevitably it leaked and ran into the bilges and things really started to get odoriferous. After a while, a black smut like a fine powder appeared on the chamber walls.

So now the walls were hot to the touch, and they gasped for breath despite the occasional hiss of oxygen and the hum of the CO_2 scrubber and the whine of a little fan above the medical lock. Galloway stared at an oval patch of sun that came in through the porthole and lay near his bare, pale, ointment-smeared feet.

"Anybody want to play some cribbage?"

"Penny a point?"

"Make it a dollar."

"No dollar-a-point cribbage," said Rodriquez. "I seen guys fight in sat over dollar-a-point cribbage."

"You done with that book yet, man? Hey, how long it take you to read one of those, anyway?"

"You busted the spine on the last one, asshole. Only other thing of mine you're touchin's this."

"Put that back, man, you're scarin' the tender."

Tiller turned his head, to see a round, mustached face peering in at them. The divers reacted instantly, throwing whatever was at hand. Things bounced off the thick glass as Kimball peered this way and that. He held up a finger and Porch thrust his own face against the glass and twisted it around. The effect must have been horrible.

Kimball vanished, and a couple seconds later the intercom popped. "You guys want something?"

"Lock in a woman."

"Lock in a dog."

"Lock in a beer."

"Fly Hannah over, man. We'll even take her."

"What's a matter? You people bored?"

"Lock us in a newspaper or somethin', man; we're going nuts in here."

Kimball didn't answer. They figured he'd left, and they settled back. The noise settled to a desultory grumbling, broken only by the hiss-squeak of Rodriquez's inhaler and a long-drawn-out fart from Porchellacchia.

Then they heard the hollow clank of the medical lock closing and the rising hiss as it was pressurized. At the same time, a queer slapping came through the steel. "What's that?" said Porch, sitting up. He scratched the tattoo on his chest.

McCray undogged the inner hatch, ready to reach in, but the white blur exploded out of it before he could move. The sea gull burst into the compartment, an outraged shriek of feathers and a hook-edged, snapping yellow beak and rubbery gray feet with little talons on them and red pissed-off eyes. This was no small bird. It was an open-sea predator with a wingspan that almost reached across the chamber, and it was ticked. The divers in their bunks recoiled and the bunks, hung on chains, went the other way and dumped them out on top of one another. The gull arched the length of the cylinder like a shell. Its wings swept a shelf clear of antiseptics and shaving mirrors, sending a shower of aspirin tablets pinging around the inside of the cylinder. Its scream was continuous, triply penetrating in the thin helium atmosphere. It kept trying to launch itself, as if airborne it could somehow escape, but its frantically milling wings seemed unable to grip the air.

"Grab the son of a bitch!" McCray got himself untangled from the mattresses and launched himself between the bunk frames. His outstretched hands missed the bird, but its beak stabbed as he went by and a red furrow ripped along his wrist. He landed on hands and knees and rolled double, arms wrapping his face. The stink of fish and bird shit filled the chamber.

Winslow stood his ground at the far end, waiting. Then, as the bird fired itself his way, he carved a slice from the air with his Big Chief. It missed the bird and Winslow reeled back as it crashed into his chest. He hit the rack of suits and slipped and went down, looking astonished.

Tiller ripped the sheet off his bunk, thinking he could catch it and bundle it up, shove it into the entry lock before it tore them all up, but it hit him before he was ready. It was like being blasted by a fishy-smelling gray-and-white jet hose. His reflexes shot him backward and the bunk edge caught him at the back of the knees. He slammed his head on the gas panel so hard, he lost everything for a couple of seconds.

When he got himself untangled, the bird and Porchellacchia were staggering around in a violent tango beside the medical lock. The Pagan was trying to stuff it back in, but it didn't want to go. Finally Porch gave up. The bird squawked as the diver's hands closed around its throat. Its wings hammered at his face. Then a gout of blood burst out onto his bare chest.

When he dropped it, its neck was not quite bitten through. The body jerked and flapped. Porchellacchia spat blood and pinfeathers and hammered on the lock, bellowing, "Kimball, you son of a bitch, I'm gonna bite your nuts off!"

"We gotta get that son of a bitch," said Winslow. He fished his knife out of the slime in the bilges and regarded it sourly.

They speculated for a while about what they were going to do to Kimball when they got out. From there, the conversation drifted to the running rivalry between divers and tenders. From there, it progressed to a woman diver at one of the companies out of Morgan City.

And from there, by some transition or segue Galloway missed, suddenly they were talking about the times they'd almost died.

Porchellacchia leaned back, narrowing his eyes. "My best pulse pounder . . . one time we were trying to set a multiple-valve guard off the port side of the *Sea Rigger*. It was rough, but Boudreaux said do it, so we hadda try, you know?

"So I'm down at three sixty feet, and this guard is a huge piece a steel thirty feet by twenty feet wide, and it's supposed to be set over a pipeline with a T. So you've got to line it up in three positions on three different sides. And the barge is rolling, so it's going up and down ten or fifteen feet by this time.

159

Time we got done fighting it and got it anchored down, come to find my hose was caught underneath it, down in the mud, and I couldn't get it out.

"We was all working long hours and the standby diver was asleep on deck when the word came up I was havin' trouble. They woke him up and got him dressed out in a matter of seconds and threw him in the water.

"Only then, the Bender tells them to hold everything. See, the standby diver could come down and give me his mask, but then what was he gonna breathe out of? We only had the one spare mask and umbilical and the storm was getting worse."

"Lemme guess," said Tiller. "You're still down there."

"No, it was Boudreaux figured that one. He had Slack Ack feed all the hose I had left down to me. I pulled that through, under where it was caught, and that got me up to about two hundred feet from the surface. I was lookin' up when I see this guy comin' out of the blue like some kinda fallin' angel. It was Bender on a bailout, riding a piece a iron down, trailing a band mask on a hose. Hadda do a no-bell change-out; that was touchy."

McCray's voice crept in. "I was on an interesting one once. Up in Alaska."

"I din't know you was in Alaska, Captain."

"Up on the North Slope, diving off a boat doing repair work on a jetty. I found this drum. And the closer I got to it, the more my skin was on fire.

"I told topside about it and my supervisor had us do a circle search and we found about twenty more. I was just burning up by then.

"So we got back on deck and they hosed us off and the supervisor called the company man. He says, 'Okay, sling one up and we'll check it out.'

"My supervisor went down—he wasn't going to send anyone else. He told us, 'When they bring it up, everybody evacuate the area except the crane operator.'

"So they slung it up. The crane operator wanted to release the drum. Sent a roustabout over. Only when he got there, he passed out. Now we got a man down on deck next to this barrel. Meanwhile, we lose comms to the supervisor and have to put the standby diver down to get him.

"I call the company man. 'Uh, we've got a problem up

here. Got a man down on deck, a man in trouble in the water. What do we do?' 'Put the drum over the side, get it in the water as quick as possible.' So the operator lowers it again. Meanwhile, we get the supervisor back on deck. He's breathing, but that's about it. Then the boat captain breaks a rule. He gets on the radio. 'We have two men down, picked up this funny-smelling drum.' Now everybody on the North Slope knows.

"The helo evacuated us all to the hospital in Barrow. Took blood samples and did tests. After a couple days, we went back to Smith Bay, but the superintendent stayed in the hospital.

"First day I got back, company man came up to me. 'You didn't find anything down there.' I said, 'I can't falsify a report. We had it on deck.' He says, 'Okay, but you only found one barrel.' I said, 'I can't do that, either.' He says, 'Well, then, you're out of here, and you're on the list.' I said, 'If that's the way you want it.' "

McCray shrugged. "So that's how come I'm diving in Louisiana instead of the North Slope."

"How about you, Wildman?" said Rodriquez.

"How about me what?"

"We was tellin' sea stories. Want to pitch in?"

Winslow shook his head. "I don't got nothing."

"Galloway?"

"Oh, I don't know," he said, and grinned. "About the closest I ever came was when Dale Kemper bought a piano."

"I hearda him."

"He bought a used piano once for twenty dollars, and the guy gave him a case of grenades he had in his garage to go with it. So that night, he and me and some other people got oiled, and Kemper dropped a grenade out of his truck as we were going over the Huey Long. Only instead of going in the river, it bounced off the guardrail. Good-bye windows, good-bye doors. He got three pieces of steel in his arm. One of 'em went right past my head. We were lucky it didn't kill us all."

Rodriquez said, "Well, only time it ever got seminervous for me was when I broke my arm."

"That was out in south Timbalier?"

"Right, live-boating for an outfit called Houston Energy Development. I was in the water at about a hundred and forty feet and this—I told them not to try to pick this up, because it weighed more than the engineer said it would—this shutoff valve housing they were replacin', it was supposed to weigh a hundred and fifty pounds. Turned out more like five hundred.

"But they get a line on and they're moving it when all of a sudden something goes haywire up on the crane and the housing jumps over my hose and starts slamming into the christmas tree. All hell breaks loose, an' this piece of junk catches my arm between it and the blowout preventer. So I tie it off with one hand and I say, 'Okay, pick me up.' And they won't. And I can't climb my hose, come up on my own, 'cause by then I only got one arm.

"So finally they decide to pick me up, after some asshole asks me how I know my arm's smashed, and I explain 'cause I can bend it both ways. So they get me up in the chamber and this guy climbs in with me, and he's going to cut the suit off, but I say, 'No, this goddamn suit cost money, man.' And somebody called my wife, and so there she was when I walked in with my arm smashed, like a dummy."

Tiller, surprised: "I didn't know you were married."

"Sure, man. Got a nice little daughter, cute as you want."

"His wife's a Cajun, ain't she, Ace?"

"Never went farther than Lafayette. Hell, she never been to the McDonald's till I married her."

"Why'd she marry some ex-con duck-ass low-rider like you?"

"Hell, Porch, we both Catholic. Plus an' you don't marry somebody from someplace else and bring 'em to Bayou City, anh?"

"What I want to know is, what language you talk at home?"

"The language of love, man. You don't do no better than a Cajun woman."

Guidry asked him, "Say, what was her name before she married you, Ace?"

"Labauve. From a place called Coteau Holmes."

"I think we might be cousins, some kind. My mother's people from there, seems I remember the name Labauve."

"You ought to have a family reunion," said Porch sarcastically.

Guidry said enthusiastically, "Yeah! Get us some gumbo and bouchettes, crawfish bisque. I do blackened redfish you won't believe, me. First, we go get us some fresh fish. My ex-uncle Maillette runs a boat out of Venice, the *Tern*. Ain't no better fishing in the world. Then we take the fish and have a cookout. How's that sound?"

"Sounds like fun," said Tiller. " 'Specially that part about goin' fishing."

"You serious? You game?"

"Sure I'm game. We'll do it," Galloway told him.

The spot of sunlight had shifted to lie on his chest. He was watching it glitter in his sweat when it was cut off by someone glancing in the porthole. A moment later, the intercom clicked. "Chamber, you hear me?"

"Your ass is grass, Archy-bald."

"You gonna regret throwin' that flying rat in here, mung-head."

"You said you were bored. Listen, just got a call from the barge. Restart in twenty minutes. Figure out who's on deck, get suited up."

"Ace? Whose turn in the barrel?"

Rodriquez sighed and reached behind his pillow. The decongestant inhaler hiss-squeaked. "Me and Jay and Pinhole, we'll take this jump."

"What we down to now?" said McCray, getting up. He stretched, and Tiller saw pain distort his face.

"Jay, you okay?"

"My ribs hurt. When that net broke—"

"Aw, does little Skiddie's wibbies hurt? Or is he just losing his nerve?"

McCray turned away from Porch and started pulling on his suit. Not looking at any of them, he said, "I'm okay. Forget it. What we down to now, Ace?"

"Five hundred feet."

"Christ."

"We're headed for the basement now, *Capitan*," said Rodriquez. "Down to seven hundred feet. Up again, trench in across the ship channel . . . then the bottom really drops out. Okay, hombre, let's ride."

As the hatch swung closed, Tiller caught a glimpse of McCray's pale, frightened face.

Sixteen

Five days later, he let go of the bell and fell ten feet to the bottom of the Gulf of Mexico. He backed away, pulling the slack of his umbilical after him.

Waiting, he swayed on his feet, eyelids sagging as he watched the others emerge into the harsh underwater lighting, eight hundred feet below the surface. Between dream and wakefulness he lost track for a moment of where they were, of what they had to do this shift. Was this the long traverse from Mile Six to the Galveston Ship Channel?

No, he remembered the channel trenching. Recalled riding the sled for days on end with the *thump-whish-thump* of ship traffic going by, sounding as if the screws were going to part his hair. He remembered the wreck they'd hit south of the channel—jagged, rusty ribs and torn steel like the teeth of a long-dead shark. They'd blown it in two with three hundred pounds of gelatin dynamite and laid the pipeline through it. Rodriquez had given them fifteen minutes each to scavenge, and several brass portholes were soaking in fresh water back on the barge.

He swayed in freezing dark, standing in mud the consistency of chocolate pudding. "Semimud," they called it. Looking out over its faintly furrowed surface. The ripples were oddly regular, two or three feet apart. When he looked up from it, he made out bluish-white work lights, wavering and blurry but clearly visible a hundred feet away, the sea was so transparently clear.

Suddenly, he had it, and he shook his head in annoyance.

164

They were on the way down now, the long grade that would end only when they reached Pandora 1000.

"Clear of the bell." Porchellacchia's voice shook with fatigue.

Rodriquez: "Clear of the lock."

McCray, his voice trailing off into a whisper, said, "Roger." The little diver had been eating Tylenol like breath mints for the last few days, but he refused to admit anything was wrong. He was staying in the bell, this dive, as safety.

It had been a cramped ride with four of them in the pot. (Winslow and Guidry were still in the chamber; you could get only four men in the bell.) McCray had had to sit on Porch's lap. But the others were too tired to rag him. Too exhausted and shaky and half-bent to say much of anything.

They trudged toward the lights like the Seven Dwarfs at dawn—only nobody was whistling. Get back on the job, he told his mind. You haven't slept in two days? Tough titty. Neither has anybody else.

The mud looked weird. When he swung the beam of his Super Q, the furrows went on out into the dark forever. And every twenty, forty yards, there was a little chunk of coral stone. He thought walking on the moon must be like this. The view was probably the same: the inside of a helmet, and a little window through which you peered out at a monotonous gray landscape. His boots plunged out of sight with every step. Pain needled his thighs as he tugged them free. He'd strained or torn too many muscles to count. Like a defensive end playing two games a day. No time to heal. Eating aspirin, swilling gallons of tepid between roast, popping the little yellow pills Kimball locked through to them—that was all that kept him going.

Galloway lifted his eyes and his forward motion stopped suddenly, leaving him bobbling in the current like a limp piece of seaweed.

A little cone of mud and sand writhed upward at their feet. As they watched, it erupted with a gout of bubbles. They rose, expanding, and the mud plume drifted away.

"Natural gas," Rodriquez said. "Ain't you never seen that before? This here's a shallow field. There's wells off to the east. It's just bubbling up through the mud, man."

They moved forward again, and it came back to him now, with the slowness of great fatigue, exactly what they had to do.

They were twenty-six miles into the lay and the end was in sight. But the closer they got, the more mercilessly Boudreaux drove them. For the past forty-eight hours, they'd worked six on and six off; not really enough time to sleep. So he hadn't, just sprawled in the chamber and stared at Porch's pinup.

The Texaco gas line headed northwest by southeast. The new Coastal DOT line tended southeast, too, but at a shallower angle. The result was the toughest kind of crossing to make: deep and long.

Seven hundred feet down . . .

They were breathing nearly pure helium now. Less than 2 percent oxygen. But the pressure was so great, even the thin gas was becoming a thick fluid that oozed in and out of his lungs.

Forget about it, he told himself again, fighting a nagging terror. Forget how deep you are. Just get the job done.

The devil that lived in a dark corner back in his mind couldn't help reminding him how much easier all this would be with a little cocaine.

The brilliance increased as they reached the work lights, dangling down from the barge on swaying lengths of weighted cable. He looked around, taking in what he had to deal with.

The gas line was half-buried, with occasional drifts of silt covering it. Twenty inches in diameter. Hoses and ropes, the jet hoses and the descent lines for the nets, plunged down from darkness to lie tangled on the bottom, weighted with shackles. Porch plodded back and forth, measuring, then knelt and unsheathed a trenching tool. Mud clouded the sea as he spaded it away, then pushed short lengths of line with eye splices at each end under the pipe. He reeved one eye through the other and shackled the down lines and keeper lines for the hoses to the free ends.

A flash: Rodriquez. He circled sideways and aimed the camera again. The pop of the strobe sounded like a ghost tapping on the outside of his helmet.

"Tiller, Porch, you guys're the biggest. Grab onto those hoses."

He grunted as he picked up the jet nozzle. There was something wrong with his elbows. Didn't think it was bends, though. They were within excursion limits, as far as he remembered. He hoped Boudreaux and Kimball were keeping track.

"Ace, gimme a hand," he muttered.

Rodriquez manhandled the hose slack out of his way as he humped the nozzle into position. Porchellacchia was on the far side of the line. The New Jerseyan got his jet running first. A scraping blizzard of mud and sand and small pebbles roared across Tiller's suit and helmet. He bent into it, digging in his boots, Rodriquez pushing his shoulders forward. He grunted, "Topside: Cut in the second jet pump."

"Topside aye. Stand by for pressure."

Half an hour fighting the hose exhausted him. He turned it over to Rodriquez and lay back in the water, sucking great gouts of gas. It was hard getting enough down his throat, and for a moment he fought the sensation of smothering. He twisted the valve to free-flow. Slow and deep, slow and deep . . . Gradually, his head sagged backward.

When somebody shook him, he flinched. He'd been dreaming he was out on *Miss Anna.* She was cutting her way through a flat dawn sea the color of rose petals. It faded as he sat up. Gas hissed across his face. He couldn't feel his arms or his legs. Great shudders worked their way up his body.

"Your turn," Ace said, panting so hard Tiller could hardly make out words. He turned from the unlighted abyss and faced the lights, accepting the heavy nozzle back. A second later, he was hanging on as it roared and bucked.

McCray was talking to topside over the interphone. Tiller kept working, cutting away the muck under the gas line, which was beginning to sag.

The cargo nets came down marked by battery-powered strobes that bounced around the inside of the muddy clouds the jets kicked up. He tried not to look. They disoriented him, and when he got disoriented, he got nauseated. Barfing in a helmet was no fun.

"Galloway, finish trenching out. Make sure it's a hundred feet both ways. We'll start on the crossing."

The mud puckered under the jet of water, then peeled away. The stream stripped old growth off the gas pipe, revealing bare, cracked-off sheathing, corrosion, patches of some stubborn marine growth that was abruptly scarlet in the sudden light.

When he told topside to shut down, his ears rang and roared even after the hose relaxed and he dropped the nozzle from numb, shaking hands. His bladder let go involuntarily. The trickle of warmth felt good. They were pumping down boiling-hot water, but it got to him at little more than skin temperature.

The others were hard at work. The cement and sand mix started hardening the second it hit the water. When it reached them, they had about thirty minutes to unload and stack the bags in the saddle-shaped bridge that would carry the transmission line over the gas line. Another reason to hurry: The lay barge, crew, tugs, and associated gear cost around forty thousand dollars an hour, and right now they were all idle, waiting on them.

Another net swayed down, flicking magnesium light over the bottom, freezing the divers as they bent or lifted. Their umbilicals wove a weird tracery of dark and light, like undersea shadow puppets. Porchellacchia got a hand hooked in the net and heaved. Tiller added his weight and it swung slowly toward the ramp. At the end of its pendulum, they yanked the releases and backpedaled frantically as hundred-pound bags of half-hardened concrete tumbled out in a dreamlike avalanche. As soon as they hit, he and Porch and Ace were in among them, slapping sacks of half-hardened rock down on one anothers' gloves in their haste. From above came the throb of screws as the barge shifted its anchors, slewing to drop the next sections of pipe.

"Net above you, stand clear."

"I see it."

"Get that line."

"Get it yourself, limp dick. Don't tell me what to do."

Finally, they staggered back, blowing and free-flowing, sinking to their knees like melting snowmen. The arched ramp lay complete under pyramids of brilliant light. Mud particles blew past, lighted for a moment, then plunged back into the eternal darkness of 130 fathoms, like snow whirling past streetlights on a winter night. Galloway saw with tired apathy the refuse and trash they'd brought to this remote part of the ocean floor: bags and wire, nets, tie-ties. They moved like this across the face of the deep, a crawling of ants that left behind a spun-out strand of hollow steel and a miles-long trail of trash. It sounded like a definition of mankind.

And now the line came down. This was the first time he'd seen it from beneath. It dropped in a scimitar curve out of the dark to mate with the earth in a blaze of light and grind of lowering sheaves and blocks and whine of motors and grate and rumble of chains. It descended at the pace of a slow walk, hundreds of tons of steel and concrete kissing deep into the mud with an excruciating screech of straightening metal. Laying itself down like a huge snake going to sleep at the bottom of the ocean.

He had a sudden picture of how it all locked together: the dark silt carried thousands of miles by the great river, raining, whirling down for eon on eon here far out at sea. Burying beneath it the swamps and forests, turning them over the millennia into the black fluid energy of oil.

All at once, he felt weird—as if he wasn't himself, but part of some big machine. Not a man, but an electron channeled willy-nilly through a circuit whose function he didn't know. And when you thought of it, how strange that it was not desire that had brought him here, or faith, or ambition, but simply the suspicion that there were dollars to be had.

As the pipeline pressed down, the mud flowed sideways with a grating sound. The descending line reached the foot of the bridge and began walking up the ramp. He watched, his teeth set. If it toppled or cracked, they'd have to do it all over again. Back the barge up, haul up half a mile of pipeline, cross the line again at a different point, and build another bridge there. On the interphone, he heard someone mutter, "Hold, you son of a bitch."

The pipeline rumbled up the bridge, tracked over it, and descended the far side. A sack of concrete worked free and tumbled away. Someone whispered, *"Mierda,"* but none of the other sacks followed.

The bridge held. He eased his breath out. "Looks like it's doin' the job," Porch said tentatively. "Ace?"

"Looks good. Lemme get some shots."

The flash licked out, etching the bottom of the sea as they looked on what they'd built, what no human eye would probably ever see again.

"Okay." Boudreaux's voice, harsh and tired, sounded in their ears. "Ace, I'm breaking Winslow off safety; put him and Guidry down for the next shift inspecting. Get everybody else back in the chamber. We're pushin' toward the end, guys, but we got miles to go."

The suited figure of Rodriquez pivoted slowly and pointed to him. He trudged forward, after the departing line, slogging in tired rage on into the eternal dark.

SEVENTEEN

But as it turned out, they torqued down the last bolt on the last riser clamp at Pandora 1000 at midnight on the thirteenth day—twenty-four hours too late. Boudreaux raged, but his attitude wasn't reflected in the chamber. They regretted missing the bonus, but more pronounced was relief at finishing without anyone getting hurt.

The relief quickly dissipated as decompression started.

From 900 feet—their storage depth for the last dives, to where the transmission line met the riser of the new platform at 1,045 feet—it took nine days to decompress. The rule was six feet an hour, and they could only decompress for sixteen hours each day. The other eight were stop time, waiting while the helium bled out of their bodies.

For the first two or three days, it wasn't too bad. They caught up on sleep first. Then Rodriquez put them to work cleaning the chamber. They scrubbed the walls and lock interiors and bilges and the inside of the bell with Betadine and hand brushes until everything gleamed. Even the aluminum duckboards were scrubbed till they looked new.

But for the last five days, they had absolutely nothing to do—nothing but get on one anothers' nerves: to brood over Porchellacchia's thunderous snoring, Rodriquez's continual sniffling, Galloway's agonized scratching at his feet, McCray's habitual nervous clearing of his throat, Winslow's crazy-sounding mutter as he read a Gideon Bible from the padlocked gear bag.

Then, as the percentage of oxygen in the chamber rose,

171

Kimball made them lock out everything flammable: books, clothes, magazines, letter-writing materials, even the redheaded pinup. He left them one pair of shorts and a hand towel apiece. They couldn't have butter with meals. They couldn't have powdered sugar or pepper.

They were close to raving when Boudreaux came on the line late on the ninth day. "Chamber, topside, you guys feelin' good?"

Nobody answered him. They lay in their bunks, staring at pale green steel and breathing 30 percent oxygen from Bibb masks.

"Just thought you'd like to know, we're gonna pop the lock in about twenty minutes."

"What time is it?" Tiller asked the grille.

"Nine in the morning. Why?"

"Sure you don't wanta keep us here till midnight, get another day's depth pay out of us?"

"Funny as shit, Galloway. The boat's gonna be here this afternoon, take us back to Summerland. Otherwise, I just might take you up on it."

"A boat? We got to go by *boat*?"

"You know you can't fly, not for seventy-two hours after you finish decompression. Okay, get packed. Twenty minutes and the hatch pops."

When they crawled out of the lock, they stopped. They stood unconsciously hunched over by the big lime green cylinder, looking around.

Tiller saw a thin reflective film on the barge's deck. At first, he didn't recognize it. Then he saw the low gray clouds of a departing squall. It was rain, but it was over now, and the sun was glowing like a hot coal falling endlessly through a blue, blue sky. He sucked the cool air into his lungs and held it. The oxygen rush made his head feel light.

"Shit," McCray muttered. "This is just so . . . damn . . . beautiful."

Boudreaux came over. He stood with them for a few silent minutes.

Porchellacchia, blinking rapidly, was torching an ultra-

172

light. He tilted his head and trickled smoke from his nostrils, bliss suffusing his pockmarked face. "Twenty-two days," he murmured. "Thirteen on the bottom, nine decompressing; twenty-two days."

"I done forty-eight once," said Boudreaux.

"What's the schedule from here, Roland?" Rodriquez asked him.

"You guys take a couple days off. Then we'll see what comes up. I got a guy coming in with a new kinda suit he wants to show us. We'll need to test that out, get smart on it."

Porch grunted, "Where's Kimball?"

"Archie an' the bell techs caught a chopper back this morning."

"That son of a bitch."

"He gets to fly, we get to load gear?"

But even frustrated vengeance didn't upset them much. Tiller felt the same. Like a corpse unexpectedly returned to life. He strolled tentatively, stretching his legs.

"Got a six-pack iced down in the gas shack, any you want a can," said Boudreaux. "Ready? Let's head over to the platform. Y'all can get cleaned up over there."

They went down the ladder to the boat, holding the handrail cautiously. It felt strange walking without a hundred pounds of suit and gear. Smells were overpowering: diesel, rain, the spicy bite of cigarette smoke.

They came out on the boat deck and stopped dead.

Their eyes traveled up, and up, and up, at a towering white iceberg of concrete decorated with fire.

Pandora 1000 was easily twice as big as 12. It loomed up out of the sea like a pyramid out of the desert, damn near as huge, damn near as permanent. Without being told, Tiller knew it went right down to the bottom as solid as what he saw.

He thought, They're not kidding, this is a major investment. Something this big, this new had to cost jillions.

The boat cast off and purred toward it. Dwarfed by one of the massive legs, a runabout rocked on a deep blue sea. Two or three husky guys in swim trunks and painful-looking red skin were holding fishing rods on the stern. Another roustabout was swimming a few yards away. As they watched, he lifted a mask from the water and blew water from a snorkel. He waved a spear gun as they went by.

"That looks like fun," Guidry said.

"Ain't you had enough a the water, Pinhole?"

"Some fresh fish, that'd be nice."

A guy from Coastal met them when they stepped out of the cage. One of the purser's assistants, he said. He frowned at the beers and the divers made them disappear. He cleared his throat. "You'll be here only a few hours, so don't destroy the rooms, please. Your boat will be here around two to take you back to Bayou City. Meanwhile, you're welcome to have lunch, relax, whatever you want. There's a weight room, sauna, swimming platform, TV room. Just ask one of the crew; they'll help you out."

They slowly became separate men with individual desires again. Galloway had a shower first, then lunch. Then he wandered out on deck, propped his foot on the rail, and looked up at the sky and down at the sea and out at the horizon.

No mud. No cold. No more Boudreaux hammering you to hurry up, hurry up, cut corners, till you knew that if anything went wrong, you might not be alive the end of the shift. No smelly feet dangling from the bunk above. No hairy asses shoved in your face.

The sun felt hot. Felt *good*.

He went back to his room and got the blanket off his bunk. Then he went back out. He unrolled the blanket and stripped his clothes off, everything, till he stood pale and white and sea-puckered. He knelt slowly, sighing, and stretched out. The concrete deck was hot under the blanket. The sun was hot on his skin.

He sighed again, closed his eyes, and looked at the sun through his closed lids. He could feel it starting to dry him out—the fungoid cracks in his toes, the scabbed patches in crotch and armpits where his suit rubbed. He drifted into the red glow. Gradually, his head rolled to the side. . . .

Somebody was shouting down below him.

He sat up, then jumped up and padded swiftly to the rail.

One of the guys he'd seen swimming was climbing the ladder from the boat—fast, his head down. "Hey! On the platform!"

Tiller shouted, "What the hell's going on?"

The man looked up through wet hair. His eyes were wide. "The other guy. He's in trouble."

174

"What other guy?"

"The diver."

Galloway started to swing a leg over the rail, then stopped himself. It was a 100-, 150-foot drop. If he hit wrong, he was dead. He spun and saw a phone box. He tore it open and dialed the number stenciled inside. A few seconds later, an alarm sounded, echoing from dozens of speakers throughout the platform.

"What's going on?" Rodriquez appeared at the top of the ladder. Porchellacchia was behind him.

The roustabout swung off the ladder, panting hard, and put his hands on his knees. "We was in the—in the water. He come down lookin' to shoot a fish. He said, 'Gonna get me one of these big albacores.' Asked if he could borry my spear gun."

"Who?"

"Guy with a mustache. I put my mask in the water and watched him. He dived a couple times. Knew what he was doin'; he was gettin' way down there. Then he saw a big one, down by the jacket. Went down after it. Then he shot it. It was a big one, all right."

"Yeah, but what—"

"Then it dived," said the roustabout.

"Holy Mother," said Rodriquez into sudden quiet. "And Guidry—"

"It dived, real fast, and he went down with it. He was slapping himself here, and here—"

"Lookin' for his knife," said Porchellacchia, looking sick. "He must of tied the line off."

"And all he had was a breath. Then the damn fish sounds—he goes to cut it—"

"Shit, he was only skin diving."

Rodriquez said grimly, "Tiller, call the pusher. Let him know what's going on. Then stand by here for the medics. Don't sound like he had much of a chance, but we'll go take a look."

They couldn't find it, but the body came up half an hour later on its own. A cook spotted it on the far side of the platform, face down. Winslow swam out to it with a line.

175

When the crane brought it up, they saw the spear line still knotted to his harness, and deep bloodless cuts on his hands where he'd tried to tear the thin ultrastrong nylon apart. And failed, and gone on down, pulled after the powerful fish.

Twenty yards on the line ended in a fray. Winslow turned it this way and that. "Cut it on part of the rig," he offered. "Fish dragged him down, turned a corner, cut it on barnacles. Or just rubbed it along the concrete."

"Not soon enough."

"Let me through, please."

It was the rig medic. They stepped back and let him do his job. A few minutes later, he and a couple of helpers took the corpse below.

It took longer than Boudreaux had expected to back-load the gear. They didn't cast off till after dark.

The boat ride back was somber. They stood by the rail or nursed coffee in the little mess, each man alone with his thoughts. Tiller kept thinking about how Guidry had saved the day in the Moon Pool, firing shot glasses till the odds got down to where they could fight their way out. He thought about how they'd worked side by side on the crossings, and blowing the wreck. You got close to a guy when you were in sat with him.

Then he thought about the narrow line between life and death, and how one little slip could push you over.

They made landfall after a night passage lighted by the flames of flare-off towers. The first things that pushed up over the horizon were the platforms being repaired and assembled in the McDermott yard. Then a little later, as they churned up the muddy brown water of the Atchafalaya, the spidery iron of the Huey Long came into view.

They came alongside the dock at Front Street a few minutes after seven. Two carryalls were waiting inside the chain-link fence. Tiller hoped Shad would be driving one, but he wasn't. The drivers, new tenders no one knew, asked them how it had gone and got mumbled replies.

Bayou City, Route 90, all looked about the same; maybe a little more traffic. A sixteen-wheeler full of pipe blasted by. Then they were speeding through the country. Charley Pride wailed from the buzzing speakers. The smells of bayou and woods. Road lilies nodded in banks of orange. Then the turnoff, and dust and gravel rattling in the wheel wells.

The lot looked different. "Hey, they put down asphalt," Porch said.

Galloway looked for Aydlett in front of the admin building but missed him again. The Suburbans swung in like boats making a pier. The doors banged and everyone piled out, forming a line in front of the office. Tiller joined it. After a few minutes, Virginia came out with paper cups and a carafe, and they had coffee there, standing in line to be paid.

When he got to the counter, the guy asked him, "Check or cash?"

"Cash. Don't have a local bank yet."

The man handed him a statement. Galloway scanned it as the others fidgeted behind him. He was unpleasantly surprised at deductions for federal tax, Social Security, unemployment insurance, medical insurance, and meals. Balanced against that was a nice chunk of change from depth bonuses. He was sorry again they hadn't made the deadline. But all in all, it wasn't a bad payday, almost eleven thousand dollars. He took it in hundreds and change, signed a ledger, and walked back through toward the shop, the wad of bills a pleasant lump against his thigh.

There was Shad, drinking from a bubbler in the corridor. His tote bag lay on the concrete beside it. As Galloway stopped he glanced up. "Look at that," Tiller said, holding up the envelope. "Eleven big ones. Not bad for twenty-two days in the can, huh?"

Shad wiped his mouth. "Not bad," he said. His voice was cool, though, and he didn't smile. "How was it offshore?"

"Grim. But we got it done."

Aydlett nodded. He picked the bag up and headed down the hall. Tiller followed. "What's going on?"

"I'm leaving. That's what's going on."

"Taking off? Must be slow in the shop."

"I talked to Hohmann yesterday. Cleaned out my locker. All I got to do is pick up my pay."

Tiller stopped there in the corridor. From back in the shop came a hiccup and clatter as a compressor started. "Wait a minute. You mean *leaving*? You're draggin' up?"

"What I said, ain't it? Put in my notice couple days ago. I called Latricia, told her I'll be back next week, could take us a few days driving from here."

"You *quit.* Why? I don't get it."

"Well, it's like this. It's a couple things, actually. I'm only making about two hundred a week—"

"Shad, we talked about this—"

"Yeah, I know, tenders are lower'n whale shit and dumber'n dirt. But that's only part of it. They don't really want me here, know what I mean?"

"No. What do you mean?"

"Maybe you wouldn't understand."

"How can I unless you tell me?"

Aydlett looked at a poster on the wall. "Well, a lot of it's petty shit. They won't let you put a mask on, without they got to wash it out afterward. You go into the chamber for training, they got to clean out the oxygen masks—every time. And, oh yeah, the little 'jokes.' Sand in the lamp guard over your bench—you turn it over, it falls all over the regulator you're rebuilding. The sign taped over your locker that says 'Suck the big one, Nigger.' And grease—that heavy industrial stuff they use on the cables— I can't pick up anything without checking for it."

Tiller looked at him. Just the way there was no expression on his friend's face told him how disturbed he was. "It's like I'm in a trough and everything flows downhill. I make up a sling, somebody else handles it, and it comes apart. I put the pin in backward, right? Shit, I know how to make up a shackle."

"I told you, Shad, every new guy goes through that. I did."

"Oh, I'm too sensitive? Okay. I got to do one dive. A deep air dive, close the valves on a pontoon. They're building a pipeline across the bottom of Lake Borgne. Band masks. A hundred fifty feet. I know how to do that, right? Gone deeper than that with you."

"Sure you have. Done good, too."

"Uh-huh. So I'm down there. I start feeling a little nitrogen. So do the other guys. They're kind of groping around. They talk them through the job from topside. Know what they say to me? Nothing. They let me hang. Come up, supervisor comes over and says, 'You didn't get much done on that dive, boy.' I say, 'No, sir, I didn't get the proper support.' He says, 'You got air, didn't you?' Shit, after that I made sure my bailout worked."

"They're assholes. Did you say anything to Hohmann—"

"I don't work that way, Till. That don't change nothing. I was looking for one guy behind it. When he come back from the hospital, people's attitudes would change. But it ain't any one. It's all of them."

He took his eyes from the wall and put them on Galloway's. "But I could maybe have stuck it out if you'd been here. You said you was going to stand by me."

"Shad, they had a job for me."

"And that's what you're here for, to make the big paycheck. I know. But it's partner this, partner that, then off you go, first day we're hired, off you go for three—goddamn—weeks. I wanted to leave the first week I got here. But you were out on the rig. I thought I'd wait. Now you're here." Aydlett grinned for the first time. "We can take that fat envelope of yours and go home."

"Man," Galloway said. It reminded him of the arguments he used to have with his ex-wife. But something warned him not to say that to Shad. "Look. We got some time off now. After that, they might offer me another job. But I don't have to take it. Once you're on the list, you can turn down a call once in a while. Let's get that trailer. Go find one right now. Then we'll get out of Bayou City. Go fishing or something. Slam down some brews—"

"It's too late."

"Oh, you made your mind up, huh? Then why are we talking?"

Aydlett looked at him for a few seconds. "Good question," he said at last. He turned and started to walk away.

"Wait a minute, damn it. I didn't mean that. I meant, I'm surprised. I was looking forward to seeing you. Now I get told you're dropping out of the plan. Leaving me flat."

"Leavin' you flat, huh? I'm dropping the ball, far as you're concerned?"

"That's what I said," Tiller told him. "You're dropping the ball."

Aydlett grabbed a wrench off a hook and threw it across the corridor. It hit the concrete so hard it made sparks. "Ain't it funny, how everybody always screwing you? You ever think about Ellie, and Bernie, and why it always goes to shit? Like why you can't keep people around who care about you?"

"Wait a minute. What's that got to do—"

"With me draggin' up? Maybe you want to think on that." Aydlett took a deep breath. "But it don't got to be that way, Till. You can come with me."

"Go back to Hatteras? Now? You got to be kidding. We owe a lot more than this. You don't know how lucky I was to get this job—"

"I was with you, when you were lookin'. Remember?" Aydlett looked around angrily, saw two white tenders coming toward them. He jerked his head toward the door. "Let's go outside."

The air was blazing hot. The new asphalt, Tiller thought, hadn't improved the climate any. Now he saw Shad's pickup, parked by the entrance to the shop.

"I was saying, we can pay off what we owe—"

"Quit talking. Listen to me."

"Okay." He relaxed, letting his hands dangle. They stood in the sunlight, and he felt himself starting to sweat.

"You been changing, Till. From what you was. It's been weird to watch. You know? It's like . . . you were an okay guy when you were a kid. Always ready for a fight, but I figured that was from your dad beating on you so much. It must of been when you were working down here, in the Patch, that's when you changed, I figure. Isn't that what Claunch was sayin'? That you come down here with Ellie and your kid, then everything changed? Started doin' drugs, then you got fired, and got mixed up with Silverberg, and Nuñez, and Christian. Now it's like you're back where it all started, and it's weird—it's like watching you change back into somebody you used to be. Am I makin' any sense?"

"No."

"Lemme try again, then. It's like you lose track of everything but one thing. Whether that one thing is drugs or some woman or money or whatever. You forget about *everything else*. You ignore the people around you, or tell yourself they're doing all right when they ain't. An' right now—right now, I think it's the money."

"Bullshit."

"No bullshit. I tell you, buddy." He reached out and

gripped Galloway's shoulder. "I'm worried. Claunch, he's right. There's somethin' rotten around this company. So ripe you can smell it. You better come back with me. Take that however much you got and we'll see what can it do, get *Miss Anna* back in the water, pay the wholesalers a little on account—"

"You think I'm greedy? You think that's all I care about, the money? Here." He took the bills out, split them in two, held half out. He was so angry, his hands were shaking. "Take it! We'll share . . . till you break out to diver."

Aydlett looked at him for a second, then down at the bills. In a soft voice, he said, "That's exactly what I'm talking about, Till. But you still don't see it, do you?"

"Take it! Goddamn it. We're partners. We'll go halves!"

"I got my own pay. Ain't as much as yours, but it'll get me home. For the last time now. You coming?"

"No."

"All right." Aydlett shrugged. "Guess that's it, then. Well, I'm all loaded. I'm taking off."

"I'll call you."

"Do that. Keep me posted, hear?"

Tiller looked after the pickup as it turned onto the highway. He waved, but he couldn't see, through the tinted windows of the cab, whether Shad waved back. He felt angry. He wanted to run after the truck and pull him out. Talk some sense into that thick defensive-end head. At the same time, he felt lonely. Shad was his last link with home. But Shad was wrong, that he thought only about the money. Hadn't he told Hohmann that if he hired him, he had to hire Aydlett, too?

"Stupid bastard," he muttered.

EIGHTEEN

He found Winslow and Porch out front, just pulling out in Winslow's van, and waved them down. The Pagan cranked the window half open. The air was on full and he had to shout to be heard over KFXY. "Thought you were draggin' up with your pal."

News traveled fast, Galloway thought. He shook his head. "He's leaving. I'm staying."

"What, he don't like it here?"

"No, and I don't blame him."

Porch shrugged. "Climb in, then. Gonna be some people over this afternoon."

When they got to the trailer, the others were already out on the deck overlooking the bayou. Ace had stopped at Slick Sam's on the way and five cases of beer were racking up bottom time in a galvanized tub of ice. Winslow hauled a sawn-in-half compressor tank out from under the deck and set it up on channel iron. "Pinhole done the welding on those," Porch said, pointing at the stand with his little finger from around a can of Miller as Wildman sprayed charcoal lighter and flicked a match. The little black pillows burst into flame. "What's that in your hand?"

"In my hand? Nothing."

"That's what I mean."

He got a beer as Porch went on. "What we'll do, we'll have some 'cue here, lay around a while, get loose, then maybe do some bars. See if there's any little ladies around. Got a couple

I can call, depends on who's in town whether they're free, if you know what I mean."

Tiller grunted. He didn't want to do the bars again, not after last time. Blacking out scared him. Doing things he didn't remember afterward. He had to cut back on the booze. Beer was enough. You didn't get drunk on beer.

Besides, he really didn't feel like it. It was as if Guidry's sudden, unnecessary death had dislocated something in his head.

That and Shad's leaving. What was all that about him changing? No, "changing back," like he was some kind of were-wolf? He was the same person. The only difference was, now he was making money. It was sour grapes. Plus, Shad was upset over the way he'd been treated at DeepTech. No doubt about it, a dive company in Louisiana wasn't a pleasant place for a black guy—any black guy.

I don't like it either, Tiller thought. But what can I do about it? He took a deep swallow of icy beer. If he'd stayed around, I'd have stood by him. But you don't sign on, then turn down the first jump they offer you.

"Till, what you want, burgers, dogs, catfish, chicken?"

"Burgers. Need any help?"

"Naw, I'll scorch 'em. Your turn next time."

"Deal." He crunched the empty and fished out another. The water novocained his fingers as he groped around under the transparent ice. He popped the top and absorbed half. Heads were bobbing over the crest of the levee. He went down the lawn, watching the grass for snakes, and got on the plank walkway and went down to the dock.

Ace and Jay were down there with two women Galloway didn't know. They were in their late twenties, early thirties. Ace introduced them: One was Edie, the other something that started with a *T*. He didn't catch it exactly. Galloway ran his eyes down swimsuits, sandals, painted toenails. They looked good after weeks on the rig. "Neighbors," McCray explained.

"We're sorry about Louis. Ace told us."

"Who? Oh . . . Louis." He realized he'd never heard Guidry's Christian name before. "You knew him?"

"Him and Edie's sister went to high school together. So this is kind of a party for him?"

"Sort of," said Galloway. He looked at McCray. "Yeah, this is a party for him."

"Well, here goes," said Rodriquez, who had stripped off his shirt. He held his hands over his head, then arched stiffly off the dock into the water.

Winslow came down the levee. The Westerner saw Ace come up, facing the jungle on the far side of the water. He put his beer on the dock and slid stealthily into the water.

"Jesus," said Edie. "Ain't there alligators in there? I never swim in the bayou."

"Did you see the spiderweb tattoos on his elbows?" said the other woman.

Rodriquez swam around, splashing, teasing the women, trying to get them to come in. Galloway started to wonder where Winslow was. He'd been under a hell of a long time. Ace slapped the water. "Hey, what you 'fraid of? There ain't nothing in here but them l'il nippy crabs. Come on in, it's—holy *shit!*"

He lunged halfway out of the murky brown water, beating frantically at his legs, and fell back. The bayou boiled as he stroked for the dock. Winslow surfaced behind him, grinning.

"*Dejate de chingaderas!* I owe you one, you gringo shithead. You better watch your back, *pendejo.*"

"Excuse me," said Edie, looking at her friend and then Tiller. "I think I'll see if Porch needs any help up there."

Galloway finished his beer. He caught the other woman's glance as she leaned back against the piling. "Tammy?" he said.

"Teagan."

"Sorry."

She smiled and closed her eyes as if inviting him to look. But something in him just didn't respond. He felt depressed, and he looked back up toward the house. He could smell the barbecuing meat.

Suddenly, he just wanted to get away. He said to them all, "What the hell are we doin' here? Haven't you had enough of this town?"

"Where you want to go, man?"

"I was thinking, go someplace different, someplace we can get some sun. Maybe do some fishing. How about Venice, like Guidry was talking about? Kind of in his memory."

From up on the levee, Porch said, "We're havin' a party. That's enough for his memory. Look, I liked the guy, but face it, he dicked up. He shouldn't a been in the water anyway, after a sat. You don't never dive without a knife. An' tying the spear line to his belt, that was plain dumb. Ain't you had enough a the water?"

"I like the water. I like boats. Okay with you?"

"A boat's a car goes on the water, okay? You want to travel, get you a bike."

Edie called from the deck. They went back up over the levee. He studied Teagan's rear as he followed her up the walkway. Maybe he could muster some interest.

Rodriquez's wife arrived and a couple of the divers from Crew One. They sat around in lawn chairs talking and drinking beer and eating burgers and chips and potato salad somebody had brought. Galloway sat a few feet away, on the steps. Every time someone laughed, he felt angry. Usually when he drank he felt better, or at least not as bad. But today, the more he drank, the worse he felt. If he could have, he'd have shucked off his skin and walked away, leaving it lying on the grass.

"So, nobody else wants to go fishing?"

"I'll come," said McCray.

"Who else?"

"Count me out."

"Forget it, man. Chill down."

Teagan looked expectant, but Galloway didn't feel like inviting her. He didn't feel like being nice or even having fun. It was as if he were locked into a big chamber that was Bayou City and he'd been pressed down too far.

"You got a car, Jay?"

"Sure. My Toyota."

He didn't really want to go with McCray. He could afford something used now—a Wrangler or Bronco, something he could kick around. But by the time he found a car, went through the paperwork, it'd be too late to drive anywhere. He took a deep breath. "Okay. Let me grab my toothbrush and let's go."

Winslow caught up to him in the bathroom. He leaned in and muttered, "You want a gun?"

185

"What?"

"I got a thirty-eight I can loan you."

Galloway stared at him. "What the hell I want a gun for, Wildman? We're just going fishing, for Christ's sake."

The Westerner shrugged and withdrew. Galloway looked after him for a moment more, then shook his head. He finished throwing his stuff into his bag and zipped it up.

They drove through the afternoon, keeping a fire lit with a cooler in the backseat of McCray's Celica. They had dinner in Gretna, then took Route 23 south along the Mississippi, crossing canals and creeks and bayous. The land was absolutely flat except for the endless grassy ramparts of the levees.

They pulled into Venice at dusk. Galloway drove through town and then back again. "You see any motels?" he asked McCray.

"None with vacancies."

"Let's stop in the marina there and ask."

The guy at the marina office sent them down the pier to something called the Teaser Clubhouse. They got a double room, then went out for more beer.

When they got back, Galloway went into the little bathroom. He had to prop himself against the walls with his arms. Then he staggered out and flopped on the bed. He popped another Miller and looked around.

Venice reminded him of Hatteras, years ago, the little motels the fishermen used to stay at in the spring and fall before real estate went through the roof. This was kind of like that, bare but clean, with a faint pungency of fish and whiskey and gas. "Not a bad idea, huh?" he asked McCray.

"I like it."

"Lots of charters here. We'll pick one out tomorrow, do some offshore trolling."

They drank for a while and talked, about the job, then about what car he should buy. McCray pointed out that it was hard to air-condition a Wrangler, said he should consider a Cherokee or a Trooper. Galloway said he had a point.

Finally, McCray asked, "So, what you think about DeepTech?"

"It's okay, I guess," he said cautiously.

"The way Boudreaux runs things? Remember when he pressed you down too fast? And you asked me why?"

"Yeah, I remember that. Wasn't too happy about it."

"They ask if you were union when they hired you?"

"No." He remembered Hannah. "It came up later, on the rig, though."

"What'd you say?"

"Said not anymore."

"Oh, you used to be?"

"I was prounion once. But when I moved down here with Ellie, you kept your mouth shut about that. If you didn't, you were on the list."

"Blacklists are illegal." McCray edged his chair closer to the bed.

"Come on. I knew fellas it happened to. Say something like 'We should have a union,' 'I worked union,'—you were history. You'd never work again."

"Do you think that's right? That we don't have a union, can't even talk about it?"

"Whoa," he said. He looked at the little diver again. "Is it *right*? Hell, you need a lawyer or something for that one. Anyway, what's a union gonna do for me? We get paid okay. We get hurt, we're taken care of." He thought of Claunch and added, "Medicalwise, anyway—cuts and breaks and things. Anyway, I'm not sure it'd fly. There's always a tender behind me ready to step up and do it if I don't want to. Divers aren't the kind of guys you make a union out of."

"Then why does California have a divers' union? And New Jersey? New York?"

"Gulf divers are different."

"Sure they are. They don't need pensions. They're never going to get hit, or make a mistake on the bottom, or get old."

"Well, that's what they think."

McCray told him, "Some guys tried to start a union once in Bayou City. One of the smaller companies voted yes. And suddenly the oil companies, they don't need this outfit anymore. Overnight, there was no work for them. It went broke.

And far as I know, none of those guys who voted yes ever jumped on the Patch again."

"How about you?" said Galloway sarcastically. "Are you union?"

"Yes. I am."

"Jesus," said Tiller. He looked at the walls as if they might have microphones in them. He sat up to face McCray. "What are you doing here?"

"Research."

"Jesus," he said again.

McCray sat forward too. "You know why that first try failed? There's no power. See, to get a union going, traditionally you'd go back to the truckers. They move everything. If the truckers don't move the gear, the pipes, the food, nothing happens. They carry a big stick. But there're no truckers' unions in Louisiana, or if there are, they don't work oil. Nationale Trucking, Palourde Truck Lines, these are non-Teamster lines. Mom and Pop owns a truck, they lease it out, and Palourde supplies the driver."

"You're no Army diver," said Galloway.

"No."

"And that about diving in Alaska—"

"That's kosher. I was up on the Slope. But I hid my affiliation."

"Why? I don't get it."

"We needed people to go up to the Alaska oil field, get experience. Then bring it back here, stir the pot, get the *U* word introduced into the vocabulary.

"See, you can't do it from inside." McCray popped another beer, and his tone became detached, as if this was something he'd explained a lot of times before. "One guy tries it? He's easy for them to break. He don't work. He either caves in to feed his family or leaves the Patch.

"And you can't do it company by company. The oil corporations will stamp on the first one and the rest will fall in line.

"So it's all got to happen at once. Guys on every shop floor. A Gulfwide strike. Then we step in, say, 'We have qualified *union* oil-field divers,' then we've got a leg to stand on. Then there's legal ammunition we can use."

"They can bring in outsiders."

"From where? East Coast, California, there's unity there. They'll have to go to the North Sea. How will that play on the news, bringing in foreign strikebreakers? Not too good, I don't think."

Galloway was beginning to realize who Jay McCray really was. "That's dangerous work, what you're doing."

"I don't tell many people." He smiled faintly. "Most of the guys—well, you know what they think about Captain Skid-mark."

"That's what, a ploy? A cover?"

"Something like that."

"Yeah, but if they find out about you—"

"Then I go back north and somebody else comes down. The clock gets set back five minutes, that's all."

"Do the other guys know this? Porch? Ace?"

"No."

"But you're telling me. Why?"

"Because the next step will be to organize. That's when we're gonna need some tough lads, Tiller."

"Uh-oh," he said. "No. That's not what I came down here for. I'm not even sure I'm on your side."

"Would you cross a picket line? No, don't answer that. I didn't ask you that. And I didn't ask you to join us."

"You were going to."

"You asked yourself." McCray grinned. "You don't have to do a damn thing. Not yet. Except maybe think about where you're gonna be when this thing comes down. Because it *is* coming down—whether I'm around for it or not.

"Now hand me another beer."

NINETEEN

The engines started before the sky was red, rumbling along the piers like thunder on the cool wind. The smells of strong coffee and cut bait mingled with exhaust and the sulfur stink of the delta marsh that stretched to the uttermost end of the land.

Tiller stood on worn, warped planks, sipping from a Styrofoam cup and looking over the Venice charter fleet—a hundred yards of slowly jostling cruisers forty or fifty feet long, with high biminied flying bridges, outriggers like the antennae of lobsters, blue canvas covers on gimballed fighting chairs, racks of stubby fiberglass rods. Middle-aged men in billed caps stood on the sterns, drinking coffee and looking east, toward the river.

He was trying to remember the name of the boat Guidry had mentioned. Or the name of—what had he called him, his "ex-uncle"? Maillette something, that was his name. But what was the boat's? *Flying Fish, C Devil, Beth Powell, Red Fin, Laura Jo.* None triggered memory, so he kept going, enjoying the wind while he had it. The marina manager had said it would break a hundred today.

He felt good this morning. Maybe it was a reaction; he'd felt so shitty yesterday. But nobody could feel morose on a day like this, filled with light and the sound of engines.

McCray, though, had woke complaining about his ribs again. Tiller told him he'd better not hold a rod, in that case. Fighting a big marlin or sailfish could put your back out even if you were in A1 shape. The little diver had decided to stay in bed.

Hell, Tiller thought, I did enough loafing in the chamber. I came out here to fish.

Or was it to look at boats? Because just the sight of them was a balm. Rakish and glossy, trembling with power, straining at their leashes of braided Dacron. He loved the sound of a marina on a working morning, echoing with the shouts of men, the clang and clatter of gear.

Why did he love boats so much? Maybe because, sail or engine, when you held a wheel in your hand, you were in control. It was the last place left where what a man decided mattered. Where you could set a goal and fight your way to it, matching your skill and the trustworthiness of your navigation against the impersonal resistance of wind and sea.

And luck. Never forget luck.

A Hatterasman without a boat was about as comfortable as a hermit crab without a shell. Hell, he remembered when you couldn't even get to Hatteras without a boat. There hadn't been a bridge until 1964. And every few years since, it had gone out, damaged by storms or hit by dredges, reminding every resident, old and new, that the natural condition of an island was isolation. In the old days, even marriages had depended on the prevailing winds. It was harder to sail north or south than east and west. So families intermarried west to east, and the wide stretches of the Pamlico and Croatan were less barriers than highways.

Well, he was on his way back. He touched his pocket with the tips of his fingers. He had enough right now to put *Miss Anna* back in the water. But he had to have something to live on till they found chartering work. Thirty thousand would be enough. Then Shad would be right: time to quit.

And maybe, once he made peace with Aydlett, he could get the rest of his life in order. If he could just get back on a sound financial footing—

He stopped there on the pier. *Tern*. That was it, wasn't it? The boat Guidry had mentioned?

She was a working craft, older than the others, her hull sooty with exhaust, but seaworthy-looking. The russet bottom paint, revealed now and then like the edge of a slip showing below a dress hem, had been freshly scrubbed not long before.

On deck, a grizzled older man and a squat younger one with plenty of curly black hair were setting up the rods. Tiller watched till they noticed him, then lifted a hand in greeting.

The old man straightened, lifting a pointed white beard. He took a shorty corncob pipe from his mouth and strolled to the stern. "You the fella does the software?"

"What? No. I'm a friend of Louis Guidry. Said to look you up if I came to Venice."

"Oh yeah? Come on aboard. How's Louis?"

Galloway had been thinking about how to answer that question. When he told the old man Louis was dead, that this was a trip they'd planned to take together, his mouth went still. He looked at the deck.

"He's my nephew, but I ain't seen him in years. Pal of yours, eh?"

"We worked together. Tiller Galloway."

"Well, I'm Maillette Ravenel. Appreciate you coming out. Afraid I've got a charter today, though. Conventioneers out of N'Orleans. You want to come along, you're welcome. Might get you on a rod later, they get tired."

"I wouldn't mind crewing. Done a lot of it up in North Carolina."

"Whereabouts in Carolina?"

"Hatteras Island."

"Prime fishin' up that way, I hear." Some pale men in shorts came down the pier, and Ravenel said, "Here's my party. Make y'self at home. We'll talk after we get offshore."

He checked the boat out while Ravenel talked to the customers. Belowdecks and forward, a galley and dining area gave onto a head and shower and a comfortable-looking bunking area. The old man lived here, judging by the ashtrays and pipe cleaners. Sliding windows let the wind stream in. The pilothouse held the usual array of offshore electronics: CB and VHF radios, radar, a new Ray Jeff loran, an Eagle sonar.

He went aft and helped the mate with the lines. A couple of the passengers looked at him, then didn't. He was part of the boat.

They cast off and headed up the Grand Pass. He stood on the foredeck, balancing against the pitching as *Tern* crossed another boat's wake. The hamlet dropped back, the faded gray buildings shrinking like the superstructures of hull-down tankers.

A few minutes later, they emerged from the pass into the far-flung horizons of the Mississippi. It was almost like being at sea. The levee was a black line that accompanied them as they maneuvered through the small boats that hugged it. The day was well started now, cloudless and already hot. Water thick and brown as cappuccino churned with the prop wash of the charter ahead. Looking past it, he saw they were only the latest in a long procession, all heading downriver. When they were clear of the bass boats, Ravenel nudged the throttles forward. The bow lifted and the wind shifted forward of the beam.

He pulled himself aft around the cabin and climbed the ladder to the flying bridge. The old man pointed wordlessly to the wheel. Galloway nodded.

When he slid both throttles all the way forward, the boat lunged like a big cat. She lifted to her step and settled there, building a white rooster tail twenty feet high. The throb and hum droned through the boat and set the rods nodding in their sockets. Below them on the afterdeck, the salesmen talked with exaggerated hand gestures. He could see their mouths moving, but no words penetrated the roar.

They ran down the river for eight or nine miles, then cut right at the great duckfooted splay of the Mississippi for the Southwest Pass. They ran between the low marshy islands, dotted with oil wells, that margined the river here at its ultimate extension. The great stream, calm till now, grew uneasy as it neared the end of its long journey.

The river ended in two great stone riprap jetties, then a tumbled chain of huge rocks washed by waves and blackened by weed and barnacles. He looked at Ravenel. The old man lowered his eyes from the derricks west of them. "Come around east, then northeast. We'll check out the East Bay."

He spun the wheel till the lubber's line met 090 and held it with quick rudder corrections as they picked up the prevailing sea. Ravenel chuckled and went below and came up with two beers.

The radio was heating up, its metal squawking filling the bridge. "How you doin' out there? Come back." "I got a double." "We got four lines busy out here by the light tower." "Nothin' doing here. Think I'll work around your way." It was just like off Diamond Shoals, back when he'd baited for Captain Cliff. There was little secrecy among charter captains. When they came back to that dock, there had to be fish to hang up. And so they helped one another.

It occurred to him that maybe that was the same thing McCray was talking about.

The young guy climbed the ladder and looked at Tiller. Ravenel said, "This here's my mate, Bill Jacobs. Tiller Galloway."

They said hi to each other. "What kind of tackle you using?" Galloway asked him.

"We use the deep-running lures here, out in blue water." Jacobs rooted around in a box. Galloway turned the plug in his fingers. "That's a Magnum Rapala," the old man said around the pipe. "Swap out the hook for a big triple-strength, use a braided wire leader. Don't snap like the single-strand, and the fish don't seem to mind."

"How deep's this run?"

"That gets down ten, twelve feet."

"At a fast troll?"

"Yeah. Sure."

"We use more surface lures in the Stream. Get four lines out there, sweep the area with bait. The soft plastic lures. You skip 'em along the waves, marlin think they're flying fish."

"Well, that works for you," said Ravenel. He shaded his eyes and peered ahead to where a forest of derricks was stubbling the sea. Galloway noticed he never looked at the loran.

"Well, guess we're here," he said. "I'll take her now."

The mate swung himself around the ladder and let go, dropping out of sight. A moment later he reappeared, leaning out over the gunwales. The bait flashed as the sea swallowed it. The engines idled, pulling the hull easily through the water. The computer salesmen carried their early beers aft.

Galloway started suddenly at a familiar twang and sizzle. Strike! The lures had only been in the water for a few seconds. Ravenel knew where to find fish, all right. The rod leaned as the line tautened. "Behind you, Bill!" the captain screamed down.

A mouth gaped a hundred feet astern, then disappeared in a flurry of spray.

The mate spun and plucked the rod from its holder. He handed it to the first fisherman to seat himself, clacked the harness on him, and stepped back. Galloway grinned. The pasty man was suddenly alone, fighting a strong silver animal on the end of a thin line.

"Holy shit! Look at that. Son of a bitch can fly!"

"That's a thirty-foot jump, all right."

"Wahoo," Ravenel shouted down, spinning the wheel, jerking the big boat around like a cow pony. "Nice sized wahoo. Play him close now."

Next it dived, and the drag screamed as the line spun out again. He leaned on the rail and waited. When the fish jumped again, it hung in the sun for the space of a breath, a long, dark, agonized needle shape between him and the light. The spray made rainbows around it. Then it fell back. It had been greedy and now it was in pain and fighting, but the hook was set too deep to shake.

Another strike. Another. "We're in a school," Ravenel howled down.

Now the mate showed a new side. From a slow-moving, bulky man, he became a whirling, ducking performer—baiting hooks, untangling the humming lines, shouting helm orders up to Ravenel.

The first fish, played out, approached the stern. Jacobs leaned over the gunwales, posing unconsciously with the gaff, a long pole tipped with curved steel. A waiting—a jab, an upward snatch, and the wahoo, silver with black tiger stripes, flew in a short arc over the transom and into the wooden fish box at the stern. It was like a magic trick. Another strike. The decks streamed ocher, a butcher's floor disciplined only by speed and skill.

After that first flurry, though, the fishing went sour. After half an hour without a tickle, Ravenel, who had been listening to the CB and frowning at the chart, jammed the throttles forward again. *Tern* bounced like a skipping stone across water that was gradually turning blue. "We'll check out the Seven Mile Rigs," he yelled.

Tiller took off his shoes and tied the laces together and hung them over a binocular box. He wiggled his toes. The air felt good on the scaly patches. "Ever do any inshore work?" he asked the old man, who had punched numbers into the auto-pilot and stepped back to relight his pipe.

"Once in a while. Redfish near the jetties and such. You call 'em red drum up in Carolina. But offshore's so good here, you don't want to work inshore, not a boat this size. We do a lot of work around the rigs. Tripletails are big now."

"That's a new one on me."

"Some call them buoy fish, or blackfish. Not too many fishermen know about 'em. They taste kind of like a freshwater bream. Lots of 'em around the rigs. You with an oil company?"

"Diving," said Galloway. "Louis and I dove together."

"That's right, you said that. Yeah, you get a lot of action around the rigs. So it ain't all bad."

"You fished all your life, huh?"

"No," said Ravenel, giving him a funny look. "Louis didn't tell you? I used to be a priest."

"He didn't tell me."

"That's how come I'm his ex-uncle. Sort of disowned by the family."

"I can identify."

"What? You're on my deaf side."

"I said, I have that problem, too."

"Oh yeah? Then you know."

They dropped back to trolling speed fifteen miles offshore. Tiller watched the sonar. He could make out fish, but he couldn't tell what kind. Apparently, Ravenel could. He put the conventioneers into a reef of tuna. Galloway went down when the salesmen tired. He pulled in two nice blackfin, then handed the rod back.

They started back around eleven, Ravenel saying they'd see what was doing closer inshore, then they'd be in good shape to run for home. By then it was hot, hot, hot, and, worse, the wind was from astern; they traveled in a cloud of their own exhaust. Tiller felt sweat running down his ribs as he climbed back up to the flying bridge.

"So, you're an oil-field diver."

"That's right."

"Like it?"

"It's a job. It's not a pretty business."

"Maybe no business is. But oil, down here, seems to be dirtier than most."

"What you mean by that?" Galloway asked him.

The old man mused, "Been that way since they first hit oil in '01, out at the Bayou Nezpique. Used to be whole islands out there would catch on fire. Natural gas seepage, then a bolt of lightning—shoom." He threw his hands upward. "Funny thing, though—it's all under Cajun land, but damn if they've made any money out of it. You ever hear of Win or Lose?"

"No."

Ravenel throttled back and punched commands into the pilot. He waved to Jacobs, pointing ahead, then splayed his fingers from his head in a makeshift crown. He came back and perched on a folding captain's chair.

"That was Huey Long's little honey-pot company, back in the thirties. Long and O. K. Allen, his lapdog governor after him, they sold the oil and gas leases for the state. The leases went to Long's cronies, then to the oil companies, but the cream of the royalties went to something called the Win or Lose Oil Company. Meaning, I guess, that whether anybody else won or lost, Long and Allen still made good. Because they owned it. Selling the state as if it were their own property. The people who lived on it, owned it, got nothing."

Tiller wondered why he'd left the priesthood, but it didn't seem like the kind of thing you asked. He waved toward the platforms. "But it brought in money. That money gets spent here."

"Some of it. But even then it don't seem to help the Cajuns. Look at marsh damage. Every navigation canal, every pipeline ditch you dig through marsh doubles its size every fourteen years. That's where the shrimp come from. No marshes, no seafood. No seafood, no fishermen. The catch is on the verge of collapse. It's only a matter of time, something pushes it over the edge. Then you'll see real misery in Louisiana."

"The oil's not going to last forever."

"I guess you can look at it that way," said Ravenel. "But what if by then there's no marsh anymore?"

"So what do you do?" Tiller asked him. "You got to make a living."

Ravenel glanced back from the horizon. "I'm not indicting the people who work oil. It feeds their families. Like you say. Just seems, it's like going up a bayou. It forks here, forks there. Every fork, you got a choice to make. But it keeps getting narrower. Sooner or later, it's too narrow to turn around. You may not like what you find at the end. But by then, it's too late."

"I'm not sure what you're saying."

"Neither am I, you know? I used to think it was original sin. That we were all cursed. Then I changed my mind."

"To what?" Galloway bent to hear him above the wind.

"Well, the older I get, the less I can say for sure, you know? I guess that was my problem in the church. People aren't ever going to be perfect. The animal just don't swim that way. But I'll guarantee you one thing: If everybody was just ten percent better"—he took his pipe out and pointed it at the sky, the sea, the land, rising now fine off the starboard bow—"this'd be Paradise. Here and now."

Jacobs shouted behind them: "Kings!"

Tiller watched the bait go over and the kingfish rise in the reddening light, watched them bite and bite. He watched them slapping and writhing in their coffin box, spewing blood and roe over the stern, the ones on top snapping at the hostile air.

Still hungry, even as their eyes glazed, and they died.

TWENTY

Porch and Winslow looked up from the tube as Tiller let himself into the trailer through the sliding doors. "How was fishing?" the Pagan asked him.

"Okay."

"What's in the bag?"

"About twenty pounds of blackfin fillets. We can grill 'em up tonight." He went into the kitchenette, watching for snakes, and put the fillets in the refrigerator.

"Where's the Captain?"

"He wanted to go by his place, check his mail. Said he'd come over later." He got a paper towel and came out of the kitchen, wiping his hands. "Anyway, that's what I did. Fish. What did y'all do last night?"

"The usual. Went out. Got drunk. Raised hell."

"What's the plan for tonight?"

"More of the same, I guess. Why? You feelin' more like yourself?"

"Maybe."

Winslow said slowly, looking at the TV, "Shook those willies, huh?"

"I guess so." He didn't understand how, but the day on the water had helped. Maybe he'd just needed to get away. "Hey, you know how to get hold of those girls? That Teagan?"

"Who?"

"Edie's pal," said Winslow.

"Oh, now you like her? She thought you were rude the

other night." Porchellacchia lowered his voice. "Not tonight. Maybe some other time."

"Why? What's going on?"

"Wildman got an idea. But we wanted to wait till you got back. Couldn't do it right, just the two of us. An' the others—I don't think this's their kind of thing, exactly."

"What's that?"

"We'll tell you later," said Winslow. "But it's about settlin' a score."

"Hey, don't do this to me. You got something cooking, let me know."

"We'll tell you tonight," said Porch. "Just stretch your air till then, okay?"

Galloway picked up the paper and flipped to the classified section. "What are we doing this afternoon?"

"Nothin'. Watchin' TV."

"Want to go out, look at some cars?"

They drove around looking at used cars for a couple of hours. Galloway saw a Jeep he liked at Hebert Brothers, an old CJ that seemed to be in decent shape except for what looked like bullet holes in the right side and the fact that somebody had painted it aluminum. But he finally put it off, since he didn't know how long they'd be ashore. There was no point buying it, then letting it sit and rust.

McCray came by the trailer around six and Galloway fired up the grille. By the time the tuna was ready, it was getting dark. They ate from paper plates, watching the stars come out over the bayou. Porch kept asking McCray whether he was tired. Finally, Jay got up and said good night, he'd see them in the morning. Around eleven, they climbed back into Winslow's van and headed into town.

"There's a daiquiri factory. Want to slide in there?"

"We better hold off. Have another beer. In the cooler there, should be some still cold."

There was no blue law in Bayou City. So that now as they rolled up Railroad Street and onto Front, the bars were lighted up and cars were cruising up and down past the piers even though it was Sunday night.

Suddenly he had the same feeling he'd had when he drove through here with Shad. Like he was seeing double, the way things were and the way they once had been.

"Remember how it was in the old days? When it was really jumping down here?"

"We wasn't here then, man. What was it like?"

"The bars along the levee, they were just rip-off joints. You could go to the beach, cash your paycheck at the bar, and spend it all in one night, just buying champagne for the girls. Sometimes they'd spike the drinks. Drag a guy out and throw him on the boat. Crews were so short then, a fella would wake up, he's a deckhand, or a cook, or a galley hand, and everybody swore he walked aboard. They'd stay out for months, fuel up at the rigs, just to keep the crews from walking off again."

Neither man said anything, and he realized they were both looking forward with great concentration. "Hey, there's the Hat. We stopping?" he asked them.

"Not there."

"So, what's going on?"

Winslow chuckled in the front seat. It was the first time Tiller had heard him laugh. He didn't like it.

They rolled on slowly, both men scanning out of the side windows. He remembered rolling this way before, in the back of a carryall, with Shad muttering in his ear, "This is stupid. These guys is frigging crazy, Till. And you're just as crazy as they are."

Winslow reached down and cut the lights. The van coasted off the road and rolled up into the lot in front of the green door. Galloway sat up. "You ain't going in there again."

"Here's a quarter," said Porch.

"What's this for?"

"See that phone booth? Get 'em out here."

"Get who out here?"

"The guys that beat on us the other night. Go on, get moving."

"What you want me to say?"

"Think of something," the Pagan said. He got out of the van and stretched. He went around to the back and opened the doors. Picked up an ax handle. He looked at Galloway. "Go on, get movin'. Or do you want out?"

He shrugged, tossed the coin in his hand, and sauntered

toward the phone. He got the number from the damp, stained Yellow Pages. When somebody answered, he could hardly hear him over the music and noise. "Yeah. Moon Pool Lounge. Who you want?"

"This's Ed. Down at the station. Gonna have three cruisers there in five minutes, do an ID check. Understand me?"

"Who's this?"

"A guy on the payroll. You hear me, about the cops? Five minutes." He hung up.

"How'd it go?"

"They'll be right out."

The door slammed open and about six men came out, tucking their shirts in hastily, looking around. They blinked and raised their hands as the headlights came on, pinning them.

"Spread 'em!" Porchellacchia shouted, grabbing two at once and throwing them over the hood of one of the cars. They knew the routine, Galloway saw. Winslow dropped from the van and halted a few paces away, one hand inside his jacket. Porch was patting them down. His hand whipped out and something clattered away in the darkness.

"Hey, Officer, what I done?"

"Shut up. There any more of you in there? Officer Oliver, bolt the door."

He started, realizing Porch was talking to him. He grabbed a trash barrel and rolled it and jammed it under the handle of the green door.

Porch grabbed the first man's shoulder and spun him around. He blinked in the glare. Porchellacchia looked back at Winslow and Galloway. They shook their heads, and the big Pagan spun him back and grabbed the next.

"That's one," said Winslow.

"Yeah," said Tiller, recognizing the one who'd said, "Welcome to the Moon Pool, cher."

Porch pulled wire from his jeans and twisted it around the man's wrists. He shoved him toward Winslow, who boosted him into the van. He grabbed the next one's hair. "I reckanize this bahstid myself."

One took his hands off the hood and started to turn. Tiller took two steps forward and jammed his bent finger into his back. "Resisting arrest, asshole?" The man bent again, cursing in a mumble.

"That's all of 'em I recognize," Porch said a second later. "Under the car, assholes! Crawl! Get under there. Let's ride!"

The van's wheels threw gravel. Then the tires caught and they bolted out onto the street. Winslow held torque till they reached the corner, burned rubber on the turn, and only then hit the lights. "Good job back there, Officer Oliver," he said.

Tiller said, "What the hell is this? What are we doing? Impersonating police, kidnapping people at gunpoint?"

"Oh no, nothin' like that. You see any guns?"

"Wildman, you got a gun?"

"Who, me?"

"What are you gonna do with them now?"

"Nothing."

"Nothing?"

"Wildman, you blindfold them?" Porch asked.

"Yeah."

"Good." The Pagan lowered his voice. "We ain't gonna do nothing with them, man. Just drive around all night with them in the back there. Stop here, open the doors, close the doors, have a drink. Stop there, open the doors, close the doors, have a drink. When we get tired, we'll drive out to the swamp and push 'em out."

"What's that gonna prove?"

Porch unbuckled his seat belt. He stood up and turned around. Over Galloway's shoulder, he called, "Hey. You hear me, back there?"

A mutter, a moan answered him.

"Just wanted to let you know. Guess you all will be dead in a little while. We're almost there."

"I didn't hear this," Tiller muttered. "I ain't saying it's not fun, but—"

"Relax. They're not gonna tell nobody," said Porchellacchia. "What they gonna say? That we gave them a ride and let 'em go? Loosen up, man. Hand me one a them beers."

Just to be sure, though, they made the Rack Box their first stop. Porch distracted the waitress while Tiller went behind the bar and set the clock back. Then Winslow asked her what time it was. They had a couple of leisurely drinks, then left.

"We'll drop you off at the Hat," said Winslow after they hit two more places, opening and then slamming the van doors at each one. "Make sure a lot of people see you, okay? And mention you saw us around. There's ever any trouble, we'll have things so fouled up, they'll never figure out where we were."

Tiller waved as they dropped him in front of the Brass Hat. He was a little sorry now he wasn't going with them.

He was glad to see that though the place wasn't exactly crowded, the bar was full. Even gladder to see Jill at the register. He peeled three fifties off the wad and shoved them across to her. "Thanks for the loan, Miss Jill."

She pushed the extra fifty back. "Tiller, please. What do you think I am, a shark? Keep the vigorish, son."

"Sorry. Tell you what." He raised his voice. "Drinks for the house!" Faces turned toward him and he waved. There, that should make them remember him.

There were some half-familiar faces here tonight. Guys he'd worked with years before. He drifted over and caught up. One was running a diving consulting firm. He was trying to understand exactly what that was when Roland Boudreaux came in.

A woman in dark glasses was with him. Boudreaux eyed him sourly as they passed. He brushed a chair and staggered. The woman caught his arm and steered him to a table in the back. Galloway noticed the black dress and then the diamonds.

The consultant started telling a long story about a tristate champion frog. Galloway laughed when it was done and told him about Kimball throwing the sea gull in the chamber. Then he got up. " 'Scuse me. My boss just came in. Better go pay my respects."

Boudreaux glanced up as he approached. Then he tilted his head back. When he put the glass down, it was empty.

"Hey, Roland."

"Hey." Boudreaux still looked annoyed, or displeased, but said pleasantly enough, "*Choux*, this here's Galloway, one a my divers. My wife."

"Arden Delisle Boudreaux." Her hand was small and soft,

but her eyes were invisible behind the dark glasses. He wished she'd take them off. He liked her shoulders. He liked her hair. Her lips curved slightly. "You look familiar, Mr. Galloway."

"I go by Tiller."

"Tiller. Have we met somewhere?"

He remembered the black Miata, the crowded fairground, long fingers on her thigh. He looked at Boudreaux's curled around the glass. Big, stubby, black-haired.

"I don't think so."

"Siddown," Boudreaux grunted. "Farrell! Two more Turkeys over here."

Tiller sipped his, remembering too late he was only drinking beer now. Well, one wouldn't hurt. Boudreaux poured his down, then lighted a cigarette.

"You work for Roland?" Arden asked him.

"That's right."

"Where are you from?"

Her voice had a soft accent, like but also unlike her husband's. He started telling her a sanitized version of his past and how he'd gotten back to Bayou City. Boudreaux interrupted him in midsentence. "You want anything?" he asked her.

"Perhaps some wine—"

"You know they don't have wine."

"A Coke. Diet."

"You ready for a swap-out, Galloway?"

"Thanks, I'm still working on this one."

"I thought you drank."

"I drink, but—"

"Two more Turkeys, and a diet Coke." Boudreaux finished the sentence with a sneer.

The diving consultant came by and started talking about an underwater beacon system he was representing. Boudreaux put him off roughly. The guy left, looking angry.

"You still livin' out there with Winslow and Porch?" the superintendent asked Tiller suddenly.

"Yeah."

"Where are they?"

"They were just here. Didn't you see 'em when you came in?"

"Understand your nigger friend dragged up."

"I don't like you calling him that." He was getting fed up

with Boudreaux's attitude. The guy was far gone; that was obvious. He was weaving just as he sat in the chair.

"You know something, Galloway? I don't much care what you like."

Tiller stood up. " 'Scuse me, Miz Boudreaux."

"Oh, sit the hell down. Your *black* friend. That better?"

He sat down as Jill brought the drinks. "Hello, Arden," she said.

"Good evening, Madame Watson."

"Who's driving tonight? Let me guess."

"You guessed right. Oh, a cherry. This is lovely."

"This is lovely," mimicked Boudreaux. Then he put his hand on Jill's. "You're a good friend, Miss Jill. Ain't many women like you, you know that?"

"You got yourself a good woman right there. Now let go my hand, Roland."

"She reminds me of my mother. *Bon comme ange.* My mother was a frigging angel, you know?" Boudreaux told Tiller.

"That so?"

"Five kids, and the son of a bitch drove off on her one day. She waited tables, kep' books for a sugar mill. Fourteen years later, he come back. Fourteen years. And he wanted dinner! I was only a kid, but I threw the son of a bitch out." He looked after Jill. "I never tol' her how much I loved her."

"Jill?"

"My mother, goddamn it. Your mother alive, Tiller?"

"She died when I was a kid. My dad remarried, but I don't get along too good with her."

"You and your dad get along?"

"No, we never did." He took a deep breath. "He's gone now, too."

"You never know how much you miss 'em till it's too late . . . *trop tard pour . . .* " His voice trailed off. He raised the glass very deliberately and drank it off.

"Roland, you've had enough."

Boudreaux said something in rapid Cajun that made his wife sit back in her chair. Tiller felt embarrassed. He got up again. "Well, it's getting late. Nice meetin' you, Miz Boudreaux—"

"You're not going, Mr. Galloway."

"Yeah, I better. We got to be at work at eight. Tomorrow's Monday."

Boudreaux sniggered. He staggered up and went into the back. They could hear him blundering into walls.

Arden leaned forward and took his hand. Tiller froze.

"Don't leave me alone with him."

"What?"

"You see what kind of shape he's in. And he'll get worse. Will you stay? To help me?"

He didn't want to, but he didn't see how he could say no. "Well . . . all right," he said.

But when Boudreaux came back, he seemed refreshed. His hair was wet and slicked back. He went to the bar and Galloway heard him arguing with the bartender. He came back with Certs and a bottle of Wild Turkey. "Want a mint?" he said.

"No thanks."

Arden refused with a shake of her head. Boudreaux crunched one between his teeth. Then he topped off Galloway's glass and raised his. "To our new diver."

"Thanks."

"You ain't drinking?"

"You don't drink to yourself."

Boudreaux looked puzzled, then hostile. He drank his glass off and poured more. A good deal of it missed.

"You can dive, anyway. But I ain't happy, that Pandora job."

"Why not?"

"I wanted that bonus." Boudreaux glared around from under knitted brows. When his gaze came back to Galloway, it was malevolent. "You bastards done a slowdown on me. Or we would of made it."

"Come on, Roland, we were working our tails off down there."

"Sure you were. That's where them portholes come from. Treasure hunting. Wreck stripping. That's why I didn't make that bonus, *choux*."

"Roland, Ace had the watch on us while we were punching those portholes out. He allowed us fifteen minutes each."

"Lazy son-of-a-bitching Mexican."

"Ace's a good diver—"

"I don't need some tube-sucker tellin' me who's a good diver!"

Tiller pushed his chair back. He was feeling the liquor, too, and he'd had enough. "Okay, Bender. Let's take it outside."

"Need another drink first. Then I'll tear your friggin' face off, asshole. Then you, bitch. My mother was a good woman. *She* was no streetwalkin' whore."

"You're not going anywhere. Take that bottle away from him!"

"In the sack, anything wears pants. Filthy, lying slut. . . . "

"Shut up. You're drunk, Roland." But she didn't sound horrified, just resigned.

"Galloway. Whassa matter? You ain't drinking."

"We're goin' outside. Discuss how I lost you your goddamned bonus."

"Hey, cool it off. Forget the bonus." Boudreaux glanced around blearily and bent forward. He whispered, "I tell you something, me. We goin' to make us a lot more money than that. An' soon. You want to be part of it? Brad and me, we cut you a deal, us."

"What the hell are you talking about?" Galloway asked him.

"Not so loud. . . . You done time, know how to keep your mouth shut. Know how to . . . talk later." He shook his head as if to clear it.

"You're drunk," his wife said again, disgust dyeing her voice. "You pig. *Sale cochon. Soulard.*"

"We talk later, us. . . . Drunk? *Gougre non, peu piqué . . .* "

Boudreaux's eyes went fixed, shining like reflective tape on a barricade. He toppled slowly forward, knocking over the bottle.

"*Merde,*" said Arden. She took a deep breath and let it out in a sigh. "Well, that's it for tonight. Help me get him outside, will you?"

The car outside wasn't the Miata; it was a new teal Firebird. They wrestled Boudreaux's soggy bulk into the rear seat. It wasn't easy. The son of a bitch was heavy, and he wasn't too steady himself. But finally he was in. He leaned against the car as Arden slid behind the wheel. "You be all right?" he asked her.

The door on his side locked, then unlocked. He looked at it and then at her. Then at the limp, snoring body in back.

"I can't get him up the steps by myself. Help me. Please?"

He got in.

They lived west of town, out toward Patterson. Tiller held the button till his window was all the way down. He leaned out, watching the darkness rush past. They didn't talk, but he could smell her perfume.

The house was huge and old, surrounded by woods. There was the black car, a gleam in the headlights under a carport. Boudreaux didn't even grunt when Tiller pulled him out by the legs. He rolled out of his grasp and slid to the grass.

Tiller slumped against the trunk. "He's too heavy. No way, I can't get him up those steps."

"Then leave him there. It won't be the first time." She turned from the front door, holding the screen, looking down. "Are you coming?"

He felt his heart shifting gears. He'd wondered on the way out. Fantasized. He looked at Boudreaux lying in the driveway. A million cicadas scraped at the inside of his head. The smell of jasmine made it hard to breathe.

"I better not," he mumbled.

"That is, what?"

"Uh, I better not come in. Got to get back."

As he stared up at her, he noticed how the porch light behind her outlined her breast through the thin material of the dress. He was tempted. She was gorgeous. Dangerous. Forbidden. Exactly the kind of woman he couldn't resist. Boudreaux was a drunken, greedy shit.

"Why not?" she said.

He stood there looking up at her for what felt to him like a long time. He wanted to, all right. But drunk as he was, he knew it wasn't the smart thing to do.

But then again, he'd done quite a few not particularly

smart things that day. Participated in an abduction; that had to count as a major felony. Got drunk when he hadn't meant to. And now was about to go to bed with his boss's wife.

The next second, the steps were creaking under his boots. He took her hand. She pressed it, opening the door.

The next moment it closed, and their lips came together.

They clung, trembling in the warm dark. He felt the heat coming off her body, the damp perfumed scent of an aroused woman. Through the open window of the front room, the insect chorus rose and fell, endless and unearthly. Then he opened his eyes to her face.

"Why?" he muttered.

"You mean him? Is that what you mean?"

"Yes."

"He brought it on himself. For years, I never looked at another man. He was the same way. Crazy-jealous. Finally, I decided, if he's going to suspect me, insult me, why not do it?"

"Then why stay with him?"

She answered a question, but not the one he'd asked. "His family hates me. To them, I'm an outsider. A foreigner. To me, they're people from another century."

"What? Aren't you—"

"I'm not Cajun. I'm French."

"Oh."

"I came here as a student and fell in love—with the country. Though I thought at the time it was with Roland."

"Why do you stay with him, then?"

She touched the necklace, earrings. "He's good to me, in his way."

"He gives you things? Is that it?"

"In Paris, we were poor. I enjoy having nice things. He enjoys giving them to me." She shrugged. "I never said I didn't appreciate him. In my way."

Tiller felt out of his depth. He felt like he was sinking, was already too deep, but he couldn't struggle. Her perfume numbed his will like nitrogen at depth. Her hands made slow circles on his back. He said, "What did he mean, there in the bar? About having some kind of deal coming down with Shattuck?"

"I don't know. Truly, I do not concern myself with how he makes his money. Only that it is there. Now, will you stay or not?"

"Stay here? What about him?"

"Let him lie, the pig. *Comme j'vous ai dit*, it won't be the first time. You can take his car. I will drive him to work in the morning in mine."

Her soft, small hands were unbuckling his belt. Her breasts brushed his chest. "Have you talked enough? Ah. You want me, don't you?"

He caught his breath. Yeah, he wanted her.

But at the same time, someone inside his head was telling him this wasn't right.

Shit, he thought. What's the matter with you? Go ahead, take her into the goddamn bedroom. Boudreaux'll never know.

But at the same time—it was weird—he was remembering what old Ravenel had told him on the *Tern*, far out in the blue Gulf. How had he put it? . . . If everybody was just ten percent better . . . Something like that.

For just a moment, swaying in the dark, he understood something about men and women, something about passion, and something about himself. About how all it took to make sense of anything was to look at it with a long-enough attention span. But even as he understood, it slipped away into the whiskey haze, like a tarpon vanishing into the blue at a hundred feet. Into that foggy light-shot Louisiana blue.

"Where are you going?"

"I gotta get back," he said. "Thanks, but I, uh . . ."

"You son of a bitch. *Sale pédé! Allez, oust!*"

Her husband was still lying where he'd fallen, his snores blending into the noises of the night woods. Tiller found the keys in the ignition. He wondered as he started the engine whether he was actually going to leave. Only when he was halfway back to town, concentrating hard to keep the weaving car on the empty road, was he really sure.

TWENTY-ONE

He felt rotten the next morning. Cursing the man who invented bourbon, he steered the Firebird into the lot and set the tires against the parking marker stenciled R. B. BOUD-REAUX.

He went in, jingling the keys in his hand like a hot potato, but the boss wasn't waiting for him as he'd expected. He didn't seem to be anywhere around. He went through the building and out into the yard.

"Hey, Till."

"Hi, guys."

The crew was sitting around, waiting for leadership. McCray looked levelly at him and Tiller gave him a nod. He squatted on his heels and waited, too.

Finally Rodriquez came out with papers in his hand. "Okay, listen a me, people. Who here got a CPR card? Let's see it. No, that's out of date. Okay, we going to do some cardio-pulmonary resuscitation—whew, can't believe I said that right the first time—training this morning."

They groaned. The assistant superintendent cut it off with, "Hey, you can't draw depth pay all the time. So let's get to it. Virginia, she will be out here in a minute, help us practice. Just joking, Porch, goddamn it!"

After review of the book, then practice on a battered dummy, Ace pulled some gear manuals and assigned mainte-nance. Tiller got to supervise Winslow and another tender, do-ing maintenance on the chamber, which had been trucked back to Summerland over the weekend. They were replacing a gasket on the medical lock when he saw the Miata arrive.

The others noticed it, too. "Ole Bender's late."

"Layin' out drunk."

"Hey, have a heart. The man spends all his time out on the rigs, makin' the Yankee dollar. He rates getting stewed once in a while, no?"

Tiller didn't say anything. He kept working. The sun was hot on his neck. They were all fish-pale from three weeks in sat, ripe for a burn.

"Hand me that rag, Wildman." He fanned it out and tucked it under his DeepTech ball cap, Foreign Legion–style. "How'd it go last night, after I left? Any surprises?"

"No," said Winslow.

An unsettling thought occurred to him. He glanced around, making sure no one else was in earshot, then muttered, "Are they *alive*, Wildman?"

"Are who what?"

"The guys we snatched. How are they?"

"We dumped them in the swamp. Like we said."

"And they're alive?"

"Far as I know. Why d'you ask?"

"Just wondered."

Boudreaux strolled out a while later. He looked inside the chamber. Tiller watched him scratching some welts on his neck. Then he ambled over.

"Galloway."

He put down the gasket compound and wiped sticky crumbs off on his pants. "Yeah," he said, keeping his voice neutral.

"Let's take a walk. Down to the pier."

The pier was on the far side of a levee. It had been grassed, but the grass hadn't taken. It stuck out of the sand withered and dead. Rusted bulldozer blades and creeper treads lined the path to the bayou. It was floored with creosoted timbers half-buried in the sand. Boudreaux gestured impatiently, motioning Galloway up beside him.

"Have a good time last night?"

"Yeah, okay."

"Where'd we saw you? I sort of remember, but—"

"I ran into you at the Hat. You were feeling no pain."

213

Boudreaux rubbed his face. "So . . . you met my wife?"

"Arden? She was with you, yeah."

The dive boss glanced sideways at him. Tiller slogged on through the sand. Heat came up in waves, shimmering the top of the levee. Some kind of mast or antenna spiked up beyond it. He dragged sweat off his forehead and flicked it off his fingertips.

"How'd my car get here?"

"Didn't she tell you? I drove it."

"How'd you get it?"

"I drove you home."

"Oh yeah? Why?"

"You passed out, Roland. Ask Miss Jill, or that asshole bartender of hers. He helped us carry you out. Your wife said she couldn't handle you alone."

"Okay, so you drove me home. Then what happened?"

"Then we tried to carry you up the stairs, put you to bed. After which, I left. She said to take the car, that she'd drive you in and you could pick it up today." He took the keys out and tossed them. Boudreaux reacted too late and they missed his hand.

"Sorry."

"Uh-huh." The boss straightened, shaking sand from them. His stare was venomous. "So you drove me home and put me to bed, huh? Then how come when I wake up, I was lyin' in the driveway, fire ants all over me?"

"Puttin' you to bed was the original idea. Like I said. But I couldn't get you up the steps. I was pretty shit-faced myself."

"Then what happened?"

What had she told him? *Had* she told him anything? He kept his face straight and his tone level as he said, "Then I left. It ain't no big deal, Roland. God knows, I been in that state myself more than once."

Boudreaux frowned. They made the crest and started down, and now he saw what the antenna belonged to. The bayou wasn't very deep here. That was why heavy gear like the chamber had to be trucked around to the Atchafalaya for loading. But it was apparently deep enough for a fifty-foot Davis.

Boudreaux cleared his throat. "You know, when you hired on, we mentioned one-atmosphere work."

"That's right."

"Said you'd had some experience."

"A few dives. Enough to know how to operate one."

"Uh-huh. Well, Coastal wants us to develop a capability. If we can, we can bid on a lot more work than we can on a pure saturation basis."

Tiller nodded. A one-atmosphere suit was a rigid shell, a miniature submarine. The diver breathed regular air at sea-level pressure. He didn't have to pressurize, so he didn't have to decompress. He didn't have the manual dexterity of a saturation diver, but Boudreaux was right: In some ways, he was more capable; he could make a deep dive for a look-see or a simple repair in a tenth the time a sat diver could.

He wondered whether this was connected somehow to the deal Boudreaux had been muttering about just before he'd passed out.

But Boudreaux was still talking. "Catch is, there's only been a couple dozen JIMs built. They're too expensive for an outfit this size. And you got to have a winch and a U-boom, all kinds of special trained guys."

The pier echoed under their boots. Still, greasy-looking water glittered between the planks. "Uh-huh," Galloway said.

"But I ran into a guy at LAGCOE, the gas and oil exposition. He had an interestin' line of talk. So I invited him to come in and show us his stuff."

They were almost to the end of the pier. It was a little cooler out here, but the sun burned off the water straight into his face. He tugged his cap down.

The boat looked new. The bow read *Janis J.* Galloway circled toward the stern as they walked the last few paces. A davit was installed on the afterdeck. From it hung a rigid diving suit. It was hinged open, like a gutted crab, and a man was bent over working on it.

Boudreaux stopped at the end of the pier, looking down. Tiller stopped, too, looking at the guy's back. A little wiry fellow with dark hair. He was really in there, digging around in the thing's innards.

While they waited, Galloway looked the suit over. It looked a little like the suits he'd trained on. The same large hemispherical helmet section, attaching without any neck to a bulging barrel of a trunk. Three small view ports looked ahead and to the sides. The legs looked stumpy, but the arms were huge, made up of bulbous cast or turned sections. They ended not in hands but in complex manipulating claws. A guy dressed out in it would be about eight feet tall and resemble the Michelin Man painted glossy white. But up close, he could see it wasn't a JIM. The head attached differently and so did the joints. The gear on the back was entirely different. In fact, it didn't look like anything he was familiar with.

Another man came back along the deck. He bowed to them and called to the one inside the suit. The guy said something in reply, his voice muffled, and started wriggling out. He stood up, holding a soldering gun in one hand. The other sleeve hung empty.

Tiller froze.

He knew this stringy little guy with the flat, high-cheekboned face. The hard dark eyes and ready, seemingly obsequious smile.

"G.Q." Lee. The druggie engineer who'd rigged the dicked-up smuggling equipment that had nearly killed him years before.

He worked for Don Juan Nuñez.

"Good morning, gentlemen. Come aboard, please."

Mastering his first impulse, to turn tail, he followed Boudreaux down a gangway that the other man, apparently a crewman, slid up to the pier. Lee stepped clear of hoses and wires, sprayed something on his hand from a can, holding it under the stump of his left arm, and wiped it on a hanging towel. He came forward with it extended. "Mr. Boudreaux, I presume."

"Roland."

"Dr. Ji Kyu Lee," said Boudreaux, waving Tiller forward from behind him. "This is—"

"Just a moment," said Lee. He frowned at Galloway, then reached up. He took Galloway's chin and aimed his head to the left, then to the right.

"Galloway," he said. "Without a beard."

"That's right."

"You know each other, huh?" said Boudreaux, looking suspiciously from Lee to Galloway.

"We did once. I have not seen you since the old days."

"Uh-huh. How's the Baptist?"

"Señor Juan Alberto Mendieta Nuñez-Sebastiano? I cannot

say, since I have not seen him in years. How has your life progressed? Well, I hope?"

"Not that well."

"Sorry to hear that. Do I recall some problem at the end of that last cruise of yours—"

"The Coast Guard was waiting when I got to Hampton Roads. I pulled five years." He looked Lee up and down. "Whoever burned me was in Nuñez's organization."

"Unfortunate. But when one deals with thugs and criminals, one must expect eventually to be beaten and robbed. That is why I terminated my association with the trade." The dark eyes gave Tiller back his stare. "As you have also, I see."

"I've been trying. They don't make it that easy to walk away."

"Well, as I said, I no longer have any association in those quarters."

"How'd you lose the arm, G.Q.?"

"Diving." Lee turned to Boudreaux. "My apologies, sir. Tiller and I will have to continue this conversation later. I'm sure it's tiresome for someone who wasn't there."

"No, it's interestin'," said Boudreaux. "To find out more about Galloway here. Knows how to keep a secret, don't he?"

Lee smiled.

"So, you want to tell us about this thing?" Boudreaux reached out and punched the suit. It swayed on its tackle, and Galloway saw it was lighter than he'd assumed.

Lee circled it, and his voice went higher. His face changed, became sharper, as if their talk up to now had been a waste of time, but now they could speak of serious things.

"I was on the *Nuestra Señora de los Dolores* expedition. Working with Dr. Pannunzio's team. I was in an articulated suit, not a JIM, but an Italian-made version. I was at eighteen hundred feet when one of the joints failed."

"Jesus," muttered Boudreaux.

"Yes. I should have died. An internal flaw in one of the castings. It cracked suddenly, and—" He shrugged and nodded toward his truncated arm.

The crewman reappeared, carrying cans of iced tea with beads of sweat rolling down them. Lee introduced him as In-Tak Ha, his technician. Galloway popped one and sucked it down. Lee kept talking, looking at the suit.

217

"As I said, any failure in the pressure shell of a one-atmosphere suit is usually fatal. But I lost only an arm. Why? Ah, that was the point that challenged me."

He waited, apparently for questions, but they both just stared. "It was the *way* it failed, you see. The articulated joints are the hardest part of the suit to manufacture. They have to resist the same pressure as the rest, but they also have to flex. A joint that does not bend, and bend easily, is no joint at all, and the diver within the suit cannot work."

Tiller nodded and Lee switched his attention to him. "So then I had an idea. What is the limiting depth for a rigid suit?"

"When it implodes, I guess."

"Correct. When it fails, it fails completely and the occupant dies. But not in the 'Brute Suit.'"

"That's what you call it?"

"I wanted a memorable name, one with commercial possibilities."

"Catchy. But what do you mean, he doesn't die?"

"The Brute Suit does not fail catastrophically. We have a phrase in engineering: 'graceful degradation.' That describes a system that fails gradually and safely, not suddenly and fatally."

"That sounds good."

"The various castings that make up the suit and joints interlock in the same way a crab's do. I discovered that only after I had designed it, but it was an interesting confirmation of the concept."

"What's it made out of?" asked Boudreaux, rapping it again.

"A little titanium, but mainly glass-reinforced plastic. Not cast metal, like the older types. Easier to handle, so you can dive off a smaller boat instead of a barge. You can run a Brute with three men. Much less expensive. 'Bottom time's the bottom line.' My slogan." He smiled modestly. "It's designed for two thousand feet. This package bolts around the waist section. Two horizontal and two vertical thrusters, powered by a three-hundred-and-sixty-volt surface supply—"

"Wait a minute," said Galloway. He had a feeling he'd missed something. "Go back a couple pages. You said it failed gradually, not suddenly. How *does* it fail?"

Lee said, "I told you that. It is designed to fail purposefully the way my suit failed by fortunate accident."

"You mean—no, that would be nuts. I thought you said—"

"It collapses at the joints first. It might amputate your arms or your legs, but it would be a clean, pinching, self-sealing shear. You would most probably live, if they got you back to the surface fast enough. Preferable to a massive pressure crush, surely?"

"My God." He stared at it in horror, then looked at Lee's sleeve, flapping in the hot wind off the bayou. "Has it been tested?"

"Of course." Lee patted the smooth carapace fondly. "I did a complete finite-element analysis during design. The fracture mechanics were most interesting. But that was not all. Computers are fine, but there are things they overlook, not so? So I constructed a one-quarter-scale proof-of-concept model. Lowered it to the equivalent of twenty-three-hundred feet."

"It held?"

"Of course not. That was not the point. It failed. But it failed perfectly."

"Galloway here went to school on rigid suits," said Boudreaux casually. "Worked in them, too, he says."

He dragged more sweat off his forehead. The sun was directly overhead now, burning off the steely mirror of the bayou. "No, I mean, has it been *tested*? Full-size? With a real live guy in it?"

"Not yet," said Boudreaux, and when Galloway looked, he saw that the Cajun was smiling. Smiling right at him.

"I'm glad to be working with you again, Tiller. And with you, Mr. Boudreaux. I'm sure we'll make a fine team."

"Wait a minute—"

Stepping over hoses and cables and spare parts, Lee plunged his lone hand into the shadowy maze of equipment inside the suit. "Let us begin with the trim controls. Pay close attention now. . . ."

TWENTY-TWO

He dangled in a world of liquid turquoise shot with rays of gold, staring through the forward port as a yellowfin moved in to investigate him. Peering up, he could just make out the black wedge of the Davis above him. Props turning slowly, the *Janis J* tossed uneasily in a gentle chop.

He was hanging thirty feet below her and it was August, a week after he'd started his training on the Brute. They were 160 miles out in the Gulf. This was his first working dive, to 1,220 feet, and for the last fifteen minutes he'd been hanging here like a giant Christmas ornament, going through final systems check before the descent.

Take it easy, he told himself. He took a sparing sip from the little water bottle by his head. You know the gear. Know what's going down. You're nowhere near the rated limits on this thing.

Yeah, but how trustworthy were Lee's calculations? And how good was the workmanship in this plastic turtle shell? If it failed, his damn goose was cooked. Even at thirty feet, a leak could drown him. At a thousand plus, pressure drove water through any crack or hole like a liquid bullet.

The suit fit like a custom coffin. He could just snake his hands up to operate switches and scratch his nose.

Suddenly his skin flushed and prickled. His body wanted out, *right now*. He fought it down, turning his head from side to side. Searching desperately for something else to think about other than where he was and where he was going.

220

They'd trained on deck first while he mastered the controls and nomenclature of the suit. He had to give Lee credit, it wasn't that hard to operate. Then a familiarization dive in the bayou, then out to Ship Shoal. The first day, he'd gone to sixty feet. The next, they'd run farther out and he went to two hundred for an hour. He'd caught some problems with the pitch control system, and Lee and Ha had fixed them, working all night. Boudreaux trained as topside supervisor and did a familiarization dive, too.

And once a shadow had fallen across the gear and they'd looked up to see Brad Shattuck. The Coastal executive had asked questions, listened carefully to Lee's explanations, and then disappeared for a long talk with Boudreaux.

The rest of Crew Two had gone back to sea, with Rodriquez moved up to supervisor—another pipeline installation. They'd given him some flak before they left, though, when they found out what he was training on. "So, Till, you gonna be a Janitor in a Drum?" He'd just grinned.

Now the training was over, and he peered down into the abyss. In his ears, the power scrubber whined steadily. The Brute had an umbilical, made up of a lift line, a power cable, and a comm cable, but no gas hose. The scrubber system recirculated the suit air, drawing it through a CO_2-absorbent canister and automatically enriching it with oxygen from the onboard supply.

Just like a space suit, he thought. Power was another story. To keep the suit light and small, Lee had left out batteries. Without power he could walk and operate his hydraulics a couple of times, but that was about it.

"This is topside back on the line. Hear us better now?"

"Yeah, a lot better. What was that, Roland?"

"My mistake. Guess I just put my plug in the wrong hole, eh, cher?"

"Oh."

"Okay, I'm turning the tape back on again. Let's get back on the checklist."

He took another sip of water to kill the dry powdered-iron taste that coated his mouth and throat. Then he switched everything else in his head off and concentrated on what Boudreaux and Lee were telling him.

"Manipulators."

He thrust his hands into the arms and got them around the control grips. Left, right, up, down. Twist left, twist right, close. The claws clicked shut. Hydraulically powered by an on-board pump, they could scissor quarter-inch steel. "Check."

"Front ballast jettison."

"Pin's in. Handle free to move."

"Rear ballast."

"Check an' ditto."

They went over the umbilical jettison, a ratchet handle and plunger behind his head. A flashing beacon he could turn on from inside. A through-water speaker, which he wouldn't need on this dive. He wiggled all the joints. They seemed to move okay, neither too much nor too little resistance.

"Okay, let's read gauges." He pulled his chin in and frowned down at the bank of meters and lights and switches at tit level. "Left to right."

"Main oxygen feed cylinder twenty-ten psi. Standby cylinder twenty-four-fifty. Oxygen select set to twenty-one percent. Suit pressure reads sixteen; exterior pressure looks like about thirty-two. Air cylinder three thousand psi."

"Switches. Top to bottom."

They always did gauges and switches in the same order, in case he had to operate them in the dark. "Main power on, scrubber on, comms on, transducer off, beacon off, pinger off, internal light off, controllers on, heater off, pumps on, thrusters off, external lights off."

That was it except for the thrusters. He tested the servos that rotated them, then turned them on and ran the pitch from plus to minus and back. The motors were controlled by foot switches. The Brute weighed almost nine hundred pounds on deck, including the operator, but only about sixty in the water. He could walk, albeit clumsily, when he was on the bottom, and in midwater he could drive the suit around with the thrusters. "Thrusters and servos check out. Thruster switch off."

"Lee says to turn on your interior light now. Then you won't dazzle when you turn it on and it's dark."

"Roger." The little bulb came on behind and above his shoulder. He adjusted the rheostat till he could see both the panel and the sea outside. "Uh, before we go, anything new on that low-pressure area?"

It was just getting into peak hurricane season, and the

Weather Service was monitoring a tropical depression off Puerto Rico pretty hard. Boudreaux growled, "Don't sweat it. It's way down south, they'll tell us in plenty of time if it heads our way. Ready in the suit?"

"Let's fly."

"Lowering away."

He couldn't feel himself descending. Lee had hydraulic take-ups on the davits and reels to damp out the motion of the boat. The only way he could tell was that occasionally he could see small life-forms in the clear water, flowing, it seemed to him, upward. That and the steady darkening of the sea were the only clues that he was descending.

The job today was inspection. They were out in South Pandora, near 1000. His job was to locate and inspect the pipeline between Pandora 1000 and one of the wells originally drilled by Met Sulphur, P-1220. They would live-boat it while he reported his findings to Boudreaux. Essentially, he'd be towed along, eyeballing and occasionally touchie-feelieing the line.

Even in shallow water, live-boating was riskier than platform or barge diving. You had to have good comms with the boat and keep your umbilical clear of the screws. This deep, the trickiest problem was positioning. Though the diver could make small adjustments on his own, basically the boat had to tow him where he needed to go. Lee had assured him it wouldn't be a problem. The Brute had a pinger that *Janis J* could track in range and bearing.

The light was fading fast now. He glanced at the pressure gauge; 230 feet. He switched the interior light off for just a second to gaze out into a deep Prussian blue.

But where he was going, there'd be no light at all. Had never been, not since the creation of the world. . . .

The thought of endless night brought Arden back again, night-haired, her lips coolly willing to his probing tongue. He still didn't understand why he hadn't gone through with it. More than once, he'd cursed himself for a fool—especially since Boudreaux suspected him anyway. But she'd relighted a fire that had been out for a while. He didn't kid himself. It wasn't love. He didn't dream about her face.

223

He flinched as her husband's voice broke in. "Should be seein' the riser pretty soon."

He cleared his throat. "Roger, watching for it."

He turned the interior light back on and checked the panel. Everything okay. Next, he checked himself. Thermal underwear, cotton sweat gear, heavy socks, and sneakers were the uniform for one-atmosphere suits. The cotton gave you absorbency, and insulation in case the heaters failed. Could save you a bruise if you busted a snubber line and got banged against the hull.

It was strange being this deep and breathing air, being able to talk in a normal voice. He felt funny, as if he wasn't really diving.

The best thing about it was the pay. A dollar a foot. He felt better as he added it up. Who needed a union? McCray talked about protection. Bullshit! All it meant was that another piece of your income went to somebody else. He couldn't see people like Porch and Ace and himself in some union hall, raising their hands meekly to vote.

When he flicked the interior light off again, there was nothing outside but black. He fumbled down the switches, found the last one, clicked it over. The outside lights came on, one on either side of his head, brilliant blue-white halogen beams. Found the control switches with his feet. The motors whined like dentist's drills as he drove the suit around.

"Riser in sight."

"You got it?"

"Looking right at it. Can see the leg off to the side. Hey, they got some tubeworms, some kind of growth here. Kind of pretty."

"Uh-huh." Boudreaux didn't sound like he wanted descriptions of marine life. "You clear of it? We lower away any faster?"

"Sure, take this elevator down."

A little jostling, all but imperceptible. He was impressed. Not a bad way to go to work, he thought.

Dr. Lee came on the line and they went over emergency procedures again. What he'd do in case of comm failure, CO_2 buildup, abnormal oxygen levels, a parted umbilical. When Lee signed off, Boudreaux must have been waiting; he came right on. "Diver, topside. Give me a pneumo."

224

"Don't have a pneumo on the Brute, Roland. Want a depth reading?"

"Yeah, a depth reading. I got to spell everything out for you?"

"Just keeping you on your toes."

"You're the one better stay on your toes, Galloway."

"Passing a thousand and seventy-five."

"See the bottom yet?"

"Just a sec. Can't aim these lights down. No, no bottom."

"Paying out, paying out . . . depth."

"Eleven hundred five."

"No bottom?"

"Not yet."

He saw the bottom just as he crashed into it. The knee joints flexed. He felt the halfhearted, treacherous resistance of soft mud. He was also starting to feel cold. The Brute's glass-reinforced plastic didn't suck heat out of the diver as fast as the cast magnesium or aluminum of the older suits. But given time, the eternal cold of the deep still penetrated.

"Time thirty," Boudreaux's voice said in his ear. Tiller grunted. Every half hour, Lee wanted all gauge readings entered in the dive log, just in case something went wrong. He started reading them out. When he came to the switch positions, he flicked the heater on.

"Any sign of the line?"

"Uh, wait one." He peered out of the left and right view ports. The backwash of the external lights showed him the sea bottom stretching away. It had the same faint rippling he'd noticed during the lay of the transmission line. These were farther apart, four to five feet. They made weird shadows. A movement caught his eye at the edge of his lights. He remembered the congers. He wasn't real familiar with what lived down here. Nothing dangerous, he was pretty sure. Especially to the armored monster he was now.

"Moving left," he said. Should be close to the riser. And thus, to the line. He started picking up his feet and putting them down. He moved, but slowly. The caramel mud sucked at his boots. The suit still had almost half a ton of mass, with him in it. Once it got going, it wanted to keep going.

A humped ridge in his work lights, cutting across the drifts. "Think I got it."

"You there yet?"

"Not far. Almost."

He slowed as he approached, finally stepping up on the pipe. He teetered, corrected too fast, and the suit finished it for him. He tumbled off in slow motion and sat down in the yielding mud.

"Darn."

"Got a problem?"

"Lost my balance." He struggled around for a while, like a nine-month-old trying to stand. He could ask them to take up on the hoist line, but he wanted to see how maneuverable he was. Finally, he rolled prone and did a sort of push-up. The claws scraped on the concrete as he levered himself to his feet. He balanced there, puffing from the effort.

"You okay?"

"Yeah." He blew a few more times, flushing the CO_2 out of his lungs. "Thought I might be able to walk the line, but don't look like it's gonna work."

"How's visibility?"

"Good. Thirty, forty feet."

Boudreaux sounded bored. He ought to be down here, Tiller thought. He was sweating. This wasn't a bad way to dive, but it was hard to forget you were clamped into a rigid shell, unable to get out by yourself. Hard to forget you were a quarter of a mile down.

"Hey, Roland, can Lee hear me? Who's got the wheel?"

"Ha."

"Bring me up ten feet. Then tell him to head out along about two-nine-five. Make it two knots, or slower, if he can maintain a heading. I'm going to try these thrusters."

He waited, looking around, till he felt his feet suck free of the mud. As soon as he left bottom, the current started blowing him off to the north. He pivoted the props and cut them on. The suit stayed canted, but he was able to motor back toward the line. Then, as he reached it, he started moving forward, along it.

"How's that? You tracking, cher?"

"Come right about five degrees. And slow down, Jesus! There, that was number thirty-nine going by. Everything looks solid so far."

"Check, joint thirty-nine."

You kept track of yourself on a line inspection by the field joints. Spaced every forty feet, the thin, rusty joint covers all pointed in the same direction. He sweated, zigging back and forth across the pipeline as he fought to balance prop thrust, current, and the tug and drag of the umbilical. "Forty-one . . . forty-two."

Struggling with the controls, he suddenly realized that this was diving, too. Maybe not skin-to-skin with the sea, but he was soaked all the same. He blinked sweat out of his eyes, trying to concentrate.

He drove along the line for the next three hours. It was tough for a while, then he got the hang of it all at once. Or maybe Ha, on the wheel, had finally figured out what he was trying to do. Anyway, he was moving. Driving down the half-buried eighteen-inch line like a semi rolling down an empty highway. A hundred and thirty joints a mile. It would be a long day. But for twelve hundred bucks, he told himself grimly, I can stick it out.

It started around joint 325. There'd been cracks here and there up till then, minor faults, missing zincs, and he'd reported them. Boudreaux had said, "Uh-huh, uh-huh. Aw right. Keep going." The tape unrolled its steady beep.

Then, all at once, there it was. Couldn't tell what had caused it, maybe damage when it was laid, invisible then. Or a flaw in the manufacture. His voice echoed in the helmet, too loud. "Pipeline damage!"

The intercom answered in Lee's voice. "What?"

"Put Bender on. Listen up, topside! Major damage. Joint three twenty-five, three twenty-six."

"Hold on a second. Okay. What you got down there?" The boss's voice asked.

"We got damage. Joints three twenty-five, three twenty-six, three twenty-seven. Tell Ha, stop the engines. I gotta check this out." He worked the foot controls and the Brute, still drag-

227

ging along behind the boat, pushed by its own and the cable's inertia, began to rotate sluggishly.

"What's going on down there?"

"Weight coating's cracked away, Roland." He licked his lips to make his voice a little less raw. The drinking water was long gone. "Big gaps. Three-foot, four-foot chunks lying on the bottom. I see dope coating. I see naked steel. I see corrosion."

His forward progress ebbed. He wheeled in a huge lazy pendulum through the black. Finally he got the suit pointed the other way. "Ha, back down. Right down your wake, okay?"

"Ha, off the phones. Off the line!"

He got his lights focused, nudged the motors left, right. "Okay, let's check this out," he muttered.

"Galloway."

"Yeah." He was almost on. There! "Back on it," he said.

"Back on what?"

"The busted sections. Looks like about three, four sections bad here. Maybe a kink while they were layin' it. It's busted up bad."

"Listen up, Galloway. *Listen to me.* We're gonna go back over those sections, hear? We're gonna do them over again, cher."

"Okay."

"An' this time, I don't want to hear nothing about any busted-off chunks. Hear me? Cracks is okay. But none of this stuff about weight coating comin' off."

Tiller leaned his knotted forehead against the inside of the helmet. "What are you telling me, Roland?"

"How much plainer I gotta explain it? You didn't see any damage. It's just like the rest of this line."

"But it isn't."

"For the last time! I'm gonna run you back over that section. And I'm gonna be listening to you. Understand me?"

He grunted. It was starting to come through. May be stupid, he thought. But I ain't dumb.

Boudreaux was ordering him to lie.

As they swept backward over the damaged portion of the line, he got a better look at the curved sections of concrete coating that had cracked off, at the rust eating through the old dope coating. The steel beneath it was tough, but nothing ferrous could resist the sea for long. Not when it was unprotected, exposed.

Kind of like he felt right now.

Okay, think, he told himself. In a few minutes, you're gonna reinspect this line. What are you gonna say? Well, what *could* he say? "Uh, Roland?"

"What?"

"What's the story here, man? I'm not sure I understand what's going on in your head."

"*Fait rien*, what's going on in my head. It's what's going on down there."

"What's going on down here is that I'm looking at a major pipeline failure, and you're tellin' me I don't see what's in front of my frigging faceplate."

"Lemme put it this way. Who's payin' for this inspection?"

"The owners, I guess. Coastal."

"Who owns the pipeline?"

"Coastal."

"Who gets their ass in a crack if it leaks?"

"Shattuck, I guess. What you want me to say? But we're inspecting it. If it craps out and leaks, it's DeepTech's—"

"Wrong. It's Coastal's problem. And Coastal's accepting the risk. Just like you're takin' a risk right now, to make a very . . . nice . . . paycheck."

"I get the message." Galloway felt as if it was starting to make sense. What Claunch and Shad had warned him was wrong with DeepTech. What Boudreaux had hinted at. And some things he'd started to notice himself, like using live guys instead of machines. Because live guys were cheaper, and to hell with the risk. Because machines couldn't be bribed or forced to lie.

"Hey, Roland. This is paying off pretty good for you, isn't it? This little arrangement between you and Shattuck?"

"It pays. Sure."

"I don't get it, though. How? Why's he want to cover up his own crappy pipeline?"

"You don't need to know that, Galloway. You done shit like this before, right? You ain't no angel. All you need is, do what I tell you."

"But I don't buy it, Roland. I mean, I see what *you* mean, and you may be right, but I don't buy it."

"You don't got no choice, cher. Turn around," Boudreaux's voice came down. He didn't sound like he wanted to discuss it anymore. "Ha's getting ready to go back."

Okay, here we are, he told himself. Stuffed into a can and dangling on the end of a power cord a thousand feet down. Time to do some fast thinking.

Say you tell Bender to hump himself. What's the worst can happen? He drops you and pulls the plug. Can you make it back to the surface? He glanced up at the ratchet handle that released the umbilical, then down at the matching handles near his waist that dropped the forward and aft weights. It would depend on how the umbilical came down. If it fell on top of him, he wouldn't make it. A thousand feet of cable was just too heavy, even if he dropped his weights.

If it fell clear, he might be able to dump the umbilical and weights. In that case, he'd make it to the surface.

But then what? Would Lee pick him up? Was he in on this, too? He was too far from the platform to make it back before he ran out of air—assuming he could find it. No power for the thrusters. Could he swim in this thing? He doubted it. Was there any way he could get out of it by himself? He mouthed the water bottle before he remembered it was empty.

He wished suddenly, desperately, that Shad had stayed. That his partner was up there tending for him.

"Hey, Roland."

"Hey what?"

"Is Dr. Lee on there? Lemme talk to G.Q."

"Forget it. He's busy."

Silence. "Boudreaux," he hissed.

"Yo, cher. You all alone down there, my friend. And now you coming up on where we made our little mistake before, no?"

He was sliding smoothly along the line. The lights illuminated it ahead of him, coming endlessly out of the night. He'd hit the flawed section pretty soon. Had to decide by then.

The trouble was, he didn't know what was going down. He had part of it figured out, but only part. Something else made him even more uneasy. Boudreaux suspected him of screwing around with Arden. So far, he'd just played dumb, ignored his digs. But what had his wife told him? Could she have told him they'd gone to bed? Taunted him with it?

It was a great setup for murder. Dangling like a plastic yo-yo on a quarter-mile string. Bolted into a hull he couldn't get out of alone. Dependent on the surface for power and light. No water, and only a few hours of oxygen. He could just see Boudreaux's shrug. *Dunno what happened, cher. He just never come up.*

Suddenly there it was, for the second time. Looming out of the black ahead, sweeping toward him: destruction, failure, possible disaster.

Boudreaux's voice, bullying, triumphant: "How's it look down there?"

Through a larynx constricted by anger and fear, he heard himself snarl, "Joint three twenty-five. Looking . . . good."

"Say again? Didn't catch that, friend."

"I said, three twenty-five, looking good. Goddamn you!"

"Three twenty-six?"

"Some—minor cracking." He swept forward over the damaged section, then, almost miraculously, there was smooth concrete again. "Three twenty-seven . . . three twenty-eight . . . good pipe down here. You asshole!"

"You doing nice work, Tiller. Run your mouth too much. But aside from that, you doing good. You know, I think you find a bonus in your envelope for this."

"Screw the bonus. Screw you, too. I want to talk to Shattuck."

"And he will be glad to talk to you, I guarantee. But remember, I'm running the tape, cher."

Christ, the tape. He felt suddenly dizzy as he remembered Boudreaux was recording all this from topside. No problem to back the cassette up, record over his earlier protests.

Until all they had was Tiller Galloway's voice saying, "Joint three twenty-five, looking good."

"Shit," he muttered.

For the rest of the inspection, he tried to calm himself by counting the money he was making. It was a nice chunk of change. The false report? Hey, Bender had you by the short hairs. You didn't have a choice.

But why had he picked him in the first place?

Galloway knew the answer to that one at least. It didn't make him feel any better.

Boudreaux and Shattuck had picked him because they figured he'd go along with whatever they had in mind. Just like anybody else would figure, looking at his record and talking to people who knew him from the old days.

Grinding his teeth, he steered along a road that appeared moment by moment ahead of him out of blackness, and disappeared into blackness astern.

TWENTY-THREE

A**ll during the hoist he nursed a cold anger. But he kept his silence, answering in clipped syllables when Boudreaux asked for data. He waited patiently, swinging beneath the boat at thirty feet, staring up. A bloom of bubbles, a form twisting swiftly toward him, trailing a line. Ha's face peered into his faceplate. A clack as the snubbing line snapped into the back of his suit, and the Korean mate was gone, clawing his way back toward the quicksilver surface.

When he was swung aboard, Lee and Ha moved busily around him, unbolting and lifting off the thruster unit, the fore and aft weight sets. Finally came a grinding as the suit hatch bolts turned.

He wriggled out into air that felt cool even though he knew the day was hot. He pushed wet hair back and gasped, "Water." Ha handed him an iced tea and he lifted it, draining it in one draft. Then he crushed it with a single savage contraction of his fist and tossed it overboard.

"Where's Boudreaux?"

"On the bridge."

"You know about this shit they're pulling, G.Q.? Are you part of this?"

Lee looked politely puzzled. Tiller yanked his socks off, stripped the soaking-wet sweatshirt over his head, and went striding forward. His heels made rapid thumps on the deck.

The Cajun was straddling the rolling deck of the flying bridge, the microphone of the VHF to his lips. He saw Tiller coming and his eyes widened. He dropped the mike as Galloway grabbed his shirt with his left hand and hit him with every ounce of strength he had left.

Boudreaux reeled away, covering instinctively. "Goddamn! Wait a second—what are you—"

He ended on an explosive wheeze as Tiller placed a left just above his belt. But it wasn't soft, like he'd expected. It was all muscle, and the big Cajun blocked the next right.

The next thing Tiller saw was one hell of a fireworks display. He grunted, dropping back, shaking his head to clear it. Boudreaux bulled in, landing two more shots before Galloway saw an opening and threw a jab through it. Boudreaux's head snapped up. The boat rolled just then and he staggered backward and into Lee's arms.

At the same instant, Tiller felt someone behind him grab both shoulders in a full nelson. But the man behind him was smaller than he was. He could break it. But as soon as he tried, the full nelson became a choke hold.

The pilothouse went dim. He lurched forward, trying to detach the technician that way, and failed. Then he slammed him back against the bulkhead. The arms let go. He staggered back toward Boudreaux, but Ha was suddenly there again, hands raised in some kind of martial-arts stance.

"Okay," he said. "Okay! Goddamn it, all I want's Boudreaux! I don't want you!"

"We don't want you, either, Tiller." Dr. Lee was still holding the panting dive boss. "But we don't do this aboard my vessel. I forbid it. Do you understand? Roland, do you understand?"

Boudreaux ducked his head, glaring. Blood made a catsup trickle down his chin. "You're bourréed, Galloway. Hear me? Finished. Never work the Patch again."

"Nobody holds a knife to my throat and walks away. I want answers, or I'm going to the Coast Guard.

"You'll get answers. Shattuck wants to talk to you. He's at Twelve, with West. First thing tomorrow—"

"No. Today." He told Lee, "We're going back to Pandora Twelve."

"We have another section to check."

"No we don't. I'm not climbing back into that thing until

I talk to the company man about what I'm seeing down there. And about Mr. Roland 'Bender' Boudreaux."

"You prick! I'm going to cut your balls off and feed them to the sharks!"

He lunged, but Ha was between them again, glancing from one to the other. Tiller stopped. So did Boudreaux.

"Wise," said Lee. "Very wise. Now, here is how we will proceed. Galloway refuses to dive again. I do not know why, but there it is. We cannot proceed without him; therefore, we must return to Pandora Twelve, as he demands. Galloway, you will go below. Mr. Boudreaux, you will go aft. If either of you refuses, I will, most reluctantly, order Ha to break his arm."

The familiar outline of Pandora Twelve loomed up out of the choppy, oily-looking sea. After the concrete iceberg of 1000, it looked small and spindly, almost antique. Below it was the equally familiar silhouette of the jet barge. Tiller watched them approach from a porthole in the galley. The surface of his iced coffee trembled, then took on an angle as the big Davis eased into a turn.

Okay, he thought. Now we'll get to the bottom of this. He still felt angry. He still felt cold.

He'd been groping around in the dark long enough.

Lee appeared in the companionway. "Tiller? We're here."

"Great."

"Can I trust you now to behave yourself with Roland? Very good. I'll drop you off at the cage. I will then clear the stage and lay off until I receive orders over channel thirty-two."

"Fine."

Lee disappeared. Tiller finished the coffee and went up on deck.

He and Boudreaux rode up in the cage side by side, not speaking. Looking down, he could see a chamber on the deck of the barge. Not the big one, the one they'd lived in for days. This was one of the twelve-foot recompression chambers. He wondered who was over there.

For some reason, he'd hoped to see Hannah when he stepped off at the cellar deck, but she wasn't there. Gassy was, though. He was wearing the exact same plaid shirt he'd worn the first time Tiller had met him, weeks before. Boudreaux asked him whether he'd seen Mr. Shattuck. He told them yeah, he was in the tool pusher's office.

Tiller started that way, then turned back. "Hey, Gassy."

"What?"

"What's the word on the low-pressure area?"

"It's a o-fficial hurricane now. But we don't gotta worry. It turned north. They think it's gonna hit south Florida someplace."

"Thanks." He gave the guy a half wave and followed Boudreaux's broad back up the ladder.

Shattuck looked up from behind Hannah's desk as they filed in. He was in a gray suit today. He didn't get up. Didn't invite them to sit. Just sat back in the chair. It creaked slightly. Tiller looked around but didn't see West.

"I asked her to step out while we talked," Shattuck murmured, noticing his glance. "Shut the door, please. Now, what's the problem? You have a contract date to meet, Roland. What's the holdup?"

"Galloway wants to talk to you. He don't like what he's bein' asked to do out on P-Twelve-twenty."

"Very well." The blond man steepled his hands, tilting his head as if listening for a faraway sound. "He's your employee, but if you can't handle him . . . Proceed, Mr. Galloway. What were you asked to do that you object to so much?"

Tiller told him. Brad Shattuck swiveled his chair as he listened, looking up at a copy of the same chart of the Pandora complex that Tiller had seen in Boudreaux's office. The owner of DeepTech leaned against the bulkhead. His nose had stopped bleeding, but Tiller was happy to see bruises blooming under his eyes.

"So, when I got to the surface, I refused to dive again till I could talk to you. I thought it was the kind of thing that, if you didn't know about, you should. And that if you did know about it, if you ordered it—well, then I'd ask why."

Shattuck waited.

"That's all," he added, a little at a loss. He stuck his hands in his pockets, found none in the sweatsuit trousers, then crossed them on his bare chest.

Shattuck swiveled away and glanced at his watch. Then he spoke, so softly that Tiller almost missed what he said.

"Galloway, do you have any idea how much Coastal has invested out here since we took over from Unocal and Met Sulphur?"

"No."

"Nearly nine hundred million dollars. Do you know how much of that went to DeepTech, for work performed? Pipe-laying inspections, platform inspections and repairs, undersea wellhead and riser installation and repairs, cleaning, connection, miscellaneous work at depth?"

He felt sweat between his shoulder blades. "No. How much?"

"How much, Roland?"

Boudreaux grunted, "Try twenty-one million bucks. Sixty percent of my gross last year."

"That's a lot."

Shattuck, still looking away: "Who requires that offshore producing equipment be inspected, Galloway? Do you know?"

"The Coast Guard?"

"Platforms, yes. But what about submerged production gear? Pipelines?"

"The federal government. MMS. EPA. Department of Transportation."

"No."

"No?"

"That's what I said."

"Well . . . isn't there some state agency—"

"In Louisiana? One more try."

Galloway thought hard. "I don't know. Who?"

"The answer is, no one. In point of fact, there *is* no requirement that offshore production facilities be inspected— other than the structural safety of the platforms themselves. That's *all*. MMS auctions the leases. After that, we operate unsupervised, unless there's some obvious major problem. Like a *big* fire."

"Okay. But then—"

"But then, why did I hire DeepTech to inspect? That what you were about to ask?"

"I guess so, yeah."

"That's obvious. I did it to establish the status of my pipeline."

"All right."

"Do you understand that, Tiller?"

"Yes."

"No, you don't." Shattuck got up and came around the desk toward him. Tiller stared into eyes blue as water frozen around a central well of utter darkness. "You don't understand a thing. What's wrong with your face?"

"Boudreaux."

"Bender?"

"He threw the first one."

"That true, Killer?"

He didn't go by that anymore, but he let it pass. "I don't like being tricked. I don't like being lied to!"

"That's enough," said Shattuck, and Tiller found his mouth closing despite himself. "I'll address that in a moment. First, let's get straight how things stand around here."

The vice president of Coastal Oil stood in front of the chart. Suddenly, Galloway saw the briefing officer again. Looking up at it, he said in a dry voice, "Met Sulphur laid the feeder lines in the One Thousand field practically overnight back during the oil embargo. No grading on the gullies. Inexpensive light pipe. They didn't plan to build for the ages. They expected to start pumping right away.

"Then the bottom fell out of the market. They were abandoned. Some of them, salt water leaked in. We've found dozens of cracks, flaws, and pressure drops in the lines between Pandora One Thousand and the satellite wells. But that's not your concern, is it?"

"Let me hear the rest. Then I'll decide."

"I wasn't asking for your blessing. But let me go on. I know about them, but I'm not going to waste time and money fixing them. They're too deep. It would be prohibitively expensive. My solution? I keep pumping. Meanwhile, I lay new lines. As they're finished, we switch over, take the old lines out of service. End of problem."

"You mean, you pay Roland not to report them."

"Oh, but you are wrong, cher," said Boudreaux. "I don't take payoffs. I don't work that way."

"Maybe not money. But you accept work."

"An' I do it. Fair and square. Just like he's telling you now."

Tiller cleared his throat. "But what if the old lines start to leak? Then what?"

Shattuck said, "That's a risk I have to accept. Actually, the probability's overwhelming they won't. Oxygen's scarce that deep. Corrosion will be minimal."

"I saw rust."

"There's a hydroid that looks very much like rust. Was it corrosion you saw? Or marine growth?"

"Wait a minute."

Shattuck said coolly, "No, *you* wait, Galloway. I'm putting major investment out here. After a hell of a long drought in offshore development. Trying to make America energy-independent again. Of course, I have to protect that investment in every way I can. Who's the best judge of whether a line's serviceable? I say it's the man who has to take the consequences if he makes a bad call."

Boudreaux said, from the wall, "I built DeepTech on service to the customer, cher. Mr. Shattuck's getting what he wants. You think this is, what, illegal? Ask a lawyer. They'll laugh at you."

Galloway felt bewildered. "Then why inspect the friggin' line at all? Why not just leave it—"

Boudreaux muttered, "You ain't figured it yet, dickhead, have you? You gotta talk to this guy one-syllable words, boss. It's for insurance. So if there *is* a leak, Mr. Shattuck can say, hey, the line was inspected, we don't know why there was a leak there. Then it ain't his fault, the insurance company antes up."

"He can say that after a leak?"

"Sure, why not?" Boudreaux grinned. "He'll have our report, sayin' it was okay as of such and such a date. And we got the tape, right from the man on the spot, to prove it."

He stood wordless. They were convincing, all right—especially Shattuck. You had to take risks in business. It was true in diving; it had to be true in oil.

He was on the verge of shrugging, saying okay, when he suddenly remembered what the old man, Ravenel, had told him. "What about the fisheries? There's a spill, it could wipe them out."

Boudreaux guffawed. "You're worried about the *fish*?"

"You ought to be," Tiller told him.

Shattuck sat again, taking back the conversation from Boudreaux like a boat captain taking the helm back from a clumsy mate. "It's not a credible failure scenario. Even if a line snapped in two, catastrophic rupture, it'd only be a few hundred barrels before West saw the pressure drop and shut down the wellhead. Not enough to hurt a flounder."

"Yeah, what about her? Does old Hannah know? She doesn't seem to be the kind that'd go along with this."

Shattuck shrugged. "There's no need for her to know."

"Doesn't that strike you as kind of underhanded? That if it's all so acceptable, it's got to be secret?"

The oilman sighed and cocked his head again, that same listening posture. "Bender, haven't you explained anything to him? Galloway, DeepTech's hourly scales are higher than the other diving companies'. You've noticed that."

"Yeah."

"And Roland only hires experienced men. Ever wonder why?"

"I thought they went together."

"Only up to a point. But I'll tell you why I think he hires people like you. It's so he can take on sensitive work and have his people treat it as privileged communication. Like an attorney-client relationship. That make sense? An individual's got a right to privacy. Doesn't a company have that same right?"

When he didn't respond, Shattuck leaned back again. "By the way. Speaking of pay scales. What did Hohmann hire you at? Didn't you hire him as a two, Roland?"

"No. He's a diver three." Boudreaux stared at Galloway, touching his lip.

"Well, that was obviously a mistake. He did a great job on the transmission line, didn't he? And now he's doing atmospheric diving, too," Shattuck prompted.

Boudreaux said reluctantly, "Got any objections to being a diver two, Galloway?"

He shrugged.

Shattuck adjusted his glasses. "I think we're close to having this straightened out. Let's review it and reach a conclusion. You saw something out of the ordinary going on. You decided to check it out with the customer. You brought it to me and I explained the situation." He picked up a mechanical pencil and screwed the point in and out and then put it down. Galloway noticed the ring again. "Now it's up to you. Accept that as part of the job."

He glanced up. "Or you can decline to participate."

"Yeah," said Boudreaux. "You want out? We can do that, too. Fly you ashore. Cut you back pay an' wave good-bye."

"Well—"

"Is that what you're saying, Galloway?"

He decided then. He needed this job. "No," he said.

"No, you're out, or no, that's not what you're saying?"

"No, that's not what I was saying."

"I didn't think so." The voice went brisk, dismissive. "Well, now we understand each other. Can we all go back to work now?"

"Not with him," Tiller said. He cocked a thumb at Boudreaux but looked steadily at Shattuck. Okay, he thought, let's toss this grenade and see what happens. "He thinks somebody's dicking his wife."

He had to admire the oilman's self-control. The only sign of tension was a faint deepening of the creases around his eyes. All Shattuck said, very quietly, was "Is that right? With Arden? Who?"

"You little shit—"

"Me," said Tiller. He kept his eyes on Shattuck. "It ain't true. That it's me, anyway. But I don't trust him on my hose. I want somebody else supervising."

"You're out of here, Galloway. That's it. You're fired, asshole."

"Then you better get ready to explain it all again to the Coast Guard, Roland. Or is it MMS that might be interested?"

Shattuck said crisply, decisively, "Look, I don't want to be bothered with this, Roland. You decide. Fire him if you like. He's your employee. But he's right. You shouldn't be diving and you shouldn't be supervising. I've told you that already. You're not a diver anymore. You're an executive, and you ought to start executing."

"I'll tell you who I want," said Tiller. "It may surprise you, but—"

He stopped, cut off by the wail of a siren. At the same moment, the rig phone started buzzing and kept on till Shattuck jerked it off the wall. "Yeah," he said. "Yeah. What? Fire? In the chamber?"

Boudreaux jumped up. Tiller spun and followed him out at a run.

B y the time they got down to the barge, the siren had stopped. So had the smoke. A plum brown plume of it was drifting slowly up on the hot air, expanding into a tenuous pall. As Boudreaux rounded the gangplank, Tiller swung over the life rail, gaining a few feet on him, and ran toward the diving area.

Winslow was there, Porch, and Ace, and a gaggle of men he didn't know, probably barge crew. He pushed through them to the rack box. "What's going on, Wildman?"

"Fire in the chamber."

"What happened?" Tiller put his hands around the port-hole to shut out the sun. He couldn't see much, just swirling darkness. Like thousands of eels . . .

"Heard a kind of thud. Looked in, he was fighting a ball of fire."

"Jesus. A flasher." The worst kind; he'd been hoping for a slow burn, insulation on a wire or something. Inhaling smoke under pressure wasn't exactly healthy, but if you got to an ox-ygen mask and flooded the chamber with extinguishing agent, you had a good chance of making it. But from what Winslow said, this was a flash fire.

Boudreaux panted up. "How'd it happen?" he asked, cup-ping the porthole and looking in, exactly as Galloway had.

"I don't know, Roland."

"Who's in there?"

"The Captain."

"And?"

"Just McCray. He said his knees hurt. So we pressed him back down."

"Alone? You pressed him down alone?"

"I wanted out," Porchellacchia said. He looked shaken. "I didn't feel like stayin' in there, go alla way back down and up again. These twelve-footers are too small for a guy my size. I didn't know it was going to—Christ. I didn't know there was gonna be a fire."

"Take it easy," said Boudreaux. "Everybody just take it easy."

Tiller had been thinking it through. At usual storage depths for saturation diving, the concentration of oxygen was too low to support combustion. "What depth was he at, Wildman?"

Winslow glanced at a clipboard. "Sixty feet."

"What was the oxygen percentage?"

"Ten percent."

"That won't support much of a fire. Or else there's more than ten percent in there."

"Then he'd be into toxicity. What are you saying? That I burned him?"

"Maybe not you, Wildman. But somebody did."

"Bullshit," said Boudreaux. "Derick, did he have a mask on? That would give you enough oxygen to support a fire."

"A mask? I don't remember. It was a big ball of fire, I'll tell you that. Like it was sitting in his lap."

"Okay, that's it," shouted West, coming around the chamber. "I got the captain calling a chopper, getting them on the line at Jo Ellen Smith Hospital. Bender, what happened?"

"Flash fire. Winslow looked in and there it was."

"What'd you do then, Derick?"

"Secured power. Then yelled my head off. Porch went for the phone."

Boudreaux said, "I'll handle this, Hannah. Winslow, you should have isolated the system. You—"

"I was doing that while I was yellin'. Shut down the gas lines, mask oxygen. Then I hit the extinguisher-system toggle."

"And?"

"Nothing. I didn't hear it go off. So I started dumping helium in."

"What have you got in there now?"

"Uh, gauge reads—seventy feet of pressure. Two percent oxygen."

Tiller was getting impatient. "Look, we got to get him out. Now. He'll suffocate, even if the smoke doesn't get him."

Boudreaux said, "You're right. Vent it, Winslow. We're going in."

"He's not done decompressing."

"We'll worry about that when we make sure he's breathing."

"Watch yourself. It might reflash," said West.

Tiller went for the lock. He shoved the barge crew away, cursing them till they backed off. There was a high, loud blast of expanding gas as Winslow blew the chamber down to sea level. Then a clank. "Atmospheric," Porchellacchia shouted. "Tiller! Take a mask!"

He didn't answer. He hauled the hatch open and scrambled in, bent double, then slammed it shut behind him.

The interior was filled with swirling brown haze. It felt clammy, and cold and hot at the same time. The sudden drop in pressure turned all the humidity into mist. The depleted atmosphere made his lungs pump faster, but the smoke was choking him. Somebody started to open the hatch again, behind him. He shouted, "Close that goddamn hatch! You let air in here, it'll reflash!" Whoever they were, they slammed it again hastily.

Small as the cylinder was, he ran into McCray before he saw him. Just a soft thing that crackled when he lifted an arm. It didn't move at all. Tiller staggered. He was panting, but there wasn't enough oxygen in what he was breathing to keep a mouse alive.

He gave up trying to see what had happened and just slung McCray over his shoulder and crawled for the hatch. He knew halfway there, he wasn't going to make it. Everything got red and black, started to spin. Then whoever had cracked the hatch before did it again. He saw light and got a sniff of air and shoved McCray out ahead of him like a sack of oats.

He rested for a second, gasping and coughing, then stuck his hand out and two or three arms came in and pulled him out, too. They carried him to a bench and set him down on it as he coughed and coughed and coughed. Then somebody put something over his face. After a startled second, he realized what it was and took five or six deep lungfuls.

When he got steadied down, he pushed the oxygen mask away. "I'm okay," he said to Porchellacchia. The Pagan's face swung to follow him as he got up and staggered across the deck to where the medics were bending over something that didn't move.

"Lemme see."

They looked at him, startled, then at each other. One said, "He ain't pretty."

"Lemme see."

When they pulled the mask off, Tiller stared for a second or two. Then turned and went back to the bench.

Porchellacchia had the pail ready when he bent over.

When he sat up again, faint but feeling better, at least in his stomach, Rodriquez was crawling out of the chamber. "What's it look like?" Boudreaux asked him.

"The Bibb mask's hanging down. All burned and melted, but it was down. The extinguishing flood handle's jammed. Like halfway between the on and off position."

"You think he pulled it?"

"Maybe, but kind of half-assed. Just enough so Wildman couldn't dump it from outside. He probably panicked."

"What?" Tiller couldn't believe what he was hearing. "What're you sayin', Ace? You saying it was his own fault?"

"Hey, everybody knows the guy was a squirrel. First thing you or me would think of, grab a mask, then hit the extinguisher flood. He probably tried to do 'em both at once and didn't do either right."

"Jay McCray was no squirrel. Anything but. What about the fire? Did he start the fire, too?"

Rodriquez put his hands out, palms up. "Calm down, man. Maybe the handle got jammed accidental, you know? I'm just tellin' you what I saw, man."

Boudreaux said, "We're all sorry, but it don't help to start accusing people, Galloway."

He fell silent and watched the medics. One of them went over to West and said something in a low voice. She nodded, looking somber. Boudreaux and Rodriquez crossed themselves. Winslow bent his head, glancing around from under his eyebrows.

Tiller felt sick again. But his stomach was empty. Maybe water would help. There was a bubbler inside the dive shack.

But as he stood, something fell out of his sweatpants. It had been caught in the waistband. Something small and black. He frowned down at it, lying there on the boot-marked, muddy, wet deck. Then he went down on one knee, frowning as he focused on it.

245

He looked around to see whether anybody was watching. They weren't.

When his fingers closed on it, it disintegrated into a smudge of fine black powder, leaving him with nothing but the visual memory of a torn corner of what had once been pasteboard. And on it, like the reversal of a negative, the faint tracings of letters.

The letters had spelled UNITED BROTHERHO before ending suddenly at a crumbling edge.

TWENTY-FOUR

He was down in the Brute Suit on the deepest dive of all, looking at a yellow smiley-face sticker someone had pasted on his tit panel, when the power failed. The lights went out. The thrusters whirred to a halt. He stamped on the controls, but nothing happened. He shouted into the intercom. No answer.

He slammed the main power switch off and then on again. Still nothing but black silence. What was going on? Had the generator on *Janis J* gone down? Now he remembered where he'd seen that smiley face before. He'd noticed one stuck on the overhead of the Sikorsky, just before it crashed. Who had he seen carrying those stickers around? Lee? Boudreaux? Rodriquez? Shattuck?

He realized suddenly that while he was wondering about stickers, he was tumbling end over end toward the bottom. Sweat broke on his forehead as the depth readout passed two thousand. The suit creaked and popped.

Time to drop some weight. He found the pin in the dark, grabbed the handle, and pulled. But instead of a bang as the weight separated, the handle rattled, attached to nothing. He tried the rear weights. That handle didn't move at all.

Okay, great; there were other ways to shed weight. He used the manipulators to shear off the transponder, the strobe, the headlights, the umbilical. The last thing he jettisoned were the manipulators themselves. He congratulated himself on his quick thinking, then realized he was suffocating.

He was cranking furiously on the manual rebreather when Lee's patent joints failed and sheared his legs off—both at once, cutting him off at the knees. Oddly, the process didn't hurt. Oddly, too, the pinched-off sections of suit, with his legs in them, fell away.

Legless, with a gentle rocking, the Brute Suit began to ascend.

As the black outside his face port yielded to gray, blue, green, his rage grew. When he found out who put that sticker on him, he'd kill him, no questions asked.

When the faceplate popped through the surface, he frantically undogged the access door. Air flooded in. He sucked it greedily through the narrow opening. The suit picked up the roll of waves and a cupful of water slopped in. He stuck his arm out and waved. He wished now he hadn't cut the transponder off. Was that a boat on the horizon? No. Oh, swell; it was a fin. Well, he was safe from that at least, inside the suit.

It rolled again, taking on a little more water.

Suddenly, it gulped a lot of water, turned over, and sank away beneath him. He tried desperately to block the incoming sea with his body, but it didn't work. The Brute slipped away under him, grew shimmering dim in the blue, disappeared—with him inside, choking and struggling as it filled with water.

Except that he was up here, too, somehow, hovering naked and alone above the empty Gulf. He looked down at the bubbles that were the only evidence of his watery grave. He knew he was dead. Oddly, that didn't bother him now. All that worried him was that Boudreaux would blame him for losing the suit.

H e came awake with a start, listening to Porch snoring in the upper bunk. First, it sounded like bull elephants being tortured; next, a grinding, like a compressor with sand in the cylinders. Then came silence, longer than anyone could possibly hold his breath. Finally, with a despairing whistle, it started all over again.

His heart was still racing from the dream. What did it mean? That was weird, about the smiley face. It made no sense at all.

Or maybe that was exactly what it meant. That what was going on made no sense.

He opened his eyes to darkness.

It occurred to him, now that he knew at least part of what DeepTech and Coastal were running, that once you started to think about it, there were a lot of things that didn't add up. They hadn't come to mind when he was facing Boudreaux and Shattuck. But McCray's death meant he had to start questioning everything.

In a little over a month, he'd been on the scene for three fatal accidents. That was too many. And there were too many other things that didn't add up, both out here in the Patch and back in Summerland.

Well, he wasn't sleepy, and the racket Porch was making didn't help. He might as well think about it now. Dump all the pieces out of the box and figure out how in hell each one fit with the others, and how, if at all, they all fit together.

He decided to start with the accidents.

First, Todds. The MMS honcho. Actually, he was talking three deaths here, not one, but he decided to set the pilot and copilot aside as incidental.

From what he'd heard during the investigation, the Sikorsky must have had some sort of transmission failure while it was approaching the platform, just as it was transitioning into vertical flight. He didn't know much about helicopters, but he knew that was when they were the most vulnerable. When they were hovering and something went wrong, they flew about as well as a crescent wrench.

So who was Todds? A senior official for Mineral Management Survey. What was he doing at Pandora? It depended on what was in that gray briefcase.

The briefcase that no one had ever seen again after Galloway shoved it out the passenger door.

Okay, what could have been in it that would make it dangerous?

And how could you drop a chopper in midair, on command?

He could think of a couple ways. The simplest was an explosively actuated cutter.

He snapped his eyes open as he remembered the Broco cutters. Yeah, that would do it. With a radio control on the platform. Somebody looking up, watching them come in. Not caring that others were in the helicopter with Todds—one of them, a new hire named Tiller Galloway.

And then that point the Sikorsky guy, Kelly, had brought up at the investigation. About flotation bags, why they hadn't inflated. That was kind of funny, too, wasn't it?

He put all that stuff into one big box in his head marked "Todds" and closed it.

Then he opened the lid on Louis "Pinhole" Guidry.

On the face of it, Guidry's death seemed about as pure accident as you could get. Guy goes spearfishing, makes a mistake, the fish takes him down. But Guidry had been a seasoned diver. And judging by his reactions at the Moon Pool, a cool head under pressure.

But nobody but Guidry could have tied the line off on his harness. And there'd been witnesses.

Galloway corrected himself: not witnesses, *a* witness—the roustabout who'd been in the water when Pinhole went down to swim, the guy who'd just happened to have a spear gun. Who'd said, no spear guns on my rig? Oh yeah, Hannah West. But Guidry had died diving off Pandora 1000.

Everybody knew Guidry loved to fish. He talked about it enough.

Or was Tiller Galloway getting paranoid?

After all, he could think of a reason for knocking off Todds. But he couldn't figure why anyone would want to kill a good diver-welder.

He put Guidry into another mental pigeonhole. Above him, Porchellacchia snuffled and began a snorting crescendo to rival an opera singer.

Now McCray. He went over what he knew, what Winslow had told him, and what he'd heard from the others after the helicopter left with Jay's body.

Porch and the Captain had come up from a bounce job, finding a welding machine that had rolled off the platform. Rather than wait their decompression time out in the bell, they'd gone into the deck chamber because it was more comfortable. When they hit fifty feet, McCray had complained about knee pain. Winslow had checked with Ace, who'd told him to blow them down again to depth of relief. That was when Porchellacchia had said he wanted out. Winslow had told him to get in the outer lock and finish his decompression there while he blew McCray back down. Porch had just emerged and was shaking out the kinks on deck when Winslow had heard the thud and peered in and saw McCray wrestling the fireball.

Suspicious, that Porch had just left when the fire broke out.

But it was McCray who'd asked to be blown back down. Did that mean he'd been a party to his own murder? Or that if he hadn't asked, both he and Porchellacchia would have been in the chamber when the fire began?

He could think of ways to cause a fire in a chamber, but not too many with only ten percent oxygen.

Motive? The only one that came to mind was the union thing. That someone had found out Jay McCray was a union organizer. But why kill him? Why not just fire him, like he'd said would happen if he was discovered? Even for a union hater like West, that made more sense. Firing him made an example the other divers could see. An "accidental" death sent no message one way or the other.

He swung himself out of the bunk and padded into the head. He frowned, standing in front of the urinal.

None of the pieces fit. The one thing he was sure of was that he was deep in a no-limits game. Like bourré, the longer he stayed, the more was in the pot. He'd started at diver three, not great money compared with the old days, but he'd been glad to get it. Now he was a two, pulling depth bonuses and a dollar a foot in the Brute. Making more but putting himself further and further over the line.

He had the feeling that someone was looking over his shoulder, and he turned his head suddenly. But of course there was no one there.

He washed his hands and went out into the bunk room. He didn't feel like trying to sleep anymore. He bent for his boots and shorts, then closed the door quietly on the mutter of sleeping men.

T he sodium work lights on the derrick threw a peach-colored glare that made the shadows green. The rumble and clang and faint, drowned shouting told him they were drilling up there. The air trembled with the roaring throb of pumps. He went down to the lower deck and stood at the rail, looking down. For the first time, he realized that the wind had risen; he was looking at restless, heaving, five-foot seas. Remembering the hurricane, he lifted his head, taking the breeze first on one cheek, then the other. About twenty knots, he judged. East by northeast.

Then he shrugged; hitting Florida, the storm shouldn't bother them here. A brush of its skirts at most.

He looked over at the superintendent's office and a thought occurred to him. He rubbed his chin as he considered it, then looked right and left. Nothing moved on the dark deck. He strolled over and tried the door.

Locked. No way to card or jimmy this sucker, either. The door was steel and felt like it was dead-bolted.

Oh well, he thought, and went back to the rail.

Then for a while, he didn't think about much of anything. He just looked out at the darkness. Not many stars tonight. Some overcast. The sea gleamed as it surged around the jacket legs.

"Gallows," someone said just behind him.

"Holy shit."

"D'I scare you? Sorry."

The voice was rough and pitched high and for a second he didn't recognize it. He couldn't see a face either, just the yellow glow of a Holden-McOwen hard hat and under it a black cutout body.

"What're you doin' out here? Thought you squids spent all your time in the sack when you weren't sleeping down there in your suits."

"Miz West. Didn't expect to see you here."

"Be funny if you didn't." She came out of the platform overhang into what light there was. Now he saw the ponytail, the stocky, strong body in overalls, heavy drillers' boots. He still couldn't see her eyes, though. "I make a round every night before I turn in. Kind of goes with being head hammer. What's going on?"

"Couldn't sleep."

"What's the trouble?"

He covered instinctively. "No trouble. Just couldn't sleep."

"It's about your buddy, ain't it? The little one. Hey, I'm sorry."

"Me, too. He was one of the good ones."

"You guys don't seem to be havin' much luck these days. An' all of that, bad."

"I was thinking that myself."

She looked past him, then put her boot on the rail, too. "Pretty night."

"Windy."

"Yeah, kind of surprised at that."

"What's the track? Of the hurricane?"

"I ain't seen a storm track lately. We got one of those machines prints out weather maps, kind of like a radio fax, pipes in from home office. But it's on the rag; all it's giving us is what looks like a bad subsurface gather."

He didn't know what a subsurface gather was. "How about the National Weather Service? They do a coastal weather broadcast—"

"Out of range out here. Maybe I'll have Gassy try to pull in something from one of the tankers. They oughta have shortwave. I wouldn't worry about it. We can take anything any pansy-ass storm can throw at us." He heard a faint jingle as she struck the rail with her hand, and he realized that *we* meant her and the platform.

He suddenly had an idea. "Uh, Miz West . . ."

"How many times I gotta tell you to call me Hannah?"

"Hannah, uh . . . who's in charge of this platform?"

"What kind 'o jackshit question's that? They drop you when you were a baby? I am. You know that."

"Thought so. For the Coastal gear, and Holden-McOwen—"

"For everything. I'm the pusher."

"So you got keys, say, to the diving spaces?"

"Sure. Why?"

"I want you to let me in Boudreaux's office."

"Oh." He saw her face turn, saw her study him. "Mind if I ask why?"

"I want to look for something."

"Why don't you ask Bender?"

Somehow it didn't surprise him that she knew Boudreaux's nickname. But it did surprise him that she didn't act shocked. He took a breath. Another hand deeper into the game. " 'Cause I don't trust him."

"Interesting," she said, still watching him.

"I won't disturb anything. I won't take anything. He won't know I've been in there." He hesitated, knowing he had to give some explanation. And to do that, he had to trust her, at least a little.

But if she wasn't what he thought—if she was part of whatever was going on here—he'd probably wake up dead tomorrow.

"I think some of these things that seem to be accidents aren't really accidents."

She didn't say anything. "Well? You gonna let me in?" he asked her.

"Maybe."

"Maybe, huh?"

"I been wondering about a couple things myself. But lemme ask you this, Gallop. What's in it for me?"

"Galloway. What's in it for you?"

"Yeah." She took her boot off the rail and turned to face him. "What's in it for me . . . big guy."

"Uh-oh," he muttered.

"Kind of romantic out here, the dark and all. Don't you think?"

He cleared his throat. "It could be considered romantic."

"But no moon. I like a moon."

"Yeah. A moon is . . . nice."

"You want a beer?"

"A beer?"

"Yeah. I got a cooler back in my stateroom."

"Damn, Hannah. First thing you said to me was, no booze, no drugs, no spear guns, no unions."

"Ain't mine. It's company. For when the mucky mucks come out to rubberneck. Makes 'em feel special, have a scotch on the rocks when the poor sweating schmuck dancin' gandy can't even have a beer."

"Scotch, huh? Any bourbon?"

"I got a nice selection," she said. Her hands were on his chest now. " 'Member what I said about not makin' secrets, who I like? People go by fast in this business. You don't want to leave them in doubt. An' I got to admit, I sort of got the hot pants for you, Gallows."

"It's Galloway."

"Uh-huh," she whispered, and he found himself being kissed. He couldn't move; his back was against the life rail. The only way he could get away was by shoving her, and he didn't want to be rude.

He was just glad she wasn't chewing tonight.

He stood in the closet-sized head attached to the pusher's stateroom. He felt dizzy. Making love to Hannah West was no sweet, slow idyll. It was more like trying to board a small boat in rough seas while wearing full gear. Earthy and violent, leaving him smelling like her all over. He peered down at the gear he was peeling off. "Safety first on the drill deck," she'd said, heavy breasts swinging as she bent to root through a drawer. "Got a preference, Trojan or Sheik? Let's do a little wildcattin', baby."

When he went back in, she was sprawled with her thighs apart, tucking a chew into her cheek. "Not so bad, huh?" she said. "Kind of different, what you're used to?"

"You're hell on wheels, Hannah." He felt used, but at the same time, he liked her. He was sorry now he'd acted reluctant.

She swung her legs down and started searching through the clothes on the floor. "Okay, my part of the deal. Here." She snapped a key off the ring and held it out.

"Thanks. I'll return it—"

"Naw, give it to Gassy. Tell 'im you found it on the deck someplace. That covers me if you dick up."

"Okay." He wanted to go but sat on the bed instead. "Listen. You better watch out for yourself, too, Hannah."

"I'm okay. This thing'll take hundred and fifty knots of wind."

"I don't mean that." He thought about what Shattuck had said: "There's no need for her to know."

But he figured there was.

When he was done telling her, she picked up a cup and spat slowly. "Did you know all that?" he asked her.

"Some of it. Knew we had some bad lines, had to be patched or replaced. I didn't think it was gonna happen anytime soon, though."

"What about the rest? Faking the inspections, that kind of stuff?"

"Well, give it to you straight, I figure Brad Shattuck's got a good reason, whatever he's doing. He's a right guy; he's treated me okay. But I don't trust that son of a bitch Boudreaux far as I can pee." She scratched her crotch thoughtfully. "I'll tell you one thing. Might fit in somewhere. Or it might not. We're pumping to deplete."

He stared at her. "Come again?"

"I'm game."

"No, I mean, tell me what that means. What you just said."

"I'll try. It's technical."

"I can understand technical stuff."

"You a reservoir engineer? Petroleum engineer? That's the kind of technical I'm talking. There's different ways to exploit a field. The ideal way's called maximum efficient rate. You use gas-cap and water drive to force the oil up. You don't get the greatest flow rate, but over time, you get the most oil. Never get all that's down there, but you try to get all you can. You with me?"

"Yeah, I follow."

"Coastal's not running Pandora and Pandora South that way. We're using gas-expansion drive. Using the gas pressure we've got down there to get lots of oil fast, and to hell with five years from now."

"I think I understand that."

"That's more'n I can say, because I don't." Her breasts looked down as she sat back. Her sleek flanks were heavy. She had the kind of body sculptors used to love, he thought. Too bad it had gone out of style. She had missing fingernails and old green bruises on her shins. She was about as different from Arden Boudreaux as you could get. Meanwhile, she was still talking about oil. "It don't make sense. Sure, prices are up a little, but that don't mean you blow off half your long-term yield to get an extra twenty percent this year. Not if he's gonna do like you say, plow long-term investment into new lines."

He got up. "Thanks. For the drink. For the key. For everything."

"My pleasure. Good luck, Galloway."

He grinned. She'd gotten it right at last. "Okay, Hannah. And watch your back."

H e stopped by the bunk room again to check, but everyone seemed to be asleep. Porch was still snoring.

He walked all the way around the lower deck. The shadows were empty. He leaned against the door stenciled R. B. BOUDREAUX for six or seven minutes. Then he put the key in and turned it quickly and let himself in.

He didn't touch the light switch, and the interior of the windowless steel box was absolute black when he closed the door. For a second, he remembered his dream. Then the bolt snapped home behind him and he remembered the Moon Pool. Neither was a good memory. He resolved to make this fast. He took out his Super Q and turned it on and set it on Boudreaux's desk, pointing up at the ceiling fixture. Enough bounced off the reflector to see tolerably well.

Okay, the safe first. Locked. No surprise there. The file cabinet. Files in the top drawer, rolls of some kind of seismograph or sonar printouts in the second. Bond paper in the third, in reams. More in the bottom drawer. Boudreaux sure liked copy paper. Or was it all paper?

Under six reams in the bottom drawer was a gray briefcase. Tiller pulled it out and propped it on the desk. Samsonite. He allowed himself a brief bitter smile, then popped the catches.

Empty.

He checked the pockets and the lining. All he found was a paper clip, rough with rust. Nothing else.

He went to the door and listened. Then he put the case back and stacked copy paper over it.

It took a little while, but he'd been shown once how to get a government-issue desk open, and this was the same design. The center drawer was the key. Finally, it popped and he went through it, then the two side drawers. Gear manuals, operations manuals, back issues of *World Oil* and *Ocean Industry* and *Louisiana Game & Fish*.

He was starting to suspect he was wasting his time. He

hoped what he wanted wasn't in the safe. He tilted the Q toward the wall clock: 4:15.

He relocked the desk and pulled the top drawer of the file cabinet out again. He rifled through the file folders.

Interesting.

There was a file folder here for each diver. He went through them quickly, picking out names. All here except Guidry and McCray.

Tiller thought, He keeps things up to date, Bender does.

He pulled his own file. Inside was his medical report. He scanned down it to Van Dine's signature at the bottom and an X in the "Passed" block. Under "Comments" was a single word: *tight*. He grimaced and put it back. Porchellacchia's file was more interesting, a private detective's report. He read the summary paragraph and put it back.

Winslow. Medical report, two photos, and two newspaper clippings. He squinted at the print, then took them over to the light.

CONVICTED KILLER TO DIE THURSDAY

RICHMOND—Desmond Clymon Winton is slated for execution this week, the second this summer at Mecklenburg Correctional Center.

Unless Governor Charles S. Robb intervenes, Winton, 29, will be put to death Thursday for robbing and murdering Lester Evans, the office manager of a Hampton grocery store.

Winton's attorney, William S. Stickney, said that the governor has been asked to intervene. "I have filed a clemency petition with the governor, on which we are awaiting word," said Stickney.

At Winton's trial, three store employees and two customers identified him as the man who shot Evans five times in the abdomen, chest, and head in front of his son, also an employee at the store. Evans did nothing to resist the robbery, witnesses said. Winton, a Nevada native, was also a suspect in killings in New York and Pennsylvania, but those charges were dropped during the trial.

The second clipping looked more recent, not new, but newer than the first.

Man in Custody in Oregon Misidentified
Murderer Who Fled Death Row Still at Large

PORTLAND—Oregon police officials confirmed today that Desmond Clymon Winton, one of four men who escaped from Virginia's death row three years ago, is the last one still at large.

Portland police explained that the man they had thought was Winton resembled him and had refused to be fingerprinted. He had been taken into custody and a court order sought for identification. They apologized to him and to the community for the accidental inclusion of his arrest report in a package prepared for reporters covering another case. He was identified and released Friday.

Winton, then 29, was to be put to death for the robbery and murder of Lester Charles Evans, the office manager of a Hampton, Virginia grocery store. The escape of Winton and three other condemned men from the maximum-security Mecklenburg Correctional Facility drew national attention and sparked a shake-up of the state prison administration.

Leonard Watters and Samuel Watters, brothers, were caught shortly after the break. James Lucas was recaptured last year after a gun battle with state police in Tennessee. Only Winton is still at large.

Oregon officials confirmed that Winton is still being sought, but declined to give details. Anyone with information in the case should notify the FBI.

Tiller pursed his lips and reread the first clipping. Then he slid them both back into Winslow's file and fanned himself with it while he thought.

Something clicked against the door, faint but sharp, like a key searching for a keyhole. He grabbed the Q and turned it off. At the same time, he dropped the folder back and eased the drawer closed. The office was now dark. He bent and

259

crawled under the desk, into the hollow where a seated man's knees would fit.

The door opened and an instant later the room light flickered on. Even under the desk, it almost blinded him. Peering under the edge, he saw boots come in. Then he heard the safe's dial being spun. It clanked open, then closed again. He hugged his knees.

His ears seemed to be picking everything up, including his heartbeat. He caught buttons being punched rapidly. Then Boudreaux's voice: "Ace? Roland. Get the guys up. Yeah, all of 'em."

A pause, then he said, "No. We got to get moving; this storm's coming down on us. Yeah, they're ready to get under way. Yeah. Yeah."

Another pause. Tiller strained to listen, but all he could hear was the wind outside. Then he heard a click and saw a spot of light moving idly around on the carpet. Shit, he thought. He'd left his Super Q on the desk.

"Sure, them too. They might need the Brute. What? Yeah, sure, he's a diver, ain't he? . . . He isn't? Well, find him, goddamn it. I want them all down there ready to go in half an hour."

Boudreaux hung up. Tiller watched the boots. They stood there for a moment more. Then they left and the lights went out.

TWENTY-FIVE

When he got back to the bunk room, lockers were banging open. Divers were dragging duffels and gear bags and shouting. He grabbed Rodriquez and asked him what was going on.

"Where the hell you been? No, don't tell me. I don't care! Get your shit together. We're getting under way for Pandora South."

"What's the hurry, Ace? I thought we had till tomorrow—"

"This *is* tomorrow. You know this business—you're either sitting on your ass or running like hell. Word is, that hurricane's speeded up and turned left. It's wiped out Miami and it's headed our way now. We got to get One Thousand buttoned up for a major storm. Get that riser stabbed in and clamped off or it'll beat itself to death against the jacket. Unnerstand? Now get moving."

"How we gonna—"

"Shut up an' get packed!" Rodriquez screamed at him, and Tiller muttered, "All right, goddamn it, take it easy."

Outside, a dull gray light seemed to radiate from the sea. The overcast was solid now and the air cool. There was no McCray to carry his hat and suit and umbilical. He collared a roustabout to help. But when they were riding down to the

Janis J, the cage swinging back and forth like a huge slow pendulum in the rising wind, the guy dropped his hat. Tiller grabbed for it, but there wasn't a chance. It fell straight into the waves foaming around the base of the platform. "Oh, freaking great," he shouted.

"Sorry, guy. Company'll buy you a new one."

"Like hell. That was my personal goddamn helmet, butterfingers. Eight hundred and fifty bucks."

The Davis was surging and rolling, engines alternately roaring and burbling as Lee held her near the landing stage. Jumping across to her was a heart-stopper, but he made it without losing anything else.

The others were at the stern, sitting on lockers and gunwales, looking curiously at the Brute Suit, which was two-blocked and lashed securely on its davit. Rodriquez glared around, counting heads, and made a go-ahead signal to the pilothouse. The Davis cast off and turned away, rolled like a pickup going over a rutted field, then steadied up, headed south. The engines changed from a burble to a hammer and spray the color of green glass leapt out in thin curved sheets from the bow.

Galloway put his hands in his pockets and stood rolling with the boat, watching Winslow. The Westerner sat with boots apart, his leather gear bag between them. When he leaned back to spit over the side, he caught Tiller's stare.

"How's it going?" said Winslow.

"Okay. How about you?"

"Okay."

Tiller turned, breaking their locked gazes, and shouted, "Hey, Porch, where's Bender?"

The big man nodded from his seat as the boat pitched. "He's prob'ly out there already. I heard a chopper come in, then leave."

"What's the plan? Ace, you know what's going on?"

"Already told you. Gotta secure that riser before the wind picks up."

"It's picking up now. We're not gonna dive in this, are we?"

"It looks bad here, that's all, *baboso.* You in the bell, hanging off that big barge, gonna be piece of cake."

"I hope you're right." He thought about his helmet next. "Ace, got a little gear problem."

"What?"

He told him. Rodriquez sighed. He pointed into the cabin. "Blue bag. Black handles."

"Jay's?"

"That's right. Should be a hat in there."

"You want me to use McCray's helmet?"

Porch grunted, "Don't worry. It ain't haunted."

"I'm not worried, goddamn it!"

"You sound worried. Hey, maybe you wear his helmet, you'll start leavin' skid marks, too."

"Any more mouth farts off you and I'll pull your goddamn lips off again, Porchellacchia."

The sea crested and hit the port side and broke, blowing warm salty spray over them all. The big Pagan spat but didn't answer.

It was thirty miles to South Pandora, but the seas kept their speed down. It was two and a half hours before they made out 1000 far ahead of the gyrating bow. Against the gray sky the giant platform shone unearthly white. The lay barge was anchored off it. As *Janis J* nosed in, losing motion as it entered the smoother water in the *Catherine Rice*'s lee, Tiller looked up at the derrick.

The marine riser was the thin-walled pipe that led from the template up to the drill floor. The drill string went down through it and drilling mud came back up. It was a long one. Hell yeah, he thought, a thousand plus feet to reach bottom here. He wondered what the problem was. Usually, it went right down and locked into the template.

Well, if everything worked the way it was supposed to, you wouldn't need divers in the Patch at all.

He didn't like the looks of the sky. It was uniformly gray now, nearly black. He couldn't even tell where the sun was. The first drops of rain were coming down.

The lay barge's side blotted out the platform. Lee leaned out, frowning, alternately gunning and backing. The Davis hit the landing platform, a little too hard, and lines sailed down from the barge.

The clouds opened as they got to the dive deck. The chamber was still in the same place he'd last seen it. Just as big. Just as green, like a huge lime. The bell was locked to it. The rain came down in steel sheets as he and Porch and Ace shed their street clothes and climbed in. Winslow threw their gear in, then climbed in himself. The interior was clean, but Tiller couldn't shake a feeling of constriction as he remembered the three weeks they'd spent here. And here they were again.

Only this time, he was a diver two. He started to count up how much he'd be making an hour, then stopped. It didn't make him feel better anymore. The rain hammered on the curved steel overhead like a hundred sailors with chipping irons. "Got everything?" Boudreaux said, peering in. Water ran off his face as if he was crying.

"Yeah."

"We're gonna press you down pretty fast. We need this gear secured. Galloway, Porch, you two get in the bell. We'll get you through the air-water interface before it gets any rougher."

"I thought it wasn't going to get any rougher."

Boudreaux grunted, "We're getting conflicting reports."

Tiller asked him, "Roland, where's the wind from?"

"What?"

"What direction's the wind coming from? I don't want to be negative about this, but if there's a possibility this goddamn hurricane is going to hit us, should we be going down?"

"Told you," murmured Porchellacchia. "Wear his helmet, leave his skid marks."

"Shut up, you tattooed—"

"Now you mention it, he's got a point," said Rodriquez. "Maybe we ought to wait."

"What is this? You going on strike, Ace?"

"Hell no, Roland, but I'm not even sure I know what we're gonna be doing down there."

"I'll tell you over the goddamn interphone. Porch, Galloway, in the bell. Get suited up!"

The hatch clanged shut. Tiller was surprised; generally, Boudreaux made them repeat back depths, stay times, and job information to make sure they were all on the same wavelength.

Porch shrugged and swung the inner hatch closed as gas began hissing in. "Sheeze, he ain't wasting no time," he muttered.

He got suited up, helped Porchellacchia with his harness, then held still while Porch helped him. They checked out their umbilicals, bailout bottles, the gas-control and hot-water panels, the onboard batteries and gas banks. Remembering his night-mare again, he checked the handles that would drop the ballast if everything went to shit. Gas continued to blast in, and when he cleared his throat, it squeaked.

The bell lurched and lifted and he felt them swing out over the side. Then they dropped. The moan of the wind vanished, replaced by silence.

He cleared his ears and glanced at the depth gauge. They weren't going down all that fast. In fact, it was kind of slow. Not that I'm complaining, he thought, remembering that first dive, when the Wildman had freaked out.

He pulled McCray's helmet out of the bag and examined it, then put it on for a moment. It smelled different from his hat. He didn't believe in haunted helmets. But he still felt funny wearing a dead man's. He took it off and set it on the curved bench. Then, just out of curiosity, he went through the rest of the stuff in McCray's bag. Knives, spare O-rings, a skin-diving face mask, three cans of warm ginger ale, dive logbook. He got his bailout bottle, and attached the whip to the helmet.

"What you doing?" Porchellacchia asked him.

"Getting rigged."

"You wearing your bailout in here?"

He wondered whether he should tell the Pagan that he wasn't really one hundred percent sure that Boudreaux wasn't going to feed them pure helium, try to asphyxiate them both right there in the bell.

Then he remembered Porch bailing out minutes before the fire. He'd better not tell anybody anything. The only guy he could trust in this whole outfit was McCray, and he'd realized it too late.

He wished again, desperately, that Shad had stayed. He'd never treat a friend that way again.

"We going down?" asked Porchellacchia, looking at the outside pressure gauge with a funny look on his face. "We been sort of hanging off here at a hundred feet."

"They're probably waiting for the blow-down to catch up

with us. No point getting to the bottom before we're at pressure."

"Yeah, guess so." He still looked puzzled. "They ain't blowing us down very fast, either."

Tiller looked at the same gauge, thinking about it. The Navy mixed-gas tables called for pressurization at no more than three feet a minute, which would be what—nine hundred feet—three hundred minutes—five hours. He didn't remember what the DeepTech manual said. Five feet a minute? That'd still take three hours.

"Better that than too fast. We're okay."

The blast of gas resumed. Porch yawned, working his jaw. Tiller looked through the logbook, then put it away. He wished they had a porthole in the bell. Even if it was too dark to see anything, you didn't feel so closed in.

Rodriquez was on the intercom. Tiller half-consciously noted that the cross-talk switch was still on; otherwise, the chamber and the bell would have to communicate indirectly, via the supervisor. "How you hombres doing down there?"

"A-okay, Ace, how you?"

"Rockin' and a-rollin'. It's raining baseballs up here. An' you can feel the barge moving."

"The *lay barge* is rolling?"

"Uh-huh."

"Hey, Roland, you on the line?"

"I'm here."

"What's that hurricane doing?"

"Don't sweat it. It's just the edge of it passing."

"Hope you're right," Tiller said. He made sure his helmet was near at hand, then leaned back and closed his eyes.

The blow-down stopped at 870 feet after four hours. They were in their suits by then. First, it had gotten hot as the atmosphere compressed, then cold. Now it was freezing.

They sat there for a half hour. Boudreaux kept saying, "Hold your horses; they're not ready for you yet. No point locking out till the riggers are ready." Tiller kept taking deep breaths. "This pot's too friggin' small," he muttered. "And—hey—are we moving? Feels like we're moving up and down—"

The intercom said, "What you complaining about, cher? Getting antsy?"

"Lay off it, Roland."

"Bet you'd rather be in some bitch's bed, huh? Maybe somebody else's wife?"

He didn't answer, just looked at Porchellacchia. The big Pagan's mouth twitched. He pointed up. Made two horns of his fingers and put them to his head.

"The hell's that mean?" Tiller grunted.

Porchellacchia grinned. "Nothin'."

To his relief, Boudreaux didn't pursue the subject. Instead, the intercom just hissed. They waited.

"Okay, they're ready. Porch, you're standby. Galloway, you lock out. Once you're out, you're at the same level as the top of the storage tanks, okay? Go along the top of those till you hit the template."

"Roland, I still don't know what you want me to do."

"Told you, the riser's gotta be stabbed. The well's off center from the drill string, okay? You be there when they lower away. You pry it a few inches this way or that way to get it to go into the bell guide. Look, just get over there and we'll talk you through it." Boudreaux sounded bored, as if none of this really mattered. Tiller had a sudden feeling something was wrong.

But he still locked out and dropped into the water. It was black as cold tar, as cold as black ice. He told Porch, back in the bell, to turn up the hot water. He felt like somebody else inside the strange helmet. Maybe he *was* somebody else.

The trek to the template took ages. He was walking on concrete, on the top of the platform base, not wading through mud, but the current was against him. Finally he found the riser and got himself positioned.

Suddenly lights came on. He flinched, then made out a camera and light pods. A TV remote, pointed at the template. Good, they could see him. He told Boudreaux to tell the platform they could lower away.

Nothing happened for a long time. He sat there idly flicking the light from McCray's Super Q around—looking at the jacket legs, looking at the tops of the storage tanks, at some cone-shaped thingies on each one, with white cables running away into the darkness.

Suddenly the riser came down and slammed into the template. He strained to push it into line, but it was a full six inches off center. The lip ground and hammered against the welded steel template. He backed off fast, imagining what would happen if he got a hand or a foot caught under it.

"That's dicked, Roland. Tell 'em to hoist again, then sway out in the direction of south, okay?"

They tried twice more and did worse every time. Finally, he shouted, "Roland, I tell 'em south, they move north! What the hell's wrong?"

"We're getting too much motion. Sea motion, rig motion."

"Are you tellin' me now that the friggin' *rig* is moving? What are we doin' down here?"

"Good question," came Boudreaux's voice. He sounded jolly. Then they heard a click.

"What the hell's going on?" said Rodriquez from the main chamber. "Hey! Roland! Where you going? I just saw him go by the porthole, up here."

"Who's running the frigging gas panel, then?"

Suddenly, Galloway felt exposed. He was all alone down here, almost nine hundred feet down, out at the end of his umbilical. A storm was going by topside strong enough to make the platform sway. And the platform was concrete, anchored on these huge concrete tanks that were, as far as he knew, filled with crude oil.

"Screw this, guys. I'm comin' back to the bell."

"Roger that," said Porch. "You need me out there?"

"No. Just start taking in slack."

His hand fumbled over his harness and found his first weight belt. He tripped it and it fell away. He bent and started pulling himself along the umbilical, hand over hand.

When he shoved his shoulders up into the bell and uncammed the helmet, the first words he heard were, "Damn, that was fast."

"I climbed my hose. Anything from topside?"

"No."

He pulled himself over to the intercom, stripping off his bailout. He shouted, "Ace, Wildman, you guys up there?"

"We're here, man."

"Anything from Bender?"

"Not a word. He just . . . left."

Tiller said rapidly, "Okay, here's how I read it. We just been abandoned. Nobody on the rack box. Nobody on the handling gear for the bell. Can you see anybody through your porthole? Anybody at all on the dive deck?"

"Nothing but rain—and dark. It's awful dark out there."

"I vote we abort this son of a bitch. Start blowing up as fast as we can."

"Porch?"

"Okay."

"Wildman? He says yeah. Okay, let's do it." Rodriquez's voice hesitated. "Wait a minute. We can open the exhaust valves up here, do a timed decompression on deck. But how about you two? How you gonna get up?"

"We're gonna cut loose and free ascend."

"I wouldn't do that, Till. You're still getting gas from here, aren't you? And what if you crash into the bottom of the barge?"

He hesitated. Ace was right. "Okay, we'll keep the umbilical. But I still think we better drop our weights and get out of here. That son of a bitch! Where the hell did he go?"

"You guys lookin' for me?" Boudreaux's voice sounded oddly furry and thick.

"Jesus, Roland, where were you?"

"Take it easy. Jus' checking things out. Okay, here's the story. Galloway, Porch, you're coming up now, you."

"Great. About time."

The bell lurched as it started up.

Boudreaux was still talking. "We're gonna lock you guys back in. Get everybody back together inna chamber. Okay?"

"Okay, Bender."

"You got it, Roland."

Tiller watched the exterior pressure needle unwind. They were rising fast. He hit the intercom. "Roland, we comin' up because of the storm?"

"No. Orders."

"Shattuck?"

"That's right."

The bell started to roll as the needle passed thirty feet. The motion grew swiftly. But Boudreaux was driving them up as fast as the motors would lift them. "He's gonna jerk us through the interface," he said to Porch. "Better hang on."

The sea released them all at once as the needle passed zero. Undamped, the bell swung, then reeled back. Now they could hear the wind. They swung again and hit something hard. The clang was deafening, like being inside a cathedral bell. Then they slammed down so hard that they bounced, and a fine dust rose.

"Lining up," said the intercom. They watched each other wordlessly. Tiller felt the barge rolling under them. He was drenched with sweat under the suit.

"You're sealed. Blowing down the outside lock." The outer hatch hissed and unsealed. They grabbed their gear and hats and crawled through fast.

Ace and Winslow were lying on their bunks. "Hey," said Rodriquez. "Nice to have you back."

Tiller shoved the two gear bags, his and McCray's, under his bunk. He checked the position of the exhaust valves and looked at the gauges. They were at a storage depth of nine hundred feet, breathing a 95/5 heliox mix. He looked out the window. The sky was black.

Gradually he relaxed. He breathed in and out, then sat down. Heavy seas and high winds were no joke, but they were safe now. On deck, with plenty of oxygen and plenty of power from the barge's powerful generators. Gradually the tension drained out of his chest into his legs, then out into the slowly heaving deck.

He glanced at Winslow. The Westerner was lying at full length, eyes closed, like a figure on a medieval tomb.

Faintly, from outside, a horn started to wail.

"What's that?" Porch muttered. "That the barge?"

Nobody answered. The blast went on and on, then ended. Tiller yawned. Another blast started. "What now?" said Rodriquez, stirring, then sitting up.

"Three blasts," said Winslow. Tiller looked at him. His eyes were open, staring up.

When the fourth blast began, Galloway jumped to his feet. Any more than three was an emergency signal. He snapped off the interior light and pressed his face to the armored porthole.

He looked across the raging sea to where a ship was emerging out of the dark and rain. His eyes went to the bridge first. There was a red light on his right and a green light on the left. Then they went to the mast. High on it, one above the other, two red lights were burning.

"Jesus God," he whispered.

The others scrambled to portholes. Now they could hear the ship's horn, too, a long-drawn-out drone.

"Shit," said Porchellacchia. "He's comin' right at us."

"What's two red lights mean?" asked Rodriquez.

Tiller cleared his throat. His voice felt like somebody else's. "It means he's not under command. His rudder's dicked or something; he can't steer."

"Why don't he stop?"

"That's a big ship there. Tanker, most likely." He felt oddly calm, considering he was watching his death and that of a lot of other people, and one of the greatest disasters in maritime history, approaching. "Fifty, eighty thousand tons. Takes him miles to stop, with his engines back full."

There was silence in the chamber for about two seconds. Then Porch was heading for the exhaust valves. Rodriquez got there just ahead of him. They had a little wrestling match before the superintendent shouted, "Knock it off, man! You open those, we're gonna blow like a piñata fulla dynamite!"

Tiller took a deep breath, preparing himself, then grabbed another look. Looking at the other ship head-on, it didn't seem to be moving. But when you looked away, then back, it had grown. Dark as it was, he could make out the lighter line of a bow wave. He figured it to be two, maybe three miles away now. Traveling, judging by that bow wave, about fifteen knots.

Unless it turned, it would hit them in eight or ten minutes. And he couldn't think of a damn thing they could do about it.

"We better get into the bell," said Rodriquez in a low, vibrating voice.

"The bell?"

"We can cut loose in it if the barge goes over. Maybe come up. The chamber—"

"We ain't got time for that, Ace."

Galloway wasn't listening. He was looking out the opposite port. Through it, he could see the white concrete pillars that were Pandora 1000.

"Roland!" Rodriquez shouted into the intercom. "You out there?"

A pause, then "Yeah. I'm here, me."

"Roland, you see that ship comin' down on us?"

"Yeah. The *Freetown Rose*."

"I don't give a shit what its name is! It's headed right for us!"

"Looks that way, Ace."

"What are we gonna do, man?"

Boudreaux's voice sounded strange, slurred. "Tell you what *I'm* gonna do, cher. The captain just passed the word to abandon ship. Get on the tugs; if you can't, lifeboats an' life jackets. Figure I'll get on *Janis J* myself. She's standing by."

Porchellacchia shouldered past Rodriquez to the intercom grille. "Yeah, great, but how about us? How we gettin' out of here?"

"I don' think you can, Porch."

Tiller looked out again. He'd hoped to see some relative motion, but he didn't. The ship was coming right down their throats. From outside came the sound of running feet and men shouting.

"You'll all die if I dump pressure. No time for an emergency decompress. Nope, can't do a thing for you, me."

"What are you talking about, man? This freaking ship is gonna *hit* us!"

Tiller pushed himself away from the bulkhead. What was that saying about the prospect of hanging concentrating the mind? He felt like that.

Because some of the pieces were starting to fit together.

" 'Scuse me," he said politely to Rodriquez. To the intercom, he said, "This ship, it's also gonna hit the platform. Pandora One Thousand. Isn't it, Bender?"

"Wouldn't surprise me."

"No, don't seem like any of this is a surprise to you. Hell, you even know the name of that ship."

"Sure do." Boudreaux laughed, and Tiller understood now: He was drunk, had probably been drinking for hours. Maybe he had to be drunk to do what he was going to do. "We been waitin' for it. Silly bastards had a breakdown coming up from Mexico."

"They'll hit the platform. And there'll be a massive oil spill."

"There will be that, cher. You know what? I guarantee, there will be that."

"What's he talking about?" Rodriquez muttered.

Tiller said to the intercom, "How about it, Roland? Want to enlighten us?"

"What? I don't got to explain nothing to you assholes. Hear me?"

He glanced out again, feeling sweat crawl his back. The ship was bigger, the side lights farther apart even as rain fog blurred them. Then they emerged again, glittering across the waves. He stared at the blunt, high bow. It was like watching a guillotine come down in slow motion. His legs wanted to run, but there was no place to go.

"Look, Bender, we don't feel like playing Twenty Questions, okay? If you're gonna tell us, tell us. If you don't know what's going on, just go ahead and shove the hell off."

As he'd hoped, the other's drunken belligerence kicked in. "Oh, I know, all right. It ain't that complicated. Jus' that I stand to make a hell of a lot of money. And the fewer people know how I got it, the better."

Fighting to keep desperation out of his voice, Tiller said, "What I don't figure is how *you* can do it. You dove with us, Roland. You drank with us. And, hell, you're a Cajun. What happens when all that oil hits the marshes? Isn't this gonna wipe out your cousins? The ones you said were still shrimpin'?"

"Those bastards are still breakin' their backs, that's their problem. Not all of us are stupid."

The words were arrogant, but he heard the defensiveness in Boudreaux's voice. Maybe a weakness there, some guilt he could hammer at. He glanced at Rodriquez. The Chino hand nodded, urging him on. Yeah, Ace understood what he was trying to do.

Hey, at least if he could keep Boudreaux talking, maybe they could take him down with them.

"So long, assholes."

"Wait, Roland. Wait. You gonna leave us here and not even let us in on it? Not how Roland Boudreaux treats guys he drank with, is it?"

"E'bien—" The slurred voice sounded unsure.

"It's us, cher. Your crew, goddamn it. Give it to us straight, man to man, that's all we're askin', okay? First thing—who killed Todds? Who blew up the chopper?"

"I rigged the cutter. Put it on the transmission the night

273

before; it was sitting there on the field. Put a Big Chief through the flotation, too."

"What was in the briefcase?"

"What briefcase?"

"The one you took out of the chopper, Roland. The one that's in your office on Pandora Twelve, the file cabinet, bottom drawer, under all the paper."

"Oh, that briefcase. Don't know that, me."

"You don't know what was in it?"

"Not me, cher. Gave it to the customer."

Galloway glanced at the others. They were staring at him as they listened. Rodriquez, a feral snarl frozen on his lips. Porchellacchia, his mouth open in astonishment. Only Winslow seemed separate, detached, sitting on his bunk with his hands on his lap.

"Okay, Roland. That's Todds. How about Guidry?"

The drunken voice went sarcastic. "Old Pinhole, he was natural causes, Till. Wasn't he? *You* were there."

"I thought he was a good diver. Almost as good as you." He glanced at Ace again.

"Good? Sure, he was wonderful. A great diver. Ask Wildman. He's right in there with you."

"Ask Winton? I mean, Winslow—"

The three men at the intercom turned involuntarily to the one on the bunk. Winslow was staring down at his hands. Tiller saw that they were starting to shake.

Boudreaux's voice turned suspicious. "How'd you know his name was Winton? Hell, what are we playing around for, anyway? You're all dead men. Dead an' buried.

"Okay, you want to know—Guidry wasn't hard. All Wildman hadda do was go down there scuba, wait for him to skin-dive down, then fake a problem. Guidry comes down to help. No tank. Just holding his breath. Wildman holds on to his harness till he quits kicking. Then ties his spear line to him and cuts it, makes it look like he got a fish too big for him."

"What about the cuts on his hands?"

"Knife'll do that good as a line."

"The roustabout?"

"On the payroll. He said what he was told to say."

"But why? What was Pinhole doing that he had to—"

"He was makin' time with the wrong woman. With Shattuck's girlfriend. Least that's what he told me."

Tiller went still inside. "His girlfriend? Who was that, Roland? Anybody we know?"

"I don't know. Who cares? The customer says Pinhole goes, he goes."

"My God," muttered Porch, beside him. Tiller risked a glance at him. He was staring out the port, his eyes bulging.

He swung back to the intercom. "Okay, next, McCray. What about Jay?"

"Phosphorus in the mask. Turn the valve on, oxygen hits it, it ignites. You know who he was? A union agitator. We don't have no use for them."

"Phosphorus," Tiller repeated. "Winton again?"

"Yep."

Porchellacchia growled, looking back toward where Winslow was still sitting on his bunk. "How about this? What you got to say?"

"He blackmailed me," the Westerner muttered. When he looked up, pleading tinted the flat voice. "Do what he said or he'd turn me in. Y'unnerstand? They get me, they'll kill me. I'll kill him, though, now. If it's the last thing I do."

Tiller turned back to the intercom. "That's murder. Five murders! Winton, I can kind of understand. He's a stone killer; he's crazy. But you gave him the orders. *Why?*"

"Told you already. Gonna come out of this rich."

"That's right, you're the guy always looking for that extra buck. But tell me this, Roland. Where's it coming from? It sounds like we're talking serious cash. Whose? Where's all this money coming from?"

"You know that. From Coastal."

"From Shattuck? Okay . . . but . . . what does he get out of an oil spill? See, it don't add up, Roland, does it? I just don't figure how it does any good for anybody."

Silence on the line. Then, "Hey, who cares? I get paid. That's bottom line for me, cher."

Porchellacchia shouted into the grille, "How about leavin' us to die? How much you getting for that, asshole?"

The slurred voice changed timbre now. Boudreaux was working himself into a rage. "That's why, right there! You all

275

know too much. Pretty soon, you start talking there in sat, bullshitting, and somebody starts putting it together. Saves time this way. . . . Well, gonna miss you fellas."

Tiller took a deep breath. This was it. He'd waited as long as he dared. Now he had to put the harpoon in. The one thing he knew that could blow this Boudreaux-Shattuck thing apart.

"Bender. Listen. You know who this girlfriend of Shattuck's is? I do. I saw 'em together. You ready for this? It's—"

But he never got to say it.

Drowning out his words, gas suddenly started to blast out through the exhaust valve at his feet. As he jumped back, another came open. His ears sizzled as the pressure started to drop. He and Rodriquez both dived at once, slamming the valves shut from inside. As they forced the valve handles over, two others jerked open on the far side of the chamber.

"He's tryin' to bend us!"

"Close all the valves. All of 'em. From our side."

From the intercom, Boudreaux's drunken mumble. "They're closin' 'em from inside. Okay, all I got to do, shut down the panel. Oxygen—off. Heat—off. Power—"

The interior light went out. The fan spun to a halt. The purr of the recirculator and scrubber, so low and continuous that they no longer noticed it, suddenly stopped.

"—Off."

"No!" Porch screamed. He battered at cast curved steel with his fists. "Bender!"

Galloway shouted, "Roland! Listen! Your wife—"

But the intercom cut him off again, going from transmit to receive as Boudreaux leaned on the lever. "What about her? I don't know which of you was screwing her. Maybe you all were! Okay, I send you all straight to hell!"

The click of the intercom going off. Forever.

Tiller spun. He looked the length of the chamber. Then he grabbed his dive harness.

"We better get strapped in, guys. This is gonna be a rough ride."

In the dim gray light, they looked at one anothers' faces: Galloway, Porchellacchia, Rodriquez, and, at the far end of the chamber, at bay, Winslow.

Or should I call him Desmond Winton? Tiller thought.

Then the ship hit them.

It all happened very slowly. Or maybe it only seemed slow. The noise came first, a grinding, tearing roar. Then after a while, the deck tilted up. They could see the red and black sides sliding by the porthole, rusty plates and weeping rivets.

The shock rippled back to the chamber and suddenly everything blurred. He felt his grip ripped free and his body catapulted spinning into the air. The harness stopped him after six inches and slammed him back against the bulkhead, nearly snapping his neck. Porchellacchia's harness broke and he flew five feet and slammed into the deck. The bunks collapsed under Winslow and fell on top of him.

When the shock rumbled away, it left silence. The chamber lay on its side, swaying. Galloway tripped his harness and crawled to the porthole. He rubbed his eyes, then looked out again, but he still saw nothing but gray.

He realized he was looking down into the sea. The barge was sagging over very slowly.

They were going down. He had to admit it: It didn't surprise him. A lay barge wasn't a warship, with watertight compartments and a crew trained in damage control. Hit on one side, abandoned, it would fill and roll and sink—with them still aboard and still under pressure, sealed in a steel tomb, bolted and chained to the deck.

With a long-drawn-out, sliding, clattering roar, the barge capsized. The light vanished. He found himself hanging upside down. And then the most terrifying thing of all happened.

It started to get dark outside the portholes.

"We're sinking," muttered Rodriquez.

The others stared at the slowly darkening circle of heavy glass. Galloway felt cold. Sinking? It was a long way down. A *long* way down. But not long enough.

Because when they got there, upside down, with the lay barge coming down on top of them—it was pretty obvious what was going to happen. Thick as the chamber walls were, they couldn't support five or six thousand tons of steel, whatever the barge weighed.

They were going to be crushed.

But he couldn't think of any way out that didn't mean they were just as dead.

He heard the others breathing, harsh, loud sounds, as if the air was already gone. In the last ebbing of light, he looked into their eyes: Porch, Rodriquez, Winton. They stared back, gripping handholds or bunk frames. No one spoke, but he could see it in their hunched shoulders, their taut, drawn mouths. They understood, too.

The sway gentled as the sea beyond the glass went black. Now they sank motionlessly, almost silently, except for the crackle and thud of crushing compartments in the huge hull above them. Gradually that, too, died away, and they sank faster, plummeting through the dark.

They stood staring at nothing, waiting to die.

Then the quiet was interrupted again. This time by a scrape, then a growing scream. The chamber jolted and rocked, and around them through the sea came the thunder of steel meeting reinforced concrete, steel snagging and tearing, like a train being dragged down a superhighway upside down. Then came a slam, a long, rumbling rattle like miles of chain running out. Finally a squealing reverberation whipped the upside-down chamber back and forth. It rocked from side to side, its chained-down skids grating and screeching against the deck, knocking the men locked inside it to their hands and knees. Then, with a long, horrifyingly loud boom, it slowly came to rest.

And then that noise, too, trailed away into creakings and rumblings. But the dark stayed.

After a while, Galloway pushed himself back to his feet. He stood half-crouched, swaying, horror making his hands numb. We're on the bottom, he thought. And somehow, still alive. But he wasn't sure whether that was good news. Trapped a thousand feet down, with a hurricane going over topside—and for all they knew, the platform wrecked, on fire, destroyed.

No air, no heat, no power. No way to let anyone know they were down here. With thousands of tons of buckled, crushed steel collapsed on top of them.

Even if they could get to the surface somehow, they'd die. The helium would come out of solution in their bodies and they'd die.

"Gas," someone said in a high, strangled, mad-sounding voice.

"What's that, Wildman?"

"They locked us in here. Now they're gonna gas us."

Tiller fumbled for the work light on his harness. He aimed it and switched it on.

The bell end of the chamber was higher than the main lock. The beam shot the length of it and lighted up Winton, standing at its bottom, straightening from his gear bag.

Something gleamed in his hand, reflecting the light: a nine-millimeter Smith & Wesson automatic.

Rodriquez screamed, "No, Wildman! Not in here! You hit one of these ports—"

"You're not locking me in here. You're not going to gas me!"

"No, Wildman! No!" But even as he shouted, Tiller knew it was too late.

Desmond Winton was far beyond reasoning with.

The dark split open with a flash and crack. Bullets whanged and caromed, bouncing off the steel walls.

At the same moment, Porchellacchia charged. Bellowing, arms out, he half-ran, half-fell toward where Winton's gun flashed again and again and again.

TWENTY-SIX

When they pulled Porch off Winton, the big Pagan was dead. No wonder, Tiller thought, looking numbly down at the pool of blood and bilge water. He'd taken at least five slugs, two through the tattoo of the Norse warrior.

But he'd gotten his hands on Winton.

The Westerner was still alive. He was trying to breathe, hands to his throat. His eyes were wide and agonized in the glare of Rodriquez's Super Q.

Ace said, "Crushed windpipe?"

"Sure looks like it."

"Anything you can do for that, Tiller?"

"Emergency tracheotomy. Or stick a tube down his throat."

"Feel like trying it?"

"Nah," Galloway said. He picked the automatic up. He thought of finishing Winton off. But powder fumes were so thick already in the chamber, they could barely breathe. He let down the hammer and set the gun back down.

"Me, neither," said Rodriquez.

Tiller found one of the blankets and put it over Porch's face. It didn't seem possible that he could be dead. "Sorry I can't do any more for you, buddy," he muttered.

He straightened and took a deep breath, putting them both behind him. He looked at Rodriquez, remembering as much as seeing the narrow dark face, the slicked-back hair, the earring. Down to two now. Well, the Chino hand was smart. He was a good diver. Maybe together they could figure some way out of here.

"Ace, any ideas?"

"First thing, we got to get something to breathe, man."

"Let's see. We got hats here in the chamber. And there're bailouts back in the bell."

"They won't last long. We got to get to the emergency gas in the pot, man."

"There's a lot more in the gas bank."

"But it's already set up to breathe, in the bell. An' the bell's the only thing we can cut loose, get out of here. I vote the bell."

"Okay, sounds good to me," Tiller said.

But when they tried the hatch to the bell, it wouldn't open. They looked at each other in dismay.

"Is it flooded?"

"I don't think so. I don't get it. We equalized when we docked."

Galloway said slowly, "Unless Bender opened the valves to the bell, too, while he was opening the ones to the chamber. That would bleed off all the internal pressure, then it'd flood on the way down."

"*Mierda.*" Rodriquez sucked a tooth. "Les' think about this, now. The barge is upside down. Nose-down, the way we are slanting. But it ain't laying on top of us or we'd be mashed. So the stern must be hung up on the—what do you call them? The big tank things. The concrete ones, at the base of the platform."

"That's good." Tiller frowned, thinking about the oil storage.

"It is?"

"Better than having it on top of us. Then we'd never get out."

Rodriquez grinned slowly. "Okay, smart guy. We get out. Then what?"

Galloway coughed and noticed that the air was getting murky. His lungs were starting to hurt, too. "I'll worry about that after we get something to breathe."

But if they couldn't open the hatches to the bell, that left only the main lock, leading out into the open sea.

"What you think's happening topside, man?"

"I don't know, Ace."

"Think that ship hit the platform like Bender said?"

"Yeah, but bouncing off the barge, it might not be so easy. I don't think that was in the original plan, having the lay barge in the way."

Rodriquez said, "My guess is, Bender wouldn't leave nothing like that to chance."

"What you mean?"

"I don't know, man. Just doesn't sound like his style. He's a diver. The way he got everything else zipped up—no, if he got to have an oil spill now, he would have some way to make sure there was a *big* oil spill."

Ace had squatted beside Winton again. Now he looked up. "Hey. Know what? He's not dead yet."

"What?"

"He's still breathing."

Tiller decided. He was going to have to open the main hatch. They were already nearly pressurized to depth, so he shouldn't be in much danger from bends or squeeze. The steps would be: one, lock out; two, swim around to the bell; three, let himself in through the lower hatch; and four, blow the bell clear, using the emergency gas it carried.

He shivered, and not just from the cold that was starting to penetrate the chamber. He couldn't think of any way to breathe while he did all this. They had helmets, but all their bailout bottles and umbilicals were in the bell.

"What you want to do about him?"

"Winton? I don't plan to do anything about him. I plan to leave him here, okay?"

Rodriquez shrugged and straightened. "Here's what I have been thinking. I'll lock out the main lock. Swim around to the bell and lock in. Okay? Grab a bailout bottle, first thing I get in there. Then—"

"That's my plan, Ace."

"No, I go. I'm more familiar with the bell."

"How do you figure? I've spent as much time in the damn pot as you have." Tiller slapped his thighs, remembering all he had on was shorts. "All right. Got a quarter?"

"No."

Finally, Rodriquez held out a closed fist. Tiller looked at it.

"One, two, three."

They regarded a pair of rocks thoughtfully. "Try again."

"One, two, three."

"Paper covers rock."

"*Mierda.*"

He pulled his suit out of the jumbled pile on the deck and stepped into it. He zipped it, thought about weights for a second, then decided, no, forget it, not this deep. He found McCray's helmet. Boots? No, flippers would be better for this job. He found a pair and strapped them on. Rodriquez handed him his Super Q silently.

"You open the hatch, Ace. I don't want to be out of breath when I bolt this helmet down."

Rodriquez bent and cracked the valve to equalize the main lock with the interior. He swung the hatch up with a grunt and stood back.

"It's flooding."

"Not far, it won't. We're pretty close to ambient."

He checked the helmet out as the dark water welled in. They watched it rise, breathing shallowly. It reached the lip of the inner door and then stopped. They could smell it, a dank, lightless, muddy smell.

"Here goes." He panted, fighting the need to cough, building up as much oxygen as he could in his bloodstream. He slipped the helmet over his head and Ace cammed it shut. Gripping the flash in his left hand, he turned around and splashed backward till the water reached his waist. Then he bent, bringing his helmet under the surface, and slid fins-first out into the sea.

He slid out, turning slowly, into liquid night. For a second, he was afraid he'd screwed up. There was nothing below him. Then he drove ahead with the fins. He was a little heavy, but not too heavy to swim. He'd guessed right.

He turned and swept the light along the chamber.

It hung from the barge, canted at about a fifteen-degree angle. Above it, the wreck stretched away out of his sight. He pointed his beam toward where he figured the platform to be, but he couldn't see anything. There was a lot of silt stirring around. Probably a lot of stuff had hit the seabed when the barge turned turtle.

283

Cold out here, he thought. He eased his first breath out and took another slowly out of the helmet itself. Slow. Easy. Everything slow and easy now.

He figured he had two or three minutes to play with before he blacked out.

He started swimming forward, upward, toward the bell.

It came into view around the chamber's curve, and he felt relieved. Neither he nor Ace had wanted to put their greatest fear into words: that the bell might have broken loose and fallen away. But there it was, hanging upside down by the chains that had kept it from sliding around on deck.

He took another breath. It was stifling already. Superlites didn't have much dead airspace in them. When you had flow, that was good; carbon dioxide couldn't build up. But when you were breathing it, well, you wished you had more.

He kicked slowly upward, got his hands on the chains, and hauled himself up in the black silence. Only it wasn't silent, not completely. A deep, bubbling rumble came from somewhere above him. A slow, reverberating boom, as if a piece of steel plate was swaying in the current. Then a single pop, or thud, that seemed closer. He listened but didn't hear that again.

He hoped the barge crew had all gotten out. He hoped there wasn't anybody still in there, in some forgotten, dogged-down compartment, full of supercompressed air.

Okay, here he was, at the bottom of the bell—only now it was the top. He had to haul hard on the lower hatch to get it open. But as soon as he let go, it fell shut again. His heart sank. He didn't have enough air to get back to the chamber.

Above him, pinned against the barge's deck by its own buoyancy, was a piece of wooden dunnage. He swam up and got it. He hauled the hatch up again, panting the exhausted hot air in his helmet. His heart was speeding up. He was getting dizzy.

He propped the hatch open with the wood, swung his legs in, and dropped inside. Then he pushed the block out and tried to secure the lower hatch. It wouldn't close. He realized belatedly that he was trying to compress water, never an easy chore. He left it and kicked at the inner hatch, gently at first, then desperately as he felt himself losing consciousness.

It unsealed with a gush of bubbles and he fell slowly into the interior of the flooded bell.

His hands jerked the whip from one of the bailout bottles he and Porch had left there. He jammed it into his helmet. He sucked desperately but got nothing, then remembered, cursed himself, and twisted the valve to full open.

Gas, rich, thick, wonderful heliox. He sucked it with eyes closed, and spasms ran down his legs and arms.

When he recovered, he closed the upper hatch, above him. This was difficult. He was pushing up, and it was heavy, but he got it closed. He flipped over the dogging handle to hold it till he pressurized. He flicked on the battery-powered interior light. He lined up valves and all at once gas was roaring in, driving the water out, the level dropping by the second. When it got down to his neck, he uncammed his helmet and lifted it off.

He grinned and hammered a fist into a palm. Rodriquez would be sitting in there sweating, wondering if he'd made it. Well, he had! He kept gas coming in till the water was below the chamber-mating hatch, then secured it. "Here comes the cavalry, Ace," he muttered.

The side hatch equalized with a hiss. It groaned as it swung open, slowly, heavily, coming up with his strength against the tilt. Water gushed out of the transfer trunk, then ebbed to a trickle. He hauled himself in and shoved the inner hatch open to the chamber.

There was no one there.

He stared stupidly, then grabbed the light and slid his legs through. There was some*thing*, though. He pointed the light down at it, heart thumping with sudden terror.

Rodriquez lay facedown a few feet from Porchellacchia.

He sank to his knees. Suddenly, it was hard to breathe, and not just because of the close air. His shaking fingers explored the bullet hole in the assistant supervisor's skull.

He staggered up suddenly and swept his light around. It probed into piles of pawed-through gear, the jumbled mass of the collapsed bunks, then glittered off the water that covered the bottom of the chamber.

No sign of Winton.

He'd gone out the lower hatch, just as Galloway had.

Like a galvanized corpse, he jerked suddenly and clambered back uphill. His feet slid on the curved wet overhead of the chamber. He gasped and clutched with fingers prickling with terror. Had to get back to the bell. Had to get back *now*—

285

From outside came a scrape, a ping, a tap.

His hands slipped on the wet hatch coaming and he fell backward, rapping his head against the folding table, which had flopped down from the bulkhead. He shook it off and climbed again, a grim, desperate monkey with blood running down the back of his head.

He rolled into the bell and hauled the hatch closed behind him. His hands were shaking. His head jangled. A faint screech caught his ear, and he glanced up. The dogging lever was turning.

He had his hand on the lock blow-down valve before he stopped himself. Blasting Winton with gas might actually help him. If he caught a bubble, he could breathe. But if he could keep him out there, Winton would drown.

He climbed, bracing one foot on the rim of the side hatch and the other on the bottom of the gas-heater panel. He reached up and grabbed the lever and yanked it back. It rotated easily for two inches, then halted.

Someone was on the other side, turning it back.

He struggled to turn it closed. He was on tiptoe. It was above him, an incredibly difficult position. The lever slid back. He braced his feet and panted and forced it a little clockwise. It moved back against his straining hands. Air started to sizzle around the edges of the hatch.

He sobbed aloud. He knew he was as strong as Winton. He had all the air he wanted. But his hands were slippery. Sweat poured down his face. The smooth metal handle slid faster and faster between his clutching, numb fingers.

Then it stopped.

He panted and planted his feet again and quickly dogged it, locking the hatch. A hammering came through the metal from the other side. Then it faded, weakened.

Tiller hung from the dogging handle, panting and coughing.

It was gone.

He waited fifteen minutes, just to make sure. No sound came from the far side of the hatch or anywhere else.

Winton was dead.

He fought down a need to retch and splashed his face with some of the cold seawater left in the bell. He rinsed his mouth. The brine reminded him he was getting thirsty. He was getting cold, too. His teeth were chattering. His calves were starting to cramp.

Okay, he told himself. You've got enough onboard gas for a few hours. You've got enough battery power you can run the heater for a while. After that, you're gonna have to either be at the surface or else hooked up to the main bank.

Either way, he'd have to go out again. But this time would be easier. This time he had a bailout and an umbilical.

He took several more deep breaths. The trouble was, he was scared.

Hey, the Great Killer Tiller, he's not supposed to get squirrely, said the little jeering voice in his head that was the only company he had now.

"But he is," he told himself aloud. "He's scared as hell."

He wondered again what was happening topside. Was the platform still standing? What was the hurricane doing? Where was Boudreaux? He'd have to live through this to find out.

He forced himself to start. He pulled the umbilicals off both racks and connected them end to end with a double male fitting from McCray's tender bag. That should be enough hose to have a good look around.

Then he thought about how to exit the bell. If he went out through the exit lock, which was now above him, he'd lose all the atmosphere in here. There was more in the bell's emergency supply, but not so much more that he felt like wasting even a cubic inch of it.

He decided to go out through the chamber instead. He looked at the hot-water panel longingly, then sighed. He checked the lineup one last time, flicked the interior light off, and turned the gas heater up as far as he could stand it. Maybe that would make up some for the lack of hot water. He opened the side lock and crawled back into the chamber, jerking his umbilical through after him.

The water was still and black at the lower end of the chamber. His breath echoed spookily as he laid out his hose. Then he paused, eyeing the pile of suits. He picked out the biggest one, Porch's, and struggled into it, over his own. That would hold the cold off a little longer. He tried to grin. McCray's helmet, Porch's suit, Winton's fins, Ace's light—he was getting to be a committee.

The voice in his head didn't think it was funny.

The sea seemed blacker this time, colder. Hypothermia was going to be a problem. Problem, hell, it was gonna kill him unless he figured something out. He could breathe, though. He had gas for about twenty hours in the bell reserve. The first thing he did was look for the gas bank.

The deck was bare. Just snapped-off chains hanging down. Staring at it, where all the tanks of oxygen and heliox mixes for different depths had been, he took a deep breath and let it out.

And all hope with it. That was that. Even decompressing twice as fast as the tables let you, it would take him two days to get topside from this depth.

The knowledge brought a strange freedom, as if he'd already died and was a ghost now, wandering the night sea. Something else occurred to him just then and he paused, alone in the black. Something Rodriquez had said before he died. Something about Boudreaux. "If he got to have an oil spill now, he would have some way to make sure there was a *big* oil spill."

Now he understood why he'd gotten a mental picture of Pandora 1000's oil-storage tanks when Ace had said that.

He'd been swimming aft slowly while he thought, following his light along the deck overhead. Now he saw the pale reflection ahead of him. A few more yards and he was at the platform again, the same place he'd tried to stab the riser.

Now the thin steel pipe lay smashed and buckled across the top of the template. Other junk had fallen, too—shattered derrick members, lengths of drill string, huge rat's nests of kinked steel cable. He took his time moving across it, keeping his umbilical clear. He didn't want to get tangled in this mess. Not before he put a stick in Boudreaux's and Shattuck's wheels.

He got to the first of the white cones and tilted it up. Just what he'd figured: a shaped charge, sited to penetrate the top of the tank beneath it.

It would be big, all right. There had to be weeks of production stored here. Hitting the beaches all at once, it would

288

make the *Torrey Canyon* or *Exxon Valdez* disasters look like a knocked-over bottle of Coppertone.

Here's one for all you shrimp out there, he thought, pulling his Big Chief. A second of sawing and the ends of the detonating line drifted apart.

He went from tank to tank, cutting the Primacord. At any moment, he knew, whoever was at the other end could set them off. It didn't worry him. It would just save him a few minutes of agonized suffocation.

When he was done, he let the current take him back to the template. He grabbed one of the bell guides and hung there, wondering, Now what? He contemplated just cutting his umbilical. Not turning on the bailout. Just letting go, letting the current sweep him away into oblivion.

Suddenly, he was bathed in light.

He squinted up into it, to see the lens of the TV remote staring down at him.

Oho, he thought. Still somebody up there on the platform. Wonder who?

He went back to thinking about letting go. The worst thing of all, he decided, was being alone. Took you long enough to learn that, he thought. But I guess you finally did.

He let go of the template. The current swiftly took charge, bearing him off across the top of the tanks. His umbilical dragged after him, scraping and clattering. Annoyed, he pulled out his knife. What had old Claunch said? "Funny thing, didn't feel too bad about it." That was how he felt. Hell, he'd figured it would happen someday, and that it would probably happen underwater. At least he'd monkey-wrenched those bastards before he went.

He grabbed his umbilical in one hand, feeling for it with the knife-blade. This was as easy as it was ever gonna get. A little dizziness, then the black.

A white-hot shaft of light lanced down from above. It flicked here and there, then probed into the wreckage around the template. It moved in, probed, then swung around toward the wreck of the lay barge.

It was so bright, he could see it almost entire. Blunt bow buried in the murky bottom. The bridge section crushed. The stern and crumpled frame of the stinger resting on the oil tanks that formed 1000's ballast and base. Lengths of pipe scattered like uncooked spaghetti. And two-thirds of the way back, the chamber and bell, locked together, hanging upside down.

Tiller let go of his umbilical. The current was carrying him over the edge of the tank, so he started swimming again. He closed the knife and let it drop to the end of its lanyard.

He decided to go over and see what was going on.

As he got closer, the light appeared to be approaching the platform. It had been above him when he first saw it. Now it was almost level, descending faster than a diver could. Some kind of submersible? Rescue vehicle? No, it hadn't been more than an hour since the collision.

"Galloway," something said through the water. It echoed and reverberated, a weird burbling sound rolling away into the darkness.

He couldn't answer, but he swam faster. The light wasn't far off now, two brilliant blue-white disks. There was so much murk and silt in the water that some of the light illuminated its source.

He stopped swimming.

It was the Brute Suit, the thrusters bolted on and running. He could hear the whine. The helmet-mounted work lights burning with all the power of 360 volts supplied from topside.

Aw, hell, he thought.

The underwater transducer spoke again, stentorian tones echoing from the jacket legs, the wreck, rolling away along the bottom. It sounded like Poseidon calling his name.

The light swung around and pinned him. He blinked and shielded his helmet with his arm.

He heard the thrusters whir up to full speed and suddenly realized he had to hide. He hauled himself back along his umbilical, the light still full on him. Finally, he ducked behind one of the massive jacket legs. It won't come in here, he thought, finning along it to drive himself upward. Not into this mess.

But he was wrong. The thrusters slowed but kept running. In the backwash of the lights, Tiller watched the other, whoever he was, cruise carefully past the leg he hid behind. Coasting in a few feet above the jumble of wire and shattered steel atop the tanks.

Then it slowed and the vertical thrusters came on—a little slow, uncoordinated. But at last, the other diver got it warped around and lowered to the top of the tank. It stood there for a few minutes. Then slowly, it bent. The claw-edged arms reached out.

Galloway tensed as he saw what it was doing. Whoever was inside the Brute was reconnecting the shaped charges. Clumsily. Slowly. But you didn't have to tie a fancy knot to connect Primacord. Just laying a strand across another was enough.

Sudden rage squeezed his heart. He let go and swam downward, kicking hard, driving himself down so fast water tore past his helmet. He came down on the bent figure's helmet with his Big Chief out and sawed at the fiberglass.

It hardly left a nick. The arm came up and the manipulator grabbed him. It closed with incredible power, and he felt the claws shear with paper-cutter ease through two layers of rubber and then the flesh of his side.

He let go fast and swam upward. The glass port below tilted back slowly to see him, and he made out the face behind it.

Boudreaux.

The Cajun wasn't real used to the Brute. And he was probably still drunk. But he was a hell of a good diver—skilled, ruthless, and strong.

All at once, Tiller realized just what he was facing. He was in standard saturation-diving dress—nothing but rubber and cloth and a helmet. Dependent for breath on a rubber hose. While below him—no, rising now, the thrusters powering him upward faster than a man could swim—was an impervious armored monster with cutter claws. Powered by electricity, powerful as hydraulics, and invulnerable to any tools or weapons he had.

He ducked into a jagged mass of wreckage, feeling like a rabbit with a wolf on its heels. He heard the thrusters whine into reverse. At any rate, Bender wouldn't follow him into this briar patch—

A snip, a click, and a roar of bubbles.

He grabbed his umbilical and hauled. The end came in. He held it up before his faceplate, seeing a neat clipped cut, as if the tough rubber and comm wire and rope had been sheared with a hydraulic cutter. Which, of course, was exactly what the manipulators were.

Okay, EGS time. He dropped the stub of hose and opened

the valve on his bailout. He had heliox again—but not very much, not at this depth. Not at the rate he was wheezing it.

He came out the other end of the tunnel of wreckage and turned and swam around the outside of the leg. He didn't figure Boudreaux could follow; if he did, he'd wind up with his lines wrapped around the leg big-time.

But when he came around the leg, he slammed into him face-first. Boudreaux had guessed exactly what he was going to do, and had done it first.

This guy's no dummy, the voice in his head told him. He's good. At least as good as you.

He wished the voice would shut up.

The arms closed on him in a deadly bear hug. He tried to slip out, but they hugged tighter. His hands scrabbled over its surface. A JIM suit had external oxygen valves. Connectors he could yank out. But the Brute was smooth, hard, featureless. He hammered on the little round faceplate with the butt of his knife. Even a crack would do the trick. It would be like nicking a Thermos bottle; compared with the pressure around them, the unpressurized interior of the one-atmosphere suit was almost a vacuum. But it was too thick, too tough.

"Nice try, cher," boomed the speaker, right next to his ear. He reversed the knife and tried sawing at the cables for the lights. No good. They were armored, too.

He wished he could tell this son of a bitch off, but there was no way to speak to him. Then he thought, Sure there is. Jamming his helmet against the Brute's, he screamed, "I'm gonna stop you, Bender."

The Cajun laughed. It sounded horrible, rumbling and rolling away into the sea.

Tiller struggled in the relentless, ever-tightening hug. He had to get free before he ran out of air. But he didn't want those cutters on him again. Some hot fluid was seeping inside his suit—blood, where they'd cut him once.

Just beyond Boudreaux's helmet, he saw a loop of the Brute's umbilical floating. No air hose, not on this suit. Just the lift line and a power cable. No point cutting those, even if he could.

Or was there?

He didn't have a lot of time to think. So he just did it— reached up and hauled the loop of cable down and pushed it into one of the open claws. Then he thrust himself away, holding one of the arms and kicking as if Boudreaux had him.

Suddenly lightning lived under the sea. A dazzling, bubbling arc that lighted the whole platform.

At the same moment, the Brute went dark, the work lights on the helmet fading to ruby sparks, then darkness. The thrusters whirred down the scale to silence.

He swam backward, blinking as his eyes adjusted. The only light now came from the TV lights on the template, behind them. When he could see again, they showed him Boudreaux staring down at his port claw. Shaking it, then slamming it against the concrete platform leg. It didn't open. The jaws had been welded together.

Galloway grinned tightly. The invulnerable monster was now a clambering turtle, helpless unless he was stupid enough to close with it. And he wasn't going to. He was just going to hamstring him. Pulling at the stub of umbilical still attached to his own helmet, he swam up and over Boudreaux. He tore the rope out of his umbilical and tied a running knot.

As he passed over the Brute's head, Boudreaux tried a crablike grab for him. Tiller avoided it with a flip of his fins, dropped the loop over the thruster pack, and pulled it taut. Then he tied a quick fisherman's bend, making the other end fast around one of the fallen I beams.

That should do it. He kicked away, looking back. The other diver was trapped, tied to the wreckage with a knot he couldn't reach. It would take a while, but he'd die down here.

The claw whipped around, faster than he expected, and caught the tip of his fin.

Struggling, kicking, he was hauled in like a hooked fish. His helmet slammed into the concrete. Boudreaux couldn't move, but he was solidly braced. Whereas Galloway was free but had nothing to kick against except the sea. He was drawn remorselessly back into the bear hug. Only this time, Boudreaux gave himself room to use the manipulator, the starboard one, the one that still worked. It had hydraulic power for one or two more strokes. Galloway felt the steel claw probing. He struggled, but his arms were caught under the Brute's armpits. The claw worked its way in relentlessly, the open blades tearing the rubber of his neck dam.

Boudreaux was going to shear his throat. And there wasn't a thing he could do about it.

Suddenly, another arm was pulling Boudreaux's back, just enough so that Tiller could wedge his elbow in between his throat and the claw. He saw a helmet above the Brute. Saw eyes behind the faceplate.

His numb lips murmured soundlessly, "*Wildman.*"

The other diver had something in his hand. Galloway stared as he thrust it against the back of Boudreaux's suit, against the tough fiberglass shell.

Winton's arm pumped, and a whirring grind came through the water.

It was the little hand-powered drill out of his tender kit.

Boudreaux must have recognized it, too, because suddenly the armored turtle became agitated. It flailed and kicked, then toppled back on top of the clinging Winton. The claw reached back, snapping and clicking. Winton's hose roared bubbles and flailed away into the dark.

But the grinding went on and on. Tiller sculled, holding himself in place with hands and sliced-up fins. He saw Boudreaux's terrified eyes rolling behind the face port.

Then the drill penetrated. It made only a little hole. The sea did the rest. Boudreaux struggled. His mouth jerked open in a soundless howl.

He was dead long before water showed behind his face port.

When Tiller pushed the Brute off Winton, he was dead, too. The gaunt face didn't move behind the faceplate, but the trace of a grim smile lingered on the thin lips.

With his last breath, Desmond Winton had had his revenge.

TWENTY-SEVEN

Two days later, he dropped through the lower lock into a blue so luminous, it made his eyes sting behind McCray's skin-diving mask. He hung there for a moment, looking up. Then, with a flick of his fins, headed for the light.

The surface, he thought, hardly daring to believe it.

After the face-off with Boudreaux, he'd followed Winton's umbilical back to find out what the Wildman had been breathing. It led to the bottom, beneath the barge, where he found the gas bank half-buried in the silt. He still didn't know how he'd done it, but Winton had managed to find an umbilical and connect it to the rack box. For better or worse, though, the Wildman had picked a nearly empty tank. He must have been on the verge of hypoxia as he reached Galloway and Boudreaux at the base of the platform, locked in that final embrace.

Sultry light flickered across the bare skin of his outstretched arms as he kicked upward.

Getting the bell free and rigged for ascent had taken the better part of a day. First, he'd detached one of the chains that held it to the deck of the barge, then reattached it to the bell's lifting pad eye. Then he'd pulled the pins on the remaining chains.

The bell dropped away, turning, but the single chain snatched it up short. It bounced around as he hovered, watching it, but ended up reoriented properly, ballast down. The current kept it out at a slight angle, swaying and turning slowly, like a hanging plant in a strong wind.

295

He let himself back inside, turned the heater on, and warmed up as much as he could, listening to the chain grate and squeak above him. He knew he was squandering the battery, using it for heat. But he was racing against hypothermia, the numbing cold gradually sapping his ability to move and even to think.

When he stopped shuddering, he reexited. He dug around in the wreck until he found rope and a big shackle. He returned to the bell and used the last of the battery to warm up once more. Meanwhile, he measured out the line, both arms outstretched. He measured it three times. It had to be right or he'd die.

When he was sure it was, he cut it. Then he exited again. He made one end of the line fast to a sturdy brace on the tool basket, near the bottom of the bell. The other end he shackled to a pad eye on the wreck. Finally, he used the remaining line to hoist two full tanks of breathing mix from the gas bank up into the bell.

Back in the bell for the last time, shaking so hard that he could barely move, he got the inner hatch closed and dogged, then pulled the pins and hammered the handles down to drop the ballast. The bell leapt upward like a released balloon and slammed into the wreck, directly above it. He hung on, helpless now, listening as the current drove it grating across the slanting deck. If it hung up, that was it. He couldn't go out again; he'd just freeze to death down here. It scraped, squealed, and then, suddenly, lurched and rolled itself free up over the turn of the gunwale.

He clung to the gas panel, watching the exterior pressure gauge dropping.

Sixty feet from the surface, the tether line jerked the ascending bell to a halt. It hung there, then slowly began rolling, picking up the motion of the swells above it. He clung grimly, fighting nausea. But he was happy, because it also began to warm up. He was tense for the first few hours, wondering whether the line would hold. But it did, and he finally allowed himself a much needed nap.

After that, all he had to do was watch the clock and the interior pressure gauge. Every hour, he cracked a valve and let a few feet of pressure bleed off into the sea.

He couldn't do a standard decompression. He didn't have

enough gas aboard for that. Even an accelerated decomp would take eighty-five hours. He was cutting that in half, flirting with the bends. He'd need a chamber when he got out. But so far, all he had was rash and some joint pain.

And now, at last, he'd left the bell and was swimming upward. . . .

He broke the surface and yanked the mask off, treading water, and almost fainted at his first breath of real air.

The storm had passed. The sunlight fell like golden rain across a sea blue as a newborn's eyes. Fleecy clouds chased one another across a brilliant sky.

He turned his head and saw that Pandora 1000 was damaged but still standing. On the far side, a boat was standing off, too far away for him to make out clearly from as low in the water as he was.

He finned slowly toward the platform, taking it easy, because he was very tired and hungry and faint from thirst—all he'd had for two days was the ginger ale in McCray's bag. As he drew closer, he saw that the damage was greater than he'd thought at first. The cranes were gone and the helo platform hung down in a limp fray of ragged steel. The derrick tilted drunkenly. There was wreckage around the legs, coated with a slime of oil. He stayed clear of it, swimming along the edges till he spotted a rope ladder hanging down. Somebody had been here already. He shed mask and fins and started climbing.

As he reached the cellar deck, he saw where the freighter's bow had bitten into it. One of the legs had buckled; here and there sections of deck had collapsed. The whole great structure was silent, abandoned. In the warm sunlight, the light breeze, it seemed spooky. He could smell oil. There were slicks of it here and there on the buckled, canted deck, but he didn't see any on the water. And he didn't see any more coming up from below.

Then he saw what he needed. He circled a huge hole in the deck and fell to his knees in a corner, gasping as he plunged his face again and again into the puddle of warm, oily, wonderful rainwater.

"Well, well. Galloway. I thought it might be worth keeping an eye out here for a couple of days."

He turned his head, to see Brad Shattuck brushing off his trousers. He was wearing a Coastal Oil hard hat and a rumpled gray suit. He wasn't wearing glasses today, and he looked tired. Through a gap in the deck, Tiller could see the boat now, riding not far away from the ladder. It looked familiar. After a second, he recognized the *Janis J.*

Then he saw the woman. She stepped out of the shadows behind Shattuck, slim and casual in jeans and a loose-fitting white blouse, white espadrilles, a calfskin belt pouch, sunglasses. Arden Boudreaux.

The executive looked around the platform, then reached unhurriedly into his back pocket. He held the .45 automatic out and away from his body, pointed at the rippled steel plating. "Get up. Where's Bender? Where are the other divers?"

Tiller got up slowly. He said, "They're all dead."

"Boudreaux? Winslow?"

"Dead."

"What happened down there?"

"They killed each other." It was the truth—sort of.

They faced each other across a gap where the support beams of the cellar deck had buckled and the plating had torn. Through it, Galloway could see the sea washing the mangled wreckage the storm and the collision had dumped on top of the platform's base.

Shattuck came a few feet closer, taking his hard hat off. He dropped it to the deck and wiped his forehead with the sleeve of his suit. Tiller took a step back as he approached.

"Boudreaux's dead? Then you're the only one left who knows what happened." He didn't sound threatening, despite the gun. Just businesslike. "We'd better talk. Review things, reach some kind of conclusion here."

"I'm game," said Tiller. He watched the gun very closely. Shattuck held it loosely, casually, not bothering to point it at him. Galloway judged he knew how to use it. He flicked his eyes to Arden Boudreaux. She stood quietly out of the way, arms crossed. He couldn't see her eyes behind the sunglasses.

Shattuck said, "You've probably got some questions. Go ahead, ask them. I want you to get the big picture, because once you do, I have an offer for you."

Tiller swallowed. He felt disoriented. The sun was too bright. But it sounded like this was his only chance. He cleared his throat of the oily taste, spat. "Okay. For starters. You set this all up—the ship, the wreck, Bender disposing of us. You set up a major oil spill. Why?"

Shattuck sucked his lip. Finally, he said, "You've figured out a lot on your own, haven't you? Okay. Here it is.

"Pandora South was expensive to develop, real expensive. And, turned out there was oil here. But not as much as the geologists thought. I was in major trouble. Coastal almost went under. But then I found some angels to help out."

Galloway remembered another glaring hot day, the taste of jambalaya and the sound of Cajun music. He remembered the scream of jets coming into a nearby airport, a Mercedes with diplomatic plates, a glimpse through an open door. . . . He said, "*Arab* angels."

Shattuck frowned, then nodded. "Uh . . . yeah. You know, I have no idea how you knew that. But you're right. Arab angels."

"But oil prices are up."

"That's right, they're up, and I was pumping as fast as I could."

Tiller remembered Hannah West's explanation of field depletion. "Too fast, actually."

"Sure, that's why everything looked so busy. Unfortunately, it's too late to help. Coastal's already gone. Raided, leveraged out, every rig and foot of pipe mortgaged. The company's a shell."

"Okay, but a *spill*—how's that gonna save it?"

"It won't."

"So what's the point?"

Shattuck said patiently, "The point is, what's going to happen to the competition."

"The competition?"

"The other offshore domestic producers. Amerada Hess, Marathon, Chevron, Conoco, Mobil. What happens to them when a million barrels of oil comes ashore on the Gulf Coast? The papers, TV, they won't leave the government any choice. First thing, they'll shut every rig in the Gulf down for inspection."

"So what? Then they come back on—"

"No. They don't 'come back on.' Shut down production, slap on more regulations after the lean years they've already had—a lot of these rigs are going to shut down. You figured out who was financing me. Take it from there. Who wins then?"

He saw it then with dawning wonder. Saw how big it really was. And yet, how inevitable that somebody would try it one day. He cleared his throat again. "The Arabs."

"Exactly. They gain five or six more points market share. Another ten or eleven cents a barrel. How much is that worth? Try five hundred billion over ten years. That's big-league, Galloway. That's how the oil game's played."

"Okay, I got that. What about Todds? What was in the briefcase?"

"Tape recordings. Wiretapped conversations between me and my principals. Justice Department turned them over to MMS to try to figure out what was going on."

"They didn't know?"

"They're not exactly eager to investigate the oil industry, Galloway. Politicians aren't too keen digging for dirt where their campaign contributions come from." Shattuck looked around carefully again. Galloway flicked his eyes around the horizon too, desperately hoping for a boat, a witness. But except for the Davis, rolling hove to a few hundred yards off, the blue circle around them was void.

"Well?"

"I don't think we're on the same side, Shattuck."

"You haven't heard my offer yet."

"Well, that's true." He licked his lips. It was hard to make it back to the light, then have it all snatched away. "What're you offering?"

"Your own company."

"What?"

Shattuck smiled thinly and waved at the wreckage below them. "This is all going to have to be cleaned up. That'll take a lot of diving. Who's going to do it for me? DeepTech was sole ownership. Now Roland's gone, it'll belong to Arden. But she's not a diver, is she? She needs a partner who knows the business." His smile deepened, eyes crinkling.

"You just said Coastal was broke."

"Not anymore. We were insured. Remember?"

"Oh."

"Don't think this setback will change things. Roland failed, but the big plan's still good. My principals are still interested. We can restage the whole thing in a year or so. And this time, with your help, we'll make sure it goes off right."

Looking at the smiling Shattuck, he understood something for the first time. Boudreaux had been a willing, venal tool. Winton had been crazy. The vice president of offshore operations, Coastal Oil, might look respectable, but he was more dangerous than the ones who killed for him.

"A partnership," he said, looking at Mrs. Boudreaux. She was smiling faintly now, leaning against a buckled beam. "Arden, what do you think about that?"

"You are not my favorite man, Galloway. But if Brad says it will be profitable, why not? You can dive. You don't seem to have any problem breaking the law. It might work out."

"What happens after the big spill, though? We go to prison."

"Not if we do it right," said Shattuck. "And next time we will. And we'll get rich. All three of us. How's that sound? Not so bad? You end up wealthy, *and* with your own diving company. Now what do you say?"

"I don't think so," Tiller said.

Shattuck sighed. He glanced at Arden, then raised the .45. He aimed with both hands, police-style.

"Time to decide, Galloway. Yes or no. Rich or dead."

He looked up at the sun. Then he looked down at the sea. The deck was empty; the horizon was empty; the sea was empty. They were alone.

"Okay," he said. "You win."

The gun held steady. "You accept?"

He sighed. "Yeah, I accept."

Shattuck dropped the muzzle beside his leg. "I thought we could reach an agreement. Don't look so down in the mouth! This is your big moment, lad."

"Partners. With her. I run the operational end, though."

"That's right. Arden? Agreed?"

She shrugged.

"Exclusive contract with Coastal."

"Exclusive. And a bonus, a *nice* bonus, when all production stops in the Gulf of Mexico."

Galloway took a step forward and put out his hand. Shattuck looked at it, still smiling, and reached out.

Galloway pulled him forward, into the gap in the deck, and let go. Shattuck gasped, toppling. His arms windmilled for balance. The gun left his hand. It spun four or five times, falling away through the air.

It hit a mass of tangled steel, bounced off, and made a splash in the water. Shattuck hit the same wreckage but didn't bounce. He didn't move at all after he hit.

"Okay, Mrs. Boudreaux," Tiller said musingly, looking down at the sprawled body, half in and half out of the breaking sea. "I guess that about wraps it up."

But when he looked up, she had unzipped the little pouch at her waist.

He blinked. It wasn't a gun. It was a black cylinder, and she was pointing it at him. More or less by reflex, he bent and snatched up a length of pipe. They crouched, facing each other across the vacancy in the deck. Wind came up through it, fanning their faces.

"What's that? Tear gas?"

"Stay away! Stay away from me or you'll find out."

Tiller eyed it and her. Then he relaxed. He straightened, shaking his head. "No. No, Arden."

"What?"

He smiled bitterly. "We need each other."

She stood still, holding the thing on him. The fact that he didn't move, neither attacked nor ran, seemed to puzzle her. "What are you talking about?" she said.

"I'm talking about the Coast Guard, MMS, the FBI, or whoever's gonna get stuck trying to make sense of this mess. If there's only one survivor, who's gonna end up with the pie in her lap? You guess."

"They will try, but—"

"With all these bodies, they'll do more than try. The only way either of us'll walk is if our stories agree. Get it? So you and me, we're just ignorant bystanders. I'm just one of the divers, not too smart, a strong back who believed everything they told him. You're the happy housewife, sent old Roland off to work every day with a kiss and a lunch pail; you had no idea he was involved in anything shady. We didn't know Todds and Guidry and McCray were murdered. We didn't know Winslow was a fugitive from justice. We didn't know Roland and Shattuck were plotting a disaster."

"What about Brad?"

"His accident, you mean? He was inspecting the platform, estimating repairs, and he slipped on a patch of oil. Understand? Alone, they'll hang us. But if we back each other up, maybe we can both get out from under."

The weapon, or whatever it was, dropped slightly. "But what was I doing here?"

"Are you kidding? Your husband's missing. You made Shattuck bring you out to see if you could find out anything. It all holds together. I'm serious, Arden. Just to show you." He looked down at the pipe. Then he tossed it. They both watched it fall.

Looking at it, he thought how maybe this was how it was supposed to end. He didn't hate Arden Boudreaux. She had her flaws, true. A greedy, ambitious woman, married to a jealous, violent man who made her life hell. She wasn't perfect or pure.

But neither was he.

And there at the end, Shattuck had been right. She *would* inherit the company. She *would* need somebody to manage it for her.

Finally, she smiled. Lowered the black rod, and slipped it back into its pouch. She took off the sunglasses, too, and hung them by one earpiece in the *V* of her blouse. "All right, Mr. Galloway. Come over here."

He saw the softness of her throat, the edged softness of her smile. Her hair was dark as the sea a thousand feet down. He felt again that he shouldn't be doing this. She was gorgeous, forbidden, dangerous. Could he trust her? But she beckoned him closer, and even as he thought he shouldn't, he was walking toward her, around the gap in the deck, carefully stepping over the jagged edges.

He was one step away when she suddenly took the cylinder out again and pointed it at his groin. Too late to react, he heard a faint whine and then a pop like the discharge of an electronic strobe.

The pain was more incredible than anything he'd ever imagined, like being stung in the balls by a thousand-pound wasp. Only it went on and on and on.

He lay face up, staring into the sun. It wasn't that he was knocked out, but the electric stun device, or whatever it was, had totally paralyzed him. He couldn't even breathe. He couldn't resist or even tense his muscles as he felt her bend down to him, pick up one leg, and cross it over the other.

He felt himself being rolled over.

Face down, he heard her murmur, directly above him, "Did you *really* think I'd let you touch me, after you killed my husband—*and* my lover?"

He couldn't move or answer, so he didn't. She said something like "Hmmph," a little derisive sound, and he felt her moving his feet again. He remembered this trick now from CPR class. Cross the ankles first and even a child could roll over the largest adult. He felt her foot on his rump, heard her grunt, and he rolled over again, this time face up. The ragged edge of the hole in the deck pressed into his side.

"Yes, of course he was a pig—and the other was not a very intelligent man, either. I thought you were attractive. I gave you a chance. Only you didn't care to become friends."

He couldn't answer. Only by every bit of concentration he had could he even get a teaspoonful of air at a time into his lungs, then out again. The rest of his body—forget it. It was on leave somewhere. She kicked him over again, and this time he felt his foot flop out and hang down into space.

Now he could hear the sea surging around the wreckage, far below, where Shattuck lay. A peaceful sound, like surf. They sold tapes of it to put you to sleep. It was the most terrifying sound he'd ever heard.

"But the stupidest of all, it is when he thought of you for my partner. As if I needed a partner! And now that he is dead, and Roland is dead, the only one left for them to deal with is me. Why should I share? I know them. I can carry it out myself."

He tried with everything he had to move his arm. To roll back from the edge, even to speak. But he couldn't. All he could do was stare up into the hard, bright sun. Her face swung forward, looking down at him. He felt her espadrille on his hip, ready to kick him gently over.

"*Au 'voir, Monsieur Galloway,*" she said. He blinked up into her face, hovering between him and the light, and saw one dark eye wink, steady and cold and irrevocable.

Something flashed in the air above their heads. A thud, a clang, a clatter. Arden Boudreaux's eyes widened. Then her pupils rolled backward and she collapsed where she stood.

The heavy steel wrench slid to a stop on the deck.

He squinted up, into the blazing sun, into the warped, sagging framework of the tilting derrick. A few seconds went by and he found it was a little easier to breathe. A few seconds after that he got one leg crossed over the other and rolled himself a foot or two from the edge. Very shakily, he pushed himself to a sitting position.

"Hello, Hannah," he croaked. "How long have you been up there?"

West leaned on the rail of the catwalk and put one boot on the edge. She shoved her hard hat back and shifted her chew, rubbing her mouth with the back of her glove. "A while. Enough to figure out what was goin' on, even if I couldn't hear everything. Had one of the choppers run me out this morning, lower me on a sling. I was makin' an inspection. Figurin' out how long it'll take to put her back in production."

"How long, you think?"

"Depends. They give her back to the sorry bastard who scooted—two months. Give her to me—two weeks."

He took some more deep breaths and staggered to his feet. "You're pretty confident."

"I'm pretty good." She grinned, but there was a trace of sadness. "Looks like I ain't so good at judgin' character, though. Too bad about Shattuck. I was climbin' down when I saw him pull the gun. I thought he was an all-right guy."

"But he wasn't," Galloway said.

"Nope. I guess not, come right down to it."

While she was climbing down, he tottered over to see whether Arden Boudreaux was still alive. Blood primed the steel under her head, but she was breathing. His fingers found a swelling knot under the long hair.

"Hell of a good-lookin' woman," West said, stepping off the ladder to stand beside him.

"Looks can be deceiving," said Galloway. He stared down for a moment more, then turned to West. "Thanks, Hannah," he said softly.

"Goddarn," she said. "Lemme get rid of this tobacco first, aw right?"

When he was through kissing her, he felt unsteady. It wasn't so much the kiss, but his balls still hurt like hell. And he really did need to get to a decompression chamber. "That G.Q., down there?" he asked her.

"Yeah." West eyed him for a second longer, then picked up her wrench and slipped it back into her tool belt. She went to the rail and cupped her hands to her mouth. "Yo! Lee! Bring that yacht a yours alongside. And get a stretcher or somethin' ready—we got a couple people hurt up here. Get in here; you ain't gonna scratch the paint!"

TWENTY-EIGHT

When he limped out of the Bayou City jail, he stood for a while on the pavement, hands in his pockets, just looking around. Around him on the street lay shattered glass, uprooted trees. Chain saws and portable generators whined. Men and women moved slowly about, cleaning up the aftermath of the storm. He thought about going back to Summerland, then thought, Why bother? DeepTech was gone. Like his job, like Porch's trailer when the hurricane had torn it and most of Bayou City apart. He was back to square one.

No, that's not exactly right, he thought. You're alive. You're free. That's worth something. More than you thought you'd end up with, when you were nine hundred feet down.

He touched the still-soggy wad of bills in his pocket. Not a big stake, but more than he'd come in on Route 90 with.

Then he noticed the little man leaning against a Hyundai, waiting.

"Hi, G.Q."

"Hello, Tiller. How are you?"

"Okay, I guess."

"Is there something wrong?"

Galloway straightened, wincing. "Took a shot to the crotch. And just got out of decompression. Still a few kinks here and there."

"I see. The police—they let you go?"

"Couldn't hold me. No witnesses. I didn't have anything

to say, 'cause it would tend to incriminate me. So there was nothing to hold me on."

"I see. And Mrs. Boudreaux?"

"Arden? They're still working on her. But she's one smart lady. And tough. I don't think they'll be able to come up with anything concrete."

"So, you are free. Excellent. Now, Tiller, is there any chance you could tell me what happened down there? It would be useful to me to know. When I redesign the suit. I assume that Boudreaux attempted to kill you."

Tiller looked around, making sure no one was near. Then he leaned close to Lee. He put his arm around him, patting his back up and down.

"I'm not wired, if that's what you're thinking," Lee said. "This is purely an engineering question."

Galloway told him. When he came to the part about the hand drill, Lee shook his head slowly.

"Thank you. I'm glad to know it was not the fault of the suit in some way. Well, well . . . and now, what are your plans?"

He thought about that. He still couldn't go back to Hatteras. And after everything that had happened, he didn't think any of the reputable diving companies would consider him employable in the Patch. "Don't really have any," he said at last. "Maybe I'll head west. Houston or someplace. How about you?"

Lee extracted his wallet and handed Galloway a card. "I have some possibilities, some plans. They might work out, they might not. But you will stay in touch, won't you? We might be able to do some work together sometime."

"Oh no. Drugs, right? You want me to work for *him* again? Forget it."

"You have a suspicious mind, Tiller. I told you, I am done with that."

"Sometimes I wonder if we'll ever be done with that, G.Q."

"You have a point. But, speaking of Nunez . . . take a look at this. You might be interested."

Galloway took the neatly clipped-out square of newspaper. It was brief, datelined Bogota, Colombia. He read it with widening eyes and a growing relief.

"In government custody," he said.

"Oh, I don't think it will be terribly onerous. Instead of a prison, he will be held at a 'special facility' in Antioquia Province, outside Medellín. I suspect that means on his own ranch. With his own cook, his own guards, his own zoo. But at least the Colombian government is starting to move against the major traffickers. He will be concentrating on preserving his own position, not worrying about old scores. For you, that is good news, I think."

He stood on the pavement, feeling lighter than he'd felt in years. "Yeah," he said. "Yeah. Well . . . in that case, I guess I'll go on back to Hatteras, see if I can pick up something there."

Lee straightened, sighed, and held out his hand. "Well . . . can I give you a lift anywhere?"

"Yeah," he said, thinking now about how to get back to Carolina. "Yeah, maybe you can."

Lee dropped him at Hebert Brothers, where the used Jeep was still for sale. After the papers were all signed, he stopped at the Chevron station and gassed up, changed a ten-dollar bill for quarters, and went out to the pay phone.

"Hi, Latricia? Tiller. Is Shad there?"

"Just a moment. I'll get him; he's out in the yard."

Aydlett sounded out of breath. "Yeah. Tiller? That you? Good to hear from you. Been thinkin' about you. How's things going?"

"Okay, I guess. How about with you?"

"Crewin' on *Dream Girl* with Billy Baum. Hard work, but I'm gettin' a hundred a day an' tips, plus all the blues, marlin, and tuna steaks you care to tote down the pier."

"Sounds okay. Think they can use another hand?"

"Hey. Hey! That mean what I think?"

"That's right." He smiled, looking out the glass doors to the brightening sky. "Put on some barbecue, Shad. I'm coming home."

About the Author

David Poyer is a sport diver, sailor, Navy reservist, and novelist. His books include *The Return of Philo T. McGiffin*, *The Med*, *The Gulf*, *The Circle*, *Winter in the Heart*, and the first two Tiller Galloway novels, *Hatteras Blue* and *Bahamas Blue*. Almost 4 million copies of his books are in print in several languages. He lives on Virginia's Eastern Shore.